Samuel Pepys, Richard Griffin Braybrooke

Diary and correspondence of Samuel Pepys from his

MS. cypher in the Pepsyian Library, with a Life and notes by Richard Lord

Braybrooke. Vol. V (April 1, 1665 - April 8, 1666)

Samuel Pepys, Richard Griffin Braybrooke

Diary and correspondence of Samuel Pepys from his
*MS. cypher in the Pepsyian Library, with a Life and notes by Richard Lord Braybrooke. Vol. V
(April 1, 1665 - April 8, 1666)*

ISBN/EAN: 9783337018450

Printed in Europe, USA, Canada, Australia, Japan

Cover: Foto ©Raphael Reischuk / pixelio.de

More available books at **www.hansebooks.com**

DIARY

AND

CORRESPONDENCE

OF

SAMUEL PEPYS, ESQ., F.R.S.

FROM HIS MS. CYPHER IN THE PEPYSIAN LIBRARY,

WITH A LIFE AND NOTES BY

RICHARD LORD BRAYBROOKE.

DECIPHERED, WITH ADDITIONAL NOTES, BY

REV. MYNORS BRIGHT, M.A.,

PRESIDENT AND SENIOR FELLOW OF MAGDALENE COLLEGE, CAMBRIDGE.

VOL. V.

APRIL 1, 1665 — APRIL 8, 1666.

NEW-YORK:

DODD, MEAD & COMPANY.

1885.

DIARY OF SAMUEL PEPYS.

APRIL 1ST, 1665. To Sir G. Carteret, whom I found with the Commissioners of Prizes dining at Captain Cocke's, in Broad Streete, very merry. Among other tricks, there did come a blind fiddler to the doore, and Sir G. Carteret did go to the doore and lead the blind fiddler by the hand in. Thence with Sir G. Carteret, Sir W. Batten, and Sir J. Minnes to my Lord Treasurer, and there did lay open the expence for the six months past, and an estimate of the seven months to come, to November next: the first arising to above 500,000*l*., and the latter will, as we judge, come to above 1,000,000*l*. But to see how my Lord Treasurer did bless himself, crying he could do no more than he could, nor give more money than he had, if the occasion and expence were never so great, which is but a sad story. And then to hear how like a passionate and ignorant asse Sir G. Carteret did harangue upon the abuse of Tickets did make me mad almost and yet was fain to hold my tongue. Thence home, vexed mightily to see how simply our greatest ministers do content themselves to understand and do things, while the King's service in the meantime lies a-bleeding. At my office late writing letters till ready to drop down asleep with my late sitting and running up and down a-days. So to bed.

2nd (Lord's day). At my office all the morning, renewing my vowes in writing and then home to dinner.

3rd. With Creed, my wife, and Mercer to a play at the Duke's, of my Lord Orrery's, called "Mustapha," [1] which being not good, made Betterton's part and Ianthe's but ordinary too, so that we were not contented with it at all. All the pleasure of the play was, the King and my Lady Castlemaine were there ; and pretty witty Nell, [2] at the King's house, and the younger Marshall sat next us ; which pleased me mightily.

4th. To the 'Change to buy a pair of cotton stockings, which I did at the husband's shop of the most pretty woman there, who did also invite me to buy some linnen of her and I was glad of the occasion, and bespoke some bands of her, intending to make her my seamstress, she being one of the prettiest and most modest looked women that ever I did see.

5th. This day was kept publiquely by the King's command, as a fast day against the Dutch warr, and I betimes with Mr. Tooker, whom I have brought into the Navy to serve us as a husband to see goods timely shipped off from hence to the Fleete and other places,

---

[1] There was another tragedy of this name, by Fulk, Lord Brook.
[2] Nell Gwynne.

and took him with me to Woolwich and Deptford, where did a very great deale of business, and then home, and there by promise find Creed, and he and my wife, Mercer and I by coach to take the ayer; and, where we have formerly been, at Hackney, did there eat some pullets we carried with us, and some things of the house; and after a game or two at shuffle-board, home, and Creed lay with me; but, being sleepy, he had no mind to talk about business, which indeed I intended, by inviting him to lie with me; and so to bed, he and I, and to sleep, being the first time I have been so much at my ease and taken so much fresh ayre these many weeks or months.

6th. With Sir G. Carteret and my Lord Brouncker attended the Duke of Albemarle about the business of money. I also went to Jervas's, my barber, for my periwigg that was mending there. Great talke of a new Comet; and it is certain one do now appear as bright as the late one at the best; but I have not seen it myself.

7th. To the Duke of Albemarle about money to be got for the Navy, or else we must shut up shop. Then to my Lord Treasurer's and there with Sir Philip Warwick till dark night, about 4 hours talking of the business of the Navy Charge and how Sir G. Carteret do order business keeping us in ignorance what he do with his money, and also Sir Philip did show me nakedly the King's condition for money for the Navy; and he do assure me, unless the King can get some noblemen or rich money-gentlemen to lend him money, or to get the City to do it, it is impossible to find money: we having already, as he says, spent one year's share of the three-years tax, which comes to 2,500,000*l.*

8th. To my Lord Chancellor's, where to have spoke with the Duke of Albemarle, but the King and Council busy, I could not; then to the Old Exchange and there of my new pretty seamstress bought four bands. The French Embassadors [1] are come incognito before their train, which will hereafter be very pompous. It is thought they come to get our King to joyne with the King of France in helping him against Flanders, and they to do the like to us against Holland. We have laine a good while with a good fleete at Harwich. The Dutch not said yet to be out. We, as high as we make our show, I am sure, are unable to set out another small fleete, if this should be worsted. Wherefore, God send us peace! I cry.

9th (Lord's day). To church with my wife in the morning, in her new light-coloured silk gowne, which is, with her new point, very noble. In the afternoon to Fanchurch, the little church in the middle of Fanchurch Streete, where a very few people and few of any rank.

10th. To the Duke of Albemarle's, and thence to White Hall to a Committee for Tangier, where new disorder about Mr. Povy's accounts, that I think I shall never be settled in my business of Treasurer for

---

[1] The French ambassadors were Henri de Bourbon, Duc de Verneuil, natural son of Henry IV. and brother of Henrietta Maria; and M. de Courtin.

him.   Here Captain Cooke met me, and did seem discontented about my boy Tom's having no time to mind his singing nor lute, which I answered him fully in, that he desired me that I would baste his coate. My Lord Brouncker took me and Sir Thomas Harvy in his coach to the Parke, which is very troublesome with the dust; and ne'er a great beauty there to-day but Mrs. Middleton.

11th. To Alderman Cheverton to treat with him about hempe. At noon dined at the Sun, behind the 'Change, with Sir Edward Deering[1] and his brother and Commissioner Pett, we having made a contract with Sir Edward this day about timber. Thence to the office, where late very busy, but with some trouble have also some hopes of profit too.

12th. To White Hall to a Committee of Tangier, where, contrary to all expectation, my Lord Ashly, being vexed with Povy's accounts, did propose it as necessary that Povy should be still continued Treasurer of Tangier till he had made up his accounts; and with such arguments as, I confess, I was not prepared to answer, but by putting off of the discourse, and so, I think, brought it right again; but it troubled me, though I think it doubtful whether I shall be much the worse for it or no, if it should come to be so. Dined at home and thence to White Hall again (where I lose most of my time now-a-days to my great trouble,

---

[1] Sir Edward Dering, of Surrenden Dering, Kent, which county he frequently represented in parliament. He was the second Baronet of his family, and some time one of the Lords of the Treasury. He died in 1684.

charge, and loss of time and benefit) and there, after the Council rose, Sir G. Carteret, my Lord Brouncker, Sir Thomas Harvy, and myself, down to my Lord Treasurer's chamber to him and the Chancellor, and the Duke of Albemarle; and there I did give them a large account of the charge of the Navy, and want of money. But strange to see how they held up their hands, crying, "What shall we do?" Says my Lord Treasurer,[1] "Why what means all this, Mr. Pepys? This is true, you say; but what would you have me to do? I have given all I can for my life. Why will not people lend their money? Why will they not trust the King as well as Oliver? Why do our prizes come to nothing, that yielded so much heretofore?" And this was all we could get, and went away without other answer, which is one of the saddest things that, at such a time as this, with the greatest action on foot that ever was in England, nothing should be minded, but let things go on of themselves and do as well as they can. So home, vexed, and going to my Lady Batten's, there found a great many women with her, in her chamber merry, my Lady Pen and her daughter, among others; where my Lady Pen flung me down upon the bed, and herself and others, one after another, upon me, and very merry we were.

13th. To Sheriff Waterman's[2] to dinner, all of us men of the office in towne, and our wives, my Lady

---

[1] The Earl of Southampton. (M. B.)

[2] George Waterman, Sheriff of London, afterwards knighted, and Lord Mayor, 1672.

Carteret and daughters, and Ladies Batten, Pen, and my wife, &c., and very good cheer we had and merry; musique at and after dinner, and a fellow danced a jigg; but when the company begun to dance, I came away lest I should be taken out; and God knows how my wife carried herself, but I left her to try her fortune.

14th. Up, and betimes to Mr. Povy, being desirous to have an end of my trouble of mind touching my Tangier business, whether he hath any desire of accepting what my Lord Ashly offered, of his becoming Treasurer again; and there I did, with a seeming most generous spirit, offer him to take it back again upon his owne terms; but he did answer to me that he would not above all things in the world, at which I was for the present satisfied; but, going away thence and speaking with Creed, he puts me in doubt that the very nature of the thing will require that he be put in again; and did give me the reasons of the auditors, which, I confess, are so plain, that I know not how to withstand them. But he did give me most ingenious advice what to do in it, and anon, my Lord Barkeley and some of the Commissioners coming together, though not in a meeting, I did procure that they should order Povy's payment of his remain of accounts to me; which order if it do pass will put a good stop to the fastening of the thing upon me. Called my wife, and with her through the city to Mile-End Greene, and eat some creame and cakes and so back home. This morning I was saluted with newes that the fleetes, ours and the Dutch, were engaged, and that the guns were heard at Walthamstow to play all yesterday, and that Captain Teddiman's legs were shot off in the Royall Catherine. But before night I hear the contrary, both by letters of my owne and messengers thence, that they were all well of our side and no enemy appears yet, and that the Royall Catherine is come to the fleete, and likely to prove as good a ship as any the King hath, of which I am heartily glad, both for Christopher Pett's sake and Captain Teddiman that is in her.

16th (Lord's day). I walked to the Rolls' Chappell, expecting to hear the great Stillingfleet [1] preach, but he did not; but a very sorry fellow, which vexed me. The sermon done, I home, where I found Mr. Andrews, and by and by comes Captain Taylor,[2] my old acquaintance at Westminster, that understands musique very well and composes mighty bravely; he brought us some things of two parts to sing, very hard; but that that is the worst, he is very conceited of them, and that though they are good makes them troublesome to one to see him every note commend and admire them. He supped with me and a good understanding man he is and a good scholler and, among other things, a great antiquary. He can, as he

---

[1] He was then preacher of the Rolls chapel, and was this year presented to the Rectory of St. Andrew's, Holborn. He was raised to the see of Worcester in 1689, and died of gout 1699. His greatest work was " Origines Sacræ, or a rational account of Natural and revealed Religion." (M. B.)

[2] See *ante*, Nov. 7, 1663.

says, show the very originall Charter to Worcester, of King Edgar's,[1] wherein he stiles himself, Rex Marium Britanniæ, &c.; which is the great text that Mr. Selden and others do quote, but imperfectly and upon trust. But he hath the very originall, which he says he will show me. This night I am told that newes is come of our taking of three Dutch men-of-warr, with the loss of one of our Captains.

17th. To the Duke of Albemarle's, where he showed me Mr. Coventry's letters, how three Dutch privateers are taken, in one whereof Everson's son is captaine. But they have killed poor Captaine Golding in The Diamond. Two of them, one of 32 and the other of 20 odd guns, did stand stoutly up against her, which hath 46, and the Yarmouth that hath 52 guns, and as many more men as they. So that they did more than we could expect, not yielding till many of their men were killed. And Everson, when he was brought before the Duke of York, and was observed to be shot through the hat, answered, that he wished it had gone

---

[1] This is the celebrated "Charta Eadgari R. de Oswaldeslawe," dat. Gloucester, 28th Dec., 964, mentioning not only the Dominion of the Sea, but also that Edgar had subdued the greatest part of Ireland, a piece of history which rests solely on the authority of this instrument. It is cited by Coke, Selden, Ussher, Dugdale, and Spelman, not to mention inferior names. Three copies existed; the finest and most complete, and probably the same which is here mentioned by Taylor, is now in the Harleian Collection in the British Museum. It is fully described in the "Dissertatio Epistolaris" (p. 86), prefixed by Hickes to his "Thesaurus Linguarum Septentrionalium," and an engraved facsimile of the whole is given by him at the end. It is right to say, that the charter is now generally considered to be a forgery, executed in later times.

through his head, rather than been taken. One thing more is written; that two of our ships the other day appearing upon the coast of Holland, they presently fired their beacons round the country to give notice. And newes is brought the King, that the Dutch Smyrna fleete is seen upon the back of Scotland; and thereupon the King hath wrote to the Duke, that he do appoint a fleete to go to the Northward to try to meet them coming home round: which God send! Thence to White Hall; where the King seeing me, did come to me, and calling me by name, did discourse with me about the ships in the River: and this is the first time that ever I knew the King did know me personally; so that hereafter I must not go thither, but with expectation to be questioned, and to be ready to give good answers. So home, and thence with Creed, who came to dine with me, to the Old James, where we dined with Sir W. Rider and Cutler, and, by and by, being called by my wife, we all to a play, "The Ghosts," [1] at the Duke's house, but a very simple play. This day was left at my house a very neat silver watch, by one Briggs, a scrivener and solicitor, at which I was angry with my wife for receiving, or, at least, for opening the box wherein it was, and so far witnessing our receipt of it, as to give the messenger 5*s.* for bringing it; but it can't be helped, and I will endeavour to do the man a kindnesse, he being a friend of my uncle Wight's.

---

[1] A Comedy, on the authority of Downes (p. 26) attributed to Mr. Holden, and probably never printed.

18th. To Sir Philip Warwick, and walked with him an houre with great delight in the Parke about Sir G. Carteret's accounts, and the endeavour that he has made to bring Sir G. Carteret to show his accounts and let the world see what he receives and what he pays. With him to my Lord Treasurer, who signed my commission for Tangier Treasurer and the docquet of my Privy Seale, for the monies to be paid to me.

19th. Up by five o'clock, and by water to White Hall; and there took coach, and with Mr. Moore to Chelsy; where, after all my fears what doubts and difficulties my Lord Privy Seale [1] would make at my Tangier Privy Seale, he did pass it at first reading, without my speaking with him. And then called me in, and was very civil to me. I passed my time in contemplating (before I was called in) the picture of my Lord's son's lady, [2] a most beautiful woman, and most like to Mrs. Butler. Thence very much joyed to London back again, and found out Mr. Povy; told him this; and then went and left my Privy Seale at my Lord Treasurer's; and so to the 'Change, and thence to Trinity-House; where a great dinner of Captain Crisp, who is made an Elder Brother. And so, being very pleasant at dinner, away home, Creed with me; and there met Povy; and we to Gresham College, where we saw some experiments upon a hen, a dogg, and a cat, of the Florence poyson. The first it made for a time drunk, but it came to itself again quickly;

---

[1] John Lord Roberts.　　[2] Sarah Bodvill. See 3rd May, 1664.

the second it made vomit mightily, but no other hurt. The third I did not stay to see the effect of it, being taken out by Povy. He and I walked below together, he giving me most exceeding discouragement in the getting of money (whether by design or no I know not, for I am now come to think him a most cunning fellow in most things he do but his accounts), and made it plain to me that money will be hard to get, and that it is to be feared Backewell has a design in it to get the thing forced upon himself. This put me into a cruel melancholy to think I may lose what I have had so near my hand; but yet something may be hoped for which to-morrow will shew.

20th. This night I am told the first play is played in White Hall noon-hall, which is now turned to a house of playing.

21st. This day we hear that the Duke and the fleete are sailed yesterday. Pray God go along with them, that they have good speed in the beginning of their worke.

22nd. Mr. Cæsar, my boy's lute master, being come betimes to teach him, I did speak with him seriously about the boy, what my mind was, if he did not look after his lute and singing that I would turn him away; which I hope will do some good upon the boy. My wife making great preparation to go to Court to Chappell to-morrow. This day I have newes from Mr. Coventry that the fleete is sailed yesterday from Harwich to the coast of Holland to see what the Dutch will do. God go along with them!

23rd (Lord's day). Mr. Povy, according to promise, sent his coach betimes and I carried my wife and her woman to White Hall Chappell and set them in the Organ Loft, and I having least to untruss went to the Harp and Ball and entertained myself in talke with the mayde of the house, a pretty mayde and very modest. Thence to the Chappell and heard the famous young Stillingfleete, whom I knew at Cambridge, and is now newly admitted one of the King's chaplains; and was presented, they say, to my Lord Treasurer for St. Andrew's, Holborn, where he is now minister, with these words: that they (the Bishops of Canterbury, London, and another) believed he is the ablest young man to preach the Gospel of any since the Apostles. He did make the most plain, honest, good, grave sermon, in the most unconcerned and easy yet substantial manner, that ever I heard in my life, upon the words of Samuel to the people, " Fear the Lord in truth with all your heart, and remember the great things that he hath done for you." It being proper to this day, the day of the King's Coronation. After dinner, Creed and we by coach took the ayre in the fields beyond St. Pancras, it raining now and then, which it seems is most welcome weather, and then all to my house, where comes Mr. Hill, Andrews, and Captain Taylor and good musique, but at supper to hear the arguments we had against Taylor concerning a Corant, he saying that the law of a dancing Corant is to have every barr to end in a pricked crochet and quaver, which I denied, was very strange. It proceeded till

I vexed him, but all parted friends. After supper, Creed and I together to bed, in Mercer's bed, and so to sleep.

24th. To the Duke of Albemarle, where very busy. To my Lady Sandwich's to dinner, where my wife by agreement. After dinner alone, my Lady told me, with the prettiest kind of doubtfullnesse, whether it would be fit for her with respect to Creed to do it, that is, in the world, that Creed had broke his desire to her of being a servant to Mrs. Betty Pickering, and placed it upon encouragement which he had from some discourse of her ladyship, commending of her virtues to him, which, poor lady, she meant most innocently. She did give him a cold answer, but not so severe as it ought to have been; and, it seems, as the lady since to my Lady confesses, he had wrote a letter to her, which she answered slightly, and was resolved to contemn any motion of his therein. My Lady takes the thing very ill, as it is fit she should; but I advise her to stop all future occasions of the world's taking notice of his coming thither so often as of late he hath done. But to think that he should have this devilish presumption to aime at a lady so near to my Lord is strange, both for his modesty and discretion. Thence to the Cocke-pitt, and there walked an houre with my Lord Duke of Albemarle alone in his garden, where he expressed in great words his opinion of me; that I was the right hand of the Navy here, nobody but I taking any care of any thing therein; so that he should not know what could be done without me. At which

I was (from him) not a little proud. So by coach with my wife and Mercer to the Parke; but the King being there, and I now-a-days being doubtfull of being seen in any pleasure, did part from the tour, and away out of the Parke to Knightsbridge, and there eat and drank in the coach, and so home.

25th. This afternoon W. Pen, lately come from his father in the fleete, did give me an account how the fleete did sayle, about 103 in all, besides small catches, they being in sight of six or seven Dutch scouts, and sent ships in chase of them.

26th. Up, my stomach sicke with the buttered ale I did drink last night. So walked to Povy's, and there I did receive the first parcel of money as Treasurer of Tangier, and did give my receipt for it, which was about 2,800*l.* value in Tallys,[1] and then I away to White Hall, talking, with Povy alone, about my opinion of Creed's indiscretion in looking after Mrs. Pickering, desiring him to make no more a sport of it, but to correct him, if he finds that he continues to owne any such thing. This I did by my Lady's desire, and do intend to pursue the stop of it. So to the Carrier's by Cripplegate, to see whether my

---

[1] " *Tally.* French, tailler, to cut. A stick notched or cut in conformity to another stick, and used to keep accounts by.

> " So right his judgement was cut fit,
> And made a *tally* to his wit."
>
> Butler, *Hudibras*, iii. 2, 395.

" The only talents in esteem at present are those of the Exchange Alley; one tally is worth a grove of bays." — *Garth. Latham's Dictionary.*

(M. B.)

mother be come to towne or no, I expecting her to-day, but she is not come. So to dinner to my Lady Sandwich's, and after dinner did spend an houre or two with her talking again about Creed's folly; but strange it is that he should dare to propose this business himself of Mrs. Pickering to my Lady, and to tell my Lady that he did it for her virtue sake, not minding her money, for he could have a wife with more, but, for that, he did intend to depend upon her Ladyship to get as much of her father and mother for her as she could; and that, which he did, was by encouragement from discourse of her Ladyship's; he also had wrote to Mrs. Pickering, but she did give him a slighting answer back again. But I do very much fear that Mrs. Pickering's honour, if the world comes to take notice of it, may be wronged by it.

27th. Creed dined with me; and, after dinner, walked in the garden, he telling me that my Lord Treasurer now begins to be scrupulous, and will know what becomes of the 26,000*l.* saved by my Lord Peterborough, before he parts with any more money, which puts us into new doubts, and me into a great fear, that all my cake will be doe [1] still. But I am well prepared for it to bear it, being not clear whether

---

[1] An obsolete proverb, signifying to lose one's hopes, a cake coming out of the oven in a state of dough being considered spoiled.

> "*My cake is dough;* but I'll in among the rest;
> Out of hope of all, but my share in the feast."
> SHAKESPEARE, *Taming of the Shrew*, act v. sc. 1.
> (M. B.)

it will be more for my profit to have it, or go without it, as my profits of the Navy are likely now to be. This night William Hewer is returned from Harwich, where he hath been paying off of some ships this fortnight, and went to sea a good way with the fleete, which was 96 in company then, men of warr, besides some come in, and following them since, which makes now above 100, whom God bless!

28th. Up by 5 o'clock, and by appointment with Creed by 6 at his chamber. After some discourse of the reason of the difficulty that Sir Philip Warwick makes in issuing a warrant for my striking of tallys, namely the having a clear account of the 26,000*l.* saved by my Lord of Peterborough, we parted, and I to Sir Philip Warwick, who did give me an account of his demurr, which I applied myself to remove by taking Creed with me to my Lord Ashly, from whom, contrary to all expectation, I received a very kind answer, just as we could have wished it, that he would satisfy my Lord Treasurer. Thence very well satisfied I home, and down the River to visit the victualling-ships, where I find all out of order. And came home to dinner, and then to write a letter to the Duke of Albemarle about them, and carried it myself to the Council-chamber, where it was read; and when they rose, my Lord Chancellor passing by stroked me on the head, and told me that the Board had read my letter, and taken order for the punishing of the' watermen for not appearing on board the ships. And so did the King afterwards, who do now know me so well, that he never sees me but he speaks to me about our Navy business. Thence got my Lord Ashly to my Lord Treasurer below in his chamber and there removed the scruple, and by and by brought Mr. Sherwin to Sir Philip Warwick and did the like.

29th. Troubled in my mind to hear that Sir W. Batten and Sir J. Minnes do take notice that I am now-a-days much from the office, upon no office business, which vexes me, and will make me mind my business the better, I hope in God ; but what troubles me more is, that I do omit to write, as I should do, to Mr. Coventry, which I must not do, though this night I minded it so little as to sleep in the middle of my letter to him, and committed forty blotts and blurrs, but of this I hope never more to be guilty, if I have not already given him sufficient offence.

30th (Lord's day). I with great joy find myself to have gained this month above 100*l.* clear, and in the whole to be worth above 1,400*l.* Down to Woolwich and Deptford, and made it late home, and so to supper and to bed. Thus I end this month in great content as to my estate and gettings : in much trouble as to the pains I have taken, and the rubs I expect yet to meet with, about the business of Tangier. The fleete, with about 106 ships upon the coast of Holland, in sight of the Dutch, within the Texel. Great fears of the sicknesse here in the City, it being said that two or three houses are already shut up. God preserve us all !

May 1st. I met my Lord Brouncker, Sir Robert

Murray, Dean Wilkins, and Mr. Hooke, going by coach to Colonel Blunt's [1] to dinner. So they stopped and took me with them. Landed at the Tower-wharf, and thence by water to Greenwich; and there coaches met us; and to his house, a very stately sight for situation and brave plantations; and among others, a vine-yard, the first that ever I did see. No extraordinary dinner, nor any other entertainment good; but only after dinner to the tryal of some experiments about making of coaches easy. And several we tried; but one did prove mighty easy, (not here for me to describe, but the whole body of the coach lies upon one long spring,) and we all, one after another, rid in it; and it is very fine and likely to take. Thence to Deptford, and in to Mr. Evelyn's,[2] which is a most beautiful place; but it being dark and late, I staid not; but Dean Wilkins and Mr. Hooke and I, walked to Redriffe; and noble discourse all day long did please me.

2nd. Sir W. Batten and my Lady and my wife by appointment yesterday to the Rhenish winehouse at the Steelyard, and there eat a couple of lobsters and some prawns, and pretty merry, especially to see us

---

[1] Wricklesmarsh, in the parish of Charlton, which belonged, in 1617, to Edward Blount, Esq., whose family alienated it towards the end of the seventeenth century. The old mansion was pulled down by Sir Gregory Page, Bart., who erected a magnificent stone structure on the site; which, devolving to his great nephew, Sir Gregory Page Turner, shared the same fate as the former house, having been sold in lots in 1784. The site of Colonel Blount's house is now covered with villas, and is called Blackheath Park.

[2] Sayes Court, the well-known residence of John Evelyn, Esq.

four together again after a year's distance between one another. Hither by and by came Mrs. Esther, that lived formerly with my Lady Batten, now well married to a priest, come to see my Lady.

3rd. To the Inne again by Cripplegate, expecting my mother's coming to towne, but she is not come this weeke neither, the coach being too full. So to the 'Change and thence home to dinner, and so out to Gresham College, and saw a cat killed with the Duke of Florence's poyson, and saw it proved that the oyle of tobacco drawn by one of the Society do the same effect, and is judged to be the same thing with the poyson both in colour and smell and effect. Thence parted, and to White Hall to the Council-chamber about an order touching the Navy, our being empowered to commit seamen or Masters that do not, being hired or pressed, follow their worke, but they could give us none. My Lord Chief-Justice Hide did die suddenly this week, a day or two ago, of an apoplexy.

5th. To Deptford, and after dinner to Mr. Evelyn's ; he being abroad, we walked in his garden, and a lovely noble ground he hath indeed. And among other rarities, a hive of bees, so as being hived in glass, you may see the bees making their honey and combs mighty pleasantly. This day, after I had suffered my owne haire to grow long, in order to wearing it, I find the convenience of periwiggs is so great, that I have cut off all short again, and will keep to periwiggs.

7th (Lord's day). Up, and to church with my wife. After sermon comes Mr. Hill, and a gentleman, a friend of his, one Mr. Scott, that sings well also, and then comes Mr. Andrews, and we all sung and supped, and then to sing again, and passed the Sunday very pleasantly and soberly, and so to prayers and to bed. Yesterday begun my wife to learn to limn of one Browne, which Mr. Hill helps her to, and, by her beginning, upon some eyes, I think she will do very fine things, and I shall take great delight in it.

8th. To the Duke of Albemarle's, and there did much business, and thence to the 'Change, and thence off with Sir W. Warren to an ordinary, where we dined and sat talking of most useful discourse, and then home, and very busy till late.

9th. At noon comes Mrs. The. Turner, and dines with us, and my wife's painting master staid and dined, and I take great pleasure in thinking that my wife will really come to something in the business. This day we have newes of eight ships being taken by some of ours going into the Texel, their two men of warr, that convoyed them, running in. They came from about Ireland, round to the North.

10th. To the Cocke-pitt, where the Duke did give Sir W. Batten and me an account of the late taking of eight ships, and of his intent to come back to the Gunfleete with the fleete presently; which creates us much work and haste therein, against the fleete comes. And thence to the Guard in Southwarke, there to get some soldiers, by the Duke's order, to go keep pressmen on board our ships. Then home, and there found my poor mother come out of the country to-day in good health, and I am glad to see her, but my business, which I am sorry for, keeps me from paying the respect I ought to her at her first coming, she being grown very weak in her judgment, and doting again in her discourse, through age and some trouble in her family.

12th. By water to the Exchequer, and strike my tallys [1] for 17,500*l.*, which methinks is so great a testimony of the goodness of God to me, that I, from a mean clerke there, should come to strike tallys myself for that sum, and in the authority that I do now, is a very stupendous mercy to me. But to see how every little fellow looks after his fees, and to get what he can for everything, is a strange consideration;

---

[1] The use of tallies, so frequently alluded to in the Diary, having been discontinued, some explanation of the term may not be considered unacceptable. Formerly, accounts were kept, and large sums of money paid and received, by the King's Exchequer, with little other form than the exchange or delivery of tallies, pieces of wood notched or scored, corresponding blocks being kept by the parties to the account: and from this usage one of the head officers of the Exchequer was called the Tallier, or Teller. These tallies were often negotiable; Adam Smith, in his "Wealth of Nations," book 11, ch. xi., says that "in 1696 *tallies* had been at forty and fifty and sixty per cent. discount, and bank-notes at twenty per cent." The system of tallies was discontinued about twenty years ago; and the destruction of the old Houses of Parliament, in the night of Oct. 16, 1834, is thought to have been occasioned by the overheating of the flues, when the furnaces were employed to consume the tallies, rendered useless by the alteration in the mode of keeping the Exchequer accounts. In the "Times" newspaper of the 1st November following appeared an article on "Tallies," which embraces all that can be said on the subject; but although well worthy of being read it is too long for insertion in these pages. It ends with the words, "Yet one word more — Tallyho!" It was written by Wm. Hone.

the King's fees that he must pay himself for this 17,-500*l.* coming to above 100*l.* Thence called my wife at Unthank's to the New Exchange and elsewhere to buy a lace band for me, but we did not buy, but I find it so necessary to have some handsome clothes that I cannot but lay out some money thereupon. Thence to my watchmaker, where he has put it in order, and a good and brave piece it is, and he tells me worth 14*l.*, which is a greater present than I valued it. After dinner comes my cozen, Thomas Pepys,[1] of Hatcham, to receive some money of my Lord Sandwich's, and there I paid him what was due to him, upon my uncle's score, but, contrary to my expectation, did get him to sign and seale to my sale of lands for payment of debts.

13th. To the 'Change, after office, and received my watch from the watchmaker, and a very fine one it is, given me by Briggs, the Scrivener. But, Lord! to see how much of my old folly and childishnesse hangs upon me still that I cannot forbear carrying my watch in my hand in the coach all this afternoon, and seeing what o'clock it is one hundred times, and am apt to think with myself, how could I be so long without one; though I remember since, I had one, and found it a trouble, and resolved to carry one no more about me while I lived. Home to supper and to bed, being troubled at a letter from Mr. Cholmly from Tangier, wherein he do advise me how people are at

---

[1] Thomas Pepys, of Hatcham Barnes, Surrey, Master of the Jewel Office to Charles II. and in the next reign.

worke to overthrow our Victualling business, by which I shall lose 300*l*. per annum. I am much obliged to him for this secret kindnesse.

14th. Up, and with my wife to church, it being Whit-sunday; my wife very fine in a new yellow bird's-eye hood, as the fashion is now. We had a most sorry sermon; so home to dinner, my mother having her new suit brought home, which makes her very fine. After dinner my wife and she and Mercer to Thomas Pepys's wife's christening of his first child, and I took a coach, and to Wanstead, the house where Sir H. Mildmay died, and now Sir Robert Brookes [1] lives, having bought it of the Duke of York, it being forfeited to him. A fine seat, but an old-fashioned house; and being not full of people looks desolately. I all the afternoon in the coach reading the treasonous book of the Court of King James, printed a great while ago, and worth reading, though ill intended.[2] As soon as I came home, upon a letter from the Duke of Albemarle, I took boat at about 12 at night, and down the river in a gally, my boy and I, down to the Hope and so up again, sleeping and waking, with great pleasure, my business to call upon every one of

15th. Our victualling ships to set them agoing, and

----

[1] Sir Robert Brookes, Lord of the Manor of Wanstead, from 1662 to 1667. M. P. for Aldborough in Suffolk. He afterwards retired to France, and died there in bad circumstances. From a letter among the Pepys MSS., Sir Robert Brookes appears to have been drowned in the river at Lyons.

[2] The work alluded to is Sir Anthony Weldon's.

so home, and after dinner to the King's playhouse, all alone, and saw "Love's Maistresse."[1] Some pretty things and good variety in it, but no or little fancy. Thence to the Duke of Albemarle to give him account of my day's works, where he shewed me letters from Sir G. Downing, of four days' date, that the Dutch are come out and joyned, well-manned, and resolved to board our best ships, and fight for certain they will. Thence called at the Harp and Ball, where the mayde, Mary, is very formosa ; but, Lord ! to see in what readiness I am, upon the expiring of my vowes this day, to begin to run into all my pleasures and neglect of business.

17th. To Langford's where I never was since my brother died there. I find my wife and Mercer, having with him agreed upon two rich silk suits for me, which is fit for me to have, but yet the money is too much, I doubt, to lay out altogether ; but it is done, and so let it be, it being the expense of the world that I can the best bear with and the worst spare. Sir J. Minnes and I had an angry bout this afternoon with Commissioner Pett about his neglecting his duty and absenting himself, unknown to us, from his place at Chatham, but a false man I every day find him more and more, and in this full of equivocation. The fleete we doubt not come to Harwich by this time. The Duchesse of York went down yesterday to meet the Duke.

---

[1] Or, "The Queen's Masque " (printed 1636), by Thomas Heywood. (M. B.)

18th. To the Duke of Albemarle, where we did examine Nixon and Stanesby, about their late running from two Dutchmen; for which they are committed to a vessel to carry them to the fleete to be tried. A most fowle unhandsome thing as ever was heard, for plain cowardice on Nixon's part. Thence with the Duke of Albemarle in his coach to my Lord Treasurer, and there was before the King (who ever now calls me by my name) and Lord Chancellor, and many other great Lords, discoursing about insuring of some of the King's goods, wherein the King accepted of my motion that we should; and so away, well pleased. Then abroad to speak with Sir G. Carteret; but, Lord! to see how fraile a man I am, subject to my vanities, that can hardly forbear, though pressed with never so much business, my pursuing of pleasure, but home I got and there very busy very late. Among other things consulting with Mr. Andrews about our Tangier business, wherein we are like to meet with some trouble, and my Lord Bellasses's endeavour to supplant us, which vexes my mind; but, however, our undertaking is so honourable that we shall stand a tug for it I think.

19th. To White Hall, where the Committee for Tangier met, and there that that troubles me most is my Lord Arlington calls to me privately and asks me whether I had ever said to any body that I desired to leave this employment, having not time to look after it. I told him, No, for that the thing being settled it will not require much time to look after it. He told

me then he would do me right to the King, for he had
been told so, which I desired him to do, and by and
by he called me to him again and asked me whether
I had no friend about the Duke, asking me (I making
a stand) whether Mr. Coventry was not my friend. I
told him I had received many friendships from him.
He then advised me to procure that the Duke would
in his next letter write to him to continue me in my
place and remove any obstruction; which I told him
I would, and thanked him. So parted, vexed at the
first and amazed at this business of my Lord Arlington's. Thence to the Exchequer, and there got my
tallys for 17,500*l.*, the first payment I ever had out
of the Exchequer, and at the Legg spent 14*s.* upon
my old acquaintance, some of them the clerks, and
away home with my tallys in a coach, fearful every
step of having one of them fall out, or snatched from
me. Sir W. Warren did give me several good hints
and principles not to do anything suddenly, but consult my pillow upon my Treasurership of Tangier, and
every great thing of my life, before I resolve anything
in it. Away home, and not being fit for business I
took my wife and Mercer down by water to Greenwich
at 8 at night, it being very fine and cool and moonshine
afterwards. Mighty pleasant passage it was, there eat
a cake or two, and so home by 10 or 11 at night, and
then to bed, my mind not settled what to think.

21st (Lord's day). This day is brought home one
of my new silk suits, the plain one, but very rich camelott and noble. I tried it and it pleases me, but

did not wear it, being I would not go out to-day to church.

22nd. Down to the ships, which now are hindered from going down to the fleete (to our great shame and sorrow) with their provisions, the wind being against them. So to the Duke of Albemarle and thence down by water to Deptford, it being Trinity Monday, and so the day of choosing the Master of Trinity House for the next yeare, where, to my great content, I find that, contrary to the practice and design of Sir W. Batten, to breake the rule and custom of the Company in choosing their Masters by succession, he would have brought in Sir W. Rider or Sir W. Pen, over the head of Hurleston (who is a knave too besides, I believe), the younger brothers did all oppose it against the elder, and with great heat did carry it for Hurleston, which I know will vex him to the heart. Thence, the election being over, to church, where an idle sermon from that conceited fellow, Dr. Britton, saving that his advice to unity, and laying aside all envy and enmity among them was very apposite. Thence walked to Redriffe, and so to the Trinity House, and a great dinner, as is usual. So to my office where till late, and then home to bed being much troubled in mind for several things, first, for the condition of the fleete for lacke of provisions, the blame this office lies under and the shame that they deserve to have brought upon them for the ships not being gone out of the river, and then for my business of Tangier which is not settled, and lastly for fear that

I am observed not to have attended the office business of late as much as I ought to do, though there has been nothing but my attendance on Tangier that has occasioned my absence, and that of late not much.

23rd. Late comes Sir Arthur Ingram [1] to my office, to tell me that, by letters from Amsterdam of the 28th of this month (their style),[2] the Dutch fleete, being about 100 men-of-war, besides fire-ships, &c., did set out upon the 23rd and 24th inst. Being divided into seven squadrons, viz. 1. General Opdam. 2. Cottenar,[3] of Rotterdam. 3. Trump. 4. Schram, of Horne. 5. Stillingworth, of Freezland. 6. Everson. 7. One other, not named, of Zealand.

24th. To the Coffee-house, where all the newes is of the Dutch being gone out, and of the plague growing upon us in this towne ; and of remedies against it : some saying one thing, some another. After dinner Creed and I to Colvills, thinking to shew him all the respect we could by obliging him in carrying him 5 tallys of 5000*l.* to secure him for so much credit he has formerly given Povy to Tangier, but he, like an impertinent fool, cavills at it, but most ignorantly that ever I heard man in my life.

---

[1] Sir Arthur Ingram, Knight, of Knottingley, Surveyor of the Customs at Hull.

[2] The Gregorian calendar was adopted in most parts of Europe in 1582, or soon after, and in England not till 1751. Then an Act of Parliament was passed which made the day after the 2nd of September, 1752, the 14th. This Act caused riots among the common people, who cried out, "Give us back our eleven days!" (M. B.)

[3] Died of his wounds after the sea-fight in 1665.

26th. Creed dined with me, and he and I afterward to Alderman Backewell's to try him about supplying us with money, which he denied at first and last also, saving that he spoke a little fairer at the end than before. But the truth is I do fear I shall have a great deale of trouble in getting of money. In the evening by water to the Duke of Albemarle, whom I found mightily off the hooks, that the ships are not gone out of the River; which vexed me to see, insomuch that I am afeard that we must expect some change or addition of new officers brought upon us, so that I must from this time forward resolve to make myself appear eminently serviceable in attending at my office duly and no where else, which makes me wish with all my heart that I had never anything to do with the business of Tangier.

28th (Lord's day). I hear that Nixon is condemned to be shot to death, for his cowardice, by a Council of War. At noon to Sir Philip Warwick's to dinner, where abundance of company came in unexpectedly; and here I saw one pretty piece of household stuff, as the company increaseth, to put a larger leaf upon an ovall table. After dinner much good discourse with Sir Philip, who I find, I think, a most pious, good man, and a professor of a philosophicall manner of life and principles like Epictetus, whom he cites in many things. Thence to my Lady Sandwich's, where, to my shame, I had not been a great while. Here, upon my telling her a story of my Lord Rochester's [1]

---

[1] John, second Earl of Rochester, celebrated for his wit and profligacy. Ob. 1680.

running away on Friday night last with Mrs. Mallett,[1] the great beauty and fortune of the North, who had supped at White Hall with Mrs. Stewart, and was going home to her lodgings with her grandfather, my Lord Haly,[2] by coach; and was at Charing Cross seized on by both horse and footmen, and forcibly taken from him, and put into a coach with six horses, and two women provided to receive her, and carried away. Upon immediate pursuit, my Lord of Rochester (for whom the King had spoke to the lady often, but with no success) was taken at Uxbridge; but the lady is not yet heard of, and the King mighty angry, and the Lord sent to the Tower. Hereupon my Lady did confess to me, as a great secret, her being concerned in this story. For if this match breaks between my Lord Rochester and her, then, by the consent of all her friends, my Lord Hinchingbroke stands fair, and is invited for her. She is worth, and will be at her mother's death (who keeps but a little from her), 2,500*l.* per annum. Pray God give a good success to it! But my poor Lady who is afeard of the sickness, and resolved to be gone into the country, is forced to stay in towne a day or two, or three about it, to see the event of it. Thence to see my Lady Pen, where my wife and I were shown a fine rarity; of fishes kept

---

[1] Elizabeth, daughter of John Mallett, Esq., of Enmere, co. Somerset; married soon afterwards to the Earl of Rochester.

[2] Sir Francis Hawley of Buckland House, co. Somerset, created a Baronet 1642, and in 1646 an Irish Peer, by the title of Baron Hawley of Donamore; in 1671 he was chosen M.P. for St. Michael's, and in 1673 became a Gentleman of the Bedchamber to the Duke of York. Ob. 1684, aged 76.

in a glass of water, that will live so for ever; and finely marked they are, being foreign.[1]

29th. To the Swan, and there drank at Herbert's, and so by coach home, it being kept a great holiday through the City, for the birth and restoration of the King.   Home to dinner, and then with my wife, mother, and Mercer in one boat, and I in another, down to Woolwich.   We have everywhere taken some prizes.   Our merchants have good luck to come home safe; Colliers from the North, and some Streights' men just now.   And our Hambrough ships, of whom we were so much afeard, are safe in Hambrough. Our fleete resolved to sail out again from Harwich in a day or two.

30th. To dinner to Sir G. Carteret's, to talk upon the business of insuring our goods upon the Hambrough ships.   Here a very fine, neat French dinner, without much cost, we being all alone with my Lady and one of the house with her; and then in the evenning, by coach, with my wife and mother and Mercer, our usual tour by coach, and eat at the old house at Islington: but, Lord! to see how my mother found herself talk upon every object to think of old stories. Here I met with one that tells me that Jack Cole, my old schoolfellow, is dead and buried lately of a consumption, who was a great crony of mine.   So back again home.   Hear to my great trouble that our Hambrough ships, valued of the King's goods and the

---

merchants' (though but little of the former) to 200,-000*l.*, are lost. By and by, about 11 at night, called into the garden by my Lady Pen and daughter, and there walked with them and my wife till almost twelve.

31st. To the 'Change, where great the noise and trouble of having our Hambrough ships lost; and that very much placed upon Mr. Coventry's forgetting to give notice to them of the going away of our fleete from the coast of Holland. But all without reason, for he did; but the merchants not being ready, staid longer than the time ordered for the convoy to stay, which was ten days. To Huysman's the Painter, who I intend shall draw my wife, but he was not within, but I saw several very good pictures.

June 1st. After dinner I put on my new camelott suit; the best that ever I wore in my life, the suit costing me above 24*l.* In this I went with Creed to Goldsmiths' Hall, to the burial of Sir Thomas Viner;[1] which Hall, and Haberdashers' also, was so full of people, that we were fain for ease and coolness to go forth to Pater Noster Row, to choose a silke to make me a plain ordinary suit. That done, we walked to Cornehill, and there at Mr. Cade's stood in the balcon and saw all the funeral, which was with the blue-coat boys and old men, all the Aldermen, and Lord Mayor

---

[1] Sheriff of London, 1648; when Lord Mayor, in 1654, he was knighted by Cromwell (Ludlow's "Memoirs"), and made baronet, 1660. He was a goldsmith, and dying 11th May, 1665, was buried in St. Mary Woolnoth, in Lombard Street.

&c., and the number of the company very great; the greatest I ever did see for a taverne.

2nd. In the afternoon went with my tallys, made a fair end with Colvill and Viner, delivering them 5,000*l.* tallys to each and very quietly had credit given me upon other tallys of Mr. Colvill for 2,000*l.* and good words for more, and of Mr. Viner too. Thence to visit the Duke of Albemarle, and thence my Lady Sandwich and Lord Crew. Thence home and there met an expresse from Sir W. Batten at Harwich, that the fleete is all sailed from Solebay, having spied the Dutch fleete at sea, and that, if the calms hinder not, they must needs now be engaged with them. Another letter also came to me from Mr. Hater, committed by the Council this afternoon to the Gate House, upon the misfortune of having his name used by one, without his knowledge or privity, for the receiving of some powder that he had bought. Up to Court about these two, and for the former was led up to my Lady Castlemaine's lodgings, where the King and she and others were at supper, and there I read the letter and returned; and then to Sir G. Carteret about Hater, and shall have him released to-morrow, upon my giving bail for his appearance. Sir G. Carteret did go on purpose to the King to ask this, and it was granted.

3rd. To White Hall, and upon entering into recognizances, he for 200*l.* and Mr. Hunt and I for 100*l.* each for his appearance upon demand, Mr. Hater was released, it costing him, I think, above 3*l.* I thence home, vexed to be kept from the office all the morning, which I had not been in many months before, if not some years. All this day by all people upon the River, and almost every where else hereabout were heard the guns, our two fleets for certain being engaged ; which was confirmed by letters from Harwich, but nothing particular : and all our hearts full of concernment for the Duke, and I particularly for my Lord Sandwich and Mr. Coventry after his Royall Highnesse.

4th (Lord's day). At my chamber all the forenoon, at evening my accounts, which I could not do sooner, for the last month, and, blessed be God! am worth 1,400*l.* odd money, something more than ever I was yet in the world. Newes come that our fleete is pursuing the Dutch, who, either by cunning, or by being worsted, do give ground, but nothing more for certain.

5th. To White Hall to a Committee of Tangier, where I offered my accounts with great acceptation, and so had some good words and honour by it, and one or two things done to my content in my business of Treasurer, but I do clearly see that we shall lose our business of victualling. Great talke of the Dutch being fled and we in pursuit of them, and that our ship Charity is lost upon our Captain's, Wilkinson, and Lieutenant's yielding, but of this there is no certainty, save the report of some of the sicke men of the Charity, turned adrift in a boat and taken up and brought on shore yesterday to Sole Bay, and the newes hereof brought by Sir Henry Felton.[1] This

---

[1] Sir Henry Felton, of Playford, Suffolk, Bart., who married Susanne, daughter of Sir Lionel Talmash, of Helmingham, Bart. Their second son,

morning I had great discourse with my Lord Barkeley about Mr. Hater, towards whom from a great passion reproaching him with being a fanatique and dangerous for me to keepe, I did bring him to be mighty calme and to ask my pardon for what he had thought of him and to desire me to ask his pardon of Hater himself for the ill words he did give him the other day alone at White Hall (which was, that he had always thought him a man that was no good friend to the King, but did never think it would breake out in a thing of this nature), and did advise him to declare his innocence to the Council and pray for his examinaſion and vindication. Of which I shall consider and say no more, but remember one compliment that in great kindness to me he did give me, extolling my care and diligence, that he did love me heartily for my owne sake, and more that he did wish me whatsoever I thought for Mr. Coventry's sake, for though the world did think them enemies, and to have an ill aspect, one to another, yet he did love him with all his heart, which was a strange manner of noble compliment, confessing his owning me as a confidant and favourite of Mr. Coventry's.

6th. To my Lady Sandwich's; who, poor lady, expects every hour to hear of my Lord; but in the best temper, neither confident nor troubled with fear, that I ever did see in my life. She tells me my Lord Rochester is now declaredly out of hopes of Mrs.

Sir Thomas Felton, married Lady Elizabeth Howard, daughter and co-heir of James, Lord Howard de Walden, and third Earl of Suffolk.

Mallett, and now she is to receive notice in a day or two how the King stands inclined to the giving leave for my Lord Hinchingbroke to look after her, and that being done to bring it to an end shortly.

7th. This morning my wife and mother rose about two o'clock; and with Mercer, Mary, the boy, and W. Hewer, as they had designed, took boat and down to refresh themselves on the water to Gravesend. To the Dolphin Taverne, where Sir J. Minnes, Lord Brouncker, Sir Thomas Harvy, and myself dined, upon Sir G. Carteret's charge, and very merry we were, Sir Thomas Harvy being a very drolle. Thence to the office, and meeting Creed away with him to my Lord Treasurer's, there thinking to have met the goldsmiths, but did not, and so appointed another time for my Lord to speak to them to advance us some money. Thence, it being the hottest day that ever I felt in my life, and it is confessed so by all other people the hottest they ever knew in England in the beginning of June, we to the New Exchange, and there drunk whey, with much entreaty getting it for our money, and they would not be entreated to let us have one glasse more. So took water and to Fox-Hall, to the Spring garden, and there walked an houre or two with great pleasure, saving our minds ill at ease concerning the fleete and my Lord Sandwich, that we have no newes of them, and ill reports run up and down of his being killed, but without ground. Here staid pleasantly walking and spending but 6*d.* till nine at night. By water home, where, weary with walking and with the mighty heat of the weather, and for my wife's not coming home, I staying walking in the garden till twelve at night, when it begun to lighten exceedingly, through the greatnesse of the heat. Then despairing of her coming home, I to bed. This day, much against my will, I did in Drury Lane see two or three houses marked with a red cross upon the doors, and "Lord have mercy upon us" writ there; which was a sad sight to me, being the first of the kind that, to my remembrance, I ever saw. It put me into an ill conception of myself and my smell, so that I was forced to buy some roll-tobacco to smell to and chaw, which took away the apprehension.

8th. About five o'clock my wife came home, it having lightened all night hard, and one great shower of rain. She came and lay upon the bed; I up and to the office all the morning. I alone at home to dinner, my wife, mother, and Mercer dining at W. Joyce's; I giving her a caution to go round by the Half Moone to his house, because of the plague. I to my Lord Treasurer's by appointment of Sir Thomas Ingram's, to meet the Goldsmiths; where I met with the great news at last newly come, brought by Bab. May [1] from the Duke of York, that we have totally

---

[1] Although the two Mays are so frequently mentioned in these pages, and by almost every contemporary annalist, no authentic account of their parentage has been traced; nor is it clear whether they were brothers, or in any way related. There is, however, a strong presumption that they sprung from a family of the same name, seated at Rawmere, in Sussex, one of whom, Jeffrey May, acquired property at Sutton Cheynell, in Leicestershire, in 1574, which was sold by the representatives of Baptist May in 1712, under an Act

routed the Dutch; that the Duke himself, the Prince, my Lord Sandwich, and Mr. Coventry are all well: which did put me into such joy, that I forgot almost all other thoughts. By and by comes Alderman Maynell and Mr. Viner, and there my Lord Treasurer did intreat them to furnish me with money upon my tallys, Sir Philip Warwick before my Lord delivering the King's changing of the hand from Mr. Povy to me, whom he called a very sober person, and one

---

passed for the payment of his debts. But though Nichols ("Hist. of Leicestershire," vol. iv. part ii. p. 548) gives a detailed pedigree of the Mays, he could not ascertain whose son Baptist May was, who held the office of Privy Purse to Charles II.; and he does not even allude to Hugh May. It is stated in Collins' "Peerage," vol. ii. p. 560, edit. 1741, that during their flight after the battle of Worcester, James Duke of York delivered his George, which had been a present from the Queen his mother, to Mr. Hugh May, who preserved it through all difficulties, and afterwards returned it to his Royal Highness in Holland. Soon after 1662 Hugh May was established as an architect, and employed at Windsor, and in erecting stables at Cornbury, and in building Berkeley House, Piccadilly, and Cassiobury. (Evelyn's "Diary.") He also held a place under Sir John Denham, the Surveyor of the Works, whom he expected to succeed; but the office becoming vacant, by the knight's death in 1667, was given to Sir Christopher Wren, and May was promised an annuity of £300 out of the Works, to make up for his disappointment. Whatever may have been his professional merits, he is not even named in Horace Walpole's list of Architects; and we know nothing more of his career, except that in 1683 he was busy in building a house at Chiswick for Sir Stephen Fox. Baptist May's history is soon told :—He was born about 1627, and after the Restoration belonged to the Duke of York's household; but he was promoted by the King to the office of Keeper of the Privy Purse, and became the confidant of Charles's amours. He was also made a Page of the Bed-chamber, which place he lost, having contrived to offend his royal master. In 1689–90, we find him returned at the general election as Burgess for Windsor, with Sir Christopher Wren : they were, however, both unseated by petition. Baptist died the 2nd of May, 1693, and lies buried in St. George's Chapel, where the slab inscribed to his memory is still to be seen.

whom the Lord Treasurer would owne in all things that
I should concern myself with them in the business of
money.   They did at present declare they could not
part with money at present.   My Lord did press them
very hard and I hope upon their considering we shall
get some of them.   Thence with great joy to the
Cocke-pitt; where the Duke of Albemarle, like a man
out of himself with content, new-told me all; and
by and by comes a letter from Mr. Coventry's own
hand to him, which he never opened (which was a
strange thing), but did give it me to open and read,
and consider what was fit for our office to do in it,
and leave the letter with Sir W. Clerke; which upon
such a time and occasion was a strange piece of indif-
ference, hardly pardonable.   I copied out the letter,
and did also take minutes out of Sir W. Clerke's other
letters; and the sum of the newes is : —

VICTORY OVER THE DUTCH, JUNE 3rd, 1665.[1]

This day they engaged; the Dutch neglecting greatly
the opportunity of the wind they had of us, by which
they lost the benefit of their fire-ships.   The Earl of
Falmouth, Muskerry, and Mr. Richard Boyle[2] killed
on board the Duke's ship, the Royall Charles, with
one shot : their blood and brains flying in the Duke's
face; and the head of Mr. Boyle striking down the
Duke, as some say.   Earle of Marlborough, Port-

----

[1] See Sir John Denham's "Advice to a Painter," concerning the Dutch
War, in "Poems on State Affairs," vol. i. p. 24.

[2] Second son to the Earl of Burlington.

land,[1] Rear-Admirall Sansum [2] (to Prince Rupert) killed, and Capt. Kirby and Ableson. Sir John Lawson [3] wounded on the knee; hath had some bones taken out, and is likely to be well again. Upon receiving the hurt, he sent to the Duke for another to command the Royal Oake. The Duke sent Jordan [4] out of the St. George, who did brave things in her. Capt. Jer. Smith of the Mary was second to the Duke, and stepped between him and Captain Seaton of the Urania (76 guns and 400 men), who had sworn to board the Duke; killed him, 200 men, and took the

---

[1] Charles Weston, third Earl of Portland.

[2] " Robert Sansum, Commander of ye Resolution, being Rear-Ad^l, of ye White." — Pepys's *Collections of Signs Manual.*

[3] When Opdam's ship blew up, a shot from it mortally wounded Sir John Lawson, which is thus alluded to in the " Poems on State Affairs," vol. i. p. 28: —

> " Destiny allowed
> Him his revenge, to make his death more proud.
> A fatal bullet from his side did range,
> And battered *Lawson;* oh, too dear exchange!
> He led our fleet that day too short a space,
> But lost his knee: since died, in glorious race:
> *Lawson,* whose valour beyond Fate did go,
> And still fights *Opdam* in the lake below."

In the same poem, Lord Falmouth's death is thus noticed: —

> " Falmouth was there, I know not what to act;
> Some say 'twas to grow Duke, too, by contract:
> An untaught bullet, in its wanton scope,
> Dashes him all to pieces, and his *Hope.*
> Such was his rise, such was his fall, unpraised;
> A chance-shot sooner took him than chance raised:
> His shattered head the fearless Duke distains,
> And gave the last first proof that he had brains."

[4] Afterwards Sir Joseph Jordan, Commander of the Royal Sovereign, and Vice Admiral of the Red, 1672. He was knighted on the 1st July, 1665.

ship; himself losing 99 men, and never an officer saved but himself lieutenant. His master indeed is saved, with his leg cut off. Admirall Opdam blown up, Trump killed, and said by Holmes; all the rest of their admiralls, as they say, but Everson (whom they dare not trust for his affection to the Prince of Orange), are killed: we having taken and sunk, as is believed, about 24 of their best ships; killed and taken near 8 or 10,000 men, and lost, we think, not above 700. A greater victory never known in the world. They are all fled, some 43 got into the Texell, and others elsewhere, and we in pursuit of the rest. Thence, with my heart full of joy, home, and to my office a little; then to my Lady Pen's, where they are all joyed and not a little puffed up at the good successe of their father; and good service indeed is said to have been done by him. Had a great bonfire at the gate; and I with my Lady Pen's people and others to Mrs. Turner's great room, and then down into the streete. I did give the boy 4*s.* among them, and mighty merry. So home to bed, with my heart at great rest and quiett, saving that the consideration of the victory is too great for me presently to comprehend.

9th. To White Hall, and in my way met with Mr. Moore, who eases me in one point wherein I was troubled; which was, that I heard of nothing said or done by my Lord Sandwich: but he tells me that Mr. Cowling, my Lord Chamberlain's secretary, did hear the King say that my Lord Sandwich had done nobly and worthily.[1] The King, it seems, is much troubled at the fall of my Lord Falmouth; but I do not meet with any man else that so much as wishes him alive again, the world conceiving him a man of too much pleasure to do the King any good, or offer any good office to him. But I hear of all hands he is confessed to have been a man of great honour, that did show it in this his going with the Duke, the most that ever any man did. Home, where my people busy to make ready a supper against night for some guests, in lieu of my stone-feast. With my taylor to buy a silke suit,[2] which though I had one lately, yet I do, for joy of the good newes we have lately had of our victory over the Dutch, which makes me willing to spare myself something extraordinary in clothes; and after long resolution of having nothing but black, I did buy a coloured silk ferrandin.[3] So home, where by and by comes Mr. Honiwood and Mrs. Wilde, and Roger Pepys and Mrs. Turner, The. and Joyce. We had a very good venison pasty, this being instead of my stone-feast the last March, and very merry we were, and so they parted. So to bed, glad it was over.

10th. In the evening home to supper; and there, to my great trouble, hear that the plague is come into the City (though it hath these three or four weeks since its beginning been wholly out of the City); but

---

[1] See Charles II.'s letter of thanks to Lord Sandwich, in Ellis's "Letters," vol. iii. p. 327, first series.

[2] See "Life," vol. i.

[3] See note, Jan. 28th, 1662-3. (M. B.)

where should it begin but in my good friend and
neighbour's Dr. Burnett,[1] in Fanchurch Street: which
in both points troubles me mightily. To bed, being
troubled at the sicknesse, and my head filled also with
other business enough, and particularly how to put my
things and estate in order, in case it should please
God to call me away, which God dispose of to his
glory.

11th (Lord's day). Up, and expected long a new
suit; but, coming not, dressed myself in my late new
black silke camelott suit; and, when fully ready, comes
my new one of coloured ferrandin, which my wife puts
me out of love with, which vexes me. At noon, by
invitation, comes my two cozen Joyces and their wives,
my aunt James and he-cozen Harman, his wife being
ill. I had a good dinner for them, and as merry as I
could be in such company. They being gone, I out
of doors a little, to show, forsooth, my new suit, and
in going I saw poor Dr. Burnett's door shut; but he
hath, I hear, gained great good-will among his neighbours; for he discovered it himself first, and caused
himself to be shut up of his own accord: which was
very handsome. In the evening comes Mr. Andrews
and his wife and Mr. Hill, and staid and played, and
sung and supped, most excellent pretty company, so
pleasant, ingenious, and harmless, I cannot desire
better.

12th. Up, and in my yesterday's new suit to the

---

[1] He was a physician.

Duke of Albemarle, and after a turne in White Hall returned, and with my taylor bought some gold lace for my sleeve hands in Pater Noster Row. The Duke of York is sent for last night and expected to be here to-morrow.

13th. At noon with Sir G. Carteret to my Lord Mayor's to dinner, where much company in a little room. His name, Sir John Lawrence. Here were at table three Sir Richard Brownes, viz. : he of the Council, a clerk, and the Alderman,[1] and his son ; and there was a little grandson also Richard, who will hereafter be Sir Richard Browne. The Alderman did here openly tell in boasting how he had, only upon suspicion of disturbances, if there had been any bad newes from sea, clapped up several persons that he was afeard of; and that he had several times done the like and would do, and take no bail where he saw it unsafe for the King. But by and by he said that he was now sued in the Exchequer by a man for false imprisonment, that he had, upon the same score, imprisoned while he was Mayor four years ago, and asked advice upon it. I told him I believed there was none, and told my story of Field, at which he was troubled, and said that it was then unsafe for any man to serve the King, and, I believed, knows not what to do

---

[1] Alderman Sir Richard Browne, Bart., was Lord Mayor in 1661–62, and Major-General of the Trained-bands: see *ante*, Feb. 22, 1659–60. His son was Sir Richard Browne, Knight. Sir Richard Browne, the Clerk of the Council, noticed Jan. 25, 1661–62, was of a different family. The Lord Mayor was seated at Debden Hall, in Essex, which he had purchased soon after 1660, and the estate was alienated by his son, the second baronet.

therein; but that Sir Richard Browne, of the Councill, advised him to speak with my Lord Chancellor about it. My Lord Mayor very respectfull to me; and so I after dinner away and found Sir J. Minnes ready with his coach and four horses at our office gate, for him and me to go out of towne to meet the Duke of York coming from Harwich to-night, and so as far as Ilford, and there 'light. By and by comes to us Sir John Shaw and Mr. Neale, that married the rich widow Gold, upon the same errand. After eating a dish of creame, we took coach again, hearing nothing of the Duke, and away home, a most pleasant evening and road. All our discourse in our way was Sir J. Minnes's telling me passages of the late King's and his father's, which I was mightily pleased to hear for information, though the pride of some persons and vice of most was but a sad story to tell how that brought the whole kingdom and King to ruine.

14th. To my Lord Treasurer's, and waited in the lobby three long hours for to speake with him, but missed him, which may teach me how I make others wait. Home to dinner and staid Mr. Hater with me, and after dinner drew up a petition for Mr. Hater to present to the Councill about his troublesome business of powder, desiring a trial that his absence may be vindicated. I met with Mr. Cowling, who observed to me how he finds every body silent in the praise of my Lord Sandwich, to set up the Duke and the Prince; but that the Duke did both to the King and my Lord Chancellor write abundantly of my Lord's courage and service. And I this day met with a letter of Captain Ferrers, wherein he tells us my Lord was with his ship in all the heat of the day, and did most worthily. To Westminster; and there saw my Lord Marlborough brought to be buried,[1] several Lords of the Council carrying him, and with the herald in some state.

15th. Up, and put on my new stuff suit with close knees, which becomes me most nobly, as my wife says. At the office all day. At noon, put on my first laced band, all lace; and to Kate Joyce's to dinner, where my mother, wife, and abundance of their friends, and good usage. At Woolwich, discoursed with Mr. Sheldon about my bringing my wife down for a month or two to his house, which he approves of, and, I think, will be convenient. This day the Newes-book (upon Mr. Moore's showing L'Estrange[2] Captain Ferrers's letters) did do my Lord Sandwich great right as to the late victory. The Duke of York not yet come to towne. The towne grows very sickly, and people to be afeard of it; there dying this last week of the plague 112, from 43 the week before, whereof but one in Fanchurch-streete, and one in Broad-streete, by the Treasurer's office.

16th. After dinner, and doing some business at the

---

[1] He was buried in Westminster Abbey.

[2] Sir Roger L'Estrange, knighted by James II., as he said, in consequence of his services and unshaken loyalty to the crown. In 1663 he published "The Public Intelligencer," a newspaper, which was laid aside when the "London Gazette," first published at Oxford, made its appearance, 1665. He also wrote many political tracts and other works. (M. B.)

office, I to White Hall, where the Court is full of the Duke and his courtiers returned from sea. All fat and lusty, and ruddy by being in the sun. I kissed his hands, and we waited all the afternoon. By and by saw Mr. Coventry, which rejoiced my very heart. Anon he and I, from all the rest of the company, walked into the Matted Gallery; where after many expressions of love, we fell to talk of business. Among other things, how my Lord Sandwich, both in his counsells and personal service, hath done most honourably and serviceably. Sir J. Lawson is come to Greenwich; but his wound in his knee yet very bad. Jonas Poole, in the Vantguard, did basely, so as to be, or will be, turned out of his ship. Captain Holmes expecting upon Sansum's death to be made Rear-admirall to the Prince (but Harman [1] is put in) hath delivered up to the Duke his commission, which the Duke took and tore. He, it seems, had bid the Prince, who first told him of Holmes's intention, that he should dissuade him from it; for that he was resolved to take it if he offered it. Yet Holmes would do it, like a rash, proud coxcombe. But he is rich, and hath, it seems, sought an occasion of leaving the service. Several of our captains have done ill. The great ships are the ships do the business, they quite deadening the enemy. They run away upon sight of

---

[1] John Harman, afterwards knighted. He had served with great reputation in several naval fights, and was desperately wounded in 1673, while engaged with a Dutch man-of-war, which he captured. He survived the action some years, but never recovered his health.

the Prince. It is strange to see how people do already slight Sir William Barkeley,[1] my Lord FitzHarding's brother, who, three months since, was the delight of the Court. Captain Smith of the Mary the Duke talks mightily of; and some great thing will be done for him. Strange to hear how the Dutch do relate, as the Duke says, that they are the conquerors; and bonfires are made in Dunkirke in their behalf; though a clearer victory can never be expected. Mr. Coventry thinks they cannot have lost less than 6,000 men, and we not dead above 200, and wounded about 400; in all about 600. Captain Grove, the Duke told us this day, hath done the basest thing at Lowestoffe, in hearing of the guns, and could not (as others) be got out, but staid there; for which he will be tried; and is reckoned a prating coxcombe, and of no courage.

17th. At the office find Sir W. Pen come home, who looks very well; and I am gladder to see him than otherwise I should be because of my hearing so

---

[1] Commander of the Swiftsure in this action, and killed in the sea-fight the following year, when Vice-Admiral of the Blue. See June 16th, 1666. Sir William Berkeley received the honour of knighthood Oct. 12th, 1664. His behaviour, after the death of his brother, Lord Falmouth, is severely commented on in " Poems on State Affairs," vol. i. p. 29: —

> " *Berkeley* had heard it soon, and thought not good
> To venture more of Royal *Harding's* blood;
> To be immortal he was not of age,
> And did e'en now the *Indian Prize* presage;
> And judged it safe and decent, cost what cost,
> To lose the day, *since his dear brother's lost.*
> With his whole squadron straight away he bore,
> And, like good boy, promised to fight no more."

well of him for his serviceablenesse in this late great action. It struck me very deep this afternoon going with a hackney coach from my Lord Treasurer's [1] down Holborne, the coachman I found to drive easily and easily, at last stood still, and came down hardly able to stand, and told me that he was suddenly struck very sicke, and almost blind, he could not see; so I 'light and went into another coach, with a sad heart for the poor man and trouble for myself, lest he should have been struck with the plague, being at the end of the towne that I took him up; but God have mercy upon us all! Sir John Lawson, I hear, is worse than yesterday: the King went to see him to-day most kindly. It seems his wound is not very bad; but he hath a fever, a thrush, and a hickup, all three together, which are, it seems, very bad symptoms.

18th (Lord's day). Up, and to church, where Sir W. Pen was the first time since he came from sea, after the battle. Mr. Mills made a sorry sermon to prove that there was a world to come after this. Sir W. Batten and my Lady are returned from Harwich. I went to see them, and it is pretty to see how we appear kind one to another, though neither of us care 2*d.* one for another. Home to supper, and there coming a hasty letter from Commissioner Pett for pressing of some calkers (as I would ever on his Majesty's service), with all speed, I made a warrant presently and issued it.

---

[1] Lord Southampton lived on the north side of Bloomsbury Square. His house was afterwards Bedford House.

19th. After dinner to my little new goldsmith's,[1] whose wife indeed is one of the prettiest, modest black women that ever I saw. I paid for a dozen of silver salts 6*l.* 14*s.* 6*d.* Thence with Sir W. Pen down to Greenwich to see Sir J. Lawson, who is better, but continues ill; his hickupp not being yet gone, could have little discourse with him.

20th. Thankes-giving-day for victory over the Dutch. Busy all the morning till church time, and there heard a mean sorry sermon of Mr. Mills. Then to the Dolphin Taverne, where all we officers of the Navy met with the Commissioners of the Ordnance by agreement, and dined: where good musique at my direction. Our club came to 34*s.* a man, nine of us. By water to Fox-hall, and there walked an hour alone, observing the several humours of the citizens that were there this holy-day, pulling of cherries,[2] and God knows what. This day I informed myself that there died four or five at Westminster of the plague in one alley in several houses upon Sunday last, Bell Alley, over against the Palace-gate; yet people do think that the number will be fewer in the towne than it was the last weeke. The Dutch are come out again with 20 sail under Bankert; supposed gone to the Northward to meete their East India fleete.

21st. I find our tallys will not be money in less than sixteen months, which is a sad thing for the King to pay all that interest for every penny he

---

[1] Colvill. (M. B.)   [2] The game of bob-cherry.

spends; and, which is strange, the goldsmiths with whom I spoke, do declare that they will not be moved to part with money upon the increase of their consideration of ten per cent. which they have, and therefore desire I would not move in it, and indeed the consequence would be very ill to the King, and have its ill consequences follow us through all the King's revenue.   I find all the towne almost going out of towne, the coaches and waggons being all full of people going into the country.

22nd. In great pain whether to send my mother into the country to-day or no, I hearing, by my people, that she, poor wretch, hath a mind to stay a little longer, and I cannot blame her, considering what a life she will through her own folly lead when she comes home again, unlike the pleasure and liberty she has had here.   At last I resolved to put it to her, and she agreed to go, because of the sicknesse in the towne, and my intentions of removing my wife.   So I did give her money and took a kind leave of her.   She was to the last unwilling to go, but would not say so, but put it off till she lost her place in the coach, and was fain to ride in the waggon part.

23rd. To a Committee for Tangier, where unknown to me comes my Lord of Sandwich, who, it seems, came to towne last night.   After the Committee was up, my Lord Sandwich did take me aside in the robe-chamber, telling me how much the Duke and Mr. Coventry did, both in the fleete and here, make of him, and that in some opposition to the Prince; and

as a more private message, he told me that he hath
been with them both when they have made sport of
the Prince and laughed at him : yet that all the discourse of the towne, and the printed relation, should
not give him one word of honour my Lord thinks very
strange ; he assuring me, that though by accident the
Prince was in the van in the beginning of the fight
for the first pass, yet all the rest of the day my Lord
was in the van, and continued so. That notwithstanding all this noise of the Prince, he had hardly a shot
in his side or a man killed, whereas he hath above 30
in her hull, and not one mast whole nor yard ; but the
most battered ship of the fleet, and lost most men,
saving Captain Smith of the Mary. That the most the
Duke did was almost out of gun-shot ; but that, indeed,
the Duke did come up to my Lord's rescue after he had
a great while fought with four of them. How poorly
Sir John Lawson performed, notwithstanding all that
was said of him ; and how his ship turned out of the
way, while Sir J. Lawson himself was upon the deck,
to the endangering of the whole fleete. It therefore
troubles my Lord that Mr. Coventry should not mention a word of him in his relation. I did, in answer,
offer that I was sure the relation was not compiled by
Mr. Coventry, but by L'Estrange, out of several letters,
as I could witness ; and that Mr. Coventry's letter that
he did give the Duke of Albemarle did give him as
much right as the Prince, for I myself read it first
and then copied it out, which I promised to show my
Lord, with which he was somewhat satisfied. From

that discourse my Lord did begin to tell me how much he was concerned to dispose of his children, and would have my advice and help; and propounded to match my Lady Jemimah to Sir G. Carteret's eldest son,[1] which I approved of, and did undertake the speaking with him about it as from myself, which my Lord liked. To one Finch,[2] one of the Commissioners for the Excise, to be informed about some things of the Excise, in order to our settling matters therein better for us for our Tangier business. I find him a very discreet, grave person. Creed and I took boat and to Fox Hall, where we spent two or three hours talking of several matters very soberly and contentfully to me, which, with the ayre and pleasure of the garden, was a great refreshment to me, and, methinks, that which we ought to joy ourselves in. Home by hackney-coach, which is become a very dangerous passage now-a-days, the sickness encreasing mightily.

24th. To Dr. Clerke's, and there I in the best manner I could, broke my errand about a match between Sir G. Carteret's eldest son and my Lord Sandwich's eldest daughter, which he (as I knew he would) took with great content: and we both agreed that my Lord and he, being both men relating to the sea, under a kind aspect of His Majesty, already good friends, and both virtuous and good familys, their alliance might be of good use to us; and he did undertake to find

---

[1] Philip Carteret, afterwards knighted. He perished on board Lord Sandwich's flag-ship at the battle of Solebay.

[2] Daniel Finch.

out Sir George this morning, and put the business in execution. So being both well pleased with the proposition, I saw his niece there and made her sing me two or three songs very prettily, and so home to the office. At noon Captain Ferrers and Mr. Moore dined with me, who do give me the best conversation in general, and as good an account of the particular service of the Prince and my Lord of Sandwich in the late sea-fight as I could desire. So I to White Hall, where I with Creed and Povy attended my Lord Treasurer, and did prevail with him to let us have an assignment for 15 or 20,000*l.*, which, I hope, will do our business for Tangier. To Sir G. Carteret, and in the best manner I could, and most obligingly, moved the business : he received it with great respect and content, and thanks to me, and promised that he would do what he possibly could for his son, to render him fit for my Lord's daughter, and showed great kindness to me, and sense of my kindness to him herein. Sir William Pen told me this day that Mr. Coventry is to be sworn a Privy Counsellor, at which my soul is glad.

25th. To White Hall, where, after I had again visited Sir G. Carteret, and received his (and now his Lady's) full content in my proposal, I went to my Lord Sandwich, and having told him how Sir G. Carteret received it, he did direct me to return to Sir G. Carteret, and give him thanks for his kind reception of this offer, and that he would the next day be willing to enter discourse with him about the business.

My Lord, I perceive, intends to give 5,000*l.* with her, and expects about 800*l. per annum* joynture. So by water home and to supper and bed, being weary with long walking at Court, but had a Psalm or two with my boy and Mercer, which pleased me mightily. This night Sir G. Carteret told me with great kindnesse that the order of the Council did run for the making of Hater and Whitfield incapable of any serving the King again. Before I went to White Hall I went down to Greenwich by water, thinking to have visited Sir J. Lawson, where, when I come, I find that he died this morning; and indeed the nation hath a great loss; though I cannot, without dissembling, say that I am sorry for it, for he was a man never kind to me at all. Being at White Hall, I visited Mr. Coventry, who, among other talk, entered about the great question now in the House about the Duke's going to sea again; about which the whole House is divided. He did concur with me that, for the Duke's honour and safety, it were best, after so great a service and victory and danger, not to go again; and, above all, that the life of the Duke cannot but be a security to the Crowne; if he were away, it being more easy to attempt anything upon the King; but how the fleete will be governed without him, the Prince [1] being a man of no government and severe in council, that no ordinary man can offer any advice against his; saying truly that it had been better he had gone to Guinny,

---

[1] Prince Rupert. (M. B.)

and that were he away, it were easy to say how matters might be ordered, my Lord Sandwich being a man of temper and judgment as much as any man he ever knew, and that upon good observation he said this, and that his temper must correct the Prince's. But I perceive he is much troubled what will be the event of the question. So I left him.

26th. To the Committee of Tangier, where my Lord Treasurer was, the first and only time he ever was there, and did promise us 15,000*l.* for Tangier and no more, which will be short. Thence with Creed to the King's head,[1] and there dined with him at the ordinary, and good sport with one Mr. Nicholls, a prating coxcombe, that would be thought a poet, but would not be got to repeat any of his verses. Thence I home, and there find my wife's brother and his wife, a pretty little modest woman, where they dined with my wife. He did come to desire my assistance for a living, and, upon his good promises of care, and that it should be no burden to me, I did say and promise I would think of something for him, and the rather because his wife seems a pretty discreet young thing, and humble, and he, above all things, desirous to do something to maintain her, telling me sad stories of what she endured with him in Holland, and I hope it will not be burdensome. The plague encreases mightily, I this day seeing a house, at a bitt-maker's over against St. Clement's Church, in the open street, shut up; which is a sad sight.

---

[1] At the corner of Chancery Lane.

28th. I did take my leave of Sir William Coventry, who, it seems, was knighted and sworn a Privy-Counsellor two days since ; who with his old kindness treated me, and I believe I shall ever find him a noble friend. Sir G. Carteret tells me how all things proceed between my Lord Sandwich and himself to full content, and both sides depend upon having the match finished presently, and professed great kindnesse to me, and said that now we were something akin. I am mightily, both with respect to myself and much more of my Lord's family, glad of this alliance. In my way to Westminster Hall, I observed several plague houses in King's Street and near the Palace. I was fearful of going to any house but I did to the Swan, and thence to White Hall, giving the waterman a shilling, because a young fellow and belonging to the Plymouth. My Lord Sandwich is gone towards the sea to-day, it being a sudden resolution, I having taken no leave of him.

29th. By water to White Hall, where the Court full of waggons and people ready to go out of towne. This end of the towne every day grows very bad of the plague. The Mortality Bill is come to 267 ; which is about ninety more than the last : and of these but four in the City, which is a great blessing to us. Took leave again of Mr. Coventry ; though I hope the Duke is not gone to stay, and so do others too. Home, calling at Somerset House, where all are packing up too : the Queene-Mother setting out for France this day to drink Bourbon waters this year, she being in a consumption; and intends not to come till winter come twelve-months.[1]

30th. To White Hall, to the Duke of Albemarle, who I find at Secretary Bennet's, there being now no other great Statesman, I think, but my Lord Chancellor, in towne. I received several commands from them, among others, to provide some bread and cheese for the garrison at Guernsey, which they promised to see me paid for. In the afternoon I down to Woolwich and after me my wife and Mercer, whom I led to Mr. Sheldon's, to see his house, and I find it a very pretty place for them to be at. Back by water and in the dark and against tide shot the bridge,[2] groping with their pole for the way, which troubled me before I got through. So home, about one or two o'clock in the morning, my family at a great losse what was become of me. Thus this book of two years ends. Myself and family in good health, consisting of myself and wife, Mercer, her woman, Mary, Alce, and Susan our maids, and Tom my boy. In a sickly time of the plague growing on. Having upon my hands the troublesome care of the Treasury of Tangier, with great sums drawn upon me, and nothing to pay them with : also the business of the office great. Considering of removing my wife to Woolwich; she lately busy in

---

[1] She never came to England again, though she lived some years after. She died at Colombe, near Paris, in August, 1669, and her son, the Duke of York, pronounced this eulogium on her: " She excelled in all the qualities of a good wife, of a good mother, and a good Christian." — MACPHERSON'S *Original Papers*, vol. i. (M. B.)

[2] See note, 8th August, 1662.

learning to paint, with great pleasure and successe. All other things well; especially a new interest I am making, by a match in hand between the eldest son of Sir G. Carteret, and my Lady Jemimah Montagu. The Duke of York gone down to the fleete, but all suppose not with intent to stay there, as it is not fit, all men conceive, he should.

July 1st. To the Duke of Albemarle's, by appointment, to give him an account of some disorder in the Yarde at Portsmouth, by workmen's going away of their owne accord, for lacke of money, to get work of hay-making, or any thing else to earne themselves bread. Thence to Westminster, where I hear the sickness encreases greatly. Sad at the newes that seven or eight houses in Bazing Hall street, are shut up of the plague.

2nd (Lord's day). Sir G. Carteret did send me word that the business between my Lord and him is fully agreed on, and is mightily liked of by the King and the Duke of York. I hear that Sir J. Lawson[1] was buried last night at St. Dunstan's by us, without any company at all, and that the condition of his family is but very poor.

3rd. Late at the office and so home resolving from this night forwards to close all my letters, if possible, and end all my business at the office by daylight, and put all my affairs in the world in good order, the season growing so sickly, that it is much to be feared

---

[1] In the register of the Old Church, at Greenwich, is the following entry: " Sir John Lawson carried away, June 27, 1665."

how a man can escape having a share with others in it, for which the good Lord God bless me, or to be fitted to receive it.

4th. At noon to the 'Change and thence to the Dolphin, where a good dinner at the cost of one Mr. Osbaston, who lost a wager a good while since and now it is spent. The wager was that ten of our ships should not have a fight with ten of the enemy's before Michaelmas. I hear this day the Duke and Prince Rupert are both come back from sea, and neither of them go back again. The latter I much wonder at but it seems the towne reports so, and I am very glad of it. This morning I did a piece of good work with Sir W. Warren, ending the business of the lotterys, wherein honestly I think I shall get above 100*l*. Bankert, it seems, is come home with the little fleete he has been abroad with, without doing any thing, so that there is nobody of an enemy at sea. We are in great hopes of meeting with the Dutch East India fleete, which is mighty rich, or with De Ruyter, who is so also. Sir Richard Ford told me this day, at table, a fine account, how the Dutch were like to have been mastered by the present Prince of Orange his father to be besieged in Amsterdam,[1] having drawn an army of foot into the towne, and horse near to the towne by

---

[1] *Sic orig.* The period alluded to is 1650, when the States, General disbanded part of the forces which the Prince of Orange (William) wished to retain. The Prince attempted, but unsuccessfully, to possess himself of Amsterdam. In the same year he died, at the early age of twenty-four some say of the small-pox, others, with Sir Richard Ford, say of poison.

night, within three miles, and they never knew of it ; but by chance the Hamburgh post in the night fell among the horse, and heard their design, and knowing the way, it being very dark and rainy, better than they, went from them, and did give notice to the towne before the others could reach the towne, and so were saved. It seems this De Witt and another family, the Beckarts, were among the chief of the familys that were enemys to the Prince, and were afterwards suppressed by the Prince, and continued so till he was, as they say, poysoned ; and then they turned all again, as it was, against the young Prince, and have so carried it to this day, it being about 12 and 14 years, and De Witt in the head of them.

5th. Up, and advised about sending of my wife's bedding and things to Woolwich, in order to her removal thither. In the afternoon I abroad to St. James's and there with Mr. Coventry a good while, and understand how matters are ordered in the fleete that is, my Lord Sandwich goes Admiral ; under him Sir G. Ascue, and Sir T. Teddiman : Vice-Admiral, Sir W. Pen ; and under him Sir W. Barkeley, and Sir Jos. Jordan : [1] Rear-Admiral, Sir Thomas Allen ; and under him Sir Christopher Mings, [2] and Captain Harman. From thence walked round to White Hall, the

---

[1] Sir Jos. Jordan commanded the Royal Sovereign as Vice-Admiral of the Red, in 1672; and distinguished himself in the battle of Solebay, and on other occasions. He had just been knighted.

[2] Sir Christopher Mings, the son of a shoemaker, bred to the sea-service; he rose to the rank of an Admiral. He was killed in the fight with the Dutch, June, 1666.

Parke being quite locked up; and I observed a house shut up this day in the Pell Mell, where heretofore in Cromwell's time we young men used to keep our weekly clubs. And so to White Hall to Sir G. Carteret; we went to Deptford, all the way talking, first, how matters are quite concluded with all possible content between my Lord and him and signed and sealed, so that my Lady Sandwich is to come thither to-morrow or next day, and the young lady is sent for, and all likely to be ended between them in a very little while, with mighty joy on both sides, and the King, Duke, Lord Chancellor, and all mightily pleased. Thence to newes, wherein I find that Sir G. Carteret do now take all my Lord Sandwich's business to heart, and makes it the same with his owne. He tells me how at Chatham it was proposed to my Lord Sandwich to be joined with the Prince in the command of the fleete, which he was most willing to; but when it came to the Prince, he was quite against it; saying, there could be no government, but that it would be better to have two fleetes, and neither under the command of the other, which he would not agree to. So the King was not pleased; but, without any unkindnesse, did order the fleete to be ordered as above, as to the Admirals and commands: so the Prince is come up; and Sir G. Carteret, I remember, had this word thence, that, says he, by this means, though the King told him that it would be but for this expedition, yet I believe we shall keepe him out for altogether. He tells me how my Lord was much troubled at Sir W.

Pen's being ordered forth, as it seems he is, to go to Solebay, and with the best fleete he can, to go forth, and no notice taken of my Lord Sandwich going after him, and having the command over him. By water to Woolwich, where I found my wife come, and her two mayds, and very prettily accommodated they will be; and I left them going to supper, grieved in my heart to part with my wife, being worse by much without her, though some trouble there is in having the care of a family at home in this plague time.

6th. By water to White Hall to Sir G. Carteret about money for the office, a sad thought, for in a little while all must go to wracke, winter coming on apace, when a great sum must be ready to pay part of the fleete, and so far we are from it that we have not enough to stop the mouths of poor people and their hands from falling about our eares here almost in the office. God give a good end to it! Sir G. Carteret told me one considerable thing: Alderman Backewell is ordered abroad upon some private score with a great sum of money; wherein I was instrumental the other day in shipping him away. It seems some of his creditors have taken notice of it, and he was like to be broke yesterday in his absence; Sir G. Carteret telling me that the King and the kingdom must as good as fall with that man at this time; and that he was forced to get 4,000*l.* himself to answer Backewell's people's occasions, or he must have broke; but committed this to me as a great secret and which I am heartily sorry for. Thence after a little merry discourse of our marrying business, I parted and to see my Lord Brouncker, who is not well. I could not see him, nor had much mind, one of the great houses within two doors of him being shut up : and Lord ! the number of houses visited, which this day I observed through the town quite round in my way by Long Lane and London Wall. Thence to Sir W. Batten, and spent the evening at supper ; and, among other discourse, the rashness of Sir John Lawson, for breeding up his daughter so high and proud, refusing a man of great interest, Sir W. Barkeley, to match her with a melancholy fellow, Coll. Norton's son, of no interest nor good nature nor generosity at all, giving her 6,000*l.*, when the other [1] would have taken her with two ; when he himself knew that he was not worth the money himself in all the world, he did give her that portion, and is since dead, and left his wife and two daughters beggars, and the other gone away with 6,000*l.*, and no content in it, through the ill qualities of her father-in-law and husband, who, it seems, though a pretty woman, contracted for her as if he had been buying a horse ; and, worst of all, is now of no use to serve the mother and two little sisters in any stead at Court, whereas, the other might have done what he would for her : so here is an end of this family's pride, which, with good care, might have been what they would, and done well. Sir W. Pen, it seems, sailed last night from Solebay with about sixty

---

[1] Whose death is mentioned, 29th August, 1666.

sail of ship, and my Lord Sandwich in the Prince and some others, it seems, going after them to overtake them.

7th. Up, and having set my neighbour, Mr. Hudson, wine coopers, at work drawing out a tierce of wine for the sending of some of it to my wife, I abroad, only taking notice to what a condition it has pleased God to bring me that at this time I have two tierces of Claret, two quarter casks of Canary, and a smaller vessel of Sack; a vessel of Tent, another of Malaga, and another of white wine, all in my wine cellar together; which, I believe, none of my friends of my name now alive ever had of his owne at one time. Home, taking some new books, 5*l.* worth home to my great content.

8th. All day very diligent at the office, ended my letters by 9 at night, and then fitted myself to go down to Woolwich to my wife which I did, but strange to think what a fine night I had down, but before I had been one minute on shore, the mightiest storm came of wind and rain that almost could be for a quarter of an houre and so left.

9th (Lord's day). To Sir G. Carteret, and there find my Lady [Sandwich] in her chamber, not very well, but looks the worst almost that ever I did see her in my life. It seems her drinking of the water at Tunbridge did almost kill her before she could with most violent physique get it out of her body again. We are received with most extraordinary kindnesse by my Lady Carteret and her children, and dined most nobly. I took occasion to have much discourse with Mr. Ph. Carteret, and find him a very modest man; and I think verily of mighty good nature, and pretty understanding. He did give me a good account of the fight with the Dutch. About three o'clock I, leaving my wife there, took boat and home, and there shifted myself into my black silke suit, and having promised Harman yesterday, I to his house, which I find very mean, and mean company. His wife very ill; I could not see her. Here I, with her father and Kate Joyce, who was also very ill, were godfathers and godmother to his boy, and was christened Will. Mr. Meriton [1] christened him. The most observable thing I found there to my content, was to hear him and his clerk tell me that in this parish of Michell's, Cornhill, one of the middle-most parishes and a great one of the towne, there hath, notwithstanding this sickliness, been buried of any disease, man, woman, or child, not one for thirteen months last past; which is very strange. And the like in a good degree in most other parishes, I hear, saving only of the plague in them, but in this neither the plague nor any other disease. So back again home and reshifted myself, and so down to my Lady Carteret's, where mighty merry and great pleasantnesse between my Lady Sandwich and the young ladies and me, and all of us mighty merry, there never having been in the world sure a greater business of general content than

---

[1] Joseph Meriton, instituted to the rectory of St. Michael, Cornhill, 1663, of which he continued incumbent nearly forty years.

this match proposed between Mr. Carteret and my Lady Jemimah. But withal it is mighty pretty to think how my poor Lady Sandwich, between her and me, is doubtfull whether her daughter will like of it or no, and how troubled she is for fear of it, which I do not fear at all, and desire her not to do it, but her fear is the most discreet and pretty that ever I did see. Here late, and then my wife and I with most hearty kindnesse from my Lady Carteret by boat to Woolwich, came thither about 12 at night, and so to bed.

10th. Away by water to the Duke of Albemarle's, where he tells me that I must be at Hampton Court anon. So I home, and having a coach of Mr. Povy's attending me, by appointment, in order to my coming to dine at his country house at Brainford, where he and his family is, I went and Mr. Tasbrough with me therein, it being a pretty chariot, but most inconvenient as to the horses throwing dust and dirt into one's eyes and upon one's clothes. There I staid a quarter of an houre. Creed rode before, and Mr. Povy and I after him in the chariot; and I was set down by him at the Parke pale, where one of his saddle horses was ready for me, he himself not daring to come into the house or be seen, because that a servant of his, out of his house, happened to be sicke, but is not yet dead, but was never suffered to come into his house after he was ill. But this opportunity was taken to injure Povy, and most horribly he is abused by some persons hereupon, and his fortune, I believe, quite broke; but that he hath a good heart to bear, or a cunning one to conceal his evil. There I met with Sir W. Coventry, and by and by was heard by my Lord Chancellor and Treasurer about our Tangier money, and my Lord Treasurer had ordered me to forbear meddling with the 15,000*l.* he offered me the other day, but, upon opening the case to them, they did offer it again, and so I think I shall have it, but my Lord General must give his consent in it, this money having been promised to him, and he very angry at the proposal. Here though I have not been in many years, yet I lacke time to stay, besides that it is, I perceive, an unpleasing thing to be at Court, everybody being fearful one of another, and all so sad, enquiring after the plague, so that I stole away by my horse to Kingston, and there with trouble was forced to press two sturdy rogues to carry me to London, and met at the Waterside with Mr. Charnocke, Sir Philip Warwick's clerke, who had been in company and was quite foxed.[1] I took him with me in my boat, and so away to Richmond, and there, by night, walked with him to Mortlake, a very pretty walk, and there staid a good while, and so

11th. All night down by water, a most pleasant passage, and came thither by two o'clock, and so walked from the Old Swan home, and there to bed to my Will, being very weary, and he lodging at my desire in my house. At 6 o'clock up and to Westminster, where and all the towne besides the plague

---

[1] Drunk.

encreases. So to the Duke of Albemarle, and there with much ado did get his consent in part to my having the money promised for Tangier, and the other part did not concur. To the evening 'Change, and there hear all the towne full that Ostend is delivered to us, and that Alderman Backewell did go with 50,-000*l.* to that purpose. But the truth of it I do not know, but something I believe there is extraordinary in his going. So to the office, and so away to bed, taking some Venice treacle, feeling myself out of order.

12th. After doing what business I could in the morning, it being a solemn fast-day for the plague growing upon us, I took boat and down to Deptford, where I stood with great pleasure an houre or two by my Lady Sandwich's bedside, talking to her (she lying prettily in bed) of my Lady Jemimah's being from my Lady Pickering's when our letters came to that place ; she being at my Lord Montagu's, at Boughton. The truth is, I had received letters of it two days ago, but had dropped them, and was in a very extraordinary straite what to do for them, or what account to give my Lady, but sent to every place ; I sent to Mortlake, where I had been the night before, and there they were found, which with mighty joy came safe to me ; but all ending with satisfaction to my Lady and me, though I find my Lady Carteret not much pleased with this delay, and principally because of the plague, which renders it unsafe to stay long at Deptford. I eat a bit, my Lady Carteret being the most kind lady in the world, and so took boat, and a fresh boat at the Tower, and so up the river, against tide all the way, I having lost it by staying prating to and with my Lady, and, from before one, made it seven ere we got to Hampton Court; and when I came there all business was over, saving my finding Mr. Coventry at his chamber, and so away to my boat, and all night upon the water and came home by two o'clock, shooting the bridge at that time of night. Heard Mr. Williamson repeat at Hampton Court to-day how the King of France hath lately set out a most high arrest against the Pope,[1] which is reckoned very lofty and high.

13th. By water, at night late, to Sir G. Carteret's,[2] but there being no oars to carry me, I was fain to call a skuller that had a gentleman already in it, and he proved a man of love to musique, and he and I sung

---

[1] The rupture between Alexander VII. and Louis XIV. was healed in 1664, by the treaty signed at Pisa, on the 12th Feb. On the 9th of August the Pope's nephew, Cardinal Chigi, made his entry into Paris, as Legate, to give the King satisfaction for the insult offered at Rome by the Corsican guard to the Duc de Créqui, the French Ambassador: see 25th Jan., 1662-63. Cardinal Imperiali, Governor of Rome, asked pardon of the King in person, and all the hard conditions of the treaty were fulfilled. But no *arrêt* against the Pope was set forth in 1665. On the contrary, Alexander, now wishing to please the King, issued a Constitution on the 2nd of Feb., 1665, ordering all the clergy of France, without any exception, to sign a formulary condemning the famous five propositions extracted from the works of Jansenius; and on the 29th of April, the King in person ordered the Parliament to register the bull. The Jansenist party, of course, demurred to this proceeding: the Bishops of Alais, Angers, Beauvais, and Pamiers, issuing mandates calling upon their clergy to refuse. It was against these mandates, as being contrary to the King's declaration and the Pope's intentions, that the *arrêt* was directed.

[2] At the Treasurer's house at Deptford, Sir G. Carteret's official residence.

together the way down with great pleasure, and an incident extraordinary to be met with. Above 700 died of the plague this week.

14th. All the morning at the Exchequer endeavouring to strike tallys for money, and mightily vexed to see how people attend there, some out of towne, and others drowsy, and to others it was late, so that the King's business suffers ten times more than all their service is worth. So I am put off to to-morrow. In the evening I by water to Sir G. Carteret's, and there find my Lady Sandwich and her buying things for my Lady Jem's wedding: and my Lady Jem is beyond expectation come to Dagenhams ¹ where Mr. Carteret is to go to visit her to-morrow; and my proposal of waiting on him, he being to go alone to all persons strangers to him, was well accepted, and so I go with him. But Lord! to see how kind my Lady Carteret is to her! Sends her most rich jewells, and provides bedding and things of all sorts most richly for her, which makes my Lady and me out of our wits almost to see the kindnesse she treats us all with, as if they

---

¹ Dagenhams, near Romford, the seat of Lady Wright, widow of Sir Henry Wright, and sister of Lady Sandwich. (See 27th March, 1660.) This estate was devised by Anne, daughter of Sir Henry and Lady Wright, widow first of Sir Robert Pye, of Berkshire, and afterwards of William Rider, Esq., only surviving child of Sir Henry Wright, to her first cousin, Edward Carteret, Postmaster-General, third son of Sir Philip Carteret and Lady Jemimah Montagu, whose daughters, in 1749, sold it to Henry Muilman; in 1772 it was again disposed of to Mr. Neave, grandfather of the present proprietor (Sir Richard Digby Neave, Bart.), who pulled down the old house built by Sir Henry Wright, and erected the present mansion on a different site. See Lysons's "Environs," vol. iv. p. 191.

would buy the young lady. Thence away home and so to bed, to be up betimes by the helpe of a larum watch, which by chance I borrowed of my watchmaker to-day, while my owne is mending.

15th. To Deptford, and anon took boat and Mr. Carteret and I to the ferry-place at Greenwich, and there staid an hour crossing the water to and again to get our coach and horses over; and by and by set out, and so toward Dagenhams. But Lord! what silly discourse we had as to love-matters, he being the most awkerd man I ever met with in my life as to that business. Thither we come, and by that time it begun to be dark, and were kindly received by Lady Wright and my Lord Crew. And to discourse they went, my Lord discoursing with him, asking of him questions of travell, which he answered well enough in a few words; but nothing to the lady from him at all. To supper, and after supper to talk again, he yet taking no notice of the lady. My Lord would have had me have consented to leaving the young people together to-night, to begin their amours, his staying being but to be little. But I advised against it, lest the lady might be too much surprised. So they led him up to his chamber, where I staid a little, to know how he liked the lady, which he told me he did mightily; but Lord! in the dullest insipid manner that ever lover did. So I bid him good night, and down to prayers with my Lord Crew's family, and after prayers, my Lord and Lady Wright, and I, to consult what to do; and it was agreed at last to have them go to church

together, as the family used to do, though his lame-
ness was a great objection against it.   But at last my
Lady Jem. sent me word by my Lady Wright that it
would be better to do just as they used to do before
his coming ; and therefore she desired to go to church,
which was yielded then to.

16th (Lord's day). I up, having lain with Mr.
Moore in the chaplain's chamber.   And having trimmed myself, down to Mr. Carteret ; and he being
ready we down and walked in the gallery an hour or
two, it being a most noble and pretty house that ever,
for the bigness, I saw.   Here I taught him what to
do : to take the lady always by the hand to lead her,
and telling him that I would find opportunity to leave
them two together, he should make these and these
compliments, and also take a time to do the like to
Lord Crew and Lady Wright.   After I had instructed
him, which he thanked me for, owning that he needed
my teaching him, my Lord Crew came down and
family, the young lady among the rest ; and so by
coaches to church four miles off ; where a pretty good
sermon, and a declaration of penitence of a man that
had undergone the Churche's censure for his wicked
life.   Thence back again by coach, Mr. Carteret having not had the confidence to take his lady once by
the hand, coming or going, which I told him of when
we came home, and he will hereafter do it.   So to
dinner.   My Lord excellent discourse.   Then to walk
in the gallery, and to sit down.   By and by my Lady
Wright and I go out (and then my Lord Crew, he not

by design), and lastly my Lady Crew came out, and left the young people together. And a little pretty daughter of my Lady Wright's most innocently came out afterwards, and shut the door to, as if she had done it, poor child, by inspiration; which made us without have good sport to laugh at. They together an hour, and by and by church-time, whither he led her into the coach and into the church, where several handsome ladies. But it was most extraordinary hot that ever I knew it. So home again and to walk in the gardens, where we left the young couple a second time; and my Lady Wright and I to walk together, who tells me that some more new clothes must of necessity be made for Lady Jemimah, which and other things I took care of. Anon to supper, and excellent discourse and dispute between my Lord Crew and the chaplin, who is a good scholler, but a nonconformist. Here this evening I spoke with Mrs. Carter, my old acquaintance, that hath lived with my Lady these twelve or thirteen years, the sum of all whose discourse and others for her, is, that I would get her a good husband; which I have promised, but know not when I shall perform. After Mr. Carteret was carried to his chamber, we to prayers and then to bed.

17th. Up all of us, and to billiards; my Lady Wright, Mr. Carteret, myself, and every body. By and by the young couple left together. Anon to dinner; and after dinner Mr. Carteret took my advice about giving to the servants, and I led him to give 10*l.* among them, which he did, by leaving it to the chief

man-servant, Mr. Medows, to do for him.   Before we
went, I took my Lady Jem. apart, and would know
how she liked this gentleman, and whether she was
under any difficulty concerning him.   She blushed,
and hid her face awhile ; but at last I forced her to
tell me.   She answered that she could readily obey
what her father and mother had done ; which was all
she could say, or I expect.   So anon I took leave, and
for London.   But, Lord ! to see, among other things,
how all these great people here are afeard of London,
being doubtfull of anything that comes from thence, or
that hath lately been there, that I was forced to say
that I lived wholly at Woolwich.   In our way Mr.
Carteret did give me mighty thanks for my care and
pains for him, and is mightily pleased, though the
truth is, my Lady Jem. hath carried herself with mighty
discretion and gravity, not being forward at all in any
degree, but mighty serious in her answers to him, as
by what he says and I observed, I collect.   To London to my office and so to Deptford, where mighty
welcome, and brought the good newes of all being
pleased to them.   Mighty mirth at my giving them
an account of all ; but the young man could not be
got to say one word before me or my Lady Sandwich
of his adventures, but, by what he afterwards related
to his father and mother and sisters, he gives an
account that pleases them mightily.   Here Sir G.
Carteret would have me lie all night, which I did
most nobly, better than ever I did in my life, Sir G.
Carteret being mighty kind to me, leading me to my

chamber; and all their care now is, to have the business ended, and they have reason, because the sicknesse puts all out of order, and they cannot safely stay where they are.

18th. To the 'Change, where a little business and a very thin Exchange; and so walked through London to the Temple, where I took water for Westminster to the Duke of Albemarle, to wait on him, and so to Westminster Hall, and there paid for my newes-books, and did give Mrs. Michell, who is going out of towne because of the sicknesse, and her husband, a pint of wine. I was much troubled this day to hear at Westminster how the officers do bury the dead in the open Tuttle-fields, pretending want of room elsewhere; whereas the new chappell churchyard was walled-in at the publick charge in the last plague-time, merely for want of room and now none, but such as are able to pay dear for it, can be buried there.

19th. To the Exchequer, and there with much trouble got my tallys, and by water down to Deptford, where I find all ¹ full of joy, and preparing to go to Dagenhams to-morrow.

20th. Up, in a boat to the Tower, and there to the office, where we sat all the morning. So down to Deptford and there dined, and after dinner saw my Lady Sandwich and Mr. Carteret and his two sisters over the water, going to Dagenhams, and my Lady

---

¹ The Carterets.

Carteret toward Cranburne.[1]   So all the company broke up in most extraordinary joy, wherein I am mighty contented that I have had the good fortune to be so instrumental, and I think it will be of good use to me.   So walked to Redriffe, where I hear the sickness is, and indeed is scattered almost every where, there dying 1,089 of the plague this week.   My Lady Carteret did this day give me a bottle of plague-water home with me.   I received yesterday a letter from my Lord Sandwich, giving me thanks for my care about their marriage business, and desiring it to be dispatched, that no disappointment may happen therein. Lord ! to see how the plague spreads.   It being now all over King's Streete, at the Axe, and next door to it, and in other places.

21st.   To the goldsmiths, to see what money I could get upon my present tallys upon the advance of the Excise, and I hope I shall get 10,000*l.*   Alderman Backewell is at sea.   Sir R. Viner came to towne but this morning.   So Colvill was the only man I could yet speak withal to get any money of.   So to Anthony Joyce's, and there broke to him my desire to have Pall married to Harman, whose wife, poor woman, is lately dead, to my trouble, I loving her very much, and he will consider it.   So home and late at my chamber, setting some papers in order; the plague growing very raging, and my apprehensions of it great.

---

[1] A royal lodge in Windsor Forest, where Sir G. Carteret was residing. (M. B.)

22nd. As soon as up I among my goldsmiths, Sir Robert Viner and Colvill, and there got 10,000*l.* of my new tallys accepted, and so I made it my work to find out Mr. Mervin and sent for others to come with their bills of Exchange. After dinner I to Sir R. Viner's, by his invitation in the morning, and got near 5,000*l.* more accepted, and so from this day the whole, or near 15,000*l.* lies upon interest. Thence I by water to Westminster and the Duke of Albemarle being gone to dinner to my Lord of Canterbury's, I thither, and there walked and viewed the new hall,[1] a new old-fashion hall as possible. Begun, and means left for the ending of it, by Bishop Juxon. Not coming proper to speak with him, I to Fox-hall, where to the Spring garden ; but I do not see one guest there, the town being so empty of anybody to come thither. Only, while I was there, a poor woman came to scold with the master of the house that a kinswoman, I think, of her's, that was newly dead of the plague, might be buried in the church-yard ; for, for her part, she should not be buried in the commons, as they said she should. I by coach home, not meeting with but two coaches, and but two carts from White Hall to my own house, that I could observe ; and the streets mighty thin of people. I met this noon with Dr. Burnett, who told me, and I find in the news-book this week that he posted upon the 'Change, that whoever did spread the report that, instead of dying

---

[1] The hall spoken of was converted into the archiepiscopal library by the late Archbishop Howley.

of the plague, his servant was by him killed, it was forgery, and shewed me the acknowledgment of the master of the pest-house, that his servant died of a bubo on his right groine, and two spots on his right thigh, which is the plague. All the news is great: that we must of necessity fall out with France, for He will side with the Dutch against us. That Alderman Backewell is gone over (which indeed he is) with money, and that Ostend is in our present possession. But it is strange to see how poor Alderman Backewell is like to be put to it in his absence, Mr. Shaw his right hand being ill. And the Alderman's absence gives doubts to people, and I perceive they are in great straits for money, besides what Sir G. Carteret told me about fourteen days ago. Our fleet under my Lord Sandwich being about the latitude $55\frac{1}{2}$ (which is a great secret) to the Northward of the Texell.

23rd (Lord's day). Called by Mr. Cutler, by appointment, and with him in his coach and four horses over London Bridge to Kingston, a very pleasant journey, and at Hampton Court by nine o'clock, and in our way very good and various discourse, as he is a man, that though I think he be a knave, as the world thinks him, yet a man of great experience and worthy to be heard discourse. When we came there we to Sir W. Coventry's chamber, and there discoursed long with him, he and I alone, I observing with a little trouble that he is too great now to expect too much familiarity with. I followed the King to chappell, and there heard a good sermon; and after sermon with my Lord Arlington, Sir Thomas Ingram and others, spoke to the Duke about Tangier, but not to much purpose. I was not invited any whither to dinner, though a stranger, which did also trouble me ; but yet I must remember it is a Court, and indeed where most are strangers ; but, however, Cutler carried me to Mr. Marriott's the house-keeper, and there we had a very good dinner and good company, among others Lilly, the painter. Thence to the councill-chamber, but the councill begun late to sit, so that when I was free and came to look for Cutler, he was gone with his coach, without leaving any word with any body to tell me so ; so that I was forced with great trouble to walk up and down looking of him, and at last forced to get a boat to carry me to Kingston, and there, after eating a bit at a neat inne, which pleased me well, I took boat, and slept all the way, without intermission, from thence to Queenhithe, where, it being about two o'clock, too late and too soon to go home to bed, I lay and slept till about four,

24th. And then up and home, and there dressed myself, and by appointment to Deptford, to Sir G. Carteret's between six and seven o'clock, where I found him and my Lady almost ready, and by and by went over to the ferry, and took coach and six horses nobly for Dagenhams, himself and lady and their little daughter, Louisonne,[1] and myself in the

---

[1] Louisa Marguerite Carteret, afterwards married to Sir Robert Atkins, of Seperton, Gloucestershire.

coach; where, when we came, we were bravely entertained and spent the day most pleasantly with the
young ladies, and I so merry as never more. Here
with great content all the day, as I think I ever
passed a day in my life, because of the contentful-
nesse of our errand, and the noblenesse of the company and our manner of going. But I find Mr.
Carteret yet as backward almost in his caresses, as he
was the first day. At night, about seven o'clock, took
coach again; but, Lord! to see in what a pleasant
humour Sir G. Carteret hath been both coming and
going; so light, so fond, so merry, so boyish, so much
content he takes in this business, it is one of the
greatest wonders I ever saw in my mind. But once
in serious discourse he did say that, if he knew his
son to be a debauchee, as many and most are now-a-
days about the Court, he would tell it, and my Lady
Jem. should not have him; and so enlarged both he
and she about the baseness and looseness of the
Court, and told several stories of the Duke of Monmouth, and Richmond, and some great person, my
Lord of Ormond's second son,[1] married to a lady[2] of
extraordinary quality, fit and that might have been
made a wife for the King himself, about six months
since; and discoursed how much this would oblige
the Kingdom if the King would banish some of these

---

[1] See note, 4th February, 1664-5.

[2] Lady Mary Stewart, only surviving child of James, Duke of Richmond
and Lennox, who died in 1665, and heir to her brother Esme, who deceased
in 1666. She survived till 1688.

great persons publiquely from the Court, and wished it with all their hearts. We set out so late that it grew dark, so we doubted the losing of our way; and a long time it was, or seemed, before we could get to the waterside, and that about eleven at night, where, when we came, all merry, we found no ferry-boat was there, nor no oares to carry us to Deptford. However, afterwards oares was called from the other side at Greenwich; but, when it came, a frolique, being mighty merry, took us, and there we would sleep all night in the coach in the Isle of Doggs. So we did, there being now with us my Lady Scott,[1] and with great pleasure drew up the glasses, and slept till daylight, and then some victuals and wine being brought us, we ate a bit, and so up and took boat, merry as might be; and when come to Sir G. Carteret's, there all to bed.

25th. Our good humour in every body continuing, and there I slept till seven o'clock. Then up and to the office, well refreshed. At noon to the 'Change, which was very thin, but sad the story of the plague in the City, it growing mightily. This day my Lord Brouncker did give me Mr. Grant's book upon the Bills of Mortality, new printed and enlarged.[2] Thence to my office awhile, full of business, and thence by coach to the Duke of Albemarle's not meeting one coach going nor coming from my house thither and

---

[1] Caroline, second daughter of Sir George Carteret, wife of Sir Thomas Scott of Scott's Hall, Kent. See *ante*, July 30, 1663.

[2] See note 24th March, 1662.

back again, which is very strange. Mightily troubled all this afternoon with masters coming to me about Bills of Exchange and my signing them upon my Goldsmiths, but I did send for them all and hope to ease myself this weeke of all the clamour. This day came a letter to me from Paris from my Lord Hinchingbroke, about his coming over; and I have sent this night an order from the Duke of Albemarle for a ship of 36 guns to go to Calais to fetch him.[1]

26th. To Greenwich to the Park, where I hear the King and Duke are come by water this morn from Hampton Court. They asked me several questions. The King mightily pleased with his new buildings there. I followed them to Castle's ship in building, and there met Sir W. Batten, and thence to Sir G. Carteret's, where all the morning with them; they not having any but the Duke of Monmouth, and Sir W. Killigrew,[2] and one gentleman, and a page more. Great variety of talk, and was often led to speak to the King and Duke. By and by they to dinner, and all to dinner and sat down to the King saving myself, which, though I could not in modesty expect, yet, God forgive my pride! I was sorry I was there, that Sir W. Batten should say that he could sit down where I could not, though he had twenty times more reason than I, but this was my pride and folly. I down and walked with Mr. Castle, he and I by and by to dinner mighty nobly, and the King having dined, he came

---

[1] For the letter see the " Correspondence."
[2] Vice-Chamberlain to the Queen.

down, and I went in the barge with him, I sitting at the door. Down to Woolwich (and there I just saw and kissed my wife, and saw some of her painting, which is very curious ; and away again to the King) and back again with him in the barge, hearing him and the Duke talk, and seeing and observing their manner of discourse. And God forgive me ! though I admire them with all the duty possible, yet the more a man considers and observes them, the less he finds of difference between them and other men, though (blessed be God !) they are both princes of great nobleness and spirits. The Duke of Monmouth is the most skittish leaping gallant that ever I saw, always in action, vaulting or leaping, or clambering. Thence mighty full of the honour of this day, took coach and to Kate Joyce's, and spoke with Anthony, who tells me he likes well of my proposal for Pall to Harman, but I fear that less than 500*l.* will not be taken and that I shall not be able to give. After a little other discourse and the sad news of the death of so many in the parish of the plague, forty last night, the bell always going, I back to the Exchange, where I went up and sat talking with my beauty, Mrs. Batelier, a great while, who is indeed one of the finest women I ever saw in my life. I home to set my Journall for these four days in order, they being four days of as great content and honour and pleasure to me as ever I hope to wish or desire, or think any body else can wish. For methinks if a man would but reflect upon this and think that all these things are ordered by

God Almighty to make me contented and even this very marriage now on foot is one of the things intended to find me content in in my life and matter of mirth methinks it should make one mightily more satisfied in the world than he is. This day poor Robin Shaw at Backewell's died, and Backewell himself now in Flanders. The King himself asked about Shaw, and being told he was dead, said he was very sorry for it. The sickness is got into our parish this week, and is got, indeed, every where; so that I begin to think of setting things in order, which I pray God enable me to put both as to soul and body.

27th. By water to Fox Hall, and there Mr. Gauden's coach took me up, and so both to Hampton Court, where I saw the King and Queene set out towards Salisbury, and after them the Duke and Duchesse, whose hands I did kiss. And it was the first time I did ever, or did see any body else, kiss her hand, and it was a most fine white and fat hand. But it was pretty to see the young pretty ladies dressed like men, in velvet coats, caps with ribbands, and with laced bands, just like men. Only the Duchesse herself it did not become. They gone, we with great content took coach again, and hungry came to Clapham about one o'clock, and Creed there too before us, where a good dinner, the house having dined, and so to walk up and down in the gardens, mighty pleasant. By and by comes by promise to me Sir G. Carteret, and viewed the house [1] above and below, and sat and

---

[1] Mr. Gauden's house at Clapham.   (M. B.)

drank there, and I had a little opportunity to kiss and spend some time with the ladies above, his daughter, a buxom lass, and his sister Fissant, a serious lady, and a little daughter of hers, that begins to sing prettily. Thence, with mighty pleasure, with Sir G. Carteret by coach, with great discourse of kindnesse with him to my Lord Sandwich, and to me also; and I every day see more good by the alliance. Almost at Deptford I 'light and walked over to Halfway House, and so home, in my way being shown my cozen Patience's house, which seems, at distance, a pretty house. At home met the weekly Bill, where above 1,000 encreased in the Bill, and of them, in all about 1,700 of the plague, which hath made the officers this day resolve of sitting at Deptford, which puts me to some consideration what to do.

28th. Up betimes, and down to Deptford. Set out with my Lady all alone with her with six horses to Dagenhams; going by water to the Ferry. And a pleasant going, and good discourse; and when there, very merry, and the young couple now well acquainted. But Lord! to see in what fear all the people here do live. How they are afeard of us that come to them, insomuch that I am troubled at it, and wish myself away. But some cause they have; for the chaplin, with whom but a week or two ago we were here mighty high disputing, is since fallen into a fever and dead, being gone hence to a friend's a good way off. A sober and a healthful man. These considerations make us all hasten the marriage, and resolve it upon Monday next, which is three days before we intended it. Mighty merry all of us and in the evening with full content took coach again and home, and thence I down to Woolwich, where found my wife well.

29th. Up betimes, and after viewing some of my wife's pictures, which now she is come to do very finely to my great satisfaction beyond what I could ever look for, I by water to the office. At noon to dinner, where I hear that my Will is come in thither and laid down upon my bed, ill of the headake, which put me into extraordinary fear; and I studied all I could to get him out of the house and set my people to work to do it without discouraging him, and myself went forth to the Old Exchange to pay my fair Batelier for some linnen, and took leave of her, they breaking up shop for a while; and so by coach to Kate Joyce's, and there used all the vehemence and rhetorique I could to get her husband to let her go down to Brampton, but I could not prevail with him; he urging some simple reasons, but most that of profit, minding the house, and the distance, if either of them should be ill. However, I did my best, and more than I had a mind to do, but that I saw him so resolved against it, while she was mightily troubled at it. At last he yielded she should go to Windsor, to some friends there. So I took my leave of them, believing that it is great odds that we ever all see one another again; for I dare not go any more to that end of the towne. So home in some ease of mind that Will is gone to his lodging and that he is likely to do well, it being only the headake.

30th (Lord's day). Up, and in my night gowne, cap and neckcloth, undressed all day long, lost not a minute, but in my chamber, setting my Tangier accounts to rights. The Lord be praised for it! Will was with me to-day, and is very well again. It was a sad noise to hear our bell to toll and ring so often to-day, either for deaths or burials; I think five or six times.

31st. Up, and very betimes by six o'clock at Deptford, and there find Sir G. Carteret, and my Lady ready to go: I being in my new coloured silk suit, and coat trimmed with gold buttons and gold broad lace round my hands, very rich and fine. By water to the Ferry, where, when we come, no coach there; and tide of ebb so far spent as the horse-boat could not get off on the other side the river to bring away the coach. So we were fain to stay there in the unlucky Isle of Doggs, in a chill place, the morning cool, and wind fresh, above two if not three hours to our great discontent. Yet being upon a pleasant errand, and seeing that it could not be helped, we did bear it very patiently; and it was worth my observing, to see how upon these two scores, Sir G. Carteret, the most passionate man in the world, and that was in greatest haste to be gone, did bear with it, and very pleasant all the while, at least not troubled much so as to fret and storm at it. Anon the coach comes: in the mean time there coming a News thither with his horse to go over, that told us he did come from Islington this morning ; and that Proctor the vintner [1] of the Miter in Wood-street, and his son, are dead this morning there, of the plague ; he having laid out abundance of money there, and was the greatest vintner for some time in London for great entertainments. We, fearing the canonicall hour would be past before we got thither, did with a great deal of unwillingness send away the license and wedding ring. So that when we come, though we drove hard with six horses, yet we found them gone from home ; and going towards the church, met them coming from church, which troubled us. But, however, that trouble was soon over ; hearing it was well done : they being both in their old clothes ; my Lord Crew giving her, there being three coach fulls of them. The young lady mighty sad, which troubled me ; but yet I think it was only her gravity in a little greater degree than usual. All saluted her, but I did not till my Lady Sandwich did ask me whether I had saluted her or no. So to dinner, and very merry we were ; but yet in such a sober way as never almost any wedding was in so great families : but it was much better. After dinner company divided, some to cards, others to talk. My Lady Sandwich and I up to settle accounts, and pay her some money. And mighty kind she is to me, and would fain have had me gone down for company with her to Hinchingbroke ; but for my

---

[1] 1665, Aug. 1. Mr. William Proctor, vintner, at y[e] Mitre, in Wood Street, with his young son, died at Islington (insolvent) *ex peste.* — SMITH'S *Obituary,* p. 64.

life I cannot. At night to supper, and so to talk ; and which, methought, was the most extraordinary thing, all of us to prayers as usual, and the young bride and bridegroom too : and so after prayers, soberly to bed ; only I got into the bridegroom's chamber while he undressed himself, and there was very merry, till he was called to the bride's chamber, and into bed they went. I kissed the bride in bed, and so the curtaines drawne with the greatest gravity that could be, and so good night. But the modesty and gravity of this business was so decent, that it was to me indeed ten times more delightful than if it had been twenty times more merry and jovial. Whereas I feared I must have sat up all night, we did here all get good beds, and I lay in the same I did before with Mr. Brisband, who is a good scholler and sober man ; and we lay in bed, getting him to give me an account of Rome, which is the most delightfull talke a man can have of any traveller : and so to sleep. Thus I ended this month with the greatest joy that ever I did any in my life, because I have spent the greatest part of it with abundance of joy, and honour, and pleasant journeys, and brave entertainments, and without cost of money ; and at last live to see the business ended with great content on all sides. This evening with Mr. Brisband, speaking of enchantments and spells, I telling him some of my charms ; he told me this of his owne knowledge, at Bourdeaux, in France. The words were these :

> Voyci un Corps mort,
> Royde come un Baston,

Froid comme Marbre,
Leger come un esprit,
Levon le au nom de Jesus Christ.

He saw four little girles, very young ones, all kneeling, each of them, upon one knee ; and one begun the first line, whispering in the eare of the next, and the second to the third, and the third to the fourth, and she to the first. Then the first begun the second line, and so round quite through, and, putting each one finger only to a boy that lay flat upon his back on the ground, as if he was dead ; at the end of the words, they did with their four fingers raise this boy as high as they could reach, and Mr. Brisband being there, and wondering at it, as also being afeard to see it, for they would have had him to have bore a part in saying the words, in the roome of one of the little girles that was so young that they could hardly make her learn to repeat the words, did, for feare there might be some sleight used in it by the boy, or that the boy might be light, call the cook of the house, a very lusty fellow, as Sir G. Carteret's cook, who is very big and they did raise him in just the same manner.[1] This is one of the stran-

---

[1] One of the most extraordinary pages in Sir David Brewster's "Letters on Natural Magic," is the experiment in which a heavy man is raised with the greatest facility when he is lifted up the instant that his own lungs and those of the persons who raise him are inflated with air. Thus, the heaviest person in the party lies down upon two chairs, his legs being supported by the one and his back by the other. Four persons, one at each leg and one at each shoulder, then try to raise him, the person to be raised giving two signals by clapping his hands. At the first signal he himself and the four lifters begin to draw a long and full breath, and when the inhalation is completed, or the lungs filled, the second signal is given for raising the person from the chair. To

gest things I ever heard, but he tells it me of his owne knowledge, and I do heartily believe it to be true. I enquired of him whether they were Protestant or Catholique girles; and he told me they were Protestant, which made it the more strange to me. Thus we end this month, as I said, after the greatest glut of content that ever I had; only under some difficulty because of the plague, which grows mightily upon us, the last week being about 1,700 or 1,800 of the plague. My Lord Sandwich at sea with a fleet of about 100 sail, to the Northward, expecting De Ruyter, or the Dutch East India fleet. My Lord Hinchingbroke coming over from France, and will meet his sister at Scott's-hall.[1]   Myself having obliged both these fam-

---

his own surprise, and that of his bearers, he rises with the greatest facility, as though he were no heavier than a feather. Sir David Brewster states that he has seen this inexplicable experiment performed more than once, and he appealed for testimony to Sir Walter Scott, who had repeatedly seen the experiment, and performed the part both of the load and the bearer. It was first shown in England by Major H., who saw it performed in a large party at Venice, under the direction of an officer of the American navy.

Sir David Brewster (in a letter to "Notes and Queries," No. 143) further remarks that "the inhalation of the lifters the moment the effort is made is doubtless essential, and for this reason: when we make a great effort, either in pulling or lifting, we always fill the chest with air previous to the effort; and when the inhalation is completed, we close the *rima glottidis* to keep the air in the lungs. The chest being thus expanded, the pulling or lifting muscles have received, as it were, a fulcrum round which their power is exerted, and we can thus lift the greatest weight which the muscles are capable of doing. When the chest collapses by the escape of the air, the lifters lose their muscular power; re-inhalation of air by the liftee can certainly add nothing to the power of the lifters, or diminish his own weight, which is only increased by the weight of the air which he inhales." — Timbs' *Curiosities of Science.* (M. B.)

[1] Evelyn's Diary, 2nd August, 1663. "This evening I accompanied Mr.

ilies in this business very much ; as both my Lady and Sir G. Carteret and his Lady do confess exceedingly, and the latter do also now call me cozen, which I am glad of. So God preserve us all friends long, and continue health among us.

August 1st. Lay long; then up and my Lord Crew and Sir G. Carteret being gone abroad, I first to see the bridegroom and bride, and found them both up, and he gone to dress himself. Thence down and Mr. Brisband and I to billiards : anon come my Lord and Sir G. Carteret in, who have been looking abroad and visiting some farms that Sir G. Carteret hath thereabouts, and, among other things, report the greatest stories of the bigness of the calfes they find there, ready to sell to the butchers, as big, they say, as little cowes, and that they do give them a piece of chalke to licke, which they hold makes them white in the flesh within. Very merry at dinner and so to talk and laugh after dinner full of content on all sides. Anon about five o'clock, Sir G. Carteret and his lady and I took coach with the greatest joy and kindnesse that could be from the two familys or that ever I saw with so much appearance, and, I believe, reality in all my life. Drove hard, and it was night ere we got to Deptford, where, with much kindnesse from them to

Treasurer and Vice-Chamberlain Carteret to his lately married son-in-law's, Sir Thomas Scott, to Scott's Hall. We took barge as far as Gravesend, thence by post to Rochester, whence in coach and six horses to Scott's Hall, a right noble seat, uniformly built, with a handsome gallery. It stands in a park well stored, the land fat and good." (M. B.)

me, I left them, and home to the office, where I find all well.

2nd. Up, it being a publique fast, as being the first Wednesday of the month, for the plague; I within doors all day, and upon my monthly accounts late, and there to my great joy settled almost all my private matters of money in my books clearly and I did find myself really worth 1,900*l.*, for which the great God of Heaven and Earth be praised !

3rd. Up, and betimes to Deptford to G. Carteret's, where not liking the horse that had been hired by Mr. Unthwayt for me, I did desire Sir G. Carteret to let me ride his new 40*l.* horse, which he did and so I left my hacquenee behind, and so after staying a good while in their bedchamber while they were dressing themselves, discoursing merrily, I parted and to the ferry, where I was forced to stay a great while before I could get my horse brought over, and then mounted and rode very finely to Dagenhams; all the way people, citizens, walking to and again to enquire how the plague is in the City this week by the Bill; which by chance, at Greenwich, I had heard was 2,020 of the plague, and 3,000 and odd of all diseases; but methought it was a sad question to be so often asked me. Coming to Dagenhams, I there met our company coming out of the house, having staid as long as they could for me; so I let them go a little before, and went and took leave of my Lady Sandwich, good woman, who seems very sensible of my service in this late business, and having her directions in some things, among others, to get Sir G. Carteret and my Lord to settle the portion, and what Sir G. Carteret is to settle, into land, soon as may be, she not liking that it should lie long undone, for fear of death on either side. So took leave of her, and then down to the buttery, and eat a piece of cold venison pie, and drank and took some bread and cheese in my hand; and so mounted after them, Mr. Marr very kindly staying to lead me the way. By and by met my Lord Crew returning; Mr. Marr telling me by the way how a mayde servant of Mr. John Wright's (who lives thereabouts) falling sick of the plague, she was removed to an out-house, and a nurse appointed to look to her; who, being once absent, the mayde got out of the house at the window, and ran away. The nurse coming and knocking, and having no answer, believed she was dead, and went and told Mr. Wright so; who and his lady were in great strait what to do to get her buried. At last resolved to go to Burntwood [1] hard by, being in the parish, and there get people to do it. But they would not; so he went home full of trouble, and in the way met the wench walking over the common, which frighted him worse than before; and was forced to send people to take her, which he did; and they got one of the pest coaches and put her into it to carry her to a pest house. And passing in a narrow lane, Sir Anthony Browne,[2] with his brother and some friends in the coach, met this coach with the curtains

---

[1] Brentwood.

[2] He commanded a troop of horse in the Train-bands, 1662.

drawn close. The brother being a young man, and believing there might be some lady in it that would not be seen, and the way being narrow, he thrust his head out of his own into her coach, and to look, and there saw somebody look very ill, and in a sick dress, and stunk mightily; which the coachman also cried out upon. And presently they come up to some people that stood looking after it, and told our gallants that it was a mayde of Mr. Wright's carried away sick of the plague; which put the young gentleman into a fright had almost cost him his life, but is now well again. I, overtaking our young people, 'light, and into the coach to them, where mighty merry all the way; and anon come to the Blockehouse,[1] over against Gravesend, where we staid a great while, in a little drinking-house. Sent back our coaches to Dagenhams. I, by and by, by boat to Gravesend, where no newes of Sir G. Carteret come yet; so back again, and fetched them all over, but the two saddle-horses that were to go with us, which could not be brought over in the horse-boat, the wind and tide being against us, without towing; so we had some difference with some watermen, who would not tow them over under 20*s.*, whereupon I swore to send one of them to sea and will do it. Anon some others come to me and did it for 10*s.* By and by comes Sir G. Carteret, and so we set out for Chatham: in my way overtaking some company, wherein was a lady, very pretty, riding

---

[1] Tilbury Fort.

singly, her husband in company with her. We fell into talke, and I read a copy of verses which her husband showed me, and he discommended, but the lady commended: and I read them, so as to make the husband turn to commend them. By and by he and I fell into acquaintance, having known me formerly at the Exchequer. His name is Nokes, over against Bow Church. He was servant to Alderman Dashwood. We promised to meet, if ever we come both to London again; and, at parting, I had a fair salute on horseback, in Rochester Street, of the lady, and so parted. Came to Chatham mighty merry and anon to supper. My Lady Carteret came thither in a coach, by herself, before us. Great mind they have to buy a little hacquenee that I rode on from Greenwich, for a woman's horse. So anon to bed. Mr. Brisband and I together to my great content.

4th. Up at five o'clock, and by six walked out alone, with my Lady Slaning,[1] to the Docke Yard, where walked up and down, and so to Mr. Pett's, who led us into his garden, and there the lady, the best humoured woman in the world, and a devout woman (I having spied her on her knees half an houre this morning in her chamber), clambered up to the top of the banquetting-house to gather nuts; and so to the Hill-house to breakfast and mighty merry. Then they took coach, and Sir G. Carteret kissed me himself heartily, and my Lady several

---

[1] Sir G. Carteret's eldest daughter, married in 1663 to Sir Nicholas Slaning. (M. B.)

times, with great kindnesse, and then the young ladies, and so with much joy, bade "God be with you!" and an end I think it will be to my mirthe for a great while, it having been the passage of my whole life the most pleasing for the time, considering the quality and nature of the business, and my noble usage in the doing of it, and very many fine journys, entertainments and great company. So home, and found all things well and letters from Dover that my Lord Hinchingbroke is arrived at Dover and would be at Scott's hall[1] this night, where the whole company will meet. I wish myself with them. After writing a few letters I took boat and down to Woolwich very late, and there found my wife and her woman upon the key hearing a fellow in a barge, that lay by, fiddle. So I to them and in, very merry, and to bed.

5th. In the morning up, and my wife showed me several things of her doing, especially one fine woman's Persian head mighty finely done, beyond what I could expect of her; and so away by water, having ordered in the yarde six or eight bargemen to be whipped, who had last night stolen some of the King's cordage from out of the yarde. De Ruyter is come

---

[1] Scott's Hall was in the parish of Smeeth, near Ashford, in Kent; it was long the residence of William Baliol *le Scot*, a brother of John Baliol, King of Scotland. At this time it belonged to Sir Thomas Scott, son-in-law of Sir George Carteret: see July 30, 1663, and July 24, 1665. The property was sold in 1784 to John Honywood, and afterwards alienated to the late Sir Edward Knatchbull, Bart., who pulled down the house. Hasted says it was of the time of Henry VIII.; but from rough sketches of the building, in the possession of one of the Scott family, who lived to be nearly ninety, it was conjectured to have been much more ancient.

81447

home, with all his fleete, which is very ill newes, considering the charge we have been at in keeping a fleete to the northward so long besides the great expectation of snapping him, wherein my Lord Sandwich will I doubt suffer some dishonour.   I am told also of a great ryott upon Thursday last in Cheapside; Colonel Danvers, a delinquent, having been taken, and in his way to the Tower was rescued from the captain of the guard, and carried away; only one of the rescuers being taken.

6th (Lord's day). Dressed and had my head combed by my little girle. So to my business in my chamber. In the evening, it raining hard, down to Woolwich.

7th. Up, and with great pleasure looking over my wife's pictures, and then to see my Lady Pen, and after being a little merry with her she went forth and I staid there talking with Mrs. Pegg [Pen] and looking over her pictures, and commended them; but, Lord! so far short of my wife's, as no comparison.   By appointment Mr. Andrews came to speake with me about their Tangier business, and so having done with him and dined, I home by water, where by appointment I met Dr. Twisden, Mr. Povy, &c., about settling their business of money; but such confusion I never met with, nor could anything be agreed on, but parted like a company of fools, I vexed to lose so much time and pains to no purpose. They gone, comes Rayner, the boat-maker, about some business, and brings a piece of plate with him, which I refused to take of him, thinking indeed that the poor man has no reason nor encouragement from our dealings with him to give any of us any presents. He gone, there comes Luellin, about Mr. Deering's business of planke, to have the contract perfected, and offers me twenty pieces in gold, as Deering had done some time since himself, but I both then and now refused it, resolving not to be bribed to dispatch business, but will have it done however out of hand forthwith. So he gone, I to supper and to bed.

8th. To my office a little, and then to the Duke of Albemarle's about some business. The streets mighty empty all the way, now even in London, which is a sad sight. And to Westminster Hall, where talking, hearing very sad stories from Mrs. Mumford; among others, of Mr. Michell's son's family. And poor Will, that used to sell us ale at the Hall-door, his wife and three children died, all, I think, in a day. So home through the City again, wishing I may have taken no ill in going; but I will go, I think, no more thither. The news of De Ruyter's coming home is certain; and told to the great disadvantage of our fleete, and the praise of De Ruyter; but it cannot be helped, nor do I know what to say to it.

9th. Betimes to my office, where Tom Hater to the writing of letters with me, which have for a good while been in arreare, and we close at it all day till night, only made a little step out for half an houre in the morning to the Exchequer about speaking of tallys, but no good done therein, people being most out of towne. At night, after reading a little in Cowley's poems, my head being disturbed with over-much business to-day, I to bed.

10th. Called upon early by my she-cozen Porter, the turner's wife, to tell me that her husband was carried to the Tower, for buying of some of the King's powder, and would have my helpe, but I could give her none, not daring any more to appear in the business, having too much trouble therein lately. By and by to the office, where we sat all the morning; in great trouble to see the Bill this week rise so high, to above 4,000 in all, and of them above 3,000 of the plague. And an odd story of Alderman Bence's stumbling at night over a dead corps in the streete, and going home and telling his wife, she at the fright, being with child, fell sicke and died of the plague. We sat late, and then by invitation to Sir G. Smith's to dinner, where very good company and good cheer. Captain Cocke was there and Jack Fenn, but to our great wonder Alderman Bence, and tells us that not a word of all this is true, but by his owne story his wife has been ill and he fain to leave his house and comes not to her, which continued a trouble to me all the time I was there. Home, to draw over anew my will, which I had bound myself by oath to dispatch by to-morrow night; the towne growing so unhealthy, that a man cannot depend upon living two days.

11th. To the Exchequer, about striking new tallys, and I find the Exchequer, by proclamation, removing to Nonsuch.[1]   Back again and at my papers, and putting up my books into chests and settling my house and all things in the best and speediest order I can, lest it should please God to take me away, or force me to leave my house.   I find that so long as I keepe myself in company at meals and do there eat lustily (which I cannot do alone, having no love to eating, but my mind runs upon my business), I am as well as can be, but when I come to be alone, I do not eat in time, nor can nor with any good heart, and I immediately begin to be full of wind, which brings my pain, till I come to fill my belly adays again, then am presently well.

12th. At noon am sent for by Sir G. Carteret, to meet him and my Lord Hinchingbroke at Deptford, but my Lord did not come thither, he having crossed the river at Gravesend to Dagenhams, whither I dare not follow him, they being afeard of me ; but Sir G. Carteret says, he is a most sweet youth in every circumstance. Sir G. Carteret being in haste of going to the Duke of Albemarle and the Archbishop, he was pettish. So he gone, I down to Greenwich and sent away the Bezan, thinking to go with my wife to-night to come back again to-morrow night to the Soveraigne at the buoy off the Nore. The people die so, that now it seems they are fain to carry the dead to be

---

1 Nonsuch House, near Epsom, where the Exchequer money was kept during the time of the plague. Of this favourite summer residence of Queen Elizabeth not a vestige remains but the " avenue planted with rows of fine elms." (M. B.)

buried by day-light, the nights not sufficing to do it in. And my Lord Mayor commands people to be within at nine at night all, as they say, that the sick may have liberty to go abroad for ayre. There is one also dead out of one of our ships at Deptford, which troubles us mightily; the Providence, fire-ship, which was just fitted to go to sea. But they tell me to-day no more sick on board. And this day W. Bodham tells me that one is dead at Woolwich, not far from the Rope-yard. I am told, too, that a wife of one of the groomes at Court is dead at Salisbury; so that the King and Queene are speedily to be all gone to Milton.[1] So God preserve us !

13th (Lord's day). It being very wet all day, clearing all matters in packing up my papers and books, and giving instructions in writing to my executors, thereby perfecting the whole business of my will, to my very great joy; so that I shall be in much better state of soul, I hope, if it should please the Lord to call me away this sickly time. To bed with a mind as free as to the business of the world as if I were not worth 100*l.* in the whole world, every thing being evened under my hand in my books and papers. Upon the whole I find myself worth, besides Brampton estate, the sum of 2,164*l.*, for which the Lord be praised !

14th. Down to Deptford to Sir G. Carteret, where

---

[1] Wilton, near Salisbury, then the seat of Philip, fifth Earl of Pembroke, who married Catherine, daughter of Sir Wm. Villiers, of Brookesley, cousin of the Duke of Buckingham. [In the MS. the reading is Milton. (M. B.)]

with him a great while, and a great deale of private talke concerning my Lord Sandwich's and his matters, and chiefly of Lord Sandwich's giving him great deale of advice why he should not bring his son in to look after his business, and more to be a Commissioner of the Navy, which he listened to and liked, and told me how much the King was his good Master and was sure would not deny him that or any thing else greater, and I find him a very cunning man whatever at other times he seems to be, and among other things he told me that he was not for the fanfaroone [1] to make a show with a great title, as he might have had long since, but the main thing to get an estate; and another thing, speaking of minding of business, " By G—d," says he, " I will and have already almost brought it to that pass, that the King shall not be able to whip a cat, but I must be at the tayle of it." Meaning so necessary he is, and the King and my Lord Treasurer and all do confess it; which, while I mind my business, is my own case in this office of the Navy, and I hope shall be more, if God give me life and health. To Sir W. Batten's, where very merry, good cheer, and up and down the garden with great content to me, and, after dinner, beat Captain Cocke at billiards, won about 8*s.* of him and my Lord Brouncker. So in the evening after much pleasure back again and by water to Woolwich, where supped

---

[1] *Fanfaroone,* from the French, *fanfaron,* swaggerer, boaster. *Fanfaronade,* swaggering, ostentation. " The Bishop copied this proceeding from the *fanfaronade* of Monsieur Boufflers." — SWIFT. (M. B.)

with my wife. This night I did present my wife with the dyamond ring, awhile since given me by Mr. Vine's brother, for helping him to be a purser, valued at about 10*l.*, the first thing of that nature I did ever give her. Great fears we have that the plague will be a great Bill this weeke.

15th. Up by 4 o'clock and walked to Greenwich, and something put my last night's dream of Lady Castlemayne into my head, which I think is the best that ever was dreamt, and I dreamt that this could not be awake, but that it was only a dream; but that since it was a dream, and that I took so much real pleasure in it, what a happy thing it would be if when we are in our graves (as Shakespeare resembles it) we could dream, and dream but such dreams as this, that we should not need to be so fearful of death, as we are this plague time. To Sir G. Carteret's; among other things he has ordered Rider and Cutler to put into my hands copper to the value of 5,000*l.*, which is to raise part of the money he is to lay out for a purchase for my Lady Jemimah. Thence he and I to Sir J. Minnes by invitation upon a venison pasty; but my pleasure lay in getting some bills signed by Sir G. Carteret and promise of present payment from Mr. Fenn, which do rejoice my heart, it being one of the heaviest things I had upon me, that so much of the little I have should lie (viz. near 1,000*l.*) in the King's hands. Here very merry and so broke up and I by water to the Duke of Albemarle, with whom I spoke a great deale in private, they being designed to send a fleete of ships privately to the Streights. It was dark before I could get home, and so land at Church-yard stairs, where, to my great trouble, I met a dead corps of the plague, in the narrow ally just bringing down a little pair of stairs. But I thank God I was not much disturbed at it. However, I shall beware of being late abroad again.

16th. To the Exchange, where I have not been a great while. But, Lord! how sad a sight it is to see the streets empty of people, and very few upon the 'Change. Jealous of every door that one sees shut up, lest it should be the plague; and about us two shops in three, if not more, generally shut up. Very contrary newes to-day upon the 'Change, some that our fleete has taken some of the Dutch East India ships, others that we did attaque it at Bergen and were repulsed, others that our fleete is in great danger after this attaque by meeting with the great body now gone out of Holland, almost 100 sayle of men of warr. Every body is at a great losse and nobody can tell. This day I had the ill news from Dagenhams, that my poor lord of Hinchingbroke his indisposition is turned to the small-pox. Poor gentleman that he should be come from France so soon to fall sick, and of that disease too, when he should be gone to see a fine lady, his mistresse. I am most heartily sorry for it.

17th. By boat to Greenwich to the Bezan yacht, where Sir W. Batten, Sir J. Minnes, my Lord Brouncker and myself embarked in the yacht and down we went most pleasantly, and noble discourse I had with my

Lord Brouncker, who is a most excellent person. Short of Gravesend it grew calme, and so we came to an anchor and to supper mighty merry, and then, as we grew sleepy, upon velvet cushions of the King's that belong to the yacht fell to sleep.

18th. Up about 5 o'clock and dressed ourselves, and to sayle again down to the Soveraigne at the buoy of the Nore, a noble ship, now rigged and fitted and manned; we did not stay long, but to enquire after her readinesse and thence to Sheernesse, where we walked up and down, laying out the ground to be taken in for a yard to lay provisions for cleaning and repairing of ships, and a most proper place it is for the purpose.[1]   Thence with great pleasure up the Meadeway, our yacht contending with Commissioner Pett's, wherein he met us from Chatham, and he had the best of it.   Here I came by, but had not tide enough to stop at Quinbrough, with mighty pleasure spent the day in doing all and seeing these places, which I had never done before.   So to the Hill house at Chatham and there dined, and after dinner spent some time discoursing of business.   Among others arguing with the Commissioner about his proposing the laying out so much money upon Sheernesse, unless it be to the slighting of Chatham yarde, for it is much a better place than Chatham, which however the King is not at present in purse to do.   I late

----

[1] The yard and fortifications of Sheerness were designed and first "staked out" by Sir Bernard de Gomme (see 24th March, 1667). The original plan is in the British Museum.

in the darke to Gravesend, where great is the plague, and I troubled to stay there so long for the tide. At 10 at night I took boat alone, and to the Tower docks about three o'clock in the morning. So knocked up my people, and to bed.

19th. Slept till 8 o'clock, and then up and met with letters from the King and Lord Arlington, for the removal of our office to Greenwich. I also wrote letters, and made myself ready to go to Sir G. Carteret, at Windsor; and having borrowed a horse of Mr. Blackbrough, sent him to wait for me at the Duke of Albemarle's door: when, on a sudden, a letter comes to us from the Duke of Albemarle, to tell us that the fleete is all come back to Solebay, and are presently to be dispatched back again. Whereupon I presently by water to the Duke of Albemarle to know what news; and there I saw a letter from my Lord Sandwich to the Duke of Albemarle, and also from Sir W. Coventry and Captain Teddiman; how my Lord having commanded Teddiman with twenty-two ships (of which but fifteen could get thither, and of those fifteen but eight or nine could come up to play) to go to Bergen;[1] where, after several messages

---

[1] A view of this attack on Bergen, " described from the life in Aug., 1661, by C. H.," being a contemporary coloured drawing, on vellum, showing the range of the ships engaged, is in the British Museum. See Sir Gilbert Talbot's narrative of this action, Harleian MS., No. 6,859, and Lord Rochester's account of it, in a letter to his mother. — WORDSWORTH'S *Eccl. Biog.* 4th ed. vol. iv. p. 611. The affair of Bergen did not escape Denham's satiric lash:

—— " all our navy 'scaped so sound of limb,
That a short space served to refresh and trim:

to and fro from the Governor of the Castle, urging that Teddiman ought not to come thither with more than five ships, and desiring time to think of it, all the while he suffering the Dutch ships to land their guns to their best advantage; Teddiman on the second pretence, began to play at the Dutch ships, (whereof ten East India-men,) and in three hours' time (the

----

And a tame fleet of theirs [1] doth convoy want
Laden with both the Indies and Levant:
Paint but this one scene more, the world's our own,
And Halcyon *Sandwich* doth command alone:
To *Bergen* we with confidence make haste,
And secret spoils by hope already taste;
Tho' *Clifford* in the character appear
Of supra-cargo to our fleet, and there
Wearing a signet ready to clap on,
And seize all for his master *Arlington.*
Ruyter, whose little squadron skimmed the seas,
And wasted our remotest colonies,
With ships all foul, returned upon our way:
Sandwich would not disperse nor yet delay;
And therefore, like commander grave and wise,
To 'scape his sight and fight, shut both his eyes:
And for more state and sureness, *Cuttance,* true,
The left eye closeth, the right *Montagu;*
And even *Clifford* proffered in his zeal,
To make all safe, to apply to both his seal.
Ulysses so, till Syrens he had past,
Would by his mates be pinioned to the mast.
Now can our navy view the wished port,
But there (to see the fortune!) was a fort:
Sandwich would not be beaten nor yet beat:
Fools only fight, the prudent use to treat.
His cousin Montagu, by court-disaster,
Dwindled into the wooden-horse's master.
To speak of peace seemed amongst all most proper,
Had *Talbot* then treated of nought but copper:

[1] The Dutch.

town and castle, without any provocation, playing on our ships,) they did cut all our cables, so as the wind being off the land, did force us to go out, and rendered our fire-ships useless ; without doing any thing, but what hurt of course our guns must have done them : we having lost five commanders, besides Mr. Edward Montagu,[1] and Mr. Windham.[2] Our fleete is come home to our great grief with not above five weeks' dry, and six days' wet provisions : however, must go out again ; and the Duke hath ordered the Soveraigne,[3] and all other ships ready, to go out to

---

Or what are forts, when void of ammunition?
With friends or foes what would we more condition?
Yet we three days, till the Dutch furnished all,
Men, powder, money, cannon, treat with wall!
Then *Tydiman*, finding the Danes would not,
Sent in six captains bravely to be shot.
And Montagu, though drest like any bride,
And aboard him too, yet was reached and died.
Sad was the chance, and yet a deeper care
Wrinkled his membranes under forehead fair,
The Dutch armado yet hath th' impudence
To put to sea, to waft their merchants thence,
For, as if all their ships of walnut were,
The more we beat them, still the more they bear:
But a good pilot, and a favouring wind,
Brings *Sandwich* back, and once again did blind."

Advice to a Painter.

[1] " Mr. Edward Montagu was killed in the action at Bergen, and is much lamented by his friends." — EARL OF ARLINGTON's *Letters*, vol. ii. p. 87.

[2] This Mr. Windham had entered into a formal engagement with the Earl of Rochester, " not without ceremonies of religion, that if either of them died, he should appear, and give the other notice of the future state, if there was any." He was probably one of the brothers of Sir Wm. Wyndham, Bart. See Wordsworth's " Ecclesiastical Biography," 4th edit. vol. iv. p. 615.

[3] " The Sovereign of the Seas " was built at Woolwich, in 1637, of timber

the fleete to strengthen them.   This news troubles us all, but cannot be helped.   Having read all this news, and received commands of the Duke with great content, he giving me the words which to my great joy he hath several times said to me, that his greatest reliance is upon me.   And my Lord Craven also did come out to talk with me, and told me that I am in mighty esteem with the Duke, for which I bless God.   Home ; and having given my fellow-officers an account hereof, to Chatham, and wrote other letters, I by water to Charing-Cross, to the post-house, and there the people tell me they are shut up ; and so I went to the new post-house, and there got a guide and horses to Hounslow, where I was mightily taken with a little girle, the daughter of the master of the house, which, if she lives, will make a great beauty. Here I met with a fine fellow who, while I staid for my horses, did enquire newes, but I could not make him remember Bergen in Norway, in 6 or 7 times telling, so ignorant he was.   So to Stanes, and there by this time it was dark night, and got a guide who lost his way in the forest, till by help of the moone (which recompences me for all the pains I ever took about studying of her motions,) I led my guide into the way back again ; and so we made a man rise that

---

which had been stripped of its bark, while growing in the spring, and not felled till the second autumn afterwards; and it is observed by Dr. Plot ("Phil. Trans." for 1691) in his discourse on the most seasonable time for felling timber, written by the advice of Pepys, that after forty-seven years, "all the ancient timber then remaining in her, it was no easy matter to drive a nail into it."—*Quarterly Review*, vol. viii. p. 35.

kept a gate, and so he carried us to Cranborne.[1] Where in the dark I perceive an old house new building with a great deal of rubbish, and was fain to go up a ladder to Sir G. Carteret's chamber. And there in his bed I sat down, and told him all my bad newes, which troubled him mightily: but yet we were very merry, and made the best of it; and being myself weary did take leave, and after having spoken with Mr. Fenn[2] in bed, I to bed in my Lady's chamber that she uses to lie in, and where the Duchesse of York, that now is, was born. So to sleep; being very well, but weary, and the better by having carried with me a bottle of strong water; whereof now and then a sip did me good.

20th (Lord's day). Sir G. Carteret came and walked by my bedside half an houre, talking and telling me how my Lord is unblameable in all this ill-successe, he having followed orders; and that all ought to be imputed to the falsenesse of the King of Denmark, who, he told me as a secret, had promised to deliver up the Dutch ships to us, and we expected no less; and swears it will, and will easily, be the ruin of him and his kingdom, if we fall out with him, as we must in honour do; but that all that can be must be to get the fleete out again to intercept De Witt, who certainly will be coming home with the East India fleete, he being gone thither. He being gone, I up and to walk forth

---

[1] One of the lodges belonging to the Crown in Windsor Forest.

[2] Nicholas Fenne is mentioned as a Commissioner of the Victualling Office, 1683. — PEPYS, *MS. Letters.*

to see the place; and I find it to be a very noble seat in a noble forest, with the noblest prospect towards Windsor, and round about over many countys, that can be desired; but otherwise a very melancholy place, and little variety save only trees. I had thoughts of going home by water and of seeing Windsor Chappell and Castle, but finding at my coming in that Sir G. Carteret did prevent me in speaking for my sudden return to look after business, I did presently eat a bit off the spit about 10 o'clock, and so took horse for Stanes, and thence to Brainford to Mr. Povy's. Mr. Povy not being at home I lost my labour, only eat and drank there with his lady, and told my bad newes, and hear the plague is round about them there. So away to Brainford; and there at the inn that goes down to the water-side, I 'light and paid off my post-horses, and so slipped on my shoes, and laid my things by, the tide not serving, and to church, where a dull sermon, and many Londoners. After church to my inn, and eat and drank, and so about seven o'clock by water, and got between nine and ten to Queenhive,[1] very dark. And I could not get my waterman to go elsewhere for fear of the plague. Thence with a lanthorn, in great fear of meeting of dead corpses, carried to be buried; but, blessed be God, met none, but did see now and then a linke (which is the mark of them) at a distance.

21st. Called up, by message from Lord Brouncker

---

[1] Queenhithe.

and the rest of my fellows, that they will meet me at the Duke of Albemarle's this morning; so I up, and weary, however, got thither before them, and spoke with my Lord, and with him and other gentlemen to walk in the Parke, where, I perceive, he spends much of his time, having no whither else to go; and here I hear him speake of some Presbyter people that he caused to be apprehended yesterday, at a private meeting in Covent Garden, which he would have released upon paying 5*l.* per man to the poor, but it was answered, they would not pay anything; so he ordered them to another prison from the guard. By and by comes my fellow-officers, and the Duke walked in, and to counsel with us; and that being done we departed, and Sir W. Batten and I to the office, where, after I had done a little business, I to his house to dinner, whither comes Captain Cocke, for whose epicurisme a dish of patriges was sent for, and still gives me reason to think is the greatest epicure in the world. After dinner I by water to Sir W. Warren's and with him two hours talking of things to his and my profit and particularly good advice from him what use to make of Sir G. Carteret's kindnesse to me and my interest in him with exceeding good cautions for my not using it too much nor obliging him to fear by prying into his secrets which it were easy for me to do. Thence to my Lord Brouncker, at Greenwich, to looke after the lodgings appointed for us there for our office, which do by no means please me, they being in the heart of all the labourers and workmen there, which makes it as unsafe as to be, I think, at London. Mr. Hugh May, who is a most ingenuous man, did show us the lodgings, and his acquaintance I am desirous of.   Messengers went to get a boat for me, to carry me to Woolwich, but all to no purpose ; so I was forced to walk it in the darke, at ten o'clock at night, with Sir J. Minnes's George with me, being mightily troubled for fear of the doggs at Coome farme, and more for fear of rogues by the way, and yet more because of the plague which is there, which is very strange, it being a single house, all alone from the towne, but it seems they use to admit beggars, for their owne safety, to lie in their barns and they brought it to them ; but I bless God I got about eleven of the clock well to my wife, and giving 4*s.* in recompence to George I to my wife, and having first viewed her last piece of drawing since I saw her, which is seven or eight days, which pleases me beyond any thing in the world, to bed with great content but weary.

22nd. Up, and after much pleasant talke and being importuned by my wife and her two mayds, which are both good wenches, for me to buy a necklace of pearle for her, and I promising to give her one of 6o*l.* in two years at furthest, and in less if she pleases me in her painting, I went away and walked to Greenwich, in my way seeing a coffin with a dead body therein, dead of the plague, lying in an open close belonging to Coome farme, which was carried out last night, and the parish have not appointed any body to bury it ; but only set a watch there day and night, that nobody should go thither or come thence : this disease making us more cruel to one another than if we are doggs. Walked to Redriffe, troubled to go through the little lane, where the plague is, but did and took water and home, where all well.

23rd. Busy writing letters, and received a very kind and good one from my Lord Sandwich of his arrival with the fleete at Solebay, and the joy he has at my last newes he met with, of the marriage of my Lady Jemimah ; and he tells me more, the good newes that all our ships, which were in such danger that nobody would insure them, from the Eastland,[1] were all safe arrived, which I am sure is a great piece of good luck, being in much more danger than those of the Hambrough which were lost and their value much greater at this time to us.

25th. This day I am told that Dr. Burnett,[2] my physician, is this morning dead of the plague ; which is strange, his man dying so long ago, and his house this month open again. Now himself dead. Poor unfortunate man !

----

[1] Baltic Sea.

[2] See *ante*, August 24th 1662. He was reported to have fallen a victim to his zeal. " Dr. Burnett, Dr. Glover, and one or two more of the College of Physicians, with Dr. O'Dowd, which was licensed by my Lord's Grace of Canterbury, some surgeons, apothecaries, and Johnson, the chemist, died all very suddenly. Some say (but God forbid that I should report it for truth) that these, in a consultation together, if not all, yet the greatest part of them, attempted to open a dead corpse which was full of the tokens ; and being in hand with the dissected body, some fell down dead immediately, and others did not outlive the next day at noon."—J. Tillison to Dr. Sancroft, 14th Sept. 1665, in 2 *Ellis*, iv. 37.

26th. Down by water to Greenwich, I found Mr. Andrews and Mr. Yeabsly, and we walked together talking about their business. We parted at my Lord Brouncker's doore, where I went in, having never been there before, and there he made a noble entertainment for Sir J. Minnes, myself, and Captain Cocke, none else saving some painted lady that dined there, I know not who she is.[1] But very merry we were, and after dinner into the garden, and to see his and her chamber, where some good pictures, and a very handsome young woman for my lady's woman. Thence I by water home, in my way seeing a man taken up dead, out of the hold of a small catch that lay at Deptford. I doubt it might be the plague, which with the thought of Dr. Burnett, did something disturb me, so that I did not what I intended and should have done, but home sooner than ordinary, and after supper, to read melancholy alone, and then to bed.

28th. To Mr. Colvill, the goldsmith's, having not for some days been in the streets ; but now how few people I see, and those looking like people that had taken leave of the world. I there and made even all accounts in the world between him and I, in a very good condition, and I would have done the like with Sir R. Viner, but he is out of towne, the sicknesse being every where thereabouts. I to the Exchange, and I think there was not fifty people upon it, and but few more like to be as they told me. Thus I

---

[1] Mrs. Williams, Lord Brouncker's mistress. (M. B.)

think to take adieu to-day of the London streets, unless it be to go again to Viner's. I think I have 1,800*l.* and more in the house, and, blessed be God! no money out but what I can very well command and that but very little, which is much the best posture I ever was in in my life, both as to the quantity and the certainty I have of the money I am worth; having most of it in my hand. But then this is a trouble to me what to do with it, being myself this day going to be wholly at Woolwich; but for the present I am resolved to venture it in an iron chest, at least for a while. Just now comes newes that the fleete is gone, or going this day, out again, for which God be praised! and my Lord Sandwich hath done himself great right in it, in getting so soon out again. Pray God, he may meet the enemy. To Woolwich, where I met my wife walking to the waterside with her paynter, Mr. Browne, and her mayds. There I met Commissioner Pett, and my Lord Brouncker, and the lady at his house had been there to-day, to see her.

29th. To Greenwich, and called at Sir Theophilus Biddulph's, a sober, discreet man, to discourse of the preventing of the plague in Greenwich, and Woolwich, and Deptford, where in every place it begins to grow very great.

30th. Abroad, and met with Hadley, our clerke, who, upon my asking how the plague goes, told me it encreases much, and much in our parish; for, says he, there died nine this week, though I have returned but six: which is a very ill practice, and makes me think it is so in other places ; and therefore the plague much greater than people take it to be. I went forth and walked towards Moorefields to see (God forbid my presumption !) whether I could see any dead corps going to the grave ; but, as God would have it, did not. But, Lord ! how every body's looks, and discourse in the street is of death, and nothing else, and few people going up and down, that the towne is like a place distressed and forsaken. After one turne there back again to Viner's, and there found my business ready for me, and evened all reckonings with them to this day to my great content. So home, and all day till very late at night setting my Tangier and private accounts in order, which I did in both, and in the latter to my great joy do find myself yet in the much best condition that ever I was in, finding myself worth 2,180*l.* and odd, besides plate and goods, which I value at 250*l.* more, which is a very great blessing to me. The Lord make me thankfull !

31st. Up ; and, after putting several things in order to my removal, to Woolwich ; the plague having a great encrease this week, beyond all expectation of almost 2,000, making the general Bill 7,000, odd 100 ; and the plague above 6,000. Thus this month ends with great sadness upon the publick, through the greatness of the plague every where through the kingdom almost. Every day sadder and sadder news of its encrease. In the City died this week 7,496, and of them 6,102 of the plague. But it is feared that the true number of the dead this week is near 10,000 ; partly from the poor that cannot be taken notice of, through the greatness of the number, and partly from the Quakers and others that will not have any bell ring for them. Our fleete gone out to find the Dutch, we having about 100 sail in our fleete, and in them the Soveraigne one; so that it is a better fleete than the former with which the Duke was. All our fear is that the Dutch should be got in before them; which would be a very great sorrow to the publick, and to me particularly, for my Lord Sandwich's sake. A great deal of money being spent, and the kingdom not in a condition to spare, nor a parliament without much difficulty to meet to give more. And to that; to have it said, what hath been done by our late fleetes? As to myself I am very well, only in fear of the plague, and as much of an ague by being forced to go early and late to Woolwich, and my family to lie there continually. My late gettings have been very great to my great content, and am likely to have yet a few more profitable jobbs in a little while; for which Tangier and Sir W. Warren I am wholly obliged to.

Sept. 1st. Up, and to visit my Lady Pen and her daughter at the Ropeyarde where I did breakfast with them and sat chatting a good while. To London, there put many more things in order for my total remove. At the Duke of Albemarle's I overheard some examinations of the late plot that is discoursed of and a great deale of do there is about it. Among other discourses, I heard read, in the presence of the Duke, an examination and discourse of Sir Philip

Howard's,[1] with one of the plotting party. In many places these words being, "Then said Sir P. Howard, 'If you so come over to the King, and be faithfull to him, you shall be maintained, and be set up with a horse and armes,'" and I know not what. And then said such a one, "Yes, I will be true to the King." "But, damn me," said Sir Philip, "will you so and so?" And thus I believe twelve times Sir P. Howard answered him a "damn me," which was a fine way of rhetorique to persuade a Quaker or Anabaptist from his persuasion. And this was read in the hearing of Sir P. Howard, before the Duke and twenty more officers, and they made sport of it, only without any reproach, or he being anything ashamed of it. But it ended, I remember, at last that such a one (the plotter) did at last bid them remember that he had not told them what King he would be faithfull to.

3rd (Lord's day). Up; and put on my coloured silk suit very fine, and my new periwigg, bought a good while since, but durst not wear, because the plague was in Westminster when I bought it; and it is a wonder what will be the fashion after the plague is done, as to periwiggs, for nobody will dare to buy any haire, for fear of the infection, that it had been cut off the heads of people dead of the plague. To church, where a sorry dull parson, and so home and most excellent company with Mr. Hill and discourse of musique. I took my Lady Pen home, and her

---

[1] Seventh son of Sir Thomas Howard, first Earl of Berkshire, the direct ancestor of the present Earl of Suffolk, to whom both the titles descended.

daughter Pegg, and merry we were; and after dinner I made my wife show them her pictures, which
did mad Pegg Pen, who learnt of the same man [1] and
cannot do so well. After dinner left them and I by
water to Greenwich, where much ado to be suffered to
come into the towne because of the sicknesse, for fear
I should come from London, till I told them who I
was. So up to the church, where at the door I find
Captain Cocke in my Lord Brouncker's coach, and he
came out and walked with me in the church-yarde till
the church was done, talking of the ill government of
our Kingdom, nobody setting to heart the business
of the Kingdom, but every body minding their particular profit or pleasures, the King himself minding
nothing but his ease and so we let things go to wracke.
This arose upon considering what we shall do for
money when the fleete comes in, and more if the fleete
should not meet with the Dutch, which will put a disgrace upon the King's actions, so as the Parliament and
Kingdom will have the less mind to give more money,
besides, so bad an account of the last money, we fear,
will be given, not half of it being spent, as it ought to
be, upon the Navy. Besides, it is said that at this
day our Lord Treasurer cannot tell what the profit of
Chimney money is, what it comes to per annum, nor
looks whether that or any other part of the revenue be
duly gathered as it ought; the very money that should
pay the City the 200,000*l.* they lent the King, being

---

[1] Brown.

all gathered and in the hands of the Receiver and has been long and yet not brought up to pay the City, whereas we are coming to borrow 4 or 500,000*l.* more of the City, which will never be lent as is to be feared. Church being done, my Lord Brouncker, Sir J. Minnes, and I up to the Vestry at the desire of the Justices of the Peace, in order to the doing something for the keeping of the plague from growing; but Lord ! to consider the madness of the people of the town, who will (because they are forbid) come in crowds along with the dead corpses to see them buried ; but we agreed on some orders for the prevention thereof. Among other stories, one was very passionate, methought, of a complaint brought against a man in the towne for taking a child from London from an infected house. Alderman Hooker told us it was the child of a very able citizen in Gracious Street, a saddler, who had buried all the rest of his children of the plague, and himself and wife now being shut up and in despair of escaping, did desire only to save the life of this little child ; and so prevailed to have it received stark-naked into the arms of a friend, who brought it (having put it into new fresh clothes) to Greenwich ; where upon hearing the story, we did agree it should be permitted to be received and kept in the towne. By water to Woolwich, in great apprehensions of an ague. Here was my Lord Brouncker's lady of pleasure,[1] who, I perceive, goes every where

---

[1] Mrs. Williams.

with him; and he, I find, is obliged to carry her, and make all the courtship to her that can be.

4th. Walked home, my Lord Brouncker giving me a very neat cane to walk with; but it troubled me to pass by Coome farme where about twenty-one people have died of the plague, and three or four days since I saw a dead corps in a coffin lie in the Close unburied, and a watch is constantly kept there night and day to keep the people in, the plague making us cruel, as doggs, one to another.

5th. Up, and walked with some Captains and others talking to me to Greenwich, they calling out upon Captain Teddiman's management of the business of Bergen, that he staid treating too long while he saw the Dutch fitting themselves, and that at first he might have taken every ship, and done what he would with them. How true I cannot tell. Here we sat very late and for want of money, which lies heavy upon us, did nothing of business almost. Thence home with my Lord Brouncker to dinner where very merry with him and his doxy.[1] After dinner comes Colonel Blunt[2] in his new chariot made with springs; as that was of wicker, wherein a while since we rode at his house. And he hath rode, he says, now this journey, many miles in it with one horse, and out-drives any coach, and out-goes any horse, and so easy, he says. So for curiosity I went into it to try it, and up the hill[3] to the heath, and over the cart-ruts and

---

[1] His mistress. (M. B.)   [2] Of Wricklesmarsh.
[3] Shooter's Hill. Blackheath.

found it pretty well, but not so easy as he pretends. Home pretty betimes and there found W. Pen, and he staid supper with us and mighty merry talking of his travells and the French humours, &c., and so parted and to bed.

6th. To London, to pack up more things; and there I saw fires burning in the street, as it is through the whole City, by the Lord Mayor's order. Thence by water to the Duke of Albemarle's : all the way fires on each side of the Thames, and strange to see in broad daylight two or three burials upon the Bankeside, one at the very heels of another : doubtless all of the plague; and yet at least forty or fifty people going along with every one of them. The Duke mighty pleasant with me; telling me that he is certainly informed that the Dutch were not come home upon the 1st instant, and so he hopes our fleete may meet with them.

7th. Up by 5 of the clock, mighty full of fear of an ague, but was obliged to go, and so by water wrapping myself up warm to the Tower, and there sent for the Weekly Bill, and find 8,252 dead in all, and of them 6,978 of the plague; which is a most dreadful number, and shows reason to fear that the plague hath got that hold that it will yet continue among us. Thence to Brainford, reading "The Villaine," a pretty good play, all the way. There a coach of Mr. Povy's stood ready for me, and he at his house ready to come in,[1]

---

[1] " Aug. 6, 1666. Dined with Mr. Povy, and then went with him to see a country-house he had bought near Brentford."— EVELYN's *Diary*.

and so we together merrily to Swakely[1] to Sir R. Viner's. A very pleasant place, bought by him of Sir James Harrington's lady. He took us up and down with great respect, and showed us all his house and grounds; and it is a place not very moderne in the garden nor house, but the most uniforme in all that ever I saw; and some things to excess. Pretty to see over the screene of the hall (put up by Sir J. Harrington, a Long Parliament-man) the King's head, and my Lord of Essex[2] on one side, and Fairfax on the other; and upon the other side of the screene, the parson of the parish, and the lord of the manor and his sisters. The window-cases, door-cases, and chimnys of all the house are marble. He showed me a

---

[1] Swakeley House, in the parish of Ickenham, Middlesex, was built in 1638 by Sir Edmund Wright, whose daughter marrying Sir James Harrington, one of Charles I.'s judges, he became possessed of it, *jure uxoris*. Sir Robert Vyner, Bart., to whom the property was sold in 1665, entertained Charles II. at Guildhall, when Lord Mayor. The house is now the residence of Thomas Clarke, Esq., whose father in 1750 bought the estate of Mr. Lethieullier, to whom it had been alienated by the Vyner family. — LYSONS's *Environs.*

It was in 1674 that Sir Robert Viner entertained the King at Guildhall. When the King was stealing away towards his coach to avoid ceremony, Sir Robert pursued him hastily, and catching him fast by the hand, cried out, *"Sir, you shall stay and take the other bottle."* The airy monarch looked kindly at him over his shoulder, and with a smile and graceful air repeated this line of an old song —

"He that's drunk is as great as a king,"

and immediately turned back and complied with his landlord. — *Spectator*, No. 462. Sir R. Viner was one of the many goldsmiths ruined by the closing of the Exchequer by Charles II. The Crown was indebted to him, at the shutting of the Exchequer, nearly half a million of money, for which was awarded 25,000*l.* 9*s.* 4*d.* per annum out of the Excise. (M. B.)

[2] The Parliament General.

black boy that he had, that died of a consumption, and being dead, he caused him to be dried in an oven, and lies there entire in a box. By and by to dinner, where his lady I find yet handsome, but hath been a very handsome woman; [1] now is old. Hath brought him near 100,000*l.* and now he lives, no man in England in greater plenty, and commands both King and Council with his credit he gives them. After dinner Sir Robert led us up to his long gallery, very fine, above stairs, (and better, or such, furniture I never did see.) A most pleasant journey we had back, Povy and I, and his company most excellent in anything but business, he here giving me an account of as many persons at Court as I had a mind or thought of enquiring after. He tells me by a letter he showed me, that the King is not, nor hath been of late, very well, but quite out of humour; and, as some think, in a consumption, and weary of every thing. He showed me my Lord Arlington's house [2] that he was born in, in a towne called Harlington: and so carried me through a most pleasant country to Brainford, and there put me into my boat, and good night. So I wrapped myself warm, and by water got to Woolwich about one in the morning.

---

[1] Mary, daughter of John Whitchurch, Esq., and widow of Sir Thomas Hyde, Bart., of Albury, Herts.

[2] Dawley House, near Hounslow, long the seat of the Bennet family. Harlington, in which parish it is situated, gave the title of Baron and Earl to Sir Henry Bennet, the aspirate being dropped. The mansion was alienated by Lord Gray, Earl of Tankerville, to Viscount Bolingbrooke, since which it has often changed owners.

8th. Up, and several with me about business. Anon comes my Lord Brouncker, as I expected, and we to the enquiring into the business of the late desertion of the Shipwrights from worke, who had left us for three days together for want of money and upon this all the morning, and brought it to a pretty good issue, that they, we believe, will come to-morrow to work. To dinner, having but a mean one, yet sufficient for him, and he well enough pleased, besides that I do not desire to vie entertainments with him or any one else.

9th. At noon, by invitation, to my Lord Brouncker's, all of us, to dinner, where a good venison pasty, and mighty merry. Here was Sir W. Doyly,[1] lately come from Ipswich about the sicke and wounded, and Mr. Evelyn and Captain Cocke. My wife also was sent for by my Lord Brouncker, and was here. After dinner, my Lord and his mistress would see her home again, it being a most cursed rainy afternoon, and I, forced to go to the office on foot, was almost wet to the skin, and spoiled my silke breeches almost. Rained all the afternoon and evening, so as my letters being done, I was forced to get a bed at Captain Cocke's, where I find Sir W. Doyly, and he, and Evelyn at supper; and I with them full of discourse of the neglect of our masters, the great officers of State,

---

[1] Sir William Doyly, of Shottisham, Norfolk, knighted 1642, created a Baronet 1663. M. P. for Yarmouth. Ob 1677. He and Mr. Evelyn were at this time appointed Commissioners for the care of the sick and wounded seamen and prisoners of war.

about all business, and especially that of money: having now some thousands prisoners kept to no purpose at a great charge, and no money provided almost for the doing of it. We fell to talk largely of the want of some persons understanding to look after businesses, but all goes to rack. "For," says Captain Cocke, "my Lord Treasurer, he minds his ease, and lets things go how they will: if he can have his 8,000*l*. per annum, and a game at l'ombre, he is well. My Lord Chancellor he minds getting of money and nothing else; and my Lord Ashly[1] will rob the Devil and the Alter, but he will get money if it be to be got." But that which put us into this great melancholy, was newes brought to-day, which Captain Cocke reports as a certain truth, that all the Dutch fleete, men-of-war and merchant East India ships, are got every one in from Bergen the 3d of this month, Sunday last; which will make us all ridiculous. The fleete come

---

[1] Lord Ashly, afterwards Earl of Shaftesbury, is described by Dryden, in 1681, under the character of Achitophel, as the worst of the ungrateful opponents of Charles.

> " Of these the false Achitophel was first,
>   A name to all succeeding ages curst;
>   For close designs, and crooked counsels fit,
>   Sagacious, bold, and turbulent of wit;
>   Restless, unfixed in principles and place,
>   In power unpleased, impatient of disgrace;
>   A fiery soul, which working out its way
>   Fretted the pigmy body to decay,
>   And o'erinformed the tenement of clay."

Absalom and Achitophel.

Pepys had no reason to have a better opinion of him afterwards See Life. (M. B.) ,

home with shame to require a great deale of money, which is not to be had, to discharge many men that must get the plague then or continue at greater charge on shipboard, nothing done by them to encourage the Parliament to give money, nor the Kingdom able to spare any money, if they would, at this time of the plague, so that, as things look at present, the whole state must come to ruine. Full of these melancholy thoughts, to bed; where, though I lay the softest I ever did in my life, with a downe bed, after the Danish manner, upon me, yet I slept very ill, chiefly through the thoughts of my Lord Sandwich's concernment in all this ill successe at sea.

10th (Lord's day). Walked home; being forced thereto by one of my watermen falling sick yesterday, and it was God's great mercy I did not go by water with them yesterday, for he fell sick on Saturday night, and it is to be feared of the plague. So I sent him away to London with his fellow; but another boat came to me this morning. I walked to Woolwich, and there found Mr. Hill, and he and I all the morning at musique and a song he has set of three parts, methinks, very good. My wife before I came out telling me the ill news that she hears that her father is very ill, and then I told her I feared of the plague, for that the house is shut up. And so she much troubled did desire me to send them something; and I said I would, and will do so. But before I come out there happened newes to come to me by an expresse from Mr. Coventry, telling me the most happy news

of my Lord Sandwich's meeting with part of the
Dutch ; his taking two of their East India ships, and
six or seven others, and very good prizes : [1] and that
he is in search of the rest of the fleet, which he hopes
to find upon the Wellbancke, with the loss only of the
Hector, poor Captn. Cuttle.   This newes do so overjoy me that I know not what to say enough to express
it, but the better to do it I did walk to Greenwich,
and there sending away Mr. Andrews, I to Captn.
Cocke's, where I find my Lord Brouncker and his
mistress, and Sir J. Minnes.   Where we supped ;
(there was also Sir W. Doyly and Mr. Evelyn,) but
the receipt of this newes did put us all into such
an extasy of joy, that it inspired into Sir J. Minnes
and Mr. Evelyn such a spirit of mirth, that in all my
life I never met with so merry a two hours as our
company this night was.   Among other humours, Mr.
Evelyn's repeating of some verses made up of nothing
but the various acceptations of *may* and *can*, and
doing it so aptly upon occasion of something of that
nature, and so fast, did make us all die almost with
laughing, and did so stop the mouth of Sir J. Minnes
in the middle of all his mirth, (and in a thing agreeing with his own manner of genius) that I never saw
any man so out-done in all my life ; and Sir J. Minnes's
mirth too to see himself out-done, was the crown of
all our mirth.   In this humour we sat till about ten
at night, and so my Lord and his mistress home, and

---

[1] These prizes, it will be seen, caused great trouble.

we to bed, it being one of the times of my life wherein I was the fullest of true sense of joy.

11th. Over to the ferry, where Sir W. Batten's coach was ready for us, and to Walthamstow drove merrily, excellent merry discourse in the way, and there come, a good plain venison dinner. After dinner to billiards, where I won an angel,[1] and among other sports we were merry with my pretending to have a warrant to Sir W. Hickes[2] (who was there, and was out of humour with Sir W. Doyly's having lately got a warrant for a leash of Bucks, of which we were now eating one) which vexed him, and at last would compound with me to give my Lord Brouncker half a buck now, and me a Doe for it a while hence when the season comes in, which we agreed to and had held, but that we fear Sir W. Doyly did betray our design, which spoiled all; however, my Lady Batten invited herself to dine with him this week, and she invited us all to dine with her there, which we agreed to only to vex him, he being the most niggardly fellow, it seems, in the world. Full of good victuals and mirth we set homeward in the evening, and very merry all the way. So to Greenwich, where I find my Lord Rutherford and Creed come from Court, and have brought me several orders for money to pay for

---

[1] An *angel*, a gold coin, so called because it bore the image of an angel, worth about ten shillings. (M. B.)

[2] Sir William Hickes, created a baronet 1619. Ob. 1680, aged 84. His country-seat was called Ruckholts, or Rookwood, at Layton, in Essex, where he entertained King Charles II. after hunting.

Tangier; and, among the rest 7,000*l.* and more, to this Lord, which is an excellent thing to consider, that, though they can do nothing else, they can give away the King's money upon their progresse. I did give him the best answer I could to pay him with tallys, and that is all they could get from me. By water to Woolwich, where with my wife to a game at tables,[1] and to bed.

12th. Up, and walked to the office, where we sat late. Home in the evening, where my wife shews me a letter from her brother speaking of their father being ill, like to die, which, God forgive me! did not trouble me so much as it should, though I was indeed sorry for it. I did presently resolve to send him something in a letter from my wife, viz. 20*s.* So to bed.

13th. Up, and walked to Greenwich, taking pleasure to walk with my minute watch in my hand, and I do find myself to come within two minutes constantly to the same place at the end of each quarter of an houre. Here we rendezvoused at Captain Cocke's, and there eat oysters, and so my Lord Brouncker, Sir J. Minnes, and I took boat, and in my Lord's coach to Sir W. Hickes's, whither by and by my Lady Batten and Sir William comes. It is a good seat, with a fair grove of trees by it, and the

---

[1] The old name for backgammon.

"Man's life's a game at *tables*, and he may
Mend his bad fortune by his wiser play."

Wit's Recre. i. 250.   (M. B.)

remains of a good garden; but so let to run to ruine, both house and every thing in and about it, so ill furnished and miserably looked after, I never did see in all my life. Not so much as a latch to his diningroom door; which saved him nothing, for the wind blowing into the room for want thereof, flung down a great bow pott that stood upon the side-table, and that fell upon some Venice glasses, and did him a crown's worth of hurt. He did give us the meanest dinner (of beef, shoulder and umbles of venison which he takes away from the keeper of the Forest,[1] and a few pigeons, and all in the meanest manner) that ever I did see, to the basest degree. I was only pleased at a very fine picture of the Queene-Mother, when she was young, by Vandike; a very good picture, and a lovely sweet face. Thence in the afternoon home, and landing at Greenwich I saw Mr. Pen[2] walking my way, so we walked together, and for discourse I put him into talke of France, when he took delight to tell me of his observations, some good, some impertinent, and all ill told, but it served for want of better, and so to my house. So being invited to his mother's to supper, we took Mrs. Barbara,[3] who was mighty finely

---

[1] Of which he was Ranger.

"The keeper hath the skin, head, *umbles*, chine, and *shoulders.*" — HOLINSHED, i. 204.

Falstaff. "Divide me like a bribe buck, each a haunch: I will keep the sides to myself, *my shoulders for the fellow of this walk.*" — SHAKESPEARE, *Merry Wives of Windsor*, act v. sc. 5. (M. B.)

[2] W. Penn, the Quaker. (M. B.)

[3] Daughter of Mr. Sheldon, his landlord. (M. B.)

dressed, and there after some discourse went to supper. Here pretty merry, only I had no stomach, having dined late, to eat. After supper Mr. Pen and I fell to discourse about some words in a French song my wife was saying, " D'un air tout interdit," wherein I laid 20 to one against him when he would not agree with me, though I knew myself in the right as to the sense of the word, and almost angry we were, and were an houre and more upon the dispute, till at last broke up not satisfied, and so home in their coach and so to bed.

14th. To London, where I have not been now a pretty while. But before I went from the office newes is brought by word of mouth that letters are now just brought from the fleete of our taking a great many more of the Dutch fleete, in which I did never more plainly see my command of my temper in my not admitting myself to receive any kind of joy from it till I had heard the certainty of it, and therefore went by water directly to the Duke of Albemarle, where I find a letter of the 12th from Solebay, from my Lord Sandwich, of the fleete's meeting with about eighteen more of the Dutch fleete, and his taking of most of them; and the messenger says, they had taken three after the letter was wrote and sealed; which being twenty-one, and the fourteen took the other day, is forty-five [1] sail; some of which are good, and others rich ships. And having taken a copy of my Lord's

---

[1] A mistake for thirty-five. (M. B.)

letter, I away back again to the Beare at the Bridge foot, and there called for a biscuit and a piece of cheese and gill of sacke, being forced to walk over the Bridge, toward the 'Change, and the plague being all thereabouts. Here my news was highly welcome, and I did wonder to see the 'Change so full, I believe 200 people; but not a man or merchant of any fashion, but plain men all. And Lord! to see how I did endeavour all I could to talk with as few as I could, there being now no observation of shutting up of houses infected, that to be sure we do converse and meet with people that have the plague upon them. I to Sir Robert Viner's, where my main business was about settling the business of Debusty's 5,000*l.* tallys, which I did for the present to enable me to have some money. So home, and put up several things to carry to Woolwich, and upon serious thoughts I am advised by W. Griffin to let my money and plate rest there, as being as safe as any place, nobody imagining that people would leave money in their houses now, when all their families are gone. But, Lord! to see the trouble that it puts a man to, to keep safe what with pain a man has been getting together, and there is good reason for it. Down to the office, and there wrote letters to and again about this good newes of our victory, and so by water home late. Where, when I came, I spent some thoughts upon the occurrences of this day, giving matter for as much content on one hand and melancholy on another, as any day in all my life. For the first; the finding of my money and

plate, and all safe at London, and speeding in my
business of money this day. The hearing of this good
news to such excess, after so great a despair of my
Lord's doing anything this year; adding to that, the
decrease of 500 and more, which is the first decrease
we have yet had in the sickness since it begun : and
great hopes that the next week it will be greater.
Then, on the other side, my finding that though the
Bill in general is abated, yet the City within the walls
is encreased, and likely to continue so, and is close
to our house there. My meeting dead corpses of the
plague, carried to be buried close to me at noon-day
through the City in Fanchurch-street. To see a person sick of the sores, carried close by me by Grace-
church in a hackney-coach. My finding the Angel
tavern, at the lower end of Tower-hill, shut up, and
more than that, the alehouse at the Tower-stairs, and
more than that, the person was then dying of the
plague when I was last there, a little while ago, at
night, to write a short letter, and I overheard the mistresse of the house sadly saying to her husband somebody was very ill, but did not think it was of the
plague. To hear that poor Payne, my waiter, hath
buried a child, and is dying himself. To hear that a
labourer I sent but the other day to Dagenhams, to
know how they did there, is dead of the plague ; and
that one of my own watermen, that carried me daily,
fell sick as soon as he had landed me on Friday
morning last, when I had been all night upon the
water (and I believe he did get his infection that day

at Brainford), and is now dead of the plague. To hear that Captain Lambert and Cuttle are killed in the taking these ships ; and that Mr. Sidney Montague is sick of a desperate fever at my Lady Carteret's, at Scott's-hall. To hear that Mr. Lewes hath another daughter sick. And, lastly, that both my servants, W. Hewer and Tom Edwards, have lost their fathers, both in St. Sepulchre's parish, of the plague this week, do put me into great apprehensions of melancholy, and with good reason. But I put off the thoughts of sadness as much as I can, and the rather to keep my wife in good heart and family also. After supper (having eaten nothing all this day) upon a fine tench of Mr. Sheldon's taking, we to bed.

15th. Up, it being a cold misling morning, and so by water to the office. By and by sent my waterman to see how Sir W. Warren do, who is sicke, and for which I have reason to be very sorry, he being the friend I have got most by of most friends in England but the King: who returns me that he is pretty well again, his disease being an ague. Thence with Captain Cocke, and there drank a cup of good drink, which I am fain to allow myself during this plague time, by advice of all, and not contrary to my oathe, my physician being dead, and chyrurgeon out of the way, whose advice I am obliged to take. In much pain to think what I shall do this winter time ; for go every day to Woolwich I cannot, without endangering my life ; and staying from my wife at Greenwich is not handsome.

16th. Up, and walked to Greenwich reading a play, and to the office, where I find Sir J. Minnes gone to the fleete, like a doating foole, to do no good, but proclaim himself an asse; for no service he can do here, nor inform my Lord, who is come in thither to the buoy of the Nore, in anything worth his knowledge. At noon to dinner to my Lord Brouncker, and very merry we were, only that the discourse of the likelihood of the encrease of the plague this weeke makes us a little sad, but then again the thoughts of the late prizes make us glad. At night to Captain Cocke's, meaning to lie there, it being late, and he not being at home, I walked to him to my Lord Brouncker's, and there staid a while, they being at tables;[1] and so by and by parted, and walked to his house; and, after a mess of good broth, to bed, in great pleasure, his company being most excellent.

17th (Lord's day). Up, and before I went out of my chamber did draw a musique scale, in order to my having it at any time ready in my hand to turn to for exercise, for I have a great mind in this Vacation to perfect myself in my scale, in order to my practising of composition. Being ready we to church, where a company of fine people, and a fine Church, and very good sermon, Mr. Plume[2] being a very excellent scholler and preacher. Thence with Captain

---

[1] Better known, at present, by the name of "backgammon." See note, Sept. 11th.

[2] Thomas Plume, D.D., Vicar of Greenwich, 1662, and installed Archdeacon of Rochester, 1679. Ob. 1704.

Cocke, in his coach, home to dinner, whither comes by invitation my Lord Brouncker and his mistresse and very good company we were, but in dinner time comes Sir J. Minnes from the fleete, like a simple weak man, having nothing to say of what he has done there, but tells us of what value he imagines the prizes to be. But this did put me upon a desire of going thither; and, moving of it to my Lord, we presently agreed upon it to go this very tide, we two and Captain Cocke. So I walked to Woolwich to trim and shift myself and by the time I was ready they came down in the Bezan yacht and so I aboard and my boy Tom and there very merrily we sailed to below Gravesend, and there come to anchor for all night, and supped and talked, and with much pleasure at last settled ourselves to sleep having very good lodging upon cushions in the cabbin.

18th. By break of day we come to within sight of the fleete, which was a very fine thing to behold, being above 100 ships, great and small; with the flag-ships of each squadron, distinguished by their several flags on their main, fore, or mizen masts. Among others, the Soveraigne, Charles, and Prince; in the last of which my Lord Sandwich was. And so we come on board, and we find my Lord Sandwich newly up in his night-gown very well. He received us kindly; telling us the state of the fleet, lacking provisions, having no beer at all, nor have had most of them these three weeks or month, and but few days dry provisions. And indeed he tells us that he believes no fleete was ever set to sea in so ill condition of provision, as this was when it went out last. He did inform us in the business of Bergen, so as to let us see how the judgment of the world is not to be depended on in things they know not; it being a place just wide enough, and not so much hardly, for ships to go through to it, the yard-armes sticking in the very rocks. He do not, upon his best enquiry, find reason to except against any part of the management of the business by Teddiman; he having staid treating no longer than during the night, whiles he was fitting himself to fight, bringing his ship a-breast, and not a quarter of an hour longer (as is said); nor could more ships have been brought to play, as is thought. Nor could men be landed, there being 10,000 men effectively always in armes of the Danes; nor, says he, could we expect more from the Dane than he did, it being impossible to set fire on the ships but it must burn the towne. But that wherein the Dane did amisse is, that he did assist them, the Dutch, all the time, while he was treating with us, when he should have been neutrall to us both. But, however, he did demand but the treaty of us; which is, that we should not come with more than five ships. A flag of truce is said, and confessed by my Lord, that he believes it was hung out; but while they did hang it out, they did shoot at us; so that it was not seen perhaps, or fit to cease upon sight of it, while they continued actually in action against us. But the main thing my Lord wonders at, and condemns the

Dane for, is, that the blockhead, who is so much in debt to the Hollander, having now a treasure more by much than all his Crowne was worth, and that which would for ever have beggared the Hollander, should not take this time to break with the Hollander, and thereby pay his debt which must have been forgiven him, and have got the greatest treasure into his hands that ever was together in the world. By and by my Lord took me aside to discourse of his private matters, who was very free with me touching the ill condition of the fleete that it hath been in, and the good fortune that he hath had, and nothing else that these prizes are to be imputed to. He also talked with me about Mr. Coventry's dealing with him in sending Sir W. Pen away before him, which was not fair nor kind; but that he hath mastered and cajoled Sir W. Pen, that he hath been able to do nothing in the fleete, but been obedient to him; but withal tells me he is a man that is but of very mean parts, and a fellow not to be lived with, so false and base he is; which I know well enough to be very true, and did, as I had formerly done, give my Lord my knowledge of him. By and by was called a Council of Warr on board, when comes Sir W. Pen there, and Sir Christopher Mings,[1] Sir Edward Spragg, Sir Jos. Jordan,[2] Sir Thomas Teddiman, and Sir Roger Cuttance, and so

---

[1] The son of a shoemaker, bred to the sea service, and rose to the rank of an Admiral. He was killed in the naval action with the Dutch, June, 1666.

[2] Distinguished himself as an Admiral in the battle of Solebay, and on other occasions.

the necessities of the fleete for victuals, clothes, and money was discovered, but by the discourse there of all but my Lord, that is to say, the counterfeit grave nonsense of Sir W. Pen and the poor mean discourse of the rest, methinks I saw how the government and management of the greatest business of the three nations is committed to very ordinary heads, saving my Lord, and in effect is only upon him, who is able to do what he pleases with them, they not having the meanest degree of reason to be able to oppose anything that he says, and so I fear it is ordered but like all the rest of the King's publique affairs. After dinner Cocke did pray me to helpe him to 500*l.* of W. Howe, who is deputy Treasurer, wherein my Lord Brouncker and I am to be concerned and I did aske it my Lord, and he did consent to have us furnished with 500*l.*, and I did get it paid to Sir Roger Cuttance and Mr. Pierce in part for above 1,000*l.* worth of goods, Mace, Nutmegs, Cynamon, and Cloves, and he tells me we may hope to get 500*l.* by it, which God send! Great spoil, I hear, there hath been of the two East India ships, and that yet they will come into the King very rich: so that I hope this journey will be worth 100*l.* to me. After having paid this money, we took leave of my Lord and so to our Yacht again, having seen many of my friends there, and I overcome with seasickness shut my eyes and fell asleep and continued till we came into Chatham river. Among others I hear that W. Howe will grow very rich by this last business and grows very proud and insolent by it ; but it is what I ever expected. I hear by everybody how much my poor Lord Sandwich was concerned for me during my silence a while, lest I had been dead of the plague in this sickly time. At Chatham at Commissioner Pett's we did eat and drink very well and very merry we were and about 10 at night, it being moonshine and very cold, we set out his coach carrying us, and so all night travelled to Greenwich, we sometimes sleeping and then talking and laughing by the way, and with much pleasure, but that it was very horrible cold, that I was afeard of an ague. A pretty passage was that the coach stood of a sudden and the coachman came down and the horses stirring, he called, Hold ! which waked me, and the coachman at the boote [1] to do something or other and calling, Hold ! I did wake of a sudden and not knowing who he was, nor thinking of the coach-man between sleeping and waking I did take up the heart to take him by the shoulder, thinking verily he had been a thief. But when I waked I found my cowardly heart to discover a fear within me and that I should never have done it if I had been awake.

19th. About 4 or 5 of the clock we came to Green-wich, and, having first set down my Lord Brouncker, Cocke and I went to his house, it being light, and there to our great trouble we being sleepy and cold we met with the ill newes that his boy Jack was gone

---

[1] The "boots" were the two projections from the sides of the carriage, open to the air, and in which the occupants were carried sideways. See "Notes and Queries," 2nd Series, vol. viii. p. 238. (M. B.)

to bed sicke, which put Captain Cocke and me also into much trouble, the boy, as they told us, complaining of his head most, which is a bad sign it seems. So they presently betook themselves to consult whether and how to remove him. However I thought it not fit for me to discover too much fear to go away, nor had I any place to go to. So to bed I went and slept till 10 of the clock and then comes Captain Cocke to wake me and tell me that his boy was well again. With great joy I heard the newes, so I up and to the office where we did a little, and but a little business. At noon by invitation to my Lord Brouncker's where we staid till four of the clock for my Lady Batten and she not then coming we to dinner and pretty merry but disordered by her making us stay so long. After dinner I to the office and did business till night and then to Sir J. Minnes, where I find my Lady Batten come, and she and my Lord Brouncker and his mistresse, and the whole house-full there at cards. But by and by my Lord Brouncker goes away and others of the company, and when I expected Sir J. Minnes and his sister should have staid to have made Sir W. Batten and Lady sup, I find they go up in snuffe to bed without taking any manner of leave of them, but left them with Mr. Boreman.[1] The reason of this I could not presently learn, but anon I hear it is that Sir J. Minnes did expect and intend them a supper, but they without

---

[1] Afterwards Sir William Boreman. (M. B.)

respect to him did first apply themselves to Boreman, which makes all this great feude. However I staid and there supped, all of us being in great disorder from this.

20th. Up, and after being trimmed, the first time I have been touched by a barber these twelvemonths, I think, and more, went to Sir J. Minnes, where I find all out of order still, they having not seen one another till by and by Sir J. Minnes and Sir W. Batten met, to go into my Lord Brouncker's coach, and so we four to Lambeth, and thence to the Duke of Albemarle, to inform him what we have done as to the fleete, which is very little, and to receive his direction. But, Lord! what a sad time it is to see no boats upon the River; and grass grows all up and down White Hall court, and nobody but poor wretches in the streets! And, which is worst of all, the Duke showed us the number of the plague this week, brought in the last night from the Lord Mayor; that it is en-creased about 600 more than the last, which is quite contrary to all our hopes and expectations, from the coldness of the late season. For the whole general number is 8,297, and of them the plague 7,165; which is more in the whole by above 50, than the biggest Bill yet; which is very grievous to us all. Thence back again by my Lord's coach to my Lord Brouncker's house and there we dined and were mighty merry. After dinner I to the office there to write letters, to fit myself for a journey tomorrow to Nonsuch to the Exchequer by appointment. That being done I to Sir J. Minnes where I find Sir W. Batten and his Lady gone home to Walthamstow in great snuffe as to Sir J. Minnes, but yet with some necessity, hearing that a mayde-servant of their's is taken ill. Here I staid and resolved of my going in my Lord Brouncker's coach which he would have me to take, though himself cannot go with me as he intended, and so to my last night's lodging to bed very weary.

21st. Up between five and six o'clock; and by the time I was ready, my Lord's coach comes for me; and taking Will Hewer with me, who is all in mourning for his father, who is lately dead of the plague, as my boy Tom's is also, I set out, and took about 100*l.* with me to pay the fees there, and so I rode in some fear of robbing. When I came thither, I find only Mr. Ward, who led me to Burgess's bed-side, and Spicer's, who, watching of the house, as it is their turns every night, did lie long in bed to-day, and I find nothing at all done in my business which vexed me. But not seeing how to helpe it I did walk up and down with Mr. Ward to see the house; and by and by Spicer came to me and Mr. Falcon-brige and he and I to a towne near by, Yowell, there drank and set up my horses and also bespoke a dinner, and while that is dressing went with Spicer and walked up and down the house and park; and a fine place it hath heretofore been, and a fine prospect about the house. A great walk of an elme and a walnutt set one after another in order. And all the house on the outside filled with figures of stories, and good painting of Rubens' or Holben's doing. And one great thing is, that most of the house is covered, I mean the post, and quarters in the walls, covered with lead, and gilded. I walked into the ruined garden, and there found a plain little girle, kinswoman of Mr. Falconbrige, to sing very finely by the eare only, but a fine way of singing, and if I come ever to lacke a girle again I shall think of getting her. Thence to the towne, and there Spicer and W. Bowyer and I dined together and a friend of Spicer's, and a good dinner I had for them. Strange to see how young W. Bowyer looks at 41 years; one would not take him for 24 or more, and is one of the greatest wonders I ever did see. About 4 of the clock we broke up, and I took coach and home (in fear for the money I had with me, but that this friend of Spicer's, one of the Duke's guard did ride along the best part of the way with us). I got to my Lord Brouncker's before night, and there I sat and supped with him and his mistresse, and Cocke whose boy is yet ill. Thence, after losing a crowne betting at Tables, we walked home, Cocke seeing me at my new lodging. All my worke this day in the coach going and coming was to refresh myself in my musique scale, which I would fain have perfecter than ever I had yet.

22nd. To the office, but was called away by my Lord Brouncker and Sir J. Minnes, and to Blackwall, there to look after the storehouses in order to the laying of goods out of the East India ships when they

shall be unladen. That being done, we into Johnson's
house, and were much made of, eating and drinking.
But here it is observable what he tells us, that in digging the late Docke, he did 12 feet under ground find
perfect trees over-covered with earth. Nut trees, with
the branches and the very nuts upon them ; some of
whose nuts he showed us. Their shells black with
age, and their kernell, upon opening, decayed, but
their shell perfectly hard as ever. And a yew tree he
showed us, (upon which, he says, the very ivy was
taken up whole about it,) which upon cutting with an
addes,[1] we found to be rather harder than the living
tree usually is.[2] They say, very much, but I do not
know how hard a yew tree naturally is. The armes,
they say, were taken up at first whole, about the body,
which is very strange. Thence away by water, and I
walked with my Lord Brouncker home, and there at
dinner comes a letter from my Lord Sandwich to tell
me that he would this day be at Woolwich, and desired me to meet him. My Lord Brouncker presently
ordered his coach to be ready and we to Woolwich,
and my Lord Sandwich not being come, we took a
boat and about a mile off met him in his Catch, and
boarded him, and came up with him ; and, after making a little halt at my house, which I ordered, to have
my wife see him, we all together by coach to Mr. Bore-

---

[1] Adze.

[2] The same discovery was made in 1789, in digging the Brunswick Dock,
also at Blackwall, and elsewhere in the neighbourhood. See "Notes and
Queries," 1st series, vol. viii. p. 263. (M. B.)

man's, where Sir J. Minnes did receive him very handsomely, and there he is to lie ; and Sir J. Minnes did give him on the sudden, a very handsome supper and brave discourse, my Lord Brouncker, and Captain Cocke, and Captain Herbert being there, with myself. Here my Lord did witness great respect to me, and very kind expressions, and by other occasions, from one thing to another did take notice how I was overjoyed at first to see the King's letter to his Lordship, and told them how I did kiss it, and that, whatever he was, I did always love the King. This my Lord Brouncker did take such notice [of] as that he could not forbear kissing me before my Lord, professing his finding occasion every day more and more to love me. Among other discourse concerning long life, Sir J. Minnes saying that his great-grandfather was alive in Edward the Vth's time ; my Lord Sandwich did tell us how few there have been of his family since King Harry the VIIIth ; that is to say, the then Chiefe Justice,[1] and his son the Lord Montagu,[2] who was father to Sir Sydney,[3] who was his father. And yet, what is more wonderfull, he did assure us from the mouth of my Lord Montagu himself, that in King James's time, (when he had a mind to get the King to cut off the entayle of some land which was given in Harry the

---

[1] Sir Edward Montagu, ob. 1556.

[2] These are the words in the MS., and not "his son *and* the Lord Montagu," as in the former Editions. Pepys seems to have written Lord Montagu by mistake for Sir Edward Montagu.

For the pedigree of Lord Sandwich, see p. 355.

[3] Master of the Requests to Charles I.

VIIIth's time to the family, with the remainder in
the Crowne ;) he did answer the King in showing how
unlikely it was that ever it could revert to the Crown,
but that it would be a present convenience to him ;
and did show that at that time there were 4,000 persons derived from the very body of the Chiefe Justice.
It seems the number of daughters in the family having
been very great, and they too had most of them many
children, and grandchildren, and great-grandchildren.
This he tells as a most known and certain truth.
After supper, my Lord Brouncker took his leave, and
I also did mine, taking Captain Herbert home to my
lodging to lie with me, who did mighty seriously in-
quire after who was that in the black dress with my
wife yesterday, and would not believe that it was
my wife's mayde, Mercer, but it was she.

23rd. Up, and to my Lord Sandwich, who did advise alone with me how far he might trust Captain
Cocke in the business of the prize-goods,[1] my Lord
telling me that he hath taken into his hands 2 or
3,000*l.* value of them : it being a good way, he says,
to get money, and afterwards to get the King's allow-
ance thereof, it being easier, he observes, to keepe
money when got of the King than to get it when it
is too late. I advised him not to trust Cocke too far,
and did therefore offer him ready money for a 1,000*l.*

---

[1] In the British Museum, " Egerton MS.," 861, is an account showing the
value of all prizes taken during the war with the Dutch ; distinguishing the
vessels, their goods, the ports at which they were condemned, and the parties
to whose accounts the amounts were debited.

or two, which he listens to and do agree to, which is great joy to me, hoping thereby to get something. Thence by coach to Lambeth, his Lordship, and all our office, and Mr. Evelyn, to the Duke of Albemarle, where we sat down to consult of the disposing and supporting of the fleete with victuals and money, and for the sicke men and prisoners; and I did propose the taking out some goods out of the prizes, to the value of 10,000*l.*, which was accorded to, and an order, drawn up and signed by the Duke and my Lord, done in the best manner I can, but what inconveniences may arise from it, I do not yet see, but fear there may be many. Here we dined, and I did hear my Lord Craven whisper, as he is mightily possessed with a good opinion of me, much to my advantage, which my good Lord did second, and anon my Lord Craven did speak publiquely of me to the Duke, in the hearing of all the rest; and the Duke did say something of the like advantage to me; I believe, not much to the satisfaction of my brethren; but I was mightily joyed at it. Thence took leave, leaving my Lord Sandwich to go visit the Bishop of Canterbury and I home, and among other things took out all my gold to carry along with me to-night with Captain Cocke downe to the fleete, being 180*l.* and more, hoping to lay out that and a great deal more to good advantage. Thence down to Greenwich and so to my Lord Sandwich, and mighty merry and he mighty kind to me in the face of all, saying much in my favour and after supper I took leave and with Captain

Cocke set out in the yacht about ten o'clock at night. So to sleep upon beds brought by Cocke on board mighty handsome, and never slept better than upon this bed upon the floor in the Cabbin.

24th (Lord's day). Waked, and up and drank, and then to discourse; and then being about Grayes, and a very calm, curious morning, we took our wherry, and to the fishermen, and bought a great deal of fine fish, and to Gravesend to White's, and had part of it dressed; and, in the meantime, we to walk about a mile from the towne, and so back again; and there, after breakfast, one of our watermen told us he had heard of a bargain of cloves for us, and we went to a blind alehouse at the further end of the towne to a couple of wretched, dirty seamen, who, poor wretches, had got together about 37 lb. of cloves and 10 lb. of nutmeggs, and we bought them of them, the first at 5*s*. 6*d*. per lb. and the latter at 4*s*., and paid them in gold; but, Lord! to see how silly these men are in the selling of it, and easily to be persuaded almost to anything, offering a bag to us to pass as 20 lbs. of cloves, which upon weighing proved 25 lbs. But it would never have been allowed by my conscience to have wronged the poor wretches, who told us how dangerously they had got some, and dearly paid for the rest of these goods.[1]   This being done we with great content herein on board again and there Captain Cocke and I to discourse of our business, but he will not yet

---

[1] Stolen from the prizes.

be open to me, nor am I to him till I hear what he will say and do with Sir Roger Cuttance. By and by to dinner about 3 o'clock and then I in the cabbin to writing down my journall for these last seven days to my great content, it having pleased God that in this sad time of the plague every thing else has conspired to my happiness and pleasure more for these last three months than in all my life before in so little time. God preserve it and make me thankfull for it !

25th. Found ourselves come to the fleete, and so aboard the Prince ; and there, after a good while in discourse, we did agree a bargain of 5,000*l*. with Sir Roger Cuttance for my Lord Sandwich for silk, cinnamon, nutmeggs, and indigo. And I was near signing to an undertaking for the payment of the whole sum ; but I did by chance escape it ; having since, upon second thoughts, great cause to be glad of it, reflecting upon the craft and not good condition, it may be, of Captain Cocke. I could get no trifles for my wife. Anon to dinner and thence in great haste to make a short visit to Sir W. Pen, where I found them and his lady and daughter and many commanders at dinner. Among others Sir G. Askue, of whom whatever the matter is, the world is silent altogether. But a very pretty dinner there was, and after dinner Sir W. Pen made a bargain with Cocke for ten bales of silke, at 16*s*. per lb., which, as Cocke says, will be a good pennyworth, and so away to the Prince and presently comes my Lord on board from Greenwich, with whom, after a little discourse about his trusting of Cocke, we parted and to our yacht; but it being calme, we to make haste, took our wherry towards Chatham; but, it growing darke, we were put to great difficultys, our simple, yet confident waterman, not knowing a step of the way; and we found ourselves to go backward and forward, which, in the darke night and a wild place, did vex us mightily. At last we got a fisher boy by chance, and took him into the boat, and being an odde kind of boy, did vex us too; for he would not answer us aloud when we spoke to him, but did carry us safe thither, though with a mistake or two; but I wonder they were not more. In our way I was [surprised] and so were we all, at the strange nature of the sea-water in a darke night, that it seemed like fire upon every stroke of the oare, and, they say, is a sign of winde. We went to the Crowne Inne, at Rochester, and there to supper, and made ourselves merry with our poor fisher-boy, who told us he had not been in a bed the whole seven years since he came to 'prentice, and hath two or three more years to serve. After eating something, we in our clothes to bed.

26th. Up by five o'clock and got post horses and so set out for Greenwich, calling and drinking at Dartford. Being come to Greenwich and shifting myself I to the office, from whence by and by my Lord Brouncker and Sir J. Minnes set out towards Erith to take charge of the two East India ships, which I had a hand in contriving for the King's service and may do myself a good office too thereby. I to dinner with Mr. Wright to his brother-in-law at Greenwich, one of the most silly, harmless, prating old men that ever I heard in my life. Creed dined with me, and among other discourses got of me a promise of half that he could get my Lord Rutherford to give me upon clearing his business, which should not be less, he says, than 50*l.* for my half, which is a good thing, though cunningly got of him. After some letters down to Woolwich.

27th. Up, and saw and admired my wife's picture of our Saviour, now finished, which is very pretty. So by water to Greenwich, where with Creed and Lord Rutherford, and there my Lord told me that he would give me 100*l.* for my pains, which pleased me well, though Creed, like a cunning rogue, has got a promise of half of it from me. We to the King's Head, the great musique house, the first time I was ever there, and had a good breakfast and thence parted, I being much troubled to hear from Creed, that he was told at Salisbury [1] that I am become to be a great swearer and drinker, though I know the contrary; but, Lord! to see how my late little drinking of wine is taken notice of by envious men to my disadvantage. I thence to Captain Cocke's, and (he not yet come from town) to Mr. Evelyn's, where much company; and thence in his coach with him to the Duke of Albemarle by Lambeth, who was in a mighty pleasant

---

[1] To which place the Court had returned on account of the plague.

humour; there the Duke tells us that the Dutch do stay abroad, and our fleet must go out again, or be ready to do so. Here we got several things ordered as we desired for the relief of the prisoners, and sick and wounded men. Here I saw this week's Bill of Mortality, wherein, blessed be God! there is above 1,800 decrease, being the first considerable decrease we have had. Back again the same way and had most excellent discourse with Mr. Evelyn touching all manner of learning; wherein I find him a very fine gentleman, and particularly of paynting, in which he tells me the beautifull Mrs. Middleton is rare, and his own wife do brave things. He brought me to the office, whither comes unexpectedly Captain Cocke, who has brought one parcel of our goods by waggons, and at first resolved to have lodged them at our office; but then the thoughts of its being the King's house altered our resolution, and so put them at his friend's, Mr. Glanville's, and there they are safe. Would the rest of them were so too! In discourse, we come to mention my profit, and he offers me 500*l.* clear, and I demand 600*l.* We part to-night, and I lie there at Mr. Glanville's house, there being none there but a mayde-servant and a young man; being in some pain, partly from not knowing what to do in this business, having a mind to be at a certainty in my profit, and partly through his having Jacke sicke still, and his blackemore now also fallen sicke. So he being gone, I to bed.

29th. Up, and by and by comes Lushmore on horseback, and I had my horse I borrowed of Mr. Gilsthropp, Sir W. Batten's clerke, brought to me, and so we set out and rode hard and was at Nonsuch [1] by about eight o'clock, a very fine journey and a fine day. There I came just about chappell time and so I went to chappell with them and thence to the several offices about my tallys, which I find done, but strung for sums not to my purpose, and so was forced to get them to promise me to have them cut into other sums. But, Lord! what ado I had to persuade the dull fellows to it, especially Mr. Warder, Master of the Pells, and yet without any manner of reason for their scruple. But at last I did and so walked to Yowell, and there did spend a piece upon them and much mirth by a sister of the mistresse of the house, an old mayde lately married to a lieutenant of a company that quarters there, and much pleasant discourse we had and, dinner being done, we to horse again and came to Greenwich before night. I hear for certain this night upon the road that Sir Martin Noell [2] is this day dead of the plague in London, where he hath lain sick of it these eight days.

30th. To the office, and at noon to Coll. Cleggat to dinner, being invited, where a very pretty dinner to my full content and very merry. The great burden

---

[1] Nonsuch House, near Epsom.

[2] He had been a Farmer of the Excise and Customs before the Restoration. The Messenger described in "Hudibras," part iii. canto ii., 1507, as disturbing the Cabal with the account of the mobs burning Rumps, is said to have been intended for Sir Martin Noell.

we have upon us at this time at the office, is the providing for prisoners and sicke men that are recovered,
they lying before our office doors all night and all day,
poor wretches.   Having been on shore, the captains
won't receive them on board, and other ships we have
not to put them on, nor money to pay them off, or
provide for them.   God remove this difficulty !   This
made us followed all the way to this gentleman's house
and there are waited for our coming out after dinner.
Hither came Luellin to me and would force me to
take Mr. Deering's 20 pieces in gold he did offer me
a good while since, which I did, yet really and sin-
cerely against my will and content, I seeing him a man
not likely to do well in his business, nor I to reap any
comfort in having to do with, and be beholden to, a
man that minds more his pleasure and company than
his business.   Thence mighty merry and much pleased
with the dinner and company and they with me I
parted and there was set upon by the poor wretches,
whom I did give good words and some little money
to, and the poor people went away like lambs, and in
good earnest are not to be censured if their necessities drive them to bad courses of stealing or the like,
while they lacke wherewith to live.   Thence to the
office and then to Captain Cocke's, where I find Mr.
Temple, the fat blade, Sir Robert Viner's chief man.
And we three and two companions of his in the evening took ship in the Bezan and the tide carried us no
further than Woolwich about 8 at night, and so I on
shore to my wife, and there to my great trouble find

my wife out of order, and she took me downstairs and there alone did tell me her falling out with both her mayds and particularly Mary, and how Mary had to her teeth told her she would tell me of something that should stop her mouth and words of that sense. This do make me mightily out of temper, and seeing it not fit to enter into the dispute did passionately go away, thinking to go on board again. But when I came to the stairs I considered the Bezan would not go till the next ebb, and it was best to lie in a good bed and, it may be, get myself into a better humour by being with my wife. So I back again and to bed and having otherwise so many reasons to rejoice and hopes of good profit, besides considering the ill that trouble of mind and melancholy may in this sickly time bring a family into, and that if the difference were never so great, it is not a time to put away servants, I was resolved to salve up the business rather than stir in it, and so became pleasant to my wife and to bed, minding nothing of this difference. I do end this month with the greatest content, and may say that these last three months, for joy, health, and profit, have been much the greatest that ever I received in all my life in any twelve months, having nothing upon me but the consideration of the sicklinesse of the season during this great plague to mortify me. For all which the Lord God be praised !

October 1st (Lord's day). Called up about 4 of the clock and so dressed myself and on board the Bezan. We spent most of the morning talking and reading of

"The Siege of Rhodes," which is certainly (the more I read it the more I think so) the best poem that ever was wrote. We came to the fleete about two of the clock. My Lord received us mighty kindly, and, among other things, to my great joy, he did assure me that he had wrote to the King and Duke about these prize-goods, and told me that they did approve of what he had done, and that he would owne what he had done, and would have to tell all the world so, and did, under his hand, give Cocke and me his certificate of our bargains, and giving us full power of disposal of what we have so bought. This do ease my mind of all my fear. He did discourse to us of the Dutch fleete being abroad, eighty-five of them still, and are now at the Texell, he believes, in expectation of our Eastland ships coming home with masts and hempe, and our laden Hambrough ships going to Hambrough. He discoursed against them that would have us yield to no conditions but conquest over the Dutch, and seems to believe that the Dutch will call for the protection of the King of France and come under his power, which were to be wished they might be brought to do under ours by fair means, and to that end would have all Dutch men and familys, that would come hither and settled, to be declared denizens; and my Lord did whisper to me alone that things here must break in pieces, nobody minding anything, but every man his owne business of profit or pleasure, and the King some little designs of his owne, and that certainly the kingdom could not stand in this condition long, which

I fear and believe is very true. So to supper and there my Lord the kindest man to me, before all the table talking of me to my advantage and with tenderness too that it overjoyed me. So after supper Captain Cocke and I and Temple on board the Bezan, and there to cards for a while and then to read again in " Rhodes " and so to sleep. But, Lord ! the mirth which it caused me to be waked in the night by their snoring round about me ; I did laugh till I was ready to burst, and waked one of the two companions of Temple, who could not a good while tell where he was that he heard one laugh so, till he recollected himself, and I told him what it was at, and so to sleep again, they still snoring.

2nd. Having sailed all night (and I do wonder how they in the dark could find the way) we got by morning to Gillingham, and thence all walked to Chatham ; and there with Commissioner Pett viewed the Yard ; and among other things, a team of four horses came close by us, he being with me, drawing a piece of timber that I am confident one man could easily have carried upon his back. I made the horses be taken away, and a man or two to take the timber away with their hands. This the Commissioner did see, but said nothing, but I think had cause to be ashamed of. We walked to the Hill-house, where we find Sir W. Pen in bed and there much talke and much dissembling of kindnesse from him, but he is a false rogue, and I shall not trust him. Thence to Rochester, walked to the Crowne, and while dinner was getting ready, I did there walk to visit the old Castle ruins, which hath been a noble place, and there going up I did upon the stairs overtake three pretty mayds and took them up with me : but, Lord ! to see what a dreadfull thing it is to look down the precipices, for it did fright me mightily, and hinder me of much pleasure which I would have made to myself in the company of these three, if it had not been for that. The place hath been very noble and great and strong in former ages. So to walk up and down the Cathedral, and thence to the Crowne, whither Mr. Fowler, the Mayor of the towne, was come in his gowne, and is a very reverend magistrate. After I had eat a bit, I took horses and to Gravesend, and there staid not, but got a boat, the sicknesse being very much in the towne still, and so called on board my Lord Brouncker and Sir John Minnes, on board one of the East Indiamen at Erith, and there do find them full of envious complaints for the pillaging of the ships, but I did pacify them. About 8 o'clock got to Woolwich and there supped and mighty pleasant with my wife, who is, for ought I see, all friends with her mayds, and so in great joy and content to bed.

3d. To the office where nobody to meet me, Sir W. Batten being the only man and he gone this day to meet to adjourne the Parliament to Oxford. Anon by appointment comes one to tell me my Lord Rutherford is come; so I to the King's Head to him, where I find his lady, a fine young Scotch lady,[1] pretty

---

[1] Christian, daughter of Sir Alexander Urquhart, of Cromarty.

handsome and plain. My wife also, and Mercer, by and by comes, Creed bringing them ; and so presently to dinner and very merry; and after to even our accounts, and I to give him tallys, where he do allow me 100*l.*, of which to my grief the rogue Creed has trepanned me out of 50*l.* That being done, and some musique and other diversions, at last goes away my Lord and Lady, and I to Mrs. Pierce's and brought her to the King's Head and there spent a piece upon a supper for her and mighty merry and pretty discourse, she being as pretty as ever, most of our mirth being upon " my Cozen " (meaning my Lord Brouncker's ugly mistress, whom he calls cozen), and to my trouble she tells me that the fine Mrs. Middleton is noted for carrying about her body a continued sour base smell, that is very offensive, especially if she be a little hot. Here some bad musique to close the night and so away and all of us save Mrs. Belle Pierce (as pretty as ever she was almost) home. This night I hear that of our two watermen that used to carry our letters, and were well on Saturday last, one is dead, and the other dying sick of the plague ; the plague, though decreasing elsewhere, yet being greater about the Tower and thereabouts.

4th. This night comes Sir George Smith [1] to see me at the office, and tells me how the plague is decreased this week 740, for which God be praised ! but that it

----

[1] Sir George Smith, of St. Bartholomew, by the Exchange. He married Martha, daughter of John Swift of London, merchant.

encreases at our end of the town still, and says how all the towne is full of Captain Cocke's being in some ill condition about prize-goods, his goods being taken from him, and I know not what. But though this troubles me to have it said, and that it is likely to be a business in Parliament, yet I am not much concerned at it, because yet I believe this newes is all false, for he would have wrote to me sure about it. Being come to my wife, at our lodging, I did go to bed, and left my wife with her people to laugh and dance and I to sleep.

5th. Lay long in bed, among other things talking of my sister Pall, and my wife of herself is very willing that I should give her 400*l.* to her portion, and would have her married soon as we could; but this great sicknesse time do make it unfit to send for her up. I abroad to the office and thence to the Duke of Albemarle's, all my way reading a book [1] of Mr. Evelyn's translating and sending me as a present, about directions for gathering a Library; but the book is above my reach, but his epistle to my Lord Chancellor is a very fine piece. So I walked through Westminster to my old house and so down by water to Deptford and there to my Valentine.[2] Round about and next door on every side is the plague, and so away to Mr. Evelyn's to discourse of our confounded business of prisoners, and sick and wounded

---

[1] Gabriel Naudé's " Instructions concerning the erecting of a Library; " translated by Evelyn in 1661. See his " Diary," Nov. 16, 1661.

[2] Mrs. Bagwell. (M. B.)

seamen, wherein he and we are so much put out of order. And here he showed me his gardens, which are for variety of evergreens, and hedge of holly, the finest things I ever saw in my life. Thence in his coach to Greenwich, and there to my office, all the way having fine discourse of trees and the nature of vegetables. This night renewed my promises of observing my vowes as I used to do; for I find that, since I left them off, my mind is run a wool-gathering and my business neglected.

6th. Up, and having sent for Mr. Gauden he and I largely discoursed the business of his Victualling, wherein I find him ready to do anything the King would have him do. So he and I took his coach and to Lambeth and to the Duke of Albemarle about it. In our way discoursing of the business and contracting a great friendship with him, and I find he is a man most worthy to be made a friend, being very honest and gratefull, and in the freedom of our discourse he did tell me his opinion and knowledge of Sir W. Pen to be, what I know him to be, as false a man as ever was born, for so, it seems, he has been to him. He did also tell me, discoursing as how things are governed as to the King's treasure, that, having occasion for money in the country, he did offer Alderman Maynell to pay him down money here, to be paid by the Receiver in some county in the country, upon whom Maynell had assignments, in whose hands the money also lay ready. But Maynell refused it, saying that he could have his money when he would, and had rather it should lie where it do than receive it here in towne this sickly time, where he has no occasion for it. But now the evil is that he has left this money upon tallys which are become payable, but he finds that nobody looks after it, how long the money is unpaid, and whether it lies dead in the Receiver's hands or no, so the King he pays Maynell 10 per cent. while the money lies in his Receiver's hands to no purpose but the benefit of the Receiver. To my office, where very busy drawing up a letter by way of discourse to the Duke of Albemarle about my conception how the business of the Victualling should be ordered, wherein I have taken great pains, and I think have hitt the right if they will but follow it. At this very late and so home to our lodgings to bed.

7th. Did business, though not much, at the office; because of the horrible crowd and lamentable moan of the poor seamen that lie starving in the streets for lack of money. Which do trouble and perplex me to the heart; and more at noon when we were to go through them, for then a whole hundred of them followed us; some cursing, some swearing, and some praying to us. And that that made me more troubled was a letter came this afternoon from the Duke of Albemarle, signifying the Dutch to be in sight, with 80 sayle, yesterday morning, off of Solebay, coming right into the bay. God knows what they will and may do to us, we having no force abroad able to oppose them, but to be sacrificed to them. At night come two waggons from Rochester with more goods from Captain Cocke; and in housing them at Mr. Tooker's lodgings come two of the Custom-house to seize, and did seize them: but I showed them my *Transire.* However, after some hot and angry words, we locked them up, and sealed up the key, and did give it to the constable to keep till Monday, and so parted. But, Lord! to think how the poor constable came to me in the dark going home; "Sir," says he, "I have the key, and if you would have me do any service for you, send for me betimes to-morrow morning, and I will do what you would have me." Whether the fellow do this out of kindness or knavery, I cannot tell; but it is pretty to observe. Talking with him in the high way, come close by the bearers with a dead corpse of the plague; but, Lord! to see what custom is, that I am come almost to think nothing of it. So to my lodging, and there, with Mr. Hater and Will, ending a business of the state of the last six months' charge of the Navy, which we bring to 1,000,000*l.* and above, and I think we do not enlarge much in it if anything. So to bed.

8th (Lord's day). Up and, after being trimmed, to the office, whither I upon a letter from the Duke of Albemarle to me, to order as many ships forth out of the river as I can presently, to joyne to meet the Dutch; having ordered all the Captains of the ships in the river to come to me, I did some business with them, and so to Captain Cocke's to dinner, he being in the country. But here his brother Solomon was, and, for guests, myself, Sir G. Smith, and a very fine lady, one Mrs. Penington, and two more gentlemen. But, both before and after dinner, most witty discourse with this lady, who is a very fine witty lady, one of the best I ever heard speake, and indifferent handsome. There after dinner an houre or two, and so to the office, where ended my business with the Captains; and I think of twenty-two ships we shall make shift to get out seven. (God helpe us! men being sick, or provisions lacking.) This day I hear the Pope is dead;[1] and one said, that the newes is, that the King of France is stabbed, but that the former is very true, which will do great things sure, as to the troubling of that part of the world, the King of Spayne being so lately dead. And one thing more, Sir Martin Noell's lady is dead with griefe for the death of her husband and nothing else, as they say, in the world; but it seems nobody can make anything of his estate, whether he be dead worth anything or no, he having dealt in so many things, publique and private, as nobody can understand whereabouts his estate is, which is the fate of these great dealers at everything.

9th. Called upon by Sir John Shaw, to whom I did give a civil answer about our prize goods, that all his dues as one of the Farmers of the Customes are paid, and showed him our *Transire;* with which he was satisfied, and parted, ordering his servants to see the weight of them. I to the office, and there found an order for my coming presently to the Duke of Albe-

---

[1] Not true. (M. B.)

marle, and what should it be, but to tell me, that, if my Lord Sandwich do not come to towne, he do resolve to go with the fleete to sea himself, the Dutch, as he thinks, being in the Downes, and so desired me to get a pleasure boat for to take him in to-morrow morning, and do many other things, and with a great liking of me, and my management especially, as that coxcombe my Lord Craven do tell me, and I perceive it, and I am sure take pains enough to deserve it. The newes of the killing of the King of France is wholly untrue, and they say that of the Pope too.

10th. Up, and receive a stop from the Duke of Albemarle of setting out any more ships, or providing a pleasure boat for himself, which I am glad of, and do see, what I thought yesterday, that this resolution of his was a sudden one and silly. By and by comes Captain Cocke's Jacob to tell me that he is come from Chatham this morning, and that there are four waggons of goods at hand coming to towne, which troubles me. I directed him to bring them to his master's house. But before I could send him away to bring them thither, newes is brought me that they are seized on in the towne by one Captain Fisher and they will carry them to another place. So I to them and found our four waggons in the streete stopped by the church by this Fisher and company and 100 or 200 people in the streetes gazing. I did give them good words, and made modest desires of carrying the goods to Captain Cocke's but they would have them to a house of their hiring, where in a barne the goods were laid. I had transires to show for all, and the tale was right, and there I spent all the morning seeing this done. At which Fisher was vexed that I would not let it be done by any body else for the merchant, and that I must needs be concerned therein, which I did not think fit to owne. So that being done, I left the goods to be watched by men on their part and ours, and so by coach to Lambeth, and I took occasion first to go to the Duke of Albemarle to acquaint him with something of what had been done this morning in behalf of a friend absent, which did give me a good entrance and prevented their possessing the Duke with anything evil of me by their report, and by and by in comes Captain Cocke and tells his whole story. So an order was made for the putting him in possession upon giving security to be accountable for the goods, which for the present did satisfy us, and so away, giving Locke that drew the order a piece. Lord! to see how unhappily a man may fall into a necessity of bribing people to do him right in a thing, wherein he has done nothing but fair, and bought dear. This night comes Sir Christopher Mings to towne and comes to see me. He is newly come from Court,[1] and carries direction for the making a show of getting out the fleete again to go fight the Dutch, but that it will end in a fleete of 20 good sayling frigates to go to the Northward or Southward, and that will be all. He being gone, anon comes

---

[1] The Court was then at Oxford. (M. B.)

Cocke and tells me he finds him sullen and speaking very high what disrespect he had received of my [Lord Sandwich], saying that he had walked 3 or 4 hours together at that Earle's cabbin door for audience and could not be received, which, if true, I am sorry for. He tells me that Sir G. Ascue says, that he did from the beginning declare against these goods, and would not receive his dividend; and that he and Sir W. Pen are at odds about it, and that he fears Mings hath been doing ill offices to my Lord. I did to-night give my Lord an account of all this, and so home and to bed.

11th. In my chamber all the morning; comes up my landlàdy, Mrs. Clerke, to make an agreement for the time to come; and I, for the having room enough, and to keepe out strangers, and to have a place to retreat to for my wife, if the sicknesse should come to Woolwich, am contented to pay dear; so for three rooms and a dining-room, and for linen and bread and butter, at nights and mornings, I am to give her 5*l.* 10*s.* per month. To Erith, and there we met Mr. Seymour, one of the Commissioners for Prizes, and a Parliament-man, and he was mighty high, and had now seized our goods on their behalf; and he mighty imperiously would have all forfeited. But I could not but think it odd that a Parliament-man, in a serious discourse before such persons as we and my Lord Brouncker, and Sir John Minnes, should quote Hudibras, as being the book I doubt he hath read most. Cocke would have had me bound with him

for his appearing, but I did stagger at it. So against
tide and in the darke and very cold weather to Woolwich, where we had appointed to keepe the night
merrily; and so, by Captain Cocke's coach, had
brought a very pretty child, a daughter of one Mrs.
Tooker's, next door to my lodging, and so she, and
a daughter and kinsman of Mrs. Pett's made up a fine
company at my lodgings at Woolwich, where my
wife and Mercer, and Mrs. Barbara [1] danced, and
mighty merry we were, but especially at Mercer's
dancing a jigg, which she does the best I ever did
see, having the most natural way of it, and keeps time
the most perfectly I ever did see. This night is kept
in lieu of yesterday, for my wedding day of ten years; [2]
for which God be praised! being now in an extreme
good condition of health and estate and honour, and
a way of getting more money, though at this houre
under some discomposure, rather than damage, about
some prize goods that I have bought off the fleete,
in partnership with Captain Cocke; and for the discourse about the world concerning my Lord Sandwich,
that he hath done a thing so bad; and indeed it must
needs have been a very rash act; and the rather because of a Parliament now newly met to give money,
and will have some account of what hath already been
spent, besides the precedent for a General to take

---

[1] Daughter of his Woolwich landlord.

[2] The date of the registry of Pepys's marriage, given in the " Life," vol.
I., does not accord with this statement, or with that in the " Diary," Oct. 10,
1664.

what prizes he pleases, and the giving a pretence to take away much more than he intended, and all will lie upon him; and not giving to all the Commanders, as well as the Flaggs, he displeases all them, and offends even some of the Flaggs, thinking others to be better served than themselves; and lastly, puts himself out of a power of begging anything again a great while of the King. Having danced with my people as long as I saw fit to sit up, I to bed and left them to do what they would. I forgot that we had W. Hewer there, and Tom, and Golding, my barber at Greenwich for our fiddler, to whom I did give 10s.

12th. Called up before day, and so I dressed myself and down, it being horrid cold, by water to my Lord Brouncker's ship, who advised me to do so, and it was civilly to show me what the King had commanded about the prize-goods, to examine most severely all that had been done in the taking out any with or without order, without respect to my Lord Sandwich at all, and I do find that extreme ill use was made of my Lord Sandwich's order. For they did toss and tumble and spoil and breake things in the hold to a great losse and shame to come at the fine goods, and they did say in doing it that my Lord Sandwich's back was broad enough to bear it. Having learned as much as I could, which was, that the King and Duke were very severe in this point, whatever order they before had given my Lord in approbation of what he had done, and that all will come out and the King see, by the entries at the Custome

House, what all do amount to that had been taken, and so I took leave. So to Cocke, and he tells me that he hath cajolled with Seymour, who will be our friend ; but that, above all, Seymour tells him, that my Lord Duke did shew him to-day an order from Court, for having all respect paid to the Earl of Sandwich, and what goods had been delivered by his order, which do overjoy us. Good newes this week that there are about 600 less dead of the plague than the last.

13th. This morning comes Sir Jer. Smith[1] to see me in his way to Court, and a good man he is, and one that I must keep fair with, and will, it being I perceive my interest to have kindnesse with the Commanders. I by water to the Duke of Albemarle, where I find him with Lord Craven and Lieutenant of the Tower about him ; among other things, talking ot ships to get of the King to fetch coles for the poore of the city, which is a good worke. But, Lord ! to hear the silly talke between these three great people ! Yet I have no reason to find fault, the Duke and Lord Craven being my very great friends. My head is full of settling the victualling business, that I may make some profit out of it, which I hope justly to do to the King's advantage. To-night came Sir J. Bankes to me upon my letter to discourse it with me, and he did give me the advice I have taken almost as fully as if I had been directed by him what to write. The busi-

---

[1] A distinguished Naval Officer, made a Commissioner of the Navy, vice Sir W. Pen, 1669.

ness also of my Tangier accounts to be sent to Court is upon my hands in great haste ; besides, all my owne proper accounts are in great disorder, having been neglected now above a month, which grieves me, but it could not be settled sooner. These together and the feare of the sicknesse and providing for my family do fill my head very full, besides the infinite business of the office, and nobody here to look after it but myself. So late to bed.

14th. Up, and to the office, where mighty busy, especially with Mr. Gauden, with whom I shall, I think, have much to do, and by and by comes the Lieutenant of the Tower to discourse about the Cole ships. The towne, I hear, is full of talke that there are great differences in the fleete among the great Commanders, and that Mings at Oxford did impeach my Lord of something, I think about these goods, but this is but talke. But my heart and head to-night is full of the Victualling business, being overjoyed and proud at my success in my proposal about it, it being read before the King, Duke, and the Caball with complete applause and satisfaction. This Sir G. Carteret and Sir W. Coventry both writ me.

15th (Lord's day). Up, and while I staid for the barber, tried to compose a duo of counter point, and I think it will do very well, it being by Mr. Berkenshaw's rule. By and by by appointment comes Mr. Povy's coach, and, more than I expected, him himself, to fetch me to Brainford : so he and I immediately set out, having drunk a draft of mulled sacke ; and so rode most nobly, in his most pretty and best contrived chariott in the world, with many new conveniences, his never having till now, within a day or two, been yet finished; our discourse upon Tangier business, want of money, and then of publique miscarriages, nobody minding the publique, but every body himself and his lusts. Anon we come to his house, and there I eat a bit, and so with fresh horses, his noble fine horses, the best confessedly in England, the King having none such, he sent me to Sir Robert Viner's,[1] whom I met coming just from church, and he and I into his garden to discourse of money, but none is to be had, he confessing himself in great straits, and I believe it. Having this answer, and that I could not get better, we fell to publique talke, and to think how the fleete and seamen will be paid, which he protests he do not think it possible to compass, as the world is now: no money got by trade, nor the persons that have it by them in the City to be come at. The Parliament, it seems, have voted the King 1,250,000*l.* at 50,000*l.* per month, tax for the war; and voted to assist the King against the Dutch, and all that shall adhere to them; and thanks to be given him for his care of the Duke of York, which last is a very popular vote on the Duke's behalf. He tells me how the taxes of the last assessment, which should have been in good part gathered, are not yet laid, and that even in part of the City of London; and the

---

[1] At Swakeley House. See 7th Sept., 1665. (M. B.)

Chimny-money comes almost to nothing, nor any thing else looked after. Having done this I parted, my mind not eased by any money, but only that I have done my part to the King's service. And so in a very pleasant evening back to Mr. Povy's, and there supped, and after supper to talke and to sing, his man Dutton's wife singing very pleasantly (a mighty fat woman) and I wrote out one song from her and pricked the tune, both very pretty. But I did never heare one sing with so much pleasure to herself as this lady do, relishing it to her very heart, which was mighty pleasant.

16th. Up about seven o'clock; and, after drinking, and I observing Mr. Povy's being mightily mortified in his eating and drinking, and coaches and horses, he desiring to sell his best, and every thing else, his furniture of his house, he walked with me to Syon,[1] and there I took water, in our way he discoursing of the wantonnesse of the Court, and how it minds nothing else. Here I took boat and down to the Tower and to Lumbard Streete, but can get no money. So upon the Exchange which is very empty, God knows! and but mean people there. The newes for certain that the Dutch are come with their fleete before Margett, and some men were endeavouring to come on shore when the post came away, perhaps to steal some sheep.

---

[1] Sion House, granted by Edward VI. to his uncle, the Duke of Somerset. After his execution, 1552, it was forfeited, and given to the Duke of Northumberland. The Duke being beheaded in 1553, it reverted to the Crown, and was granted in 1604 to Henry Percy, Earl of Northumberland. (M. B.)

But Lord ! how Colvill talks of the business of publique revenue like a madman, and yet I doubt all true ;
that nobody minds it, but that the King and Kingdom
must speedily be undone.   Here I endeavoured to satisfy all I could, people about Bills of Exchange from
Tangier, but it is only with good words, for money I
have not, nor can get.   God knows what will become
of all the King's matters in a little time, for he runs
in debt every day, and nothing to pay them looked
after.   Thence I walked to the Tower; but, Lord !
how empty the streets are and melancholy, so many
poor sick people in the streets full of sores ; and so
many sad stories overheard as I walk, every body talking of this dead, and that man sick, and so many in
this place, and so many in that.   And they tell me
that, in Westminster, there is never a physician and
but one apothecary left, all being dead ; but that there
are great hopes of a great decrease this week : God
send it !   At the Tower found my Lord Duke [1] and
Duchesse at dinner ; so I sat down.   And much good
cheer, the Lieutenant and his lady, and several officers
with the Duke.   But, Lord ! to hear the silly talk was
there, would make one mad ; the Duke having none
almost but fools about him.   Much of their talke about
the Dutch coming on shore and spoke all in reproach
of them in whose hands the fleete is ; but, Lord helpe
him there is something will hinder him and all the
world in going to sea, which is want of victuals ; for

----

[1] Of Albemarle.   (M. B.)

we have not wherewith to answer our service; and how much better it would have been if the Duke's advice had been taken for the fleete to have gone presently out; but, God helpe the King! while no better counsels are given, and what is given no better taken. After dinner down to Greenwich having received letters from my Lord Sandwich to-day, speaking very high about the prize goods, that he would have us to fear nobody, but be very confident in what we have done, and not to confess any fault or doubt of what he hath done; for the King hath allowed it, and do now confirm it, and sent orders, as he says, for nothing to be disturbed that his Lordshipp hath ordered therein as to the division of the goods to the fleete; which do comfort us. To the Still Yarde,[1] which place, however, is now shut up of the plague; but I was there, and we now make no bones of it. Much talke there is of the Chancellor's speech and the King's at the Parliament's meeting, which are very well liked; and that we shall certainly, by their speeches, fall out with France at this time, together with the Dutch, which will find us work.

18th. Making of my accounts up of Tangier, which I did with great difficulty. However I was at it late and did it pretty perfectly, and so, after eating something, to bed, my mind eased of a great deal of figures and castings.

19th. Come to an agreement yesterday with my

---

[1] The Still Yard was formerly the resort of the Hans Town merchants. It was destroyed in the Great Fire.

landlady for 6*l.* per month, for so many rooms for myself, them,[1] and my wife and mayde, when she shall come, and to pay besides for my dyett. To the Duke of Albemarle's this evening; and among other things, spoke to him for my wife's brother, Balty, to be of his guard, which he kindly answered that he should. My business of the Victualling goes on as I would have it; and now my head is full how to make some profit of it to myself or people. To that end, when I came home, I wrote a letter to Mr. Coventry, offering myself to be the Surveyor Generall, and am apt to think he will assist me in it, but I do not set my heart much on it, though it would be a good helpe.

20th. Up, and had my last night's letters brought back to me, which troubles me, because of my accounts, lest they should be asked for before they come, which I abhor, being more ready to give than they can be to demand them: so I sent away an expresse to Oxford with them, and another to Portsmouth, with a copy of my letter to Mr. Coventry about my victualling business, for fear he should be gone from Oxford, as he intended, thither. So busy all the morning and at noon to Cocke, and dined there. He and I alone, vexed that we are not rid of all our trouble about our goods, but it is almost over.

22nd (Lord's day). To Church, in my way was meeting some letters, which make me resolve to go

---

after church to my Lord Duke of Albemarle's, so, after sermon, I took Cocke's chariott, and to Lambeth ; but, in going and getting over the water, and through White Hall, I spent so much time, the Duke had almost dined. However, fresh meat was brought for me to his table, and there I dined, and full of discourse and very kind. Here they are again talking of the prizes, and my Lord Duke did speake very broad that my Lord Sandwich and Pen should do what they would, and answer for themselves. For his part, he would lay all before the King. Here he tells me the Dutch Embassador at Oxford is clapped up, but since I hear it is not true.

23rd. Down by water, calling to see my wife, with whom very merry for ten minutes and so to Erith, where my Lord Brouncker and I kept the office. Among other things about the slopsellers, who have trusted us so long, they are not able, nor can be expected to trust us further, and I fear this winter the fleete will be undone by that particular. Thence on board the East India ship, where my Lord Brouncker had provided a great dinner, and thither comes by and by Sir J. Minnes and before him Sir W. Warren and anon a Perspective glasse maker, of whom we, every one, bought a pocket glasse. But I am troubled with the much talke and conceitedness of Mrs. Williams and her impudence, in case she be not married to my Lord. They are getting themselves ready to deliver the goods all out to the East India Company, who are to have the goods in their possession and to advance two thirds of the moderate sum thereof and sell them as well as they can and the King to give them 6 per cent. for the use of the money they shall so advance. Thence Captain Taylor with me in my boat and to the office, and there he and I reckoned; and I perceive I shall get 100*l.* profit for my services of late to him, which is a very good thing. Thence to my lodging where I found my Lord Rutherford of which I was glad. My Lord and I to business and he would have me forbear paying Alderman Backewell the money ordered him. Discourse being done, he to bed in my chamber and I to another in the house.

24th. To my Lord and sent him going to Oxford, and I to my office whither comes Sir W. Batten now newly from Oxford. I can gather nothing from him about my Lord Sandwich about the business of the prizes, he being close, but he shewed me a bill which has been read in the House making all breaking of bulke for the time to come felony, but it is a foolish Act, and will do no great matter, only is calculated to my Lord Sandwich's case. He shewed me also a good letter printed from the Bishop of Munster to the States of Holland shewing the state of their case. Here we did some business and so broke up and I to Cocke, where Mr. Evelyn was, to dinner, and there merry, yet vexed again at publique matters, and to see how little heed is had to the prisoners and sicke and wounded. Thence to my office, and no sooner there but to my great surprise am told that my Lord Sandwich is come to towne; so I presently to Boreman's, where he is and there found him: he mighty kind to me, but no opportunity of discourse private yet, which he tells me he must have with me; only his business is sudden to go to the fleete, to get out a few ships to drive away the Dutch. To the office till about 10 at night and to him again to Captain Cocke's, where he supped, and lies, and never saw him more merry, and here is Charles Harbord, who the King hath lately knighted. My Lord, to my great content, did tell me before them, that never anything was read to the King and Council, all the chief Ministers of State being there, as my letter about the Victualling was, and no more said upon it than a most thorough consent to every word was said, and directed, that it be pursued and practised.

25th. Up, and to my Lord Sandwich's, where several Commanders, of whom I took the state of all their ships, and of all could find not above four capable of going out. The truth is, the want of victuals being the whole overthrow of this yeare both at sea, and now at the Nore here and Portsmouth, where all the fleete lies. By and by comes down my Lord, and then he and I an houre together alone upon private discourse. He tells me that Mr. Coventry and he are not reconciled, but declared enemies: the only occasion of it being, he tells me, his ill usage from him about the first fight, wherein he had no right done him, which, methinks, is a poor occasion, for, in my conscience, that was no design of Coventry's. He tells me, as very private, that there are great factions at the Court between the King's party and the Duke of York's, and that the King, which is a strange difficulty, do favour my Lord in opposition to the Duke's party: that my Lord Chancellor, being, to be sure, the patron of the Duke's, it is a mystery whence it should be that Mr. Coventry is looked upon by him [Clarendon] as an enemy to him; that if he had a mind himself to be out of this employment, as Mr. Coventry, he believes, wishes, and himself and I do incline to wish it also, in many respects, yet he believes he shall not be able, because of the King, who will keepe him in on purpose, in opposition to the other party; that Prince Rupert and he are all possible friends in the world; that Coventry hath aggravated this business of the prizes, though never so great plundering in the world as while the Duke and he were at sea; and in Sir John Lawson's time he could take and pillage, and then sink a whole ship in the Streights, and Coventry say nothing to it; that my Lord Arlington is his fast friend; that the Chancellor is cold to him, and though I told him that I and the world do take my Lord Chancellor, in his speech the other day, to have said as much as could be wished, yet he thinks he did not. That my Lord Chancellor do from hence begin to be cold to him, because of his seeing him and Arlington so great: that nothing at Court is minded but faction and pleasure, and nothing intended of general good to the kingdom by anybody heartily; so that he believes with me, that in a little time confusion will certainly come over all the nation. He told me how a design was carried on a while ago, for the Duke of York to raise an army in the North, and to be the Generall of it, and all this without the knowledge or advice of the Duke of Albemarle, which when he came to know, he was so vexed, they were fain to let it fall to content him: that his matching with the family of Sir G. Carteret do make the difference greater between Coventry and him, they being enemies; that the Chancellor did, as every body else, speak well of me the other day, but yet was, at the Committee for Tangier, angry that I should offer to suffer a bill of exchange to be protested. So my Lord did bid me take heed, for that I might easily suppose I could not want enemies, no more than others. In all he speaks with the greatest trust and love and confidence in what I say or do, that a man can do. After this discourse ended we sat down to dinner and mighty merry, among other things, at the Bill brought into the House to make it felony to break bulke, which, as my Lord says well, will make that no prizes shall be taken, or, if taken, shall be sunke after plundering; and at the Act for the method of gathering this last 1,250,000*l.* now voted and how paid wherein are several strange imperfections.

26th. Sir Christopher Mings and I together by water to the Tower; and I find him a very witty well-spoken fellow, and mighty free to tell his parentage, being a shoemaker's son, to whom he is now going, and I to the 'Change, where I hear how the French have taken two and sunk one of our merchant-men in the Straights, and carried the ships to Toulon ; so that there is no expectation but we must fall out with them. The 'Change pretty full, and the town begins to be lively again, though the streets very empty, and most shops shut. So back again I and took boat and called for Sir Christopher Mings at St. Katharine's, who was followed with some ordinary friends, of which, he says, he is proud, and so down to Greenwich and did give him a good dinner and so parted, he being pretty close to me as to any business of the fleete, knowing me to be a servant of my Lord Sandwich's. He gone I to the office till night, and then they come and tell me my wife is come to towne, so I to her vexed at her coming, but it was upon innocent business, so I was pleased and made her stay, Captain Ferrers and his lady being there, and so I left them to dance, and I to the office till past nine at night, and so to them and there saw them dance very prettily, the Captain and his wife, my wife and Mrs. Barbara, and Mercer and then little Mistress Tooker and her mother. Anon to supper, and then to dance again till past twelve at night, and then we broke up and every one to bed.

27th. To Captain Cocke's, there to do some business, and then away with Cocke in his coach through Kent Streete, a miserable, wretched, poor place, people sitting sicke and muffled up with plasters at every 4 or 5 doors. So to the 'Change, and thence by water to the Duke of Albemarle's, and there much company,

but I staid and dined, and he makes mighty much of
me; and he tells us the Dutch are gone, and have
lost above 160 cables and anchors, through the last
foule weather.   Here he proposed to me from Mr.
Coventry, as I had desired of Mr. Coventry, that I
should be Surveyor-Generall of the Victualling business, which I accepted.   But, indeed, the terms in
which Mr. Coventry proposes it for me are the most
obliging that ever I could expect from any man, and
more; it saying me to be the fittest man in England,
and that he is sure, if I will undertake, I will perform
it; and that it will be also a very desirable thing that
I might have this encouragement, my encouragement
in the Navy alone being in no wise proportionable to
my pains or deserts.   This, added to the letter I had
three days since from Mr. Southerne,[1] signifying that
the Duke of York had in his master's absence opened
my letter, and commanded him to tell me that he did
approve of my being the Surveyor-General, do make
me joyful beyond myself that I cannot express it, to
see that as I do take pains, so God blesses me, and
hath sent me masters that do observe that I take
pains.   This having done here, I back by water and
to London and late with Captain Taylor, and he and I
settled all accounts between us, and I do find that
I do get above 120*l.* of him for my services within
these six months.   At it till almost one in the morning, and after supper he away and I to bed, mightily

---

[1] Secretary to Sir W. Coventry.

satisfied in all this, and in a resolution I have taken to
propose the port of London for the victualling business for Thos. Willson, by which it will be better done
and I at more ease, in case he should grumble.

28th. Up, and sent for Thos. Willson, and broke
the victualling business to him and he is mightily
contented, and so am I that I have bestowed it on
him, and so I to Mr. Boreman's, where Sir W. Batten
is, to tell him what I had proposed to Thos. Willson,
and the newes also I have this morning from Sir W.
Clerke, which is, that notwithstanding all the care the
Duke of Albemarle has taken about putting the East
India prize goods into the East India Company's
hands, and my Lord Brouncker and Sir J. Minnes
having laden out a great part of the goods, an order
is come from Court to stop all, and to have the goods
delivered to the Sub-Commissioners of prizes. At
which I am glad, because it do vex this simple weake
man, and we shall have a little reparation for the disgrace my Lord Sandwich has had in it. He tells me
also that the Parliament hath given the Duke of York
120,000*l.*,[1] to be paid him after 1,250,000*l.* is gathered
upon the tax which they have now given the King.
He tells me that the Dutch have lately launched sixteen new ships; all which is great news. Thence by
horseback with Mr. Deane to Erith, and so aboard
my Lord Brouncker and dined, and very merry with
him and good discourse between them about ship

---

[1] This sum was granted by the Commons to Charles, with a request that
he would bestow it on his brother.

building, and, after dinner and a little pleasant discourse, we away and by horse back again to Greenwich, and there I to the office very late, offering my persons for all the victualling posts much to my satisfaction. Also much other business I did to my mind, and so weary home to my lodging, and there after eating and drinking a little I to bed. The King and Court, they say, have now finally resolved to spend nothing upon clothes, but what is of the growth of England; which, if observed, will be very pleasing to the people, and very good for them.

29th (Lord's day). Up, and being ready set out with Captain Cocke in his coach toward Erith, where we dined and were very merry. After dinner we fell to discourse about the Dutch, Cocke undertaking to prove that they were able to wage warr with us three years together, which, though it may be true, yet, not being satisfied with his arguments, my Lord and I did oppose the strength of his arguments, which brought us to a great heate, he being a conceited man, but of no Logique in his head at all, which made my Lord and I mirth. Anon we parted, and back again, we hardly having a word all the way, he being so vexed at our not yielding to his persuasion. I was set down at Woolwich towne end, and walked through the towne in the darke. But in the streete did overtake and almost run upon two women crying and carrying a man's coffin between them. I suppose the husband of one of them, which, methinks, is a sad thing. Being come to Sheldon's, I found my people in the darke in the dining room, merry and laughing, and, I thought, sporting one with another, which, God helpe me ! raised my jealousy presently. I came in the darke, and one of them touching me (which afterwards I found was Su) made them shriek, and so went out up stairs, leaving them light a candle and to run out. I went out and was very vexed till I found my wife was gone with Mr. Hill and Mercer this day to see me at Greenwich, and these people were at supper, and the candle on a sudden falling out of the candlesticke (which I saw as I came through the yarde) and Mrs. Barbara being there I was well at ease again, and so bethought myself what to do, whether to go to Greenwich or stay there ; at last go I would, and so with a lanthorne, and 3 or 4 people with me, among others Mr. Browne, who was there, would go, I walked and discoursed with him about paynting and the several sorts of it. I came in good time to Greenwich, where I found Mr. Hill with my wife, and very glad I was to see him. To supper and discourse of musique and so to bed, I lying with him talking till midnight about Berkenshaw's musique rules, which I did to his great satisfaction inform him in, and so to sleep.

30th. Up, and to my office about business. At noon to dinner, and after some discourse of musique, Hill and I to the office awhile, and he to get Mr. Coleman, if he can, against night. By and by I back again home, and there find him returned with Mr. Coleman (his wife being ill) and Mr. Laneare, with whom with their Lute we had excellent company and good singing till midnight, and a good supper I did give them, but Coleman's voice is quite spoiled, and when he begins to be drunk he is excellent company, but afterwards troublesome and impertinent. Laneare sings in a melancholy method very well, and a sober man he seems to be. They being gone, we to bed, Captain Ferrers coming this day from my Lord is forced to lodge here, and I put him to Mr. Hill.

31st. To the office, where Sir W. Batten met me, and did tell me that Captain Cocke's black was dead of the plague, which I had heard of before, but took no notice. By and by Captain Cocke came to the office, and Sir W. Batten and I did send to him that he would either forbear the office, or forbear going to his owne office. However, meeting yesterday the Searchers with their rods in their hands coming from Captain Cocke's house, I did overhear them say that the fellow did not die of the plague. About nine at night I come home, and there find Mrs. Pierce come and little Frank Tooker, and Mr. Hill, and other people, a great many dancing, and anon comes Mrs. Coleman [1] and her husband and Laneare. [2] The dan-

---

[1] Probably the person mentioned in the following extract from Malone's "Account of the English Stage:" "In 1659 or 60, in imitation of foreign theatres, women were first introduced on the scene. In 1656, indeed, Mrs. Coleman, wife to Mr. Edward Coleman, represented Ianthe in the first part of the Siege of Rhodes; but the little she had to say was spoken in recitative." "Sir William Davenant's patent contained a clause permitting all women's parts to be performed by females."

[2] Nicholas Lanier, composer of the Symphonies to several of the Masques written by Ben Jonson, and performed at Court, had died, æt. 78, Nov. 4th,

cing ended and to sing, which Mrs. Coleman do, and very finely, though her voice is decayed as to strength but mighty sweet though soft, and a pleasant jolly woman, and in mighty good humour was to-night. Among other things Laneare did, at the request of Mr. Hill, bring two or three the finest prints for my wife to see that ever I did see in all my life. But for singing, among other things, we got Mrs. Coleman to sing part of the Opera, though she would not owne that ever she did get any of it without book in order to the stage; but, above all, her counterfeiting of Captain Cooke's part, in his reproaching his man with cowardice, "Base slave," &c., she do it most excellently. At it till past midnight, and then broke up. Thus we end the month merrily; and the more for that, after some fears that the plague would have increased again this week, I hear for certain that there is above 400 less, the whole number being 1,388, and of them of the plague, 1,031. Want of money in the Navy puts every thing out of order. Men grow mutinous; and nobody here to mind the business of the Navy but myself. I in great hopes of my place of Surveyor-Generall of the Victualling, which will bring me 300*l*. per annum.

1646, and was buried at St Martin's-in-the-Fields (*Somerset House Gazette,* vol. i p. 57). The Letters Patent under which the Society of Musicians was incorporated at the Restoration, mention a Lanier, possibly a son of Nicholas, as first Marshal, and four others of his name as Wardens or Assistants, of the Company. There is an engraved portrait of him in the British Museum (Addit. MS., 15,858, fol. 55), and a letter to his niece, Mrs. Richards, " at her house in the Old Aumery, Westminster."

November 1st. Lay very long in bed discoursing with Mr. Hill of most things of a man's life, and how little merit do prevail in the world, but only favour; and that, for myself, chance without merit brought me in; and that diligence only keeps me so, and will, living as I do among so many lazy people that the diligent man becomes necessary, that they cannot do anything without him, and so told him of my late business of the victualling, and what cares I am in to keepe myself having to do with people of so different factions at Court, and yet must be fair with them all, which was very pleasant discourse for me to tell, as well as he seemed to take it for him to hear. At last up, and it being a very foule day for raine and a hideous wind, yet having promised I would go by water to Erith, and bearing sayle was in danger of oversetting, but made them take down their sayle, and so cold and wet got thither, as they had ended their dinner. However, I dined well, and after dinner all on shore, my Lord Brouncker with us to Mrs. Williams's lodgings, and Sir W. Batten, Sir Edmund Pooly,[1] and others; and there, it being my Lord's birth-day, had every one a green riband tied in our hats very foolishly; and methinks mighty disgracefully for my Lord to have his folly so open to all the world with this woman. But by and by Sir W. Batten and I took coach, and so going home I saw Captain Cocke 'lighting out of his coach, and so he would

---

[1] M. P. for Bury St. Edmunds, and in the list of proposed Knights of the Royal Oak for Suffolk.

come along with me to my lodging, and there sat and supped and talked with us, but we were angry a little while about our message to him the other day about bidding him keepe from the office or his owne office, because of his black dying. I owned it and the reason of it, and would have been glad if he had been out of the house, but I could not bid him go, and so supped, and after much other talke of the sad condition and state of the King's matters we broke up, and my friend and I to bed. This night coming with Sir W. Batten into Greenwich we called upon Coll. Cleggatt, who tells us for certaine that the King of Denmark has declared to stand for the King of England, but since I hear it is wholly false.

2nd. Up, left my wife and to the office, and there to my great content Sir W. Warren came to me to settle the business of the Tangier boats wherein I shall get above 100*l*., besides 100*l*., which he gives me in the paying for them out of his owne purse. He gone, I home to my lodgings and there comes Captain Wager new returned from the Streights, who puts me in great fear for our last ships that went to Tangier with provisions, that they will be taken. A brave, stout fellow this Captain is, and I think very honest. To the office again after dinner and there late writing letters, and then about 8 at night set out from my office and fitting myself at my lodging intended to have gone this night in a Ketch down to the Fleete, but calling in my way at Sir J. Minnes's, who is come up from Erith about something about the prizes, they persuaded me not to go till the morning, it being a horrible darke and a windy night. So I back to my lodging and to bed.

3rd. Was called up about four o'clock and in the darke by lanthorne took boat and to the Ketch and set sayle, sleeping a little in the Cabbin till day and then up and fell to reading of Mr. Evelyn's book about Paynting, which is a very pretty book. Carrying good victuals and Tom with me I to breakfast about 9 o'clock, and then to read again and came to the Fleete about twelve, where I found my Lord (the Prince being gone in) on board the Royal James, Sir Thomas Allen commander, and with my Lord an houre alone discoursing what was my chief and only errand about what was adviseable for his Lordship to do in this state of things, himself being the Duke of York and Mr. Coventry's envy, and a great many more and likely never to do anything honourably but he shall be envied and the honour taken as much as can be from it. His absence lessens his interest at Court, and what is worst we never able to set out a fleete fit for him to command, or, if out, to keepe them out or fit them to do any great thing, or if that were so yet nobody at home minds him or his condition when he is abroad, and lastly the whole affairs of state looking as if they would all of a sudden break in pieces, and then what a sad thing it would be for him to be out of the way. My Lord did concur in every thing and thanked me infinitely for my visit and counsel, telling me that in every thing he concurs, but puts a query, what if the King will not think himself safe, if any man should go but him. How he should go off then? To that I had no answer ready, but the making the King see that he may be of as good use to him here while another goes forth. But for that I am not able to say much. We after this talked of some other little things and so to dinner, where my Lord infinitely kind to me, and after dinner I rose and left him with some Commanders at the table taking tobacco and I took the Bezan back with me, and with a brave gale and tide reached up that night to the Hope, taking great pleasure in learning the seamen's manner of singing when they sound the depths, and then to supper and to sleep, which I did most excellently all night, it being a horrible foule night for wind and raine.

4th. They sayled from midnight and came to Greenwich about 5 o'clock in the morning. I however lay till about 7 or 8, and so to my office, my head a little akeing, partly for want of natural rest, partly having so much business to do to-day and partly from the newes I hear that one of the little boys at my lodging is not well; and they suspect, by their sending for plaister and fume, that it may be the plague; so I sent Mr. Hater and W. Hewer to speake with the mother; but they returned to me, satisfied that there is no hurt nor danger, but the boy is well, and offers to be searched, however, I was resolved myself to abstain coming thither for a while. Sir W. Batten and myself at the office all the morning. At noon with him to dinner at Boreman's, where Mr. Seymour with us, who is a most conceited fellow and not over much in him. Here Sir W. Batten told us (what I had not heard before) that the last sitting day his cloake was taken from Mings going home to dinner, and that he was beaten by the seamen and swears he will come to Greenwich, but no more to the office till he can sit safe. After dinner I to the office and there late, and much troubled to have 100 seamen all the afternoon there, swearing below and cursing us, and breaking the glasse windows, and swear they will pull the house down on Tuesday next. I sent word of this to Court, but nothing will helpe it but money and a rope.

5th (Lord's day). Up, and after being trimmed, by water to the Cockpitt, where I heard the Duke of Albemarle's chaplin make a simple sermon : among other things, reproaching the imperfection of humane learning, he cried: "All our physicians cannot tell what an ague is, and all our arithmetique is not able to number the days of a man;" which, God knows, is not the fault of arithmetique, but that our understandings reach not the thing. To dinner, where a great deale of silly discourse, but the worst is I hear that the plague increases much at Lambeth, St. Martin's, and Westminster, and fear it will all over the city. By water to Deptford, and there made a visit to Mr. Evelyn, who, among other things, showed me most excellent painting in little ; in distemper, Indian incke, water colours : graveing ; and, above all, the whole secret of mezzo-tinto,[1] and the manner of it, which is very pretty, and good things done with it. He read to me very much also of his discourse, he hath been many years and now is about, about Gardenage; which will be a most noble and pleasant piece. He read me part of a play or two of his making, very good, but not as he conceits them, I think, to be. He showed me his Hortus Hyemalis; leaves laid up in a book of several plants kept dry, which preserve colour, however, and look very finely, better than any Herball. In fine, a most excellent person he is, and must be allowed a little for a little conceitedness; but he may well be so, being a man so much above others. He read me, though with too much gusto, some little poems of his own, that were not transcendant, yet one or two very pretty epigrams; among others, of a lady looking in at a grate, and being pecked at by an eagle that was there. Here comes in, in the middle of our discourse Captain Cocke, as drunk as a dogg, but could stand, and talke and laugh. He did so joy himself in a brave woman that he had been with all the afternoon, and who should it be but my Lady Robinson, but very troublesome he is with his noise and talke, and laughing, though very pleasant. With him in his coach to Mr. Glanville's where he sat with Mrs. Penington and myself a good while talking of

---

[1] Invented a short time before by Prince Rupert, from the accidental observation of a soldier's scraping his rusty gun. In 1660 Prince Rupert showed Evelyn "the new way of graving called mezzo-tinto."—*Evelyn's Diary*. (M. B.)

this fine woman again and then went away. Then the lady and I to very serious discourse and, among other things, of what a bonny lasse my Lady Robinson is, who is reported to be kind to the prisoners. After an houre's talke we to bed, the lady mightily troubled about a pretty little bitch she has, which is very sicke, and will eat nothing, and the worst was, I could hear her in her chamber bemoaning the bitch, and taking her into bed with her. This night I had a letter that Sir G. Carteret would be in towne to-morrow, which did much surprise me.

6th. Up, and to my office, where busy all the morning and then to dinner to Captain Cocke's with Mr. Evelyn, where very merry, only vexed after dinner to stay too long for our coach. At last, however, to Lambeth and thence the Cockpitt, where we found Sir G. Carteret come, and in with the Duke and the East India Company about settling the business of the prizes, and they have gone through with it. Then they broke up, and Sir G. Carteret came out, and thence through the garden to the water side and by water I with him in his boat down with Captain Cocke to his house at Greenwich, and while supper was getting ready Sir G. Carteret and I did walk an houre in the garden before the house, talking of my Lord Sandwich's business; what enemies he hath, and how they have endeavoured to bespatter him : and particularly about his leaving of 30 ships of the enemy, when Pen would have gone, and my Lord called him back again : which is most false. However, he says, it was purposed by some hot-heads in the House of Commons, at the same time when they voted a present to the Duke of York, to have voted 10,000*l.* to the Prince, and half-a-crowne to my Lord of Sandwich ; but nothing came of it. But, for all this, the King is most firme to my Lord, and so is my Lord Chancellor, and my Lord Arlington. The Prince, in appearance, kind ; the Duke of York silent, says no hurt ; but admits others to say it in his hearing. Sir W. Pen, the falsest rascal that ever was in the world ; and that this afternoon the Duke of Albemarle did tell him that Pen was a very cowardly rogue, and one that hath brought all these rogueish fanatick Captains into the fleete, and swears he should never go out with the fleete again. That Sir W. Coventry is most kind to Pen still ; and says nothing nor do any thing openly to the prejudice of my Lord. He agrees with me, that it is impossible for the King to set out a fleete again the next year ; and that he fears all will come to ruine, there being no money in prospect but these prizes, which will bring, it may be, 20,000*l.* but that will signify nothing in the world for it. That this late Act of Parliament for bringing the money into the Exchequer, and making of it payable out there, intended as a prejudice to him and will be his convenience hereafter and ruine the King's business, and so I fear it will and do wonder Sir W. Coventry would be led by Sir G. Downing to persuade the King and Duke to have it so, before they had thoroughly weighed all circumstances ; that for my Lord, the King has said to him lately that I was an excellent officer, and that my Lord Chancellor do, he thinks, love and esteem of me as well as he do of any man in England that he hath no more acquaintance with. So having done and received from me the sad newes that we are like to have no money here a great while, not even of the very prizes, I set up my rest [1] in giving up the King's service to be ruined and so in to supper, where pretty merry, and after supper late to Mr. Glanville's, and Sir G. Carteret to bed. I also to bed, it being very late.

7th. Up, and to Sir G. Carteret, and with him, he being very passionate to be gone, without staying a minute for breakfast, to the Duke of Albemarle's and with him by water: but, among other things, Lord ! to see how he wondered to see the river so empty of boats, nobody working at the Custome-house keys; and how fearful he is, and vexed that his man, holding a wine-glasse in his hand for him to drinke out of, did cover his hands, it being a cold, windy, rainy morning, under the waterman's coate, though he brought the waterman from six or seven miles up the river, too. Nay, he carried this glasse with him for his man to let him drink out of at the Duke of Albemarle's, where he intended to dine, though this he did to prevent sluttery; for the same reason he carried a napkin with him to Captain Cocke's, making him believe that he

---

[1] The phrase *set up my rest* is a metaphor from the once fashionable game of Primero, meaning, to stand upon the cards you have in your hand, in hopes they may prove better than those of your adversary. Hence, to make up your mind, to be determined. See Nares' " Glossary." (M. B.)

should eat with foule linnen.   Here he with the Duke
walked a good while in the Parke, and I with Fen.
Thence in and so staying till noon, I took leave of the
Duke and Sir G. Carteret, there being no good to be
done more for money, and so over the river and by
coach to Greenwich, where at Boreman's we dined,
it being late.   Thence my head being full of business
and mind out of order for thinking of the effects
which will arise from the want of money, I made an
end of my letters by eight o'clock, and so to my
lodging and there spent the evening till midnight
talking with Mrs. Penington, who is a very discreet,
understanding lady and very pretty discourse we had
and great variety, and she tells me with great sorrow
her bitch is dead this morning, died in her bed.   So
broke up and to bed.

8th. Up, and to the office, where busy among other
things to looke my warrants for the settling of the
Victualling business, the warrants being come to me
for the Surveyors of the ports and that for me also to
be Surveyor-Generall.   I did discourse largely with
Tom Willson about it and doubt not to make it a good
service to the King as well, as the King gives us very
good salarys.   It being a fast day, all people were at
church and the office quiett ; so I did much business,
and at noon adventured to my old lodging, and there
eat, but am not yet well satisfied, not seeing of Christopher, though they say he is abroad.   Thence after
dinner to the office again, and thence am sent for to
the King's Head by my Lord Rutherford, who, since

I can hope for no more convenience from him his business is troublesome to me, and therefore I did leave him as soon as I could and by water to Deptford, and, about eight o'clock at night, did take water, being glad I was out of the towne ; for the plague, it seems, rages there more than ever, and so to my lodgings, where my Lord had got a supper and the mistresse of the house and her daughters, and here staid Mrs. Pierce to speake with me about her husband's business, and I made her sup with us and then at night my Lord and I walked with her home, and so back again. My Lord and I ended all we had to say as to his business overnight, and so I took leave, and went again to Mr. Glanville's and so to bed, it being very late.

9th. Up, and did give the servants something at Mr. Glanville's and so took leave, meaning to lie to-night at my owne lodging. To my office, where busy with Mr. Gauden running over the Victualling business, and he is mightily pleased that this course is taking and seems sensible of my favour and promises kindnesse to me. At noon by water, to the King's Head at Deptford, where Captain Taylor invites Sir W. Batten, Sir John Robinson (who comes in with a great deale of company from hunting, and brought in a hare alive and a great many silly stories they tell of their sport, which pleases them mightily, and me not at all, such is the different sense of pleasure in mankind), and others upon the score of a survey of his new ship ; and strange to see how a good dinner and feasting reconciles everybody, Sir W. Batten and Sir J. Robinson being now as kind to him, and report well of his ship and proceedings, and promise money, and Sir W. Batten is a solicitor for him, but it is a strange thing to observe, they being the greatest enemys he had, and yet, I believe, has in the world in their hearts. Thence after dinner stole away and to my office, where did a great deale of business till midnight, and then to Mrs. Clerk's, to lodge again, and going home W. Hewer did tell me my wife will be here to-morrow, and hath put away Mary, which vexes me to the heart, I cannot helpe it, though it be a folly in me, and when I think seriously on it, I think my wife means no ill design in it, or, if she do, I am a foole to be troubled at it, since I cannot helpe it. The Bill of Mortality, to all our griefs, is encreased 399 this week, and the encrease generally through the whole City and suburbs, which makes us all sad.

10th. Up, and entered all my Journall since the 28th of October, having every day's passage well in my head, though it troubles me to remember it, and which I was forced to, being kept from my lodging, where my books and papers are, for several days. So to my office where till two or three o'clock busy before I could go to my lodging to dinner, then did it and to my office again. In the evening newes is brought me my wife is come: so I to her, and with her spent the evening, but with no great pleasure, I being vexed about her putting away of Mary in my absence, but yet I took no notice of it at all, but fell into other discourse, and she told me, having herself been this day at my house at London, which was boldly done, to see Mary have her things, that Mr. Harrington, our neighbour, an East country merchant is dead at Epsum of the plague, and that another neighbour of our's, Mr. Hollworthy, a very able man, is also dead by a fall in the country from his horse, his foot hanging in the stirrup, and his brains beat out.

12th (Lord's day). Up, and invited by Captain Cocke to dinner. So after being ready I went to him, and there he and I and Mr. Yard (one of the Guinny Company) dined together and very merry. After dinner I by water to the Duke of Albemarle, and there had a little discourse and business with him, chiefly to receive his commands about pilotts to be got for our Hambro' ships, that have lain at great pain and charge, some three, some four months at Harwich for a convoy. They hope here the plague will be less this weeke. Thence back by water to Captain Cocke's, and there he and I spent a great deale of the evening as we had done of the day reading and discoursing over part of Mr. Stillingfleet's " Origines Sacræ," wherein many things are very good and some frivolous.

13th. Up, and to my office, where busy all the morning and at noon to Captain Cocke's to dinner as we had appointed in order to settle our business of accounts. But here came in an Alderman, a merchant, a very merry man, and we dined, and he being gone, after dinner Cocke and I walked into the garden, and there after a little discourse he did undertake under his hand to secure me in 500*l.* profit, for my share of the profit of what we bought of the prize goods. We agreed upon the terms, which were easier on my side than I expected, and so with extraordinary inward joy we parted till the evening. So I to the office and among other business prepared a deed for him to sign and seale to me about our agreement, which at night I got him to come and sign and seale and so he and I to Glanville's and there he and I sat talking with Mrs. Penington [1] whom we found undrest in her smocke and petticoats by the fireside and there we drank and laughed. We staid here late and so I home after one of the clock.

14th. Called up by break of day by Captain Cocke, and he and I in his coach to Kent-streete (a sad

---

[1] Unmarried women are constantly styled in the Diary Mrs. or Mistress. The following is part of a letter without date, written by Isaac Penington, the famous Quaker, to this sister Judith. It seems not altogether unnecessary.

"Dear Sister,

"Is thy soul in unity with God, or art thou separated from Him? Whither art thou travelling? Oh! whither art thou travelling? Is it towards the eternal rest and peace of thy soul, or from thy soul's life towards spiritual death? Every day thou art sowing somewhat which thou must hereafter reap. What art thou daily sowing? Will the cross at last be comfortable to thee? Oh! dear sister, if thou art not able to bear the pains of the earthly body, should the Lord therein set his hand upon thee, how wilt thou bear the misery which is prepared for souls that go out of this world unrenewed in nature, and unreconciled to God?

*   *   *   *   *

"I have writ this in the pity and the love of God unto thee, who herein is seeking thy soul.

"Thy truly loving brother,

"J. P."

The Penns and Peningtons, by Maria Webb.

See note, Nov. 15th. (M. B.)

place through the plague, people sitting sicke and with plaisters about them in the street begging). To Viner's and Colvill's about money business, and so to my house; there I took 300*l.* in order to the carrying it down to my Lord Sandwich in part of the money I am to pay for Captain Cocke by our agreement. So I took it down, and down I went to Greenwich, and by and by to the Duke of Albemarle's by water late, where I find he had remembered that I had appointed to come to him this day about money, which I excused not doing sooner; but I see, a dull fellow, as he is, do sometimes remember what another thinks he minded not. My business was about getting money of the East India Company; but, Lord! to see how the Duke himself magnifies himself in what he had done with the Company; and my Lord Craven what the King could have done without my Lord Duke, and a deale of stir, but most mightily what a brave fellow I am. Back by water, it raining hard, and so to the office, and stopped my going, as I intended, to the buoy of the Nore, and great reason I had to rejoice at it, for it proved the night of as great a storm as was almost ever remembered. This day I hear that my pretty grocer's wife, Mrs. Beversham, over the way there, her husband is lately dead of the plague at Bow, which I am sorry for, for fear of losing her neighbourhood.

15th. At noon to the King's Head taverne, where all the Trinity House dined to-day, to choose a new Master in the room of Hurlestone, that is dead, and

Captain Crispe is chosen.   But, Lord! to see how Sir
W. Batten governs all and tramples upon Hurlestone,
but I am confident the Company will grow the worse
for the man's death, for now Batten, and in him a lazy,
corrupt, doting rogue, will have all the sway there.
After dinner who comes in but my lady Batten, and a
troop of a dozen women almost, and expected, as I
found afterwards, to be made mighty much of, but
nobody minded them; but the best jest was, that
when they saw themselves not regarded, they would
go away, and it was horrible foule weather; and my
Lady Batten walking through the dirty lane with new
spicke and span white shoes, she dropped one of her
goloshes in the dirt, where it stuck, and she forced to
go home without one, at which she was horribly vexed,
and I led her; and after vexing her a little more in
mirth, I parted, and to Glanville's, where I knew Sir
John Robinson, Sir G. Smith, and Captain Cocke were
gone, and there, with the company of Mrs. Penington, whose father,[1] I hear, was one of the Court of
Justice, and died prisoner, of the stone, in the Tower,
I made them, against their resolutions, to stay from

---

[1] Alderman Penington, in 1640, was elected Member of Parliament for
the City of London, and in 1642 he was chosen Lord Mayor of London, and
afterwards was appointed Lieutenant of the Tower. He was one of the Commissioners for the trial of Charles I., but he did not sign the warrant for his
execution. In 1660 he was committed to the Tower as one of the King's
judges, and his estates confiscated. In the State Papers — " Dec. 19th, 1661.
Warrant to Sir John Robinson, Lieutenant of the Tower, to deliver the corpse
of Isaac Penington, who died in prison there, to his relations." He had two
sons; Isaac, a well-known Quaker, and Arthur, who became a Romish priest;
and a daughter Judith. (M. B.)

houre to houre till it was almost midnight, and a furious, darke and rainy, and windy, stormy night, and, which was best, I, with drinking small beer, made them all drunk drinking wine, at which Sir John Robinson made great sport. But, they being gone, the lady and I very civilly sat an houre by the fireside observing the folly of this Robinson, that makes it his worke to praise himself, and all he say and do, like a heavy-headed coxcombe. The plague, blessed be God! is decreased 400; making the whole this week but 1,300 and odd; for which the Lord be praised!

16th. Up, and fitted myself for my journey down to the fleete, and sending my money and boy down by water to Eriffe,[1] I borrowed a horse of Mr. Boreman's son, and after having sat an houre laughing with my Lady Batten and Mrs. Turner, and eat and drank with them, I took horse and rode to Eriffe, where, after making a little visit to Madam Williams, who did give me information of W. Howe's having bought eight bags of precious stones taken from about the Dutch Vice-Admirall's neck, of which there were eight dyamonds which cost him 4,000*l.* sterling, in India, and hoped to have made 12,000*l.* here for them. And that this is told by one that sold him one of the bags, which hath nothing but rubys in it, which he had for 35*s.*; and that it will be proved he hath made 125*l.* of one stone that he bought. This she desired, and

---

I resolved I would give my Lord Sandwich notice of. So I on board my Lord Brouncker; and there he and Sir Edmund Pooly carried me down into the hold of the India shipp, and there did show me the greatest wealth lie in confusion that a man can see in the world. Pepper scattered through every chink, you trod upon it; and in cloves and nutmegs, I walked above the knees; whole rooms full. And silk in bales, and boxes of copper-plate, one of which I saw opened. Having seen this, which was as noble a sight as ever I saw in my life, I away on board the other ship in despair to get the pleasure-boat of the gentlemen there to carry me to the fleet. They were Mr. Ashburnham [1] and Colonell Wyndham; [2] but pleading the King's business, they did presently agree I should have it. So I presently on board, and got under sail, and had a good bedd by the shift, of Wyndham's; and so, —

17th. Sailed all night, and got down to Quinbrough water, where all the great ships are now come, and there on board my Lord, and was soon received with great content. And after some little discourse, he and I on board Sir W. Pen; and there held a council of

---

[1] John Ashburnham, a Groom of the Bedchamber to Charles I., whom he attended during the whole of the Rebellion, and afterwards filled the same post under Charles II. He was in 1661 M. P. for Sussex; and ob. 1671. The late Earl of Ashburnham, who was lineally descended from him, wrote an excellent vindication of his ancestor, against the insinuations of Clarendon and others.

[2] Colonel Francis Wyndham, a distinguished loyalist, Governor of Dunster Castle, Somersetshire. He was created a Baronet, 18th November, 1673.

Warr about many wants of the fleete, but chiefly how to get slopps and victuals for the fleete now going out to convoy our Hambro' ships, that have been so long detained for four or five months for want of convoy, which we did accommodate one way or other, and so, after much chatt, Sir W. Pen did give us a very good and neat dinner, and better, I think, than ever I did see at his owne house at home in my life, and so was the other I eat with him. After dinner much talke, and about other things, he and I about his money for his prize goods, wherein I did give him a cool answer, but so as we did not disagree in word much, and so let that fall, and so followed my Lord Sandwich, who was gone a little before me on board the Royall James. And there spent an houre, my Lord playing upon the gittarr, which he now commends above all musique in the world, because it is base enough for a single voice, and is so portable and manageable without much trouble. That being done, I got my Lord to be alone, and so I fell to acquaint him with W. Howe's business, which he had before heard a little of from Captain Cocke, but made no great matter of it, but now he do, and resolves nothing less than to lay him by the heels, and seize on all he hath, saying that for this yeare or two he has observed him so proud and conceited he could not endure him. But though I was not at all displeased with it, yet I prayed him to forbear doing anything therein till he heard from me again about it and I had made more enquiry into the truth of it. Then we fell to publique discourse, wherein was principally this: he cleared it to me beyond all doubt that Coventry is his enemy, and has been long so. So that I am over that, and my Lord told it me upon my proposal of a friendship between them, which he says is impossible. I showed him how advisable it were upon almost any terms for him to get quite off the sea employment. He answers me again that he agrees to it, but thinks the King will not let him go off. He tells me he lacks now my Lord Orrery to solicit it for him, who is very great with the King. As an infinite secret, my Lord tells me, the factions are high between the King and the Duke, and all the Court are in an uproar with their loose amours; the Duke of York being in love desperately with Mrs. Stewart. Nay, that the Duchesse herself is fallen in love with her new Master of the Horse, one Harry Sidney,[1] and another, Harry Savill.[2] So that God knows what will be the end of it. And that the Duke is not so obsequious as he used to be, but very high of late; and would be glad to be in the head of an army as Generall; and that it is said that he do propose to go and command under the King of Spayne, in Flanders. That his amours to Mrs. Stewart are told the King. So that all is like to be nought among them. That he knows that the Duke of York

---

[1] Younger son of Robert, Earl of Leicester, created Earl of Romney, 1694. He was Lord Lieutenant of Ireland, Master of the Ordnance, and Warden of the Cinque Ports in the reign of King William. Ob. 1704, unmarried.

[2] Henry Saville, some time one of the Grooms of the Bedchamber to the Duke of York.

do give leave to have him spoken slightly of in his owne hearing, and doth not oppose it, and told me from what time he hath observed this to begin. So that upon the whole my Lord do concur to wish with all his heart that he could with any honour get from off the employment. After he had given thanks to me for my kind visit and good counsel, on which he seems to set much by, I left him, and so away to my Bezan [1] again, and there to read in a pretty French book, "La Nouvelle Allegorique," upon the strife between rhetorique and its enemies, very pleasant. So, after supper, to sleepe, and sayled all night, and came to Erith before break of day.

18th. About nine of the clock, I went on shore, there to give Mrs. Williams an account of her matters, and so hired an ill-favoured horse, and away to Greenwich to my lodgings, where I hear how rude the soldiers have been in my absence, swearing what they would do with me, which troubled me, but, however, after eating a bit I to the office and there very late writing letters and so home and to bed.

19th (Lord's day). Up, and after being trimmed, alone by water to Erith, all the way with my song book singing of Mr. Lawes's long recitative song in the beginning of his book. Being come there, on board my Lord Brouncker, I find Captain Cocke and other company, the lady not well, and mighty merry we were ; Sir Edmund Pooly being very merry, and

---

[1] The yacht.

a right English gentleman, and one of the discontented Cavaliers, that think their loyalty is not considered. After dinner, all on shore to my Lady Williams, and there drank and talked; but, Lord! the most impertinent bold woman with my Lord that ever I did see. I did give her an account again of my business with my Lord touching W. Howe, and she did give me some more information about it, and examination taken about it, and so we parted and took boat, and to Woolwich, where we found my wife not well, and I out of humour begun to dislike her paynting, the last things not pleasing me so well as the former, but I blame myself for my being so little complaisant. So without eating or drinking, there being no wine (which vexed me too), we walked with a lanthorne to Greenwich and eat something at his house and so home to bed.

20th. Up before day, and so took horse for Nonsuch, with two men with me, and the ways very bad, and the weather worse, for wind and rayne. But we got in good time thither, and I did get my tallys got ready, and thence, with as many as would go, to Yowell, and there dined very well, and I saw my Besse, a very well-favoured country lass there, and after being very merry and having spent a piece I took horse, and by another way met with a very good road, but it rained hard and blew, but got home very well. Here I find Mr. Deering come to trouble me about business, which I soon dispatched and parted, he telling me that Luellin hath been dead this fortnight, of the plague, in St. Martin's Lane, which much surprised me.

21st. Up, and to the office, where all the morning doing business and at noon home to dinner and quickly back again to the office, where very busy all the evening and late sent a long discourse to Mr. Coventry by his desire about the regulating of the method of our payment of bills in the Navy, which will be very good, though, it may be, he did ayme principally at striking at Sir G. Carteret. So weary but pleased with this business being over I home to supper and to bed.

22nd. Up, and by water to the Duke of Albemarle, and there did some little business, but most to shew myself, and mightily I am yet in his and Lord Craven's books, and thence to the Swan and there drank and so down to the bridge, and so to the 'Change, where spoke with many people, and about a great deale of business, which kept me late. I heard this day that Mr. Harrington is not dead of the plague, as we believed, at which I was very glad, but most of all, to hear that the plague is come very low; that is, the whole under 1,000, and the plague 600 and odd; and great hopes of a further decrease, because of this day's being a very exceeding hard frost, and continues freezing. This day the first of the Oxford Gazettes [1] come out, which is very pretty, full of newes, and no folly in it. Wrote by William-

---

[1] No. xxiv. of the "Oxford Gazette" was the first "London Gazette." The Williamson who "wrote" it was afterwards Sir Joseph Williamson.

son.   Fear that our Hambro' ships at last cannot go because of the great frost, which we believe it is there, nor are our ships cleared at the Pillow, which will keepe them there too all this winter, I fear.   From the 'Change, which is pretty full again, I to my office and so by water to my lodging at Greenwich and dined and then to the office awhile and at night home to my lodgings, and took T. Willson and T. Hater with me, and there spent the evening till midnight discoursing and settling of our Victualling business, that thereby I might draw up instructions for the Surveyors and that we might be doing something to earne our money.   This done I late to bed.   Among other things it pleased me to have it demonstrated, that a Purser without professed cheating is a professed loser, twice as much as he gets.

23rd.   Up betimes, and so, being trimmed, I to get papers ready against Sir H. Cholmly came to me by appointment, he being newly come over from Tangier. He did by and by come, and we settled all matters about his money, and he is a most satisfied man in me, and do declare his resolution to give me 200*l.* per annum.   It continuing to be a great frost, which gives us hope for a perfect cure of the plague, he and I to walk in the parke, and there discoursed with grief of the calamity of the times; how the King's service is performed, and how Tangier is governed by a man, who, though honourable, yet do mind his ways of getting and little else compared, which will never make the place flourish.   I brought him and had a good dinner for him, and there came by chance Captain Cuttance who tells me how W. Howe is laid by the heels, and confined to the Royall Katharine, and his things all seized: and how, also, for a quarrel, which indeed the other night my Lord told me, Captain Ferrers, having cut all over the back of another of my Lord's servants, is parted from my Lord. At my lodging writing for the last twelve days my Journall and so to bed. Great expectation what mischief more the French will do us, for we must fall out. We in extraordinary lacke of money and everything else to go to sea next year. My Lord Sandwich is gone from the fleete yesterday towards Oxford.

24th. To London, and there, in my way, at my old oyster shop in Gracious Streete, bought two barrels of my fine woman of the shop, who is alive after all the plague, which now is the first observation or inquiry we make at London concerning everybody we knew before it. So to the 'Change, where very busy with several people, and mightily glad to see the 'Change so full, and hopes of another abatement still the next week. I went home with Sir G. Smith to dinner, sending for one of my barrels of oysters, which were good, though come from Colchester, where the plague hath been so much. Here a very brave dinner, though no invitation; and, Lord! to see how I am treated, that come from so mean a beginning, is matter of wonder to me. But it is God's great mercy to me, and His blessing upon my taking pains, and being punctual in my dealings. After dinner

Captain Cocke and I about some business, and then with my other barrel of oysters home to Greenwich, sent them by water to Mrs. Penington, while he and I landed, and visited Mr. Evelyn, where most excellent discourse with him; among other things he showed me a ledger of a Treasurer of the Navy, his great grandfather, just 100 years old; which I seemed mighty fond of, and he did present me with it, which I take as a great rarity;[1] and he hopes to find me more, older than it. He also showed us several letters of the old Lord of Leicester's,[2] in Queen Elizabeth's time, under the very hand-writing of Queen Elizabeth, and Queen Mary, Queen of Scotts; and others, very venerable names. But, Lord! how poorly, methinks, they wrote in those days, and in what plain uncut paper. Thence, Cocke having sent for his coach, we to Mrs. Penington, and there sat and talked and eat our oysters with great pleasure, and so home to my lodging late and to bed.

25th. Up, and busy at the office all day long, saving dinner time, and in the afternoon also very late at my office, and so home to bed. All our business is now about our Hambro' fleete, whether it can go or no this yeare, the weather being set in frosty, and the whole stay being for want of Pilotts now, which I have wrote

---

[1] This ledger is now in the British Museum, amongst some of Pepys's papers, in the Ducket Collection.

[2] There are some letters and papers answering to this description in the Pepysian Library, and amongst them an account of the Coroner's Inquest held upon the Countess of Leicester at Cumnor.

to the Trinity House about, but have so poor an account from them, that I did acquaint Sir W. Coventry with it this post.

26th (Lord's day). Up before day to dress myself to go toward Erith, which I would do by land, it being a horrible cold frost to go by water : so borrowed two horses of Mr. Howell and his friend, and with much ado set out, after my horses being frosted [1] (which I know not what it means to this day), and my boy having lost one of my spurs and stockings, carrying them to the smith's ; but I borrowed a stocking, and so got up, and Mr. Tooker with me, and rode to Erith, and there on board my Lord Brouncker, met Sir W. Warren upon his business, among others, and did a great deale, Sir J. Minnes, as God would have it, not being there to hinder us with his impertinences. Business being done, we to dinner very merry, there being there Sir Edmund Pooly, a very worthy gentleman. They are now come to the copper boxes in the prizes, and hope to have ended all this weeke. After dinner took leave, and on shore to Madam Williams, to give her an account of my Lord's letter to me about Howe, who he has clapped by the heels on suspicion of having the jewels, and she did give me my Lord Brouncker's examination of the fellow, that declares his having them, and so away, Sir W. Warren riding with me, and the way being very bad, that is, hard and slippery by reason of the frost, so we could not come to past

---

[1] Roughed, or rough-shod. (M. B.)

Woolwich to-night. To my wife at Woolwich, where I found, as I had directed, a good dinner to be made against to-morrow, and invited guests in the yarde, meaning to be merry, in order to her taking leave, for she intends to come in a day or two to me for altogether. But here, they tell me, one of the houses behind them is infected, and I was fain to stand there a great while, to have their back-doors opened, but they could not, having locked them fast, against any passing through, so was forced to pass by them again, close to their sicke beds, which they were removing out of the house, which troubled me ; so I made them uninvite their guests, and to resolve of coming all away to me to-morrow, and I walked with a lanthorne, weary as I was, to Greenwich ; but it was a fine walke, it being a hard frost, and so to Captain Cocke's, but he I found had sent for me to come to him to Mrs. Penington, and there I went, and we were very merry, and supped.

27th. Up, and being to go to wait on the Duke of Albemarle, who is to go out of towne to Oxford to-morrow, and being unwilling to go by water, it being bitter cold, walked it with my landlady's little boy Christopher to Lambeth, it being a very fine walke and calling at half the way and drank, and so to the Duke of Albemarle, who is visited by every body against his going ; and mighty kind to me : and upon my desiring his grace to give me his kind word to the Duke of York, if any occasion there were of speaking of me, he told me he had reason to do so ;

for there had been nothing done in the Navy without me. His going, I hear, is upon putting the sea business into order, and, as some say, and people of his owne family, that he is agog to go to sea himself the next year. Here I met with a letter from Sir G. Carteret, who is come to Cranborne, that he will be here this afternoon and desires me to be with him. So the Duke would have me dine with him. To dinner, he most exceeding kind to me to the observation of all that are there. At dinner comes Sir G. Carteret and dines with us. After dinner a great deal alone with Sir G. Carteret, who tells me that my Lord hath received still worse and worse usage from some base people about the Court. But the King is very kind, and the Duke do not appear the contrary; and my Lord Chancellor swore to him " by —— I will not forsake my Lord of Sandwich." Our next discourse is upon this Act for money, about which Sir G. Carteret comes to see what money can be got upon it. But none can be got, which pleases him the thoughts of, for, if the Exchequer should succeed in this, his office would faile. But I am apt to think at this time of hurry and plague and want of trade, no money will be got upon a new way which few understand. We walked, Cocke and I, through the Parke with him, and so we being to meet the Vice Chamberlayne to-morrow at Nonsuch, to treat with Sir Robert Long about the same business. I into London, it being dark night, by a hackney coach; the first I have durst to go in many a day, and with great pain now for fear.

But it being unsafe to go by water in the dark and frosty cold, and unable being weary with my morning walke to go on foot, this was my only way. Few people yet in the streets, nor shops open, here and there twenty in a place almost; though not above five or sixe o'clock at night. So to Viner's, and there heard of Cocke, and found him at the Pope's Head, drinking with Temple. I to them, where the Goldsmiths do decry the new Act, for money to be all brought into the Exchequer, and paid out thence, saying they will not advance one farthing upon it; and indeed it is their interest to say and do so. Thence Cocke and I to Sir G. Smith's, it being now night, and there up to his chamber and sat talking, and I barbing [1] against to-morrow; and anon, at nine at night, comes to us Sir G. Smith and the Lieutenant of the Tower and there they sat talking and drinking till past midnight, and mighty merry we were, the Lieutenant of the Tower being in a mighty vein of singing, and he hath a very good eare and strong voice, but no manner of skill. Sir G. Smith shewed me his lady's closett, which was very fine; and, after being very merry, here I lay in a noble chamber, and mighty highly treated, the first time I have lain in London a long time.

28th. Up before day and Cocke and I took a hackney coach appointed with four horses to take us up, and so carried us over London Bridge. But there, thinking of some business, I did light at the foot of

---

[1] *Barbing, i. e.* shaving. Also a cant term for clipping of gold, shaving it. BEN JONSON's *Alchemist*, act i. sc. 1. (M B.)

the bridge, and by helpe of a candle at a stall, where some pavers were at work, I wrote a letter to Mr. Hater, and never knew so great an instance of the usefulness of carrying pen and ink and wax about one : so we, the way being very bad, to Nonsuch, and thence to Sir Robert Long's house ; [1] a fine place, and dinner time ere we got thither ; but we had breakfasted a little at Mr. Gauden's, he being out of towne though, and there borrowed Dr. Taylor's sermons, and is a most excellent booke and worth my buying, where had a very good dinner, and curiously dressed, and here a couple of ladies, kinswomen of his, not handsome though, but rich, that knew me by report of The. Turner, and mighty merry we were. After dinner to talk of our business, the Act of Parliament, where in short I saw Sir R. Long mighty fierce in the great good qualities of it. But in that and many other things he was stiff in, I think without much judgment, or the judgment I expected from him, and already they have evaded the necessity of bringing people into the Exchequer with their bills to be paid there. Sir G. Carteret is titched [2] at this, yet resolves with

---

[1] " Nonsuch, afterwards called Worcester Park, co. Surrey. Sir Robert Long was Auditor of the Exchequer, which office was removed from Westminster to his Majesty's honour of Nonsuch, 15th August, 1665. On the 22nd Sept., 1670, the king demised the Great Park, Great Park Meadow, and the mansion house called Worcester Park, to Sir Robert Long, Bart., for ninety-nine years."—MANNING AND BRAY'S *Surrey*, vol. ii. p. 606.

[2] In Cole's Dictionary, " *Titchy*, morosus, difficilis." Also spelt *techy*, *teachy*, or *tetchy*, peevish, fretful.

" *Tetchy* and wayward was thy infancy."
SHAKESPEARE, *Richard III.* act iv. sc. 4. (M. B.)

me to make the best use we can of this Act for the King, but all our care, we think, will not render it as it should be. He did again here alone discourse with me about my Lord, and is himself strongly for my Lord's not going to sea, which I am glad to hear and did confirm him in it. He tells me too that he talked last night with the Duke of Albemarle about my Lord Sandwich, by the by making him sensible that it is his interest to preserve his old friends, which he confessed he had reason to do, for he knows that ill offices were doing of him, and that he honoured my Lord Sandwich with all his heart. After this discourse we parted, and all of us broke up and we parted. Captain Cocke and I through Wandsworth. Drank at Sir Allen Broderick's,[1] a great friend and comrade of Cocke's, whom he values above the world for a witty companion, and I believe he is so. So to Fcx-Hall and there took boat, and down to the Old Swan, and thence to Lumbard Streete, it being darke night and thence to the Tower. Took boat and down to Greenwich, Cocke and I, he home and I to the office, where did a little business, and then to my lodgings, where my wife is come, and I am well pleased with it, only much trouble in those lodgings we have, the mistresse of the house being so deadly dear in everything we have; so that we do resolve to remove home soon as we know how the plague goes this weeke, which we hope will be a good decrease. So to bed.

---

[1] Son of Sir Thomas Broderick, of Richmond, Yorkshire, and Wandsworth, Surrey, knighted by Charles II., and Surveyor-General in Ireland to that king.

29th. Up, my wife and I talking how to dispose of our goods, and resolved upon sending our two mayds Alce (who has been a day or two at Woolwich with my wife, thinking to have had a feast there) and Susan home. So my wife after dinner did take them to London with some goods, and I in the afternoon after doing other business did go also by agreement to meet Captain Cocke and from him to Sir Roger Cuttance, about the money due from Cocke to him for the late prize goods, wherein Sir Roger is troubled that he has not payment as agreed, and the other, that he must pay without being secured in the quiett possession of them, but some accommodation to both, I think, will be found. But Cocke do tell me that several have begged so much of the King to be discovered out of stolen prize goods and so I am afeard we shall hereafter have trouble, therefore I will get myself free of them as soon as I can and my money paid. Thence home to my house, calling my wife, where the poor wretch is putting things in a way to be ready for our coming home, and so by water together to Greenwich.

30th. Up and at the office all the morning. At noon comes Sir Thomas Allen, and I made him dine with me, and very friendly he is, and a good man, I think, but one that professes he loves to get and to save. He dined with me and my wife and Mrs. Barbara, whom my wife brings along with her from Woolwich for as long as she stays here. Great joy we have this week in the weekly Bill, it being come to

544 in all, and but 333 of the plague; so that we are encouraged to get to London soon as we can. And my father writes as great news of joy to them, that he saw York's waggon go again this week to London, and was full of passengers; and tells me that my aunt Bell hath been dead of the plague these seven weeks.

December 1st. This morning to the office, full of resolution to spend the whole day at business, and there, among other things, I did agree with Poynter to be my clerke for my Victualling business, and so all alone all the day long shut up in my little closett at my office, drawing up instructions, which I should long since have done for my Surveyors of the Ports, Sir W. Coventry desiring much to have them, and he might well have expected them long since. After dinner to it again, and at night had long discourse with Gibbson, who is for Yarmouth, who makes me understand so much of the victualling business and the pursers' trade, that I am ashamed I should go about the concerning myself in a business which I understand so very very little of, and made me distrust all I had been doing to-day. So I did lay it by till to-morrow morning to think of it fresh, and so home by promise to my wife, to have mirth there. So we had our neighbours, little Miss Tooker and Mrs. Daniels, to dance, and after supper I to bed, and left them merry below, which they did not part from till two or three in the morning.

2nd. Up, and discoursing with my wife, who is resolved to go to London for good and all this day, we did agree upon giving Mr. Sheldon 10*l.*, and Mrs. Barbara two pieces, and so I left her to go down thither to fetch away the rest of the things and pay him the money, and so I to the office, where very busy setting Mr. Poynter to write out my last night's worke, which pleases me this day, but yet it is pretty to reflect how much I am out of confidence with what I had done upon Gibson's discourse with me, for fear I should have done it sillily, but Poynter likes them, and Mr. Hater also, but yet I am afeard lest they should do it out of flattery, so conscious I am of my ignorance. Dined with my wife at noon and took leave of her, she being to go to London, as I said, for altogether, and I to the office, busy till past one in the morning.

3rd (Lord's day). It being Lord's day, up and dressed and to church, thinking to have sat with Sir James Bunce [1] to hear his daughter [2] and her husband sing, that are so much commended, but was prevented by being invited into Coll. Cleggatt's pew. However, there I sat, near Mr. Laneare, with whom I spoke, and in sight, by chance, and very near my fat brown beauty of our Parish, the rich merchant's lady, a very noble woman, and Madame Pierce. A good sermon of Mr. Plume's, and so to Captain Cocke's, and there dined with him, and Collonell Wyndham, a worthy gentleman, whose wife was nurse to the present King, and one that while she lived governed him

---

[1] James Bunce, an Alderman of London, 1660.   [2] Mrs. Chamberlain.

and every thing else, as Cocke says, as a minister of
state; the old King putting mighty weight and trust
upon her.[1] They talked much of matters of State
and persons, and particularly how my Lord Barkeley
hath all along been a fortunate, though a passionate
and but weak man as to policy; but as a kinsman
brought in and promoted by my Lord of St. Alban's,
and one that is the greatest vapourer in the world, this
Collonell Wyndham says; and one to whom only,
with Jacke Ashburne[2] and Colonel Legg,[3] the King's
removal to the Isle of Wight from Hampton Court
was communicated; and (though betrayed by their
knavery, or at best by their ignorance, insomuch that
they have all solemnly charged one another with their
failures therein, and have been at daggers-drawing
publickly about it), yet now none greater friends in
the world. We dined, and in comes Mrs. Owen, a
kinswoman of my Lord Brouncker's, about getting a
man discharged, which I did for her, and by and by

---

[1] Mrs. Wyndham, Charles II.'s nurse, had great influence over him, and
had many private designs of benefit and advantage to herself and her children,
and the qualifying her husband to do all acts of power without control upon
his neighbours, and laboured to procure grants or promises of reversions of
lands from the Prince, and finding that the Prince was not to transact any
such thing without the advice of the Council, she contrived to raise jealousies
and dislikes between them, and being a woman of no good breeding, and of
a country pride, *nihil muliebre præter corpus gerens*, valued herself
much upon the power and familiarity which her neighbours might see she had
with the Prince of Wales, and therefore in company would use great boldness
toward him. See Clarendon's " Hist. of Rebellion," book ix. 1645. (M. B.)

[2] This should be Ashburnham.

[3] William Legge, Groom of the Bedchamber to Charles I., and father to
the first Lord Dartmouth. He was M. P. for Southampton. Ob. 1672.

Mrs. Pierce to speake with me about her husband's business of money, and she tells us how she prevented Captain Fisher the other day in his purchase of all her husband's fine goods, as pearls and silks, that he had seized in an Apothecary's house, a friend of theirs, but she got in and broke them open and removed all before Captain Fisher came the next day to fetch them away, at which he is starke mad. She went home, and I to my lodgings. At night by agreement I fetched her again with Cocke's coach, and he came and we sat and talked together, thinking to have had Mrs. Coleman and my songsters, her husband and Laneare, but they failed me. So we to supper, and as merry as was sufficient, and my pretty little Miss with me; and so after supper walked with Pierce, and so back and to bed. But, Lord! I stand admiring of the wittinesse of her little boy, which is one of the wittiest boys, but most confident that ever I did see of a child of 9 year old or under in all my life, or indeed one twice his age almost, but all for roguish wit. So to bed.

4th. Several people to me about business, among others Captain Taylor, intended Storekeeper for Harwich, whom I did give some assistance in his dispatch by lending him money. So out and by water to London and to the 'Change, and up and down about several businesses, and after the observing (God forgive me!) one or two of my neighbour Jason's women come to towne, which did please me very well, home to my house at the office, where my wife had got a dinner for me: and it was a joyfull thing for us to meet here, for which God be praised! Here was her brother come to see her, and speake with me about business. It seems that my recommendation of him hath not only obtained his presently being admitted into the Duke of Albemarle's guards, and present pay, but also by the Duke's and Sir Philip Howard's direction, to be put as a right-hand man, and other marks of special respect, at which I am very glad, partly for him, and partly to see that I am reckoned something in my recommendations, but wish he may carry himself that I may receive no disgrace by him. So to the 'Change. Up and down again in the evening about business and to meet Captain Cocke, who waited for Mrs. Pierce (with whom he is mightily stricken), to receive and hide for her her rich goods she saved the other day from seizure. Upon the 'Change to-day Colvill tells me, from Oxford, that the King in person hath justified my Lord Sandwich to the highest degree; and is right in his favour to the uttermost. So late by water home, taking a barrel of oysters with me, and at Greenwich went and sat with Madame Penington till two in the morning, and so away to my lodging and so to bed. Over fasting all the morning has filled me mightily with wind, and nothing else has done it, that I fear a fit of the cholique.

5th. Up and to the office, where very busy about several businesses all the morning. At noon empty, yet without stomach to dinner having spoiled myself with fasting yesterday, and so filled with wind. In the afternoon by water, calling Mr. Stevens, who is with great trouble paying of seamen of their tickets at Deptford, and to London, to look for Captain Kingdon, whom we found at home about 5 o'clock. I tried him, and he promised to follow us presently to the East India house to sign papers to-night in order to the settling the business of my receiving money for Tangier. We went and stopt the officer there to shut up. He made us stay above an houre. I sent for him; he comes and brings a paper saying that he had been this houre looking for the Lord Ashley's order. When he looks for it, that is not the paper. He would go again to look; kept us waiting till almost 8 at night. Then was I to go home by water this weather and darke, and to write letters by the post, besides keeping the East India officers there so late. I sent for him again; at last he comes, and says he cannot find the paper (which is a pretty thing to lay an order for 100,000*l.* no better). I was angry; he told me I ought to give people ease at night, and all business was to be done by day. I answered him sharply, that I did not make, nor any honest man, any difference between night and day in the King's business, and this was such, and my Lord Ashley should know. He answered me short. I told him I knew the time (meaning the Rump's time) when he did other men's business with more diligence. He cried, " Nay, say not so," and stopped his mouth, not one word after. We then did our business without the order in less than eight minutes, which he made me to no purpose stay above two hours for the doing. This made him mad, and so we exchanged notes, and I had notes for 14,000*l.* of the Treasurer of the Company, and so away and by water to Greenwich and wrote my letters, and so home late to bed.

6th. Up betimes, it being fast-day; and by water to the Duke of Albemarle,[1] who came to towne from Oxford last night. He is mighty brisk, and very kind to me, and asks my advice principally in every thing. He surprises me with the news that my Lord Sandwich goes Embassador to Spayne speedily; though I know not whence this arises, yet I am heartily glad of it. He did give me several directions what to do, and so I home by water again and to church a little, thinking to have met Mrs. Pierce in order to our meeting at night; but she not there, I home and dined, and comes presently by appointment my wife, and I spent the afternoon upon a song of Solyman's words to Roxalana that I have set,[2] and so with my wife walked and Mercer to Mrs. Pierce's, where Captain Rolt and

---

[1] At the Cockpit.

[2] This song, as set to music by Pepys, is taken from the second part of the *Siege of Rhodes*, act iv. sc. 2. It is in the Pepysian Library.

> " Beauty retire; thou doest my pitty move,
> Believe my pitty, and then trust my love.
> Att first I thought her by our Prophet sent,
>   As a re-ward for valour's toiles,
>   More worth than all my Fa-ther's spoiles;
> But now, she is become my punishment.
> But thou art just, O Pow'r di-vine,
>   With niew and painfull arts
>   Of studied warr, I breake the hearts

Mrs. Knipp,[1] Mr. Coleman and his wife, and Laneare, Mrs. Worshipp[2] and her singing daughter, met; and by and by unexpectedly comes Mr. Pierce from Oxford. Here the best company for musique I ever was in, in my life, and wish I could live and die in it, both for musique and the face of Mrs. Pierce, and my wife and Knipp, who is pretty enough; but the most excellent, mad-humoured thing, and sings the noblest that ever I heard in my life, and Rolt, with her, some things together most excellently. I spent the night in extasy almost; and, having invited them to my house a day or two hence, we broke up, Pierce having told me that he is told how the King hath done my Lord Sandwich all the right imaginable, by showing him his countenance before all the world on every occasion, to remove thoughts of discontent; and that he is to go Embassador, and that the Duke of York is made generall of

---

Of half the world, and shee breakes mine,
And shee, and shee, and shee breakes mine."

I hope, in the Appendix, to give a catalogue of Pepys' large collection of music books. (M. B.)

[1] Genest, in his " History of the British Stage," vol. i., enumerates sixteen characters filled by Mrs. Knipp, at the King's House, between 1664 and 1678, when she disappears from the playbills, in which her name is spelt in six different ways. The details in the " Diary " respecting this lively actress and " her brute of a husband," whom Pepys describes as a " horse jockey," are so amusing, that any particulars of their subsequent history would have been interesting. Those readers who may wish to know what performers spoke or acted in any plays, prologues, or epilogues, mentioned by Pepys, will find information in Genest's work, above quoted; but it was not thought necessary to transplant all the particulars into these pages.

[2] Mrs. Worshipp, sister of Mrs. Clerke, wife of Dr. Clerke. See 13th Feb., 1666-7.

all forces by land and sea, and the Duke of Albemarle, lieutenant-generall. Whether the latter alterations be so, true or no, he knows not, but he is told so; but my Lord is in full favour with the King. So all home and to bed.

7th. Up and to the office, where very busy all day. Sir G. Carteret's letter tells me my Lord Sandwich is, as I was told, declared Embassador Extraordinary to Spayne, and to go with all speed away, and that his enemies have done him as much good as he could wish. At noon late to dinner, and after dinner spent till night with Mr. Gibson and Hater discoursing and making myself more fully know the trade of pursers, and what fittest to be done in their business, and so to the office till midnight writing letters, and so home, and after supper with my wife about one o'clock to bed.

8th. Up, well pleased in my mind about my Lord Sandwich, about whom I shall know more anon from Sir G. Carteret, who will be in towne, and also that the Hambrough ships after all difficulties are got out. God send them good speed! So, after being trimmed, I by water to London, to the Navy office, there to give order to my mayde to buy things to send down to Greenwich for supper to-night; and I also to buy other things, as oysters, and lemons, 6*d.* per piece, and oranges, 3*d.* That done I to the 'Change, and among many other things, especially for getting of my Tangier money, I by appointment met Mr. Gauden, and he and I to the Pope's Head Taverne, and there he did give me alone a very pretty dinner. Our business to talk of his matters and his supply of money, which was necessary for us to talk on before the Duke of Albemarle this afternoon and Sir G. Carteret. After that I offered now to pay him the 4,000*l.* remaining of his 8,000*l.* for Tangier, which he took with great kindnesse, and prayed me most frankly to give him a note for 3,500*l.* and accept the other 500*l.* for myself, which in good earnest was against my judgment to do, for I expected about 100*l.* and no more, but however he would have me do it, and ownes very great obligations to me, and the man indeed I love, and he deserves it. This put me into great joy, though with a little stay to it till we have time to settle it, for for so great a sum I was fearfull any accident might by death or otherwise defeate me, having not now time to change papers. So we rose, and by water to White Hall, where we found Sir G. Carteret with the Duke, and also Sir G. Downing, whom I had not seen in many years before. He greeted me very kindly, and I him ; though methinks I am touched, that it should be said that he was my master heretofore, as doubtless he will. So to talk of our Navy business, and particularly money business, of which there is little hopes of any present supply upon this new Act, the goldsmiths being here (and Alderman Backewell newly come from Flanders), and none offering any. So we rose without doing more than by stating the case of the Victualler, that whereas there is due to him on the last year's declaration 80,000*l.*, and the charge of this year's

amounts to 420,000*l.* and odd, he must be supplied
between this and the end of January with 150,000*l.*,
and the remainder in 40 weeks by weekly payments,
or else he cannot go through his business.   Thence
after some discourse with Sir G. Carteret, who, though
he tells me that he is glad of my Lord's being made
Embassador, and that it is the greatest courtesy his
enemies could do him; yet I find he is not heartily
merry upon it, and that it was no design of my Lord's
friends, but the prevalence of his enemies, and that
the Duke of Albemarle and Prince Rupert are like to
go to sea together the next year.   I pray God, when
my Lord is gone, they do not fall hard upon the Vice-
Chamberlain, being alone, and in so envious a place,
though this late Act and the instructions now a brew-
ing for our office as to method of payments will
destroy the profit of his place of itself without more
trouble.   Thence by water down to Greenwich, and
there found all my company come; that is, Mrs.
Knipp, and an ill, melancholy, jealous-looking fellow,
her husband, that spoke not a word to us all the night,
Pierce and his wife, and Rolt, Mrs. Worshipp and her
daughter, Coleman and his wife, and Laneare, and, to
make us perfectly happy, there comes by chance to
towne Mr. Hill to see us.   Most excellent musique
we had in abundance, and a good supper, dancing,
and a pleasant scene of Mrs. Knipp's rising sicke from
table, but whispered me it was for some hard word or
other her husband gave her just now when she laughed
and was more merry than ordinary.   But we got her

in humour again, and mighty merry; spending the night, till two in the morning, with most complete content as ever in my life. Then broke up, and we to bed, Mr. Hill and I, whom I love more and more, and he us.

9th. Called up betimes by my Lord Brouncker, who is come to towne from his long water worke at Erith last night, to go with him to the Duke of Albemarle, which by his coach I did. Our discourse upon the ill posture of the times through lacke of money. At the Duke's did some business, and I believe he was not pleased to see all the Duke's discourse and applications to me and every body else. Discoursed also with Sir G. Carteret about office business, but no money in view. Here my Lord and I staid and dined. At table the Duchesse, a damned ill-looked woman, complaining of her Lord's going to sea the next year, said these cursed words: "If my Lord had been a coward he had gone to sea no more: it may be then he might have been excused, and made an Embassador" (meaning my Lord Sandwich). This made me mad, and I believed she perceived my countenance change, and blushed herself very much. I was in hopes others had not minded it, but my Lord Brouncker, after we were come away, took notice of the words to me with displeasure. To the office, and then home to Mr. Hill, and sang, among other things, my song of "Beauty retire," which he likes, only excepts against two notes in the base, but likes the whole very well. So late to bed.

10th (Lord's day). Lay long talking, Hill and I, with great pleasure, and then up, and being ready walked to Cocke's for some newes, but heard none, only they would have us stay their dinner, and sent for my wife, who came, and very merry we were, there being Sir Edward Pooly and Mr. Evelyn. Before we had dined comes Mr. Andrews, and so after dinner home, and there we sung some things, one thing after another, late till supper, and so to bed with great pleasure.

11th. To London to the 'Change, and after discoursed with several people about business; met Mr. Gauden at the Pope's Head, where he brought Mr. Lewes and T. Willson to discourse about the Victualling business, and the alterations of the pursers' trade, for something must be done to secure the King a little better, and yet that they may have wherewithal to live. After dinner I took him aside, and perfected to my great joy my business with him, wherein he deals most nobly in giving me his hand for the 4,000*l.*, and would take my note but for 3,500*l.* This is a great blessing, and God make me thankfull truly for it. With him till it was darke putting in writing our discourse about victualling, and so parted, and I to Viner's, and there evened all accounts. The like to Colvill. Then late met Cocke and Temple[1] at the Pope's Head, and there had good discourse with Temple, who tells me that of the 80,000*l.* advanced

---

[1] See 30th September, 1665. "Mr. Temple, the fat blade, Sir Robert Viner's chief man." (M. B.)

already by the East India Company, they have had 45,000*l.* out of their hands. He discoursed largely of the quantity of money coyned, and what may be thought the real sum of money in the kingdom. He told me, too, as an instance of the thrift used in the King's business, that the tools and the interest of the money using to the King for the money he borrowed while the new invention of the mill money was perfected cost him 35,000*l.*, and in mirthe tells me that the new fashion money is good for nothing but to help the Prince if he can secretly get copper plates shut up in silver it shall never be discovered, at least not in his age. Thence Cocke and I by water, he home and I home, and there sat with Mr. Hill and my wife supping and talking and singing till midnight, and then to bed. That I may remember it the more particularly, I thought fit to insert this additional memorandum of Temple's discourse this night with me, which I took in writing from his mouth. Before the Harp and Crosse money was cried down, he and his fellow goldsmiths did make some particular trials what proportion that money bore to the old King's money, and they found that generally it came to, one with another, about 25*l.* in every 100*l.* Of this money there was, upon the calling of it in, 650,000*l.* at least brought into the Tower; and from thence he computes that the whole money of England must be full 16,250,000*l.* But for all this believes that there is above 30,000,000*l.*; he supposing that about the King's coming in (when he begun to observe the quantity of the new money) people begun to be fear-full of this money's being cried down, and so picked it out and set it a-going as fast as they could, to be rid of it ; and he thinks 30,000,000*l.* the rather, because if there were but 16,250,000*l.* the King having 2,000,-000*l.* every year, would have the whole money of the kingdom in his hands in eight years. He tells me about 350,000*l.* sterling was coined out of the French money, the proceeds of Dunkirke ; so that, with what was coined of the Crosse money, there is new coined about 1,000,000*l.* besides the gold, which is guessed at 500,000*l.* He tells me, that, though the King did deposit the French money in pawn all the while for the 350,000*l.* he was forced to borrow thereupon till the tools could be made for the new Minting in the present form. Yet the interest he paid for that time came to 35,000*l.* Viner having to his knowledge 10,000*l.* for the use of 100,000*l.* of it.

12th. I by water saving the tide through Bridge and to Sir G. Downing by appointment at Charing Crosse, who did at first mightily please me with in-forming me thoroughly the virtue and force of this Act, and indeed it is ten times better than ever I thought could have been said of it, but when he came to impose upon me that without more ado I must get by my credit people to serve in goods and lend money upon it and none could do it better than I, and the King should give me thanks particularly in it, and I could not get him to excuse me, but I must come to him though to no purpose on Saturday, and he is sure

I will bring him some bargains or other made upon this Act, it vexed me more than all the pleasure I took before, for I find he will be troublesome to me in it, if I will let him have as much of my time as he would have. So late I took leave and in the cold home to the office and to supper and to bed.

13th. Up betimes and finished my Journall for five days back and then after being ready to my Lord Brouncker by appointment there to order the disposing of some money that we have come into the office, and here to my great content I did get a bill of imprest to Captain Cocke to pay myself in part of what is coming to me from him for my Lord Sandwich's satisfaction and to my owne, and having done that did go to Mr. Pierce's where he and his wife made me drink some tea and so he and I by water together to London. So away to the 'Change, and there hear the ill news, to my great and all our great trouble, that the plague is encreased again this week, notwithstanding there hath been a day or two great frosts; but we hope it is only the effects of the late close warm weather, and if the frosts continue the next week, may fall again; but the town do thicken so much with people, that it is much if the plague do not grow again upon us. On the 'Change invited by Sheriff Hooker,[1] who keeps the poorest, mean, dirty table in a dirty house that ever I did see any Sheriff of London; and a plain, ordinary, silly man I think he is, but rich;

---

[1] Afterwards Sir William Hooker.

only his son, Mr. Lethulier, I like, for a pretty, civil, understanding merchant; and the more by much, because he happens to be husband to our noble, fat, brave lady [1] in our parish, that I and my wife admire so. Thence away to the Pope's Head Taverne, and there met first with Captain Cocke, and dispatched my business with him to my content, he being ready to sign his bill of imprest of 2,000*l.*, which glads my heart. He being gone, comes Sir W. Warren, who advised with me about a business of insurance, wherein something may be saved to him and got to me, and to that end he and I did take a coach at night and to the Cockpit, there to get the Duke of Albemarle's advice for our insuring some of our Sounde goods coming home under Harman's convoy, but he proved shy of doing it without knowledge of the Duke of York, so we back again and calling at my house to see my wife, who is well; though my great trouble is that our poor little parish is the greatest number this weeke in all the city within the walls, having six, from one the last weeke; and so by water to Greenwich.

14th. Up, and to the office a while with my Lord Brouncker, where we directed Sir W. Warren in the business of the insurance as I desired, and so at noon I to London, but the 'Change was done before I got thither, so I to the Pope's Head Taverne, and there find Mr. Gauden and Captain Beckford and Nick Osborne going to dinner and I dined with them and

---

[1] Mr. Lethieulier's lady was Anne, daughter of Sir William Hooker. See Oct. 14, 1666.

very exceeding merry we were as I had [not] been a great while, and so having seen my wife in the way I home by water and to write my letters and then home to bed.

15th. Spent all the morning with my Surveyors of the Ports for the Victualling, and there read to them what instructions I had provided for them and discoursed largely much of our business and the business of the pursers. I left them to dine with my people, and to my Lord Brouncker's, where I met with a great good dinner and Sir T. Teddiman, with whom my Lord and I were to discourse about the bringing of W. Howe to a tryall for his jewels and there till almost night and so away toward the office and in my way met with Sir James Bunch ;[1] and after asking what newes, he cried "Ah !" says he, "this is the time for you," says he, "that were for Oliver heretofore ; you are full of employment, and we, poor Cavaliers, sit still and can get nothing ; " which was a pretty reproach, I thought, but answered nothing to it, for fear of making it worse. So away and I to see Mrs. Penington, but company being to come, I staid not, but to the office a little and so home.

16th. Up, and met at the office; Sir W. Batten with us, who came from Portsmouth on Monday last, and has not been with us to see or discourse with us about any business till this day. At noon to dinner, and then I by water, it being a fearful cold, snow-

---

[1] Sir James Bunce, an Alderman of London, 1660.

ing day to Westminster to White Hall stairs to Sir G.
Downing to whom I brought the happy newes of
my having contracted, as we did this day with Sir W.
Warren, for a ship's lading of Norway goods here and
another at Harwich to the value of above 3,000*l.*,
which is the first that has been got upon the New Act,
and he is overjoyed with it and tells me he will do me
all the right to Court about it in the world, and I am
glad I have it to write to Sir W. Coventry to-night.
He would fain have me come in 200*l.* to lend upon
the Act, but I desire to be excused in doing that, it
being to little purpose for us that relate to the King to
do it, for the sum gets the King no courtesy nor credit.
So I parted from him and walked to Westminster Hall,
and there I did see Betty Howlet come after the sicknesse to the Hall. Had not opportunity to salute her,
as I desired, but was glad to see her and a very pretty
wench she is. Thence back landing at the Old Swan
and taking boat again at Billingsgate and setting
ashore at home and I to the office. Newes is come
to-day of our Sounde fleete being come, but I do not
know what Sir W. Warren has insured.

17th (Lord's day). Word brought me that Cutler's
coach is, by appointment, come to the Isle of Doggs
for me, and so I over the water; and in his coach to
Hackney, a very fine, cold, clear, frosty day. At his
house I find him with a plain little dinner, good wine,
and welcome. He is still a prating man; and the
more I know him, the less I find in him. A pretty
house he hath here indeed, of his owne building. His

old mother was an object at dinner that made me not like it; and, after dinner, to visit his sicke wife I did not also take much joy in, but very friendly he is to me, not for any kindnesse I think he has to any man, but thinking me, I perceive, a man whose friendship is to be looked after. After dinner back again and to Deptford to Mr. Evelyn's, who was not within, but I had appointed my cozen Pepys of Hatcham to meet me there, to discourse about getting his 1,000*l.* of my Lord Sandwich, having now an opportunity of my having above that sum in my hands of his. I found this a dull fellow still in all his discourse, but in this he is ready enough to embrace what I counsel him to, which is, to write importunately to my Lord and me about it and I will look after it. I do again and again declare myself a man unfit to be security for such a sum. He walked with me as far as Deptford upper towne, being mighty respectfull to me, and there parted, he telling me that this towne is still very bad of the plague. I walked to Greenwich first, to make a short visit to my Lord Brouncker, and next to Mrs. Penington and spent all the evening with her with the same freedom I used to have and very pleasant company. With her till past one of the clock.

18th. In the morning and past, and so to my lodging to bed, and betimes up, it being a fine frost, and walked it to Redriffe, calling and drinking at Half-way house, thinking, indeed, to have overtaken some of the people of our house, the women, who were to walk the same walke, but I could not. So to London, and there visited my wife, and was a little displeased to find she is so forward all of a spurt to make much of her brother and sister since my last kindnesse to him in getting him a place, but all ended well presently, and I to the 'Change and up and down to Kingdon and the goldsmith's to meet Mr. Stephens, and did get all my money matters most excellently cleared to my complete satisfaction. Passing over Cornhill I spied young Mrs. Daniel and Sarah, my landlady's daughter, who are come, as I expected, to towne, and did say they spied me and I dogged them to St. Martin's, where I passed by them buying shoes, and walked down as low as Ducke Lane, and enquired for some Spanish books, and so back again and they were gone. So to the 'Change, hoping to see them in the streete, and missing them, went back again thither and back to the 'Change, but no sight of them, so I went after my business again, and, though late, was sent to by Sir W. Warren (who heard where I was) to intreat me to come dine with him, hearing that I lacked a dinner, at the Pope's Head; and there with Mr. Hinton, the goldsmith, and others, very merry; but, Lord ! to see how Dr. Hinton came in with a gallant or two from Court, and do so call "Cozen" Mr. Hinton, the goldsmith,[1] but I that know him to be a beggar and a knave, did make great sport in my mind at it. I hence, my mind full of content in my

---

[1] "Benjamin Hinton was a goldsmith keeping running cashes at the Flower de Luce in Lumbard Street in 1671." — PRICE'S *Handbook of London Bankers.* (M. B.)

day's worke, home by water to Greenwich, the river beginning to be very full of ice, so as I was a little frighted, but got home well, it being darke. So having no mind to do any business, went home to my lodging, and there got little Miss Tooker, and Mrs. Daniel, the daughter, and Sarah to my chamber to cards and sup with me, when in comes Mr. Pierce to me, who tells me how W. Howe has been examined on shipboard by my Lord Brouncker to-day, and others, and that he has charged him out of envy with sending goods under my Lord's seale and in my Lord Brouncker's name, thereby to get them safe passage, which, he tells me, is false, but that he did use my name to that purpose, and hath acknowledged it to my Lord Brouncker, but do also confess to me that one parcel he thinks he did use my Lord Brouncker's name, which do vexe me mightily that my name should be brought in question about such things, though I did not say much to him of my discontent till I have spoke with my Lord Brouncker about it. So he being gone, being to go to Oxford to-morrow, we to cards again late, and so broke up, I having great pleasure with my little girle, Miss Tooker.

19th. Up, and to the office, where all the morning. At noon by agreement comes Hatcham Pepys to dine with me. I thought to have had him to Sir J. Minnes to a good venison pasty with the rest of my fellows, being invited, but seeing much company I went away with him and had a good dinner at home. He did give me letters he hath wrote to my Lord and Moore about my Lord's money to get it paid to my cozen, which I will make good use of. I made mighty much of him, but a sorry dull fellow he is, fit for nothing that is ingenious, nor is there a bit of kindnesse or service to be had from him. So I shall neglect him if I could get but him satisfied about this money that I may be out of bonds for my Lord to him. To see that this fellow could desire me to helpe him to some employment, if it were but 100*l.* per ann : when he is not worth less than, I believe, 20,000*l.* He gone, I to Sir J. Minnes, and thence with my Lord Brouncker on board the Bezan to examine W. Howe again, who I find upon this tryall one of much more wit and ingenuity in his answers than ever I expected, he being very cunning and discreet and well spoken in them. I said little to him or concerning him ; but, Lord ! to see how he writes to me adays, and styles me " My Honour. " So much is a man subjected and dejected under afflictions as to flatter me in that manner on this occasion. Back with my Lord to Sir J. Minnes, where I left him and the rest of a great deale of company, and so I to my office, where late writing letters and then home to bed.

20th. Up, and was trimmed, but not time enough to save my Lord Brouncker's coach or Sir J. Minnes's, and so was fain to walk to Lambeth on foot, but it was a very fine frosty walke, and great pleasure in it, but troublesome getting over the River for ice. I to the Duke of Albemarle, whither my brethren were all come, but I was not too late. There we sat in discourse upon our Navy business an houre, and thence in my Lord Brouncker's coach alone, he walking before (while I staid awhile talking with Sir G. Downing about the Act, in which he is horrid troublesome) to the Old Exchange. Thence I took Sir Ellis Layton to Captain Cocke's, where my Lord Brouncker and Lady Williams dine, and we all mighty merry; but Sir Ellis Layton one of the best companions at a meale in the world. After dinner I to the Exchange to see whether my pretty semstress be come again or no, and I find she is, saluted her over her counter in the open Exchange above, and mightily joyed to see her, poor pretty woman! I must confess I think her a great beauty. After laying out a little money there for two pair of thread stockings, cost 8*s.*, I to Lumbard Streete to see some business to-night there at the goldsmith's, among others paying in 1,258*l.*, to Viner for my Lord Sandwich's use upon Cocke's account. I was called by my Lord Brouncker in his coach with his mistresse, and so home to Greenwich, and thence I to Mrs. Penington, and had a supper from the King's Head for her, and there mighty merry and free as I used to be with her, and at last, late, I did pray her to undress herself into her nightgowne, that I might see how to have her picture drawne carelessly (for she is mighty proud of that conceit), and I would walk without in the streete till she had done. So I did walk forth, and whether I made too many turns or no in the darke cold frosty night between the two walls up to the Parke gate I know not, but she was gone to bed when I came again to the house, upon pretence of leaving some papers there, which I did on purpose by her consent. So I away home, and was there sat up for to be spoken with my young Mrs. Daniel, to pray me to speake for her husband to be a Lieutenant. I had the opportunity here of kissing her again and again, and did answer that I would be very willing to do him any kindnesse, and so parted, and I to bed, exceedingly pleased in all my matters of money this month or two, it having pleased God to bless me with several opportunities of good sums, and that I have them in effect all very well paid, or in my power to have. But two things trouble me; one, the sicknesse is increased about 80 this weeke (though in my owne parish not one has died, though six the last weeke); the other, most of all, which is, that I have had so complexed an account for these last two months for variety of layings out upon Tangier, occasions and variety of gettings that I have not made even with myself these 3 or 4 months, which do trouble me mightily, finding that I shall hardly ever come to understand them again, as I used to do my accounts when I was at home.

21st. At the office all the morning. At noon all of us dined at Captain Cocke's at a good chine of beef, and other good meat; but, being all frost-bitten, was most of it unroast; but very merry, and a good dish of fowle we dressed ourselves. Mr. Evelyn there, in very good humour. All the afternoon till night pleasant, and then I took my leave of them and to the office, where I wrote my letters, and away home, my head full of business and some trouble for my letting my accounts go so far that I have made an oathe this night for the drinking no wine, &c., on such penalties till I have passed my accounts and cleared all. Coming home and going to bed, the boy tells me his sister Daniel has provided me a supper of little birds killed by her husband, and I made her sup with me, and after supper were alone a great while, and I had the pleasure of her lips, she being a pretty woman. She gone, I to bed. This day I was come to by Mrs. Burrows, of Westminster, Lieutenant Burrows (lately dead) his wife, a most pretty woman and my old acquaintance; I had a kiss or two of her, and a most modest woman she is.

22nd. Up betimes and to my Lord Brouncker to consider the late instructions sent us for the method of our signing bills hereafter and paying them. About this all the morning, and, it appearing necessary for the Controller to have another Clerke, I recommended Poynter to him, which he accepts, and I by that means rid of one that I fear would not have been fit for my turne, though he writes very well. At noon comes Mr. Hill to towne, and finds me out here, and brings Mr. Houbland.[1] So I was compelled to leave my Lord and his dinner and company, and with them to the Beare, and dined with them and their brothers, of which Hill had his and the other two of his, and

---

[1] Houblon. (M. B.)

mighty merry and very fine company they are, and I glad to see them. After dinner I forced to take leave of them by being called by Mr. Andrews, I having sent for him, and by a fine glosse did bring him to desire tallys for what orders I have to pay him and his company for Tangier victuals, and I by that means cleared to myself 210*l.* coming to me upon their two orders, which is also a noble addition to my late profits, which have been very considerable of late, but how great I know not till I come to cast up my accounts, which burdens my mind that it should be so backward, but I am resolved to settle to nothing till I have done it. He gone, I to my Lord Brouncker's, and there spent the evening by my desire in seeing his Lordship open to pieces and make up again his watch, thereby being taught what I never knew before; and it is a thing very well worth my having seen, and am mightily pleased and satisfied with it. So I sat talking with him till late at night, somewhat vexed at a snappish answer Madam Williams did give me to herself, upon my speaking a free word to her in mirthe, calling her a mad jade. She answered, we were not so well acquainted yet. But I was more at a letter from my Lord Duke of Albemarle to-day, pressing us to continue our meetings for all Christmas, which though every body intended not to have done, yet I am concluded in it, who intended nothing else. But I see it is necessary that I do make often visits to my Lord Duke, which nothing shall hinder after I have evened my accounts, and now the river is frozen I know not how to get to him.   Thence to my lodging, making up my Journall for 8 or 9 days, and so my mind being eased of it, I to supper and to bed.   The weather hath been frosty these eight or nine days, and so we hope for an abatement of the plague the next weeke, or else God have mercy upon us! for the plague will certainly continue the next year if it do not.

23rd. At my office all the morning and home to dinner, my head full of business, and there my wife finds me unexpectedly.   But I not being at leisure to stay or talk with her, she went down by coach to Woolwich, thinking to fetch Mrs. Barbara to carry her to London to keep her Christmas with. her, and I to the office.   This day one came to me with four great turkies, as a present from Mr. Deane, at Harwich, three of which my wife carried in the evening with her to London in her coach (Mrs. Barbara not being to be got so suddenly, but will come to her the next week).

24th (Sunday). Up betimes, to my Lord Duke of Albemarle by water, and after some talke with him about business of the office with great content, and so back again and to dinner, my landlady and her daughters with me, and had mince-pies, and very merry at a mischance her young son had in tearing of his new coate quite down the outside of his sleeve in the whole cloth, one of the strangest mishaps that ever I saw in my life.   Then to church, and placed myself in the Parson's pew under the pulpit, to hear Mrs. Chamberlain in the next pew sing, who is daughter to Sir James Bunce,[1] of whom I have heard much, and indeed she sings very finely, and from church met with Sir W. Warren and he and I walked together talking about his and my businesses, getting of money as fairly as we can, and, having set him part of his way home, I walked to my Lord Brouncker, whom I heard was at Alderman Hooker's, hoping to see and salute Mrs. Lethulier, whom I did see in passing, but no opportunity of beginning acquaintance, but a very noble lady she is, however the silly alderman got her. Here we sat talking a great while. Hence with my Lord Brouncker home and sat a little with him and so home to bed. Here I saw again my beauty Lethulier. Thence to my Lord Brouncker by invitation and dined there, and so home to look over and settle my papers, both of my accounts private, and those of Tangier, which I have let go so long that it were impossible for any soul, had I died, to understand them, or ever come to any good end in them. I hope God will never suffer me to come to that disorder again.

25th (Christmas-day). To church in the morning, and there saw a wedding in the church, which I have not seen many a day; and the young people so merry one with another, and strange to see what delight we married people have to see these poor fools decoyed into our condition, every man and woman gazing and smiling at them.

---

[1] He had married Mary, daughter of Thomas Gipps, or Gibbs, of London.

26th. Up, and to the office, where Sir J. Minnes and my Lord Brouncker and I met, to give our directions to the Commanders of all the ships in the river to bring in lists of their ships' companies, with entries, discharges, &c. all the last voyage, where young Seymour, among 20 that stood bare, stood with his hat on, a proud, saucy young man. Thence with them to Mr. Cuttle's, being invited, and dined nobly and neatly; with a very pretty house and a fine turret at top, with winding stairs and the finest prospect I know about all Greenwich, save the top of the hill, and yet in some respects better than that. Here I also saw some fine writing worke of Mr. Hoare, he one that I knew long ago, an acquaintance of Mr. Tomson's at Westminster, that is this man's clerk. It is the story of the several Archbishops of Canterbury, engrossed in vellum, to hang up in Canterbury Cathedrall in tables, in lieu of the old ones, which are almost worn out.

27th. By coach to London, there home to my wife, and angry about her desiring a mayde yet, before the plague is quite over. It seems Mercer is troubled that she hath not one under her, but I will not venture my family by increasing it before it be safe. Thence about many businesses and to the goldsmiths to examine the state of my matters there, and so with Sir W. Warren took boat, and it being darke and the thaw having broke the ice, but not carried it quite away, the boat did pass through so much of it all along, and that with the crackling and noise made me fearfull indeed. So I forced the watermen to land us on Redriffe side, and so walked together till Sir W. Warren and I parted near his house and thence I walked quite over the fields home by light of linke, one of my watermen carrying it, and I reading by the light of it, it being a very fine, clear, dry night. So to Captain Cocke's, and there sat and talked, especially with his Counsellor, about his prize goods, that has done him good turne, being of the company with Captain Fisher, his name Godderson ; here I supped and so home to bed, with great content that the plague is decreased to 152, the whole being but 330.

29th. Up betimes, and all day long within doors upon my accounts, publique and private, and find the ill effect of letting them go so long without evening, that no soul could have understood them but myself, and I with much ado. But, however, my regularity in all I did and spent do helpe me and I hope to find them well.   Late at them and to bed.

30th. All the afternoon to my accounts again and there find myself, to my great joy, a great deal worth above 4,000*l.* for which the Lord be praised ! and is principally occasioned by my getting 500*l.* of Cocke, for my profit in his bargains of prize goods, and from Mr. Gauden's making me a present of 500*l.* more, when I paid him 8,000*l.* for Tangier.

31st (Lord's day). All the morning in my chamber, writing fair the state of my Tangier accounts, and so dined at home. In the afternoon to the Duke of Albemarle and thence back again by water, and so to my chamber to finish the entry of my accounts and to think of the business I am next to do, which is the stating my thoughts and putting in order my collections about the business of pursers, to see where the fault of our present constitution relating to them lies and what to propose to mend it, and upon this late and with my head full of this business to bed. Thus ends this year, to my great joy, in this manner. I have raised my estate from 1,300*l.* in this year to 4,400*l.* I have got myself greater interest, I think, by my diligence, and my employments encreased by that of Treasurer for Tangier, and Surveyor of the Victualls. It is true we have gone through great melancholy because of the great plague, and I put to great charges by it, by keeping my family long at Woolwich, and myself and another part of my family, my clerks, at my charge at Greenwich, and a mayde at London; but I hope the King will give us some satisfaction for that. But now the plague is abated almost to nothing, and I intending to get to London as fast as I can. The Dutch war goes on very ill, by reason of lack of money; having none to hope for, all being put into disorder by a new Act that is made as an experiment to bring credit to the Exchequer, for goods and money to be advanced upon the credit of that Act. I have never lived so merrily (besides that I never got so much) as I have done this plague time, by my Lord Brouncker's and Captain Cocke's good company, and the acquaintance of Mrs. Knipp, Coleman and her husband, and

Mr. Laneare, and great store of dancings we have had at my cost (which I was willing to indulge myself and wife) at my lodgings. The great evil of this year, and the only one indeed, is the fall of my Lord of Sandwich, whose mistake about the prizes hath undone him, I believe, as to interest at Court; though sent (for a little palliating it) Embassador into Spayne, which he is now fitting himself for. But the Duke of Albemarle goes with the Prince to sea this next year, and my Lord is very meanly spoken of; and, indeed, his miscarriage about the prize goods is not to be excused, to suffer a company of rogues to go away with ten times as much as himself, and the blame of all to be deservedly laid upon him. My whole family hath been well all this while, and all my friends I know of, saving my aunt Bell, who is dead, and some children of my cozen Sarah's, of the plague. But many of such as I know very well, dead; yet, to our great joy, the town fills apace, and shops begin to be open again. Pray God continue the plague's decrease! for that keeps the Court away from the place of business, and so all goes to rack as to publick matters, they at this distance not thinking of it.

1665–66.

January 1st. Called up by five o'clock, by my order, by Mr. Tooker, who wrote, while I dictated to him, my business of the Pursers; and so, without eating or drinking, till three in the afternoon, and then, to my great content, finished it.[1]   So to dinner and then to copying it over till interrupted by Sir W. Warren's coming, of whom I always learne something or other, his discourse being very good and his brains also.

2nd. Up by candlelight again, and wrote the greatest part of my business fair and so to dinner, and made an end of my fair writing and to my Lord Brouncker's, and there find Sir J. Minnes and all his company, and Mr. Boreman and Mrs. Turner, but, above all, my dear Mrs. Knipp, with whom I sang, and in perfect pleasure I was to hear her sing, and especially her little Scotch song of " Barbary Allen ; "[2] and to make our mirthe the completer, Sir J. Minnes was in the highest pitche of mirthe, and his mimicall tricks, that ever I saw, and most excellent pleasant company he is, and the best mimique that ever I saw, and certainly would have made an excellent actor, and now would be an excellent teacher of actors.   Then, it being past night, against my will took leave, but

---

[1] This document is in the British Museum (Harleian MS., 6287), and is entitled, " A letter from Mr. Pepys, dated at Greenwich, 1 Jan. 1665-6, which he calls his New Year's Gift to his hon. friend, Sir Wm. Coventry, wherein he lays down a Method for securing his Majesty a husbandly execution of the Victualling part of the Naval Expence." It consists of nineteen closely written folio pages, and is a remarkable specimen of Pepys's business habits.

[2] Entitled, " Barbara Allen's cruelty, or the young man's tragedy." It begins —

> " In Scarlet towne where I was borne,
> There was a faire maid dwellin,
> Made every youth crye, Wel-awaye!
> Her name was Barbara Allen."

PERCY'S Reliques of English Poetry.

(M. B.)

before I came to my office, longing for more of her company, I returned and met them coming home in coaches, so I got into the coach where Mrs. Knipp was and (the coach being full) upon my knees, and sung and at last set her at her house and so good night.

3rd. Up, and all the morning till three in the afternoon examining and fitting up my Purser's paper and sent it away by an Expresse. Then comes my wife, and I set her to get supper ready against I go to the Duke of Albemarle and back again ; and at the Duke's with great joy I received the good news of the decrease of the plague this week to 70, and but 253 in all ; which is the least Bill hath been known these twenty years in the City. Though the want of people in London is it, that must make it so low below the ordinary number for Bills. So home, and find all my good company I had bespoke, as Coleman and his wife, and Laneare, Knipp and her surly husband ; and good musique we had, and, among other things, Mrs. Coleman sang my words I set of " Beauty retire," and I think it is a good song, and they praise it mightily. Then to dancing and supper, and mighty merry till Mr. Rolt came in, whose pain of the tooth-ake made him no company, and spoilt ours ; so he away, and then my wife's teeth fell of akeing, and she to bed. So forced to break up all with a good song, and so to bed.

4th. Up, and to the office where my Lord Brouncker and I, against Sir W. Batten and Sir J. Minnes and the whole table, for Sir W. Warren in the business of his mast contract, and overcame them and got them to do what I had a mind to. So home to dinner and then my wife home to London by water and I to the office till 8 at night, and so to my Lord Brouncker, thinking to have been merry, having appointed a meeting for Sir J. Minnes and his company and Mrs. Knipp again, but whatever hindered I know not, but no company came, which vexed me because it disappointed me of the glut of mirthe I hoped for. However, good discourse with my Lord. So home and to bed.

5th. I with my Lord Brouncker and Mrs. Williams by coach with four horses to London, to my Lord's house [1] in Covent-Garden. But, Lord! what staring to see a nobleman's coach come to town. And porters every where bow to us; and such begging of beggars! And a delightful thing it is to see the towne full of people again; and shops begin to open, though in many places seven or eight together, and more, all shut; but yet the towne is full, compared with what it used to be. I mean the City end; for Covent-Garden and Westminster are yet very empty of people, no Court nor gentry being there. Set Mrs. Williams down at my Lord's house and he and I to Sir G. Carteret. So my Lord and he and I much talke about the Act, what credit we find upon it, but no private talke between him and I. So I to the 'Change, and

---

[1] In the Piazza, and one of the largest houses in what was then the most fashionable part of London.

to Sir G. Smith's and there dined nobly. He tells me how my Lord Bellairs complains for want of money and of him and me therein, but I value it not, for I know I do all that can be done. I away to Cornhill to expect my Lord Brouncker's coming back again, and by and by comes my Lord, and did take me up and so to Greenwich, and after sitting with them awhile at their house, home, thinking to get Mrs. Knipp, but could not, she being busy with company, but sent me a pleasant letter, writing herself "Barbary Allen." I went therefore to Mr. Boreman's for pastime, and there staid an houre or two talking with him, and reading a discourse about the River of Thames, the reason of its being choked up in several places with shelfes; which is plain is, by the encroachments made upon the River, and running out of causeways into the River at every wood-wharfe; which was not heretofore when Westminster Hall and White Hall were built, and Redriffe Church, which now are sometimes overflown with water. I had great satisfaction herein. So home and to my papers for lacke of company, but by and by comes little Miss Tooker and sat and supped with me and I kept her very late talking and making her comb my head.

6th. Up betimes and by water to the Cockpitt, there met Sir G. Carteret and, after discourse with the Duke, all together, and there saw a letter wherein Sir W. Coventry did take notice to the Duke with a commendation of my paper about Pursers, I to walke in the Parke with the Vice Chamberlain, and received

his advice about my deportment about the advancing
the credit of the Act; giving me caution to see that
we do not misguide the King by making them believe
greater matters from it than will be found. But I see
that this arises from his great trouble to see the Act
succeed, and to hear my name so much used and my
letters shown at Court about goods served us in upon
the credit of it. But I do make him believe that I do
it with all respect to him and on his behalfe too, as
indeed I do, as well as my owne, that it may not be
said that he or I do not assist therein. He tells me
that my Lord Sandwich do proceed on his journey
with the greatest kindnesse that can be imagined from
the King and Chancellor, which was joyfull newes to
me. Thence with my Lord Brouncker to Greenwich
by water to a great dinner and much company; Mr.
Cuttle and his lady and others and I went, hoping to
get Mrs. Knipp to us, having wrote a letter to her
in the morning, calling myself " Dapper Dicky," [1] in
answer to her's of " Barbary Allen," but could not,
and am told by the boy that carried my letter, that he
found her crying; but I fear she lives a sad life with
that ill-natured fellow her husband : so we had a great,
but I a melancholy dinner, having not her there, as I
hoped. After dinner to cards, and then comes notice
that my wife is come unexpectedly to me to towne.
So I to her. It is only to see what I do, and why I
come not home; and she is in the right that I would

---

[1] A song called " Dapper Dicky " is in the British Museum; it begins,
" In a barren tree." It was printed in 1710.

have a little more of Mrs. Knipp's company before I go away. My wife to fetch away my things from Woolwich, and I back to cards and after cards to choose King and Queene, and a good cake there was, but no marks found; but I privately found the clove, the mark of the knave, and privately put it into Captain Cocke's piece, which made some mirthe, because of his lately being knowne by his buying of clove and mace of the East India prizes. At night home to my lodging, where I find my wife returned with my things. It being Twelfth Night, they had got the fiddler and mighty merry they were; and I above came not to them, but when I had done my business among my papers went to bed, leaving them dancing, and choosing King and Queene.

7th (Lord's day). Up, and being trimmed I was invited by Captain Cocke, so I left my wife, having a mind to some discourse with him. He tells me of new difficulties about his goods which troubles me and I fear they will be great. He tells me too what I hear everywhere how the towne talks of my Lord Craven being to come into Sir G. Carteret's place; but sure it cannot be true. But I do fear those two families, his and my Lord Sandwich's, are quite broken. And I must now stand upon my own legs. Thence to my lodging, and considering how I am hindered by company there to do anything among my papers, I did resolve to go away to-day rather than stay to no purpose till to-morrow and so got all my things packed up and so took leave of my landlady and daughters, having paid dear for what time I have spent there, but yet having been quiett and my health, I am very well contented therewith. So with my wife and Mercer took boat and away home; but in the evening, before I went, comes Mrs. Knipp, just to speake with me privately, to excuse her not coming to me yesterday, complaining how like a devil her husband treats her, but will be with us in towne a weeke hence, and so I kissed her and parted. Being come home, my wife and I to look over our house and consider of laying out a little money to hang our bedchamber better than it is, and so resolved to go and buy something to-morrow, and so after supper with great joy in my heart for my coming once again hither to bed.

8th. Up, and my wife and I by coach to Bennett's, in Paternoster Row, few shops there being yet open, and there bought velvett for a coate, and camelott for a cloake for myself; and thence to a place to look over some fine counterfeit damasks to hang my wife's closett, and pitched upon one, and so by coach home again to dinner and all the afternoon look over my papers at home and so after supper considering the uselessnesse of laying out so much money upon my wife's closett, but only the chamber, to bed.

9th. To the office, where we met first since the plague, which God preserve us in! At noon home to dinner, where uncle Thomas with me, and in comes Pierce lately come from Oxford. He tells me how a great difference hath been between the Duke and Duchesse, he suspecting her to be naught with Mr.

Sidney. But some way or other the matter is made up; but he was banished the Court, and the Duke for many days did not speak to the Duchesse at all. He tells me that my Lord Sandwich is lost there at Court, though the King is particularly his friend. But people do speak every where slightly of him; which is a sad story to me, but I hope it may be better again. And that Sir G. Carteret is neglected, and hath great enemies at work against him. That matters must needs go bad, while all the town, and every boy in the streete, openly cries, "The King cannot go away till my Lady Castlemaine be ready to come along with him;" she being lately put to bed.[1] And that he visits her and Mrs. Stewart every morning before he eats his breakfast. All this put together makes me very sad, but yet I hope I shall do pretty well among them for all this by my not meddling with either of their matters. Then comes Mr. Gauden and he and I talked together a good while about his business, and to my great joy got him to declare that of the 500*l.* he did give me the other day, none of it was for my Treasureship for Tangier (I first telling him how matters stand between Povy and I, that he was to have half of whatever was coming to me by that office), and that he will gratify me at 2 per cent. for that when he next receives any money. He gone I with a glad heart to the office to write my letters and so home to supper and bed, my

---

[1] 28 Dec., 1665. In a fellow's chamber in Merton College, Oxford, of George Fitzroy, afterwards Duke of Northumberland.

wife mighty full of her worke she has to-day in furnishing her bedchamber.

10th. Up, and by coach to Sir G. Downing, where Mr. Gauden met me by agreement to talke upon the Act. I do find Sir G. Downing to be a mighty talker, more than is true, which I now know to be so, and suspected it before, but for all that I have good grounds to think it will succeed for goods and in time for money too, but not presently. Having done with him, I to my Lord Brouncker's house in Covent-Garden, and, among other things, it was to acquaint him with my paper of Pursers, and read it to him, and had his good liking of it. Shewed him Mr. Coventry's sense of it, which he sent me last post much to my satisfaction. Thence to the 'Change, and there hear to our grief how the plague is encreased this week from seventy to eighty-nine. We have also great fear of our Hambrough fleete, of their meeting the Dutch; as also have certain newes, that by storms Sir Jer. Smith's[1] fleet is scattered, and three of them come without masts back to Plymouth, which is another very exceeding great disappointment, and if the victualling ships are miscarried will tend to the losse of the garrison of Tangier. Thence home, in my way had the opportunity I longed for, of seeing and saluting Mrs, Stokes, my little goldsmith's wife in Paternoster Row. and there bespoke a silver chafing-dish for warming

---

[1] Admiral Sir Jeremy Smith commanded a fleet in the Straights at this time, and another in the Channel in 1668.

plates, and so home to dinner, found my wife busy about making her hangings for her chamber with the upholster. So I to the office and anon to the Duke of Albemarle, by coach at night. Here I saw Sir W. Coventry's kind letter to him concerning my paper,[1] and among others of his letters, which I saw all, and that is a strange thing, that whatever is writ to this Duke of Albemarle, all the world may see; for this very night he did give me Mr. Coventry's letter to read, soon as it came to his hand, before he had read it himself, and bid me take out of it what concerned the Navy, and many things there was in it, which I should not have thought fit for him to have let any body so suddenly see; but, among other things, find him profess himself to the Duke a friend into the inquiring further into the business of prizes, and advises that it may be publique, for the righting the King, and satisfying the people and getting the blame to be rightly laid where it should be, which strikes very hard upon my Lord Sandwich, and troubles me to read it. Besides, which vexes me more, I heard the damned Duchesse again say to twenty gentlemen publiquely in the room, that she would have Montagu sent once more to sea, before he goes his embassy, that we may see whether he will make amends for his cowardice, and repeated the answer she did give the other day in my hearing to Sir G. Downing, wishing her Lord had been a coward, for then perhaps he might have been

---

[1] Pepys's request to be Surveyor-General.

made an Embassador, and not been sent now to sea.
But one good thing she said, she cried mightily out
against the having of gentlemen Captains with feathers
and ribbands, and wished the King would send her
husband to sea with the old plain sea Captains, that
he served with formerly, that would make their ships
swim with blood, though they could not make legs [1]
as Captains now-a-days can. It grieved me to see
how slightly the Duke do every thing in the world,
and how the King and every body suffers whatever he
will to be done in the Navy, though never so much
against reason, as in the business of recalling tickets,
which will be done notwithstanding all the arguments
against it. So back again to my office, and there to
business and to bed.

11th. To the Custome House to the Farmers, there
with a letter of Sir G. Carteret's for 3,000*l.*, which they
agreed to be paid me. So away back again to the office,
and at noon to dinner all of us by invitation to Sir W.
Pen's, and much other company. Among others, Lieutenant of the Tower, and Broome, his poet, and Dr.
Whistler, and his (Sir W. Pen's) son-in-law Lowther,[2]

---

[1] Make bows, play the courtier. In former editions, "make leagues."
"He that cannot *make a leg*, put off cap, kiss his hand, and say nothing,
has neither leg, hands, lip, nor cap; and, indeed, such a fellow, to say pre-
cisely, were not for the court."—SHAKESPEARE, *All's Well that Ends
Well*, act ii. sc. 2. (M. B.)

[2] Anthony Lowther, of Marske, in Yorkshire, who shortly afterwards
married Margaret Penn, was M. P. for Appleby in 1678 and 1679. He was
buried at Walthamstow in 1692. William, his son by Margaret Penn, created
a Baronet in 1697, married the heir of Thomas Preston, of Holker, Lanca-
shire. The second Baronet married Elizabeth, daughter of William, Duke

servant [1] to Mrs. Margaret Pen, and Sir Edward Spragg, a merry man, that sang a pleasant song pleasantly. Rose from dinner before half dined, and with Mr. Mountney of the Custome House to the East India House, and there delivered to him tallys for 3,000*l.*, and received a note for the money on Sir R. Viner. So ended the matter, and back to my company, where staid a little, and thence away with Lord Brouncker for discourse sake, and he and I to Gresham College to have seen Mr. Hooke and a new invented chariott of Dr. Wilkins, but met with nobody at home. So to Dr. Wilkins, where I never was before, and very kindly received and met with Dr. Merritt, and fine discourse among them to my great joy, so sober and so ingenious. He is now upon finishing his discourse of a universal character. So away and I home to my office about my letters, and so home to supper and to bed.

12th. By coach to the Duke of Albemarle, where Sir W. Batten and I only met. Troubled at my heart to see how things are ordered there without consideration or understanding. Thence back by coach and

---

of Devonshire, and their son, dying unmarried, bequeathed Holker and other estates to his cousin, Lord George Cavendish, whence the Earl of Burlington enjoys them.

[1] Lover.

> " *Sil.* Too low a mistress for so high a *servant.*
> *Pro.* Not so, sweet lady; but too mean a *servant*
>   To have a look of such a worthy mistress."
>   SHAKESPEARE, *Two Gentlemen of Verona*, act ii. sc. 4.
>   (M. B.)

called at Wotton's, my shoemaker, lately come to towne, and bespoke shoes, as also got him to find me a taylor to make me some clothes, my owne being not yet in towne. So he helped me to a pretty man, one Mr. Penny, against St. Dunstan's Church. Thence to the 'Change and there met Mr. Moore, newly come to towne, and took him home to dinner with me and after dinner to talke, and he and I do conclude my Lord's case to be very bad and may be worse, if he do not get a pardon for his doings about the prizes and his business at Bergen, and other things done by him at sea, before he goes for Spayne. I do use all the art I can to get him to get my Lord to pay my cozen Pepys, for it is a great burden to my mind my being bound for my Lord 1,000*l.* to him. Having done discourse with him and directed him to go with my advice to my Lord expresse to-morrow to get his pardon perfected before his going, because of what I read the other night in Sir W. Coventry's letters, I to the office, and there had an extraordinary meeting of Sir J. Minnes, Sir W. Batten, and Sir W. Pen, and my Lord Brouncker and I to hear my paper read about pursers, which they did all of them with great good will and great approbation of my method and pains in all, only Sir W. Pen, who must except against every thing and remedy nothing, did except against my proposal for some reasons, which I could not understand, I confess, nor my Lord Brouncker neither, but he did detect indeed a failure or two of mine in my report about the ill condition of the present pursers, which

I did magnify in one or two little things, to which, I think, he did with reason except, but at last with all respect did declare the best thing he ever heard of this kind, but when Sir W. Batten did say, Let us that do know the practical part of the Victualling meet Sir J. Minnes, Sir W. Pen and I and see what we can do to mend all, he was so far from offering or furthering it, that he declined it and said, he must be out of towne. So as I ever knew him never did in his life ever attempt to mend any thing, but suffer all things to go on in the way they are, though never so bad, rather than improve his experience to the King's advantage. So we broke up, however they promising to meet to offer some thing in it of their opinions, and so we rose, and I and my Lord Brouncker by coach a little way for discourse sake, till our coach broke, and tumbled me over him quite down the side of the coach, falling on the ground about the stockes, but up again, and thinking it fit for my honour to have some thing reported in writing to the Duke in favour of my pains in this, lest it should be thought to be rejected as frivolous, I did move it to my Lord, and he will see it done to-morrow. So we parted, and I to the office and thence home to my poor wife, who works all day at home like a horse, at the making of her hangings for our chamber and the bed. So to supper and to bed.

13th. At the office all the morning, where my Lord Brouncker moved to have something wrote in my matter as I desired him last night, and it was ordered and will be done next sitting. Home with his Lordship to Mrs. Williams's, in Covent-Garden, to dinner (the first time I ever was there), and there met Captain Cocke; and pretty merry, though not perfectly so, because of the fear that there is of a great encrease again of the plague this week. And again my Lord Brouncker do tell us, that he hath it from Sir John Baber,[1] who is related to my Lord Craven, that my Lord Craven do look after Sir G. Carteret's place, and do reckon himself sure of it. After dinner Cocke and I together by coach to the Exchange, in our way talking of our matters, and do conclude that every thing must breake in pieces, while no better counsels govern matters than there seem to do, and that it will become him and I and all men to get their reckonings even, as soon as they can, and expect all to breake. Besides, if the plague continues among us another yeare, the Lord knows what will become of us. I set him down at the 'Change, and I home to my office. My head full of cares, but pleased with my wife's minding her worke so well, and busying herself about her house, and I trust in God if I can but clear myself of my Lord Sandwich's bond, I shall do pretty well, come what will come.

14th (Lord's day). Long in bed, till raised by my new taylor, Mr. Penny, who comes and brings me my new velvet coat, very handsome, but plain. At noon eat the second of the two cygnets Mr. Shepley

---

[1] Physician in Ordinary to the King.

sent us for a new-year's gift. This afternoon, after sermon, comes my dear fair beauty of the Exchange, Mrs. Batelier, brought by her sister, an acquaintance of Mercer's, to see my wife. I saluted her with as much pleasure as I had done any a great while. We sat and talked together an houre, with infinite pleasure to me, and so the fair creature went away, and proves one of the modestest women, and pretty, that ever I saw in my life, and my wife judges her so too.

15th. Busy all the morning in my chamber in my old cloth suit, while my usuall one is to my taylors to mend, which I had at noon again, and an answer to a letter I had sent this morning to Mrs. Pierce to go along with my wife and I down to Greenwich to-night upon an invitation to Mr. Boreman's to be merry to dance and sing with Mrs. Knipp. Being dressed, and having dined, I took coach and to Mrs. Pierce, to her new house in Covent-Garden, a very fine place and fine house. Took her thence home to my house, and so by water to Boreman's by night, where the greatest disappointment that ever I saw in my life, much company, a good supper provided, and all come with expectation of excesse of mirthe, but all blank through the waywardnesse of Mrs. Knipp, who, though she had appointed the night, could not be got to come. Not so much as her husband could get her to come; but, which was a pleasant thing in my anger, I asking him, while we were in expectation what answer one of our many messengers would bring, what he thought, whether she would come or no, he answered that, for his part, he could not so much as thinke. By and by we all to supper, which the silly master of the feast commended, but, what with my being out of humour, and the badnesse of the meate dressed, I did never eat a worse supper in my life. At last, very late, and supper done, she came undressed, but it brought me no mirthe at all; only, after all being done, without singing, or very little, and no dancing, Pierce and I to bed together, and he and I very merry to find how little and thin clothes they give us to cover us, so that we were fain to lie in our stockings and drawers, and lay all our coates and clothes upon the bed. So to sleep.

16th. Up, and leaving the women in bed together (a pretty black and white) I to London to the office, and there forgot, through business, to bespeake any dinner for my wife and Mrs. Pierce. However, by noon they came, and a dinner we had, and Kate Joyce comes to see us, with whom very merry. After dinner she and I up to my chamber, who told me her business was chiefly for my advice about her husband's leaving off his trade, which though I wish enough, yet I did advise against, for he is a man will not know how to live idle, and employment he is fit for none. Hence anon carried her and Mrs. Pierce home, and so to the Duke of Albemarle, and mighty kind he to me still. So home late at my letters, and so to bed, being mightily troubled at the newes of the plague's being encreased, and was much the saddest news that the plague hath brought me from the beginning of it; because of the lateness of the year, and the fear, we may with reason have, of its continuing with us the next summer. The total being now 375, and the plague 158.

17th. Busy all the morning, settling things against my going out of towne this night. After dinner, late took horse, having sent for Lechmere to go with me, and so he and I rode to Dagenhams in the dark. It was my Lord Crew's desire that I should come, and chiefly to discourse with me of my Lord Sandwich's matters ; and therein to persuade, what I had done already, that my Lord should sue out a pardon for his business of the prizes, as also for Bergen, and all he hath done this year past, before he begins his Embassy to Spayne. For it is to be feared that the Parliament will fly out against him and particular men, the next Session. He is glad also that my Lord is clear of his sea-imployment, though sorry as I am, only in the manner of its bringing about. By and by to supper, my Lady very kind. After supper up to wait on my Lady Crew, who is the same weake silly lady as ever, asking such saintly questions. Down to my Lord again and sat talking an houre or two, and anon to prayers the whole family, and then all to bed, I handsomely used, lying in the chamber Mr. Carteret formerly did, but sat up an houre talking sillily with Mr. Carteret and Mr. Marre, and so to bed.

18th. Up before day and thence rode to London before office time, where I met a note at the doore to invite me to supper to Mrs. Pierce's because of Mrs. Knipp, who is in towne and at her house. To the office, where, among other things, vexed with Major Norwood's coming, who takes it ill my not paying a bill of Exchange of his, but I have good reason for it, and so the less trouble, but yet troubled, so as at noon being carried by my Lord Brouncker to Captain Cocke's to dinner, where Mrs. Williams was, and Mrs. Knipp, I was not heartily merry, though a glasse of wine did a little cheer me. After dinner to the office. Anon comes to me thither my Lord Brouncker, Mrs. Williams, and Knipp. I brought down my wife in her night-gowne, she not being indeed very well, to the office to them and there by and by they parted all and my wife and I anon and Mercer, by coach, to Pierce's; where mighty merry, and sing and dance with great pleasure; and I danced, who never did in company in my life. And had a pretty supper, and spent till two in the morning, but got home well by coach, though as dark as pitch, and so to bed.

19th. It is a remarkable thing how infinitely naked all that end of the towne, Covent-Garden, is at this day of people; while the City is almost as full again of people as ever it was. To the 'Change and so home to dinner and the office, whither anon comes Sir H. Cholmley to me, and he and I to my house, there to settle his accounts with me, and so with great pleasure we agreed and great friends become, I think, and he presented me upon the foot of our accounts for this year's service for him 100*l.*, whereof Povy must have half.

20th. To the office, where upon Mr. Kinaston's coming to me about some business of Collonell Norwood's, I sent my boy home for some papers, where, he staying longer than I would have him, and being vexed at the business and to be kept from my fellows in the office longer than was fit, I became angry, and boxed my boy when he came, that I do hurt my thumb so much, that I was not able to stir all the day after, and in great pain.

21st (Lord's day). Lay almost till noon merrily and with pleasure talking with my wife in bed. Then up looking about my house, and the roome which my wife is dressing up, having new hung our bedchamber with blue, very handsome. After dinner to my Tangier accounts and there stated them against to-morrow very distinctly for the Lords to see who meet to-morrow, and so to supper and to bed.

22nd. Down the river to Greenwich to the office to fetch away some papers and thence to Deptford, where by agreement my Lord Brouncker was to come, but staid almost till noon, after I had spent an houre with W. Howe talking of my Lord Sandwich's matters and his folly in minding his pleasures too much now-a-days, and permitting himself to be governed by Cuttance to the displeasing of all the Commanders almost of the fleete, and thence we may conceive indeed the rise of all my Lord's misfortunes of late. At noon my Lord Brouncker did come, but left the keys of the chests we should open, at Sir G. Carteret's lodgings, of my Lord Sandwich's, wherein Howe's supposed jewells are ;[1] so we could not, according to my Lord Arlington's order, see them to-day; but we parted, resolving to meet here at night: my Lord Brouncker being going with Dr. Wilkins, Mr. Hooke,[2] and others,[3] to Collonell Blunt's, to consider again of the business of chariots, and to try their new invention. Which I saw here my Lord Brouncker ride in; where the coachman sits astride upon a pole over the horse, but do not touch the horse, which is a pretty odde thing; but it seems it is most easy for the horse, and, as they say, for the man also. Thence I with speede by water home and eat a bit, and took my accounts and to the Duke of Albemarle, where for all I feared of Norwood he was very civill, and Sir Thomas Ingram beyond expectation, I giving them all content and I thereby settled mightily in my mind, for I was weary of the employment, and had had thoughts of giving it over. I did also give a good stop in a business of Mr. Houblon, about getting a ship of his to go to Tangier, which during this strict embargo is a great matter, and I shall have a good reward for it, I hope. Thence by water in the darke down to Deptford, and there find my Lord Brouncker come and gone, having staid long for me. I back presently to the Crowne taverne behind the

---

[1] The jewels were stolen from the Dutch Vice-Admiral. See Nov. 16, 1665, *ante.*

[2] Dr. Robert Hooke, before mentioned, Professor of Geometry at Gresham College, and Curator of the Experiments to the Royal Society, of which he was one of the earliest and most distinguished members. Ob. 1678.

[3] See Feb. 15, 1664-5.

Exchange by appointment, and there met the first meeting of Gresham College since the plague. Dr. Goddard did fill us with talke, in defence of his and his fellow physicians going out of towne in the plague-time; saying that their particular patients were most gone out of towne, and they left at liberty; and a great deal more, &c. But what, among other fine discourse pleased me most, was Sir G. Ent [1] about Respiration; that it is not to this day known, or concluded on among physicians, nor to be done either, how the action is managed by nature, or for what use it is.

23rd. Good newes beyond all expectation of the decrease of the plague, being now but 79, and the whole but 272. So home with comfort to bed. A most furious storme all night and morning.

24th. By agreement my Lord Brouncker called me up, and though it was a very foule, windy, and rainy morning, yet down to the waterside we went, but no boat could go, the storme continued so. So my Lord to stay till fairer weather carried me into the Tower to Mr. Hore's and there we staid talking an houre, but at last we found no boat yet could go, so we to the office, where we met upon an occasion extraordinary of examining abuses of our clerks in taking money for examining of tickets, but nothing done in it. Thence my Lord and I, the weather being a little fairer, by water to Deptford to Sir G. Carteret's house,

---

[1] Sir George Ent, F.R.S., President of the College of Physicians.

where W. Howe met us, and there we opened the chests, and saw the poor sorry rubys which have caused all this ado to the undoing of W. Howe; though I am not much sorry for it, because of his pride and ill nature. About 200 of these very small stones, and a cod of muske (which it is strange I was not able to smell) is all we could find; so locked them up again, and my Lord and I, the wind being again very furious, so as we durst not go by water, walked to London quite round the bridge, no boat being able to stirre; and, Lord! what a dirty walk we had, and so strong the wind, that in the fields we many times could not carry our bodies against it, but were driven backwards. We went through Horslydowne, where I never was since a little boy, that I went to enquire after my father, whom we did give over for lost coming from Holland.[1] It was dangerous to walk the streets, the bricks and tiles falling from the houses that the whole streets were covered with them; and whole chimneys, nay, whole houses in two or three places, blowed down. But, above all, the pales on London-bridge on both sides were blown away, so that we were fain to stoop very low for fear of blow-

---

[1] From the Domestic State Papers in the Public Record Office, London. Page 327, Entry Book No. 105 of the Protector Oliver's Council of State.

Ordered by the Council, Thursday, 7th August, 1656," That passes be graunted to goe beyond ye Seas to ye p'sons following, vizt To John Pepys and his man wth necessaryes for Holland, being on the desire of Mr Samll Pepys."

Probably this was a later journey of Pepys' father to Holland, as Pepys says here he was a little boy then. (M. B.)

ing off of the bridge. We could see no boats in the Thames afloat, but what were broke loose, and carried through the bridge, it being ebbing water. And the greatest sight of all was, among other parcels of ships driven here and there in clusters together, one was quite overset and lay with her masts all along in the water, and keel above water. So I walked home, my Lord away to his house and I to dinner, Mr. Creed being come to towne and to dine with me. After dinner he and I to our accounts and very troublesome he is and with tricks which I found plainly and was vexed at; while we were together comes Sir G. Downing with Collonell Norwood, Rumball, and War-rupp to visit me. I made them drink good wine and discoursed above alone a good while with Sir G. Downing, who is very troublesome, and then with Collonell Norwood, who has a great mind to have me concerned with him in everything; which I like, but am shy of adventuring too much but will thinke of it. They gone, Creed and I to finish the settling his accounts. Thence to the office, where the Houblons and we discoursed upon a rubb which we have for one of the ships I hoped to have got to go out to Tangier for them. They being gone, I to my office-business late, and then home to supper and even sacke for lacke of a little wine, which I was forced to drink against my oathe, but without pleasure.

25th. To the Duke of Albemarle and Kate Joyce's and her husband, with whom I talked a great deale about Pall's business, and told them what portion I would give her, and they do mightily like of it and will proceed further in speaking with Harman, who has already been spoke to about it, as from them only, and he is mighty glad of it, but doubts it may be an offence to me, if I should know of it, so thinks that it do come only from Joyce, which I like the better. It is now certain that the King of France hath publickly declared war against us, and God knows how little fit we are for it. At night comes Sir W. Warren, and he and I into the garden, and talked over all our businesses. He gives me good advice not to embarke into trade (as I have had it in my thoughts about Collonell Norwood) so as to be seen to mind it, for it will do me hurte, and draw my mind off from my business and embroile my estate too soon. So to the office business, and I find him as cunning a man in all points as ever I met with in my life and mighty merry we were in the discourse of our owne trickes. So about 10 at night I home and staid with him there settling my Tangier-Boates business and talking and laughing at the folly of some of our neighbours of this office till two in the morning and so to bed.

26th. Up, and pleased mightily with what my poor wife hath been doing these eight or ten days with her owne hands, like a drudge in fitting the new hangings of our bed-chamber of blue, and putting the old red ones into my dressing-room, and so by coach to White Hall, where I had just now notice that Sir G. Carteret is come to towne. He seems pleased, but I perceive he is heartily troubled at the Act, and the report of his losing his place, and more at my not writing to him to the prejudice of the Act. But I carry all fair to him and he to me. He bemoans the Kingdom as in a sad state, and with too much reason I doubt, having so many enemys about us and no friends abroad, nor money nor love at home. Hence to the Duke of Albemarle, and there a meeting with all the officers of the Navy, where, Lord! to see how the Duke of Albemarle flatters himself with false hopes of money and victuals and all without reason. Then comes the Committee of Tangier to sit, and I there carry all before me very well. Thence with Sir J. Bankes and Mr. Gauden to the 'Change, they both very wise men. After 'Change and agreeing with Houblon about our ships, D. Gauden and I to the Pope's Head and there dined and little Chaplin (who a rich man grown). He gone after dinner, D. Gauden and I to talke of the Victualling of the Navy in what posture it is, which is very sad also for want of money. Thence home to my chamber by oathe to finish my Journall. Here Mr. Hewer came to me with 320*l.* from Sir W. Warren, whereof 220*l.* is got clearly by a late business of insurance of the Gottenburg ships, and the other 100*l.* which was due and he had promised me before to give me to my very extraordinary joy, for which I ought and do bless God and so to my office, where late and so to bed.

27th. To the office, where all the morning. At noon after a bit of dinner back to the office and there fitting myself in all points to give an account to the

Duke and Mr. Coventry in all things till three o'clock in the morning, and so to bed.

28th. And up again about six (Lord's day) and being dressed in my velvett coate and plain cravatte took a Hackney coach provided ready for me by eight o'clock and so to my Lord Brouncker's with all my papers, and there took his coach with four horses and away toward Hampton Court, having a great deale of good discourse with him, and then of getting Mr. Evelyn or Sir Robert Murray into the Navy in the room of Sir Thomas Harvey. At Brainford I light, and went into an Inne doore that stood open, but saw no people, only after I was in the house, heard a great dogg barke, and so was afeard how I should get safe back again and therefore drew my sword and scabbard out of my belt to have ready in my hand but did not need to use it, but got safe into the coach again, but lost my belt by the shift, not missing it till I came to Hampton Court. At the Wicke found Sir J. Minnes and Sir W. Batten at a lodging provided for us by our messenger, and there a good dinner ready. After dinner took coach and to Court, where we find the King, and Duke, and Lords, all in council; so we walked up and down : there being none of the ladies come, and so much the more business I hope will be done. The Council being up, out comes the King, and I kissed his hand, and he grasped me very kindly by the hand. The Duke also, I kissed his, and he mighty kind, and Sir W. Coventry. I found my Lord Sandwich there, poor man ! I see with a melancholy face, and suffers his beard to grow on his upper lip more than usual. I took him a little aside to know when I should wait on him, and where : he told me, and that it would be best to meet at his lodgings, without being seen to walk together. Which I liked very well; and, Lord! to see in what difficulty I stand, that I dare not walk with Sir W. Coventry, for fear my Lord or Sir G. Carteret should see me; nor with either of them, for fear Sir W. Coventry should. I went down into one of the Courts, and there met the King and Duke; and the Duke called me to him. And the King came to me of himself, and told me, "Mr. Pepys," says he, "I do give you thanks for your good service all this year, and I assure you I am very sensible of it." And the Duke of York did tell me with pleasure, that he had read over my discourse about pursers, and would have it ordered in my way, and so fell from one discourse to another. I walked with them quite out of the Court into the fields, and then back and to my Lord Sandwich's chamber, where I find him very melancholy and not well satis-fied, I perceive, with my carriage to Sir G. Carteret, but I did satisfy him and made him confess to me, that I have a very hard game to play; and he told me that he was sorry to see it, and the inconveniences which likely may fall upon me with him; but, for all that, I am not much afeard, if I can but keepe out of harm's way in not being found too much concerned in my Lord's or Sir G. Carteret's matters, and that I will not be if I can helpe it. He hath got over his business of the prizes, so far as to have a privy seale passed for all that was in his distribution to the officers, which I am heartily glad of; and, for the rest, he must be answerable for what he is proved to have. But for his pardon for anything else, he thinks it not seasonable to aske it, and not usefull to him; because that will not stop a Parliament's mouth, and for the King, he is sure enough of him. I did aske him whether he was sure of the interest and friendship of any great Ministers of State and he told me, yes. As we were going further, in comes my Lord Mandeville, so we were forced to breake off and I away, and we took boat, and by water to Kingston, and so to our lodgings, where a good supper and merry, only I sleepy, and therefore after supper I slunk away from the rest to bed, and lay very well and slept soundly, my mind being in a great delirium between joy for what the King and Duke have said to me and Sir W. Coventry, and trouble for my Lord Sandwich's concernments, and how hard it will be for me to preserve myself from falling hereof.

29th. Up, and to Court by coach, where to council before the Duke of York, the Duke of Albemarle with us, and after Sir W. Coventry had gone over his notes that he had provided with the Duke of Albemarle, I went over all mine with good successe, only I fear I did once offend the Duke of Albemarle, but I was much joyed to find the Duke of York so much contending for my discourse about the pursers against Sir W. Pen, who opposes it like a foole; my Lord Sand-

wich came in in the middle of the business, and, poor
man, very melancholy, methought, and said little at
all, or to the business, and sat at the lower end, just
as he came, no roome being made for him, only I did
give him my stoole, and another was reached me.
After council done, I walked to and again up and
down the house, discoursing with this and that man.
Among others tooke occasion to thanke the Duke of
York for his good opinion in general of my service,
and particularly his favour in conferring on me the
Victualling business. He told me that he knew nobody so fit as I for it, and next, he was very glad to
find that to give me for my encouragement, speaking
very kindly of me. So to Sir W. Coventry to dinner
with him, whom I took occasion to thanke for his
favour and good thoughts of what little service I did,
desiring he would do the last act of friendship in telling me of my faults also. He told me he would be
sure he would do that also, if there were any occasion
for it. So that as much as it is possible under so
great a fall of my Lord Sandwich's, and difference
between them, I may conclude that I am thoroughly
right with Sir W. Coventry. I dined with him with
a great deale of company, and much merry discourse.
I was called away before dinner ended to go to my
company who dined at our lodgings. Thither I went
with Mr. Evelyn, whom I met in his coach going that
way, but finding my company gone, but my Lord
Brouncker left his coach for me ; so Mr. Evelyn and
I into my Lord's coach, and rode together with excel-

lent discourse till we came to Clapham, talking of the vanity and vices of the Court, which makes it a most contemptible thing; and indeed in all his discourse I find him a most worthy person. Particularly he entertained me with discourse of an Infirmary, which he hath projected for the sick and wounded seamen against the next year, which I mightily approve of; and will endeavour to promote it, being a worthy thing, and of use, and will save money. He set me down at Mr. Gauden's, where I took a book and into the gardens, and there walked and read till darke. Anon comes in Creed, and after that Mr. Gauden and his sons, and then they bringing in three ladies, who were in the house, but I do not know them, his daughter and two nieces, daughters of Dr. Whistler's, with whom and Creed mighty sport at supper, the ladies very pretty and mirthfull. I perceive they know Creed's gut and stomach as well as I, and made as much mirthe as I with it at supper. After supper I made the ladies sing, and they have been taught, but, Lord! though I was forced to commend them, yet it was the saddest stuff I ever heard. However, we sat up late, and then I, in the best chamber like a prince, to bed, and Creed with me, and being sleepy talked but little.

30th. Up, and after walking a turne or two in the garden, and bid good morrow to Mr. Gauden's sons, and sent my service to the ladies, I took coach and home, finding the towne keeping the day solemnly, it being the day of the King's murther, and they being at church, I presently into the church, and a dull sermon of our young Lecturer, too bad. This is the first time I have been in this church since I left London for the plague, and it frighted me indeed to go through the church more than I thought it could have done, to see so many graves lie so high upon the churchyards where people have been buried of the plague.[1] I was much troubled at it, and do not think to go through it again a good while. So home to my wife, and we to dinner, where she entertained me with what she has lately bought of clothes for herself, and Damask linnen, and other things for the house. I did give her a serious account how matters stand with me, of favour with the King and Duke, and of danger in reference to my Lord's and Sir G. Carteret's falls, and the dissatisfaction I have heard the Duke of Albemarle has acknowledged to some-

---

[1] No fewer than 166 burials of the victims of this dreadful disease took place in the small parish of St. Olave, Hart Street, during a period of 154 days.

In July, 1665	4
" August	22
" September	63
" October	54
" November	18
" December	5
Of these there were buried in the churchyard	98
In the new churchyard	42
In vaults	12
IN THE CHURCH	7
In the *chancel* of the church	1
Buried (place of interment not specified)	6
	166

Gentleman's Magazine, Oct., 1845. (M. B.)

body, among other things, against my Lord Sandwich, that he did bring me into the Navy against his desire and endeavour for another which was our doting foole Turner. Thence from one discourse to another, and looking over my house, and other things I spent the day at home, and at night betimes to bed.

31st. To the 'Change, and brought home my cozen Pepys, whom I appointed to be here to-day, and Mr. Moore upon the business of my Lord's bond. Seeing my neighbour Mr. Knightly I did invite him home with me, and he dined with me, a very sober, pretty man he is. He is mighty solicitous, as I find many about the City that live near the churchyards, to have the churchyards covered with lime, and I think it is needfull, and ours I hope will be done. Good pleasant discourse at dinner of the practices of merchants to cheate the Customers, occasioned by Mr. Moore's being with much trouble freed of his prize goods, which he bought, which fell into the Customers' hands, and with much ado has cleared them. Mr. Knightly being gone, my cozen Pepys and Moore and I to our business, being the clearing of my Lord Sandwich's bond wherein I am bound with him to my cozen for 1,000*l.*; I have at last by my dexterity got my Lord's consent to have it paid out of the money raised by his prizes. So the bond is cancelled, and he paid me by having a note upon Sir Robert Viner, in whose hands I had lodged my Lord's money, by which I am to my extraordinary comfort eased of a liablenesse to pay the sum in case of my Lord's death, or troubles in estate, or my Lord's greater fall, which God defend!   Having settled this matter at Sir R. Viner's, I to my Lord Chancellor's new house which he is building, only to view it, hearing so much from Mr. Evelyn of it; and, indeed, it is the finest pile I ever did see in my life, and will be a glorious house. To White Hall, and to my great joy people begin to bustle up and down there, the King holding his resolution to be in towne to-morrow, and hath good encouragement, blessed be God! to do so, the plague being decreased this week to 56, and the total to 227. So after going to the Swan in the Palace, and sent for Spicer to discourse about my last Tangier tallys that have some of the words washed out with the rain, to have them new wrote, I home, and at the office, and so to supper, and to bed.

February 1st. To the office, where all the morning till late, and Mr. Coventry with us, the first time since before the plague, then hearing that my wife was gone abroad to buy things and to see her mother and father, whom she has not seen since before the plague, and no dinner provided for me ready, I walked to Captain Cocke's, knowing my Lord Brouncker dined there, and there very merry, and a good dinner. Thence my Lord and his mistresse, Madam Williams, set me down at the Exchange, and I to Alderman Backewell's to set all my reckonings straight there, which I did, and took up all my notes. So evened to this day, and thence to Sir Robert Viner's where I did the like, leaving clear in his hands just 2,000*l.* of my owne money, to be called for when I pleased. So home, and spent till one in the morning in my chamber to set right all my money matters, and so to bed.

2nd. Knowing that my Lord Sandwich is come to towne with the King and Duke, I to wait upon him, which I did, and find him in very good humour, which I am glad to see with all my heart. Having received his commands, and discoursed with Sir Roger Cuttance, who was there, and finds himself slighted by Sir W. Coventry, I advised him however to look after employment lest it be said that my Lord's friends do forsake the service after he has made them rich with the prizes. I to London, and there among other things did look over some pictures at Cade's for my house, and did carry home a silver drudger [1] for my cupboard of plate, and did call for my silver chafing dishes, but they are sent home, and the man would not be paid for them, saying that he was paid for them, already, and with much ado got him to tell me by Mr. Wayth, but I would not accept of that, but will send him his money, not knowing any courtesy I have yet done him to deserve it. So home, and with my wife looked over our plate, and picked out 40*l.* worth, I believe, to change for more usefull plate, to our great content, and then we shall have a very handsome cupboard of

---

[1] Dredger. Still in common use in kitchens. "It gives me great satisfaction to hear that the pig turned out so well . . . you had all some of the crackling and brain sauce. Did you remember to rub it with butter, and gently *dredge* it a little, just before the crisis?"—LAMB, *Letter to Coleridge.* (M. B.)

plate.   So to dinner, and then to the office, where we had a meeting extraordinary, about stating to the Duke the present debts of the Navy, for which ready money must be had, and that being done, I to my business, where late, and then home to supper, and to bed.

4th. Lord's day; and my wife and I the first time together at church since the plague, and now only because of Mr. Mills his coming home to preach his first sermon; expecting a great excuse for his leaving the parish before any body went, and now staying till all are come home; but he made but a very poor and short excuse, and a bad sermon. It was a frost, and had snowed last night, which covered the graves in the churchyard, so as I was the less afeard for going through. Here I had the content to see my noble Mrs. Lethulier, and so home to dinner, and all the afternoon at my Journall till supper, it being a long while behindhand. At supper my wife tells me that W. Joyce has been with her this evening, the first time since the plague, and tells her my aunt James is lately dead of the stone.

5th. Up, and with Sir W. Batten (at whose lodgings calling for him, I saw his Lady the first time since her coming to towne since the plague, having absented myself designedly to shew some discontent, and that I am not at all the more suppliant because of my Lord Sandwich's fall) to my Lord Brouncker's. My Lord invited me to dinner to-day to dine with Sir W. Batten and his Lady there, but lest he should thinke so little an invitation would serve my turne I refused and parted, and to the 'Change, and there met Mr. Hill, and with him the Houblons, and agreed that I must sup with them to-night. So visited my Lord Sandwich, and so to the Sun, behind the Exchange, about seven o'clock, where I find all the five brothers Houblons, and mighty fine gentlemen they are all, and used me mighty respectfully. We were mighty civilly merry, and their discourses, having been all abroad, very fine.

6th. Up, and to the office, where very busy all the morning. We met upon a report to the Duke of York of the debts of the Navy, which we finished by three o'clock, and having eat one little bit of meate, I by water before the rest to White Hall, because of a Committee for Tangier, where I did my business of stating my accounts perfectly well, and to good liking, and do not discern, but the Duke of Albemarle is my friend in his intentions notwithstanding my general fears. After that to our Navy business, where my fellow officers were called in, and did that also very well, and then broke up, and I home by coach, Tooker with me, and staid in Lumbard Streete at Viner's, and sent home for the plate which my wife and I had a mind to change, and there changed it, about 50*l.* worth, into things more usefull, whereby we shall now have a very handsome cupboard of plate. So home to the office, wrote my letters by the post, and to bed.

7th. It being fast day I staid at home all day long to set things to rights in my chamber by taking out all my books, and putting my chamber in the same condition it was before the plague.

8th. To Captain Cocke's where by and by Lord Brouncker, he having been with the King and Duke upon the water to-day, to see Greenwich house, and the yacht Castle is building of, and much good discourse.

9th. Up, and betimes to Sir Philip Warwick, who was glad to see me. Thence to Collonell Norwood's lodgings, and there set about Houblons' business about their ships. Thence to Westminster, to the Exchequer, about my Tangier business to get orders for tallys, and so to the Hall, where the first day of the Terme, and the Hall very full of people, and much more than was expected, considering the plague that hath been. Thence to the 'Change, and to the Sun behind it to dinner with Colonell Norwood and others, where strange pleasure they seem to take in their wine and meate, and discourse of it with the curiosity and joy that methinks was below men of worthe. Thence home, and there very much angry with my people till I had put all things in good forwardnesse about my supper for the Houblons, but that being done I was in good humour again. Anon the five brothers Houblons[1] came and Mr. Hill, and a very good supper we had, and good company and discourse, with great pleasure. My new plate sets off my cupboard very

---

[1] Two of these brothers, Sir James and Sir John Houblon, Knights and Aldermen, rose to great wealth; the former represented the City of London, and the latter became Lord Mayor in 1695. See note, March 22, 1664-65.

nobly. Here they were till about eleven at night with great pleasure, and a fine sight it is to see these five brothers thus loving one to another, and all industrious merchants. Our subject was principally Mr. Hill's going for them to Portugall, which was the occasion of this entertainment.

10th. To the office. This day comes first Sir Thomas Harvey after the plague, having been out of towne all this while. He was coldly received by us, and he went away before we rose also, to make himself appear yet a man less necessary. After dinner, being full of care and multitude of business, I took coach and my wife with me, and at the old Exchange bought a muffe, and so home and late at my letters, and so to supper and to bed, being now-a-days, for these four or five months, mightily troubled with my snoring in my sleep, and know not how to remedy it.

11th (Lord's day). Up, and put on a new black cloth suit to an old coate that I make to be in mourning at Court, where they are all, for the King of Spayne.[1] To church I and at noon dined well, and then by water to White Hall, and there I to the Parke, and walked two or three turnes of the Pell Mell with the company about the King and Duke; the Duke speaking to me a good deal. There met Lord Brouncker and Mr. Coventry, and discoursed about the Navy business; and all of us much at a loss that we yet can hear nothing of Sir Jeremy Smith's fleete,

---

[1] Philip IV. died 17th Sept., 1665.

that went away to the Streights the middle of December, through all the storms that we have had since, that have driven back three or four of them with their masts by the board. Yesterday come out the King's Declaration of War against the French,[1] but with such mild invitations of both them and the Dutch to come over hither with promise of their protection, that every body wonders at it. Thence home with my Lord Brouncker for discourse sake, and so my wife and I mighty pleasant discourse, supped and to bed. My wife and I are much thoughtfull now-a-days about Pall's coming up in order to a husband.

12th. Up, and very busy to perform an oathe in finishing my Journall this morning for 7 or 8 days past. Then to several people attending upon business. Then comes Mr. Cæsar, my boy's lute-master, whom I have not seen since the plague before, but he hath been in Westminster all this while very well; and tells me in the height of it, how bold people there were, to go in sport to one another's burials; and in spite too, ill people would breathe in the faces (out of their windows) of well people going by. Then to dinner, and so to the 'Change, and so by coach to my Lord Treasurer's, there to meet my Lord Sandwich, but missed; met him at my Lord Chancellor's, and

---

[1] "It was proclaimed by the Herald-at-Arms, and two of his brethren, His Majesty's Serjeants-at-Arms, with other usual officers (with His Majesty's Trumpeters attending), before his Royal Palace at Whitehall : and afterwards (the Lord Mayor and his brethren assisting) at Temple Bar, and other the usual parts of the city."— *The London Gazette*, Feb. 8-12, 1665-6.

there talked with him about his accounts, and then about Sir G. Carteret, and I find by him that Sir G. Carteret has a worse game to play than my Lord Sandwich, for people are jeering at him, and he cries out of the business of Sir W. Coventry, who strikes at all and do all. Then to my bookseller's, and then received some books I have new bought, and here late choosing some more to new bind, having resolved to give myself 10*l.* in books, and so home to the office and then to supper, where Mr. Hill was and supped with us, and good discourse; an excellent person he still appears to me. He gone, we to bed.

13th. At noon to the 'Change, and thence after business dined at the Sheriffe's (Hooker) being carried by Mr. Lethulier, where to my heart's content I met with his wife, a most beautifull fat woman. I had a salute of her, and after dinner some discourse the Sheriffe and I about a parcel of tallys I am buying of him. I away home, and there at the office all the afternoon till late at night, and then away home to supper and to bed. Ill newes this night that the plague is encreased this week, and in many places else about the towne, and at Chatham and elsewhere.

14th (St. Valentine's day). This morning called up by Mr. Hill, who, my wife thought, had been come to be her Valentine; she, it seems, having drawne him last night, but it proved not. However, calling him up to our bed-side, my wife challenged him. Up, and made myself ready, and so with him by coach to my Lord Sandwich's by appointment to deliver Mr.

Howe's accounts to my Lord. Which done, my Lord did give me hearty and large studied thanks for all my kindnesse to him and care of him and his business. I after profession of all duty to his Lordship took occasion to bemoane myself that I should fall into such a difficulty about Sir G. Carteret, as not to be for him, but I must be against Sir W. Coventry, and therefore desired to be neutral, which my Lord approved and confessed reasonable, but desired me to befriend him privately. Having done in private with my Lord I brought Mr. Hill to kisse his hands, to whom my Lord professed great respect on my score. My Lord being gone, I took Mr. Hill to my Lord Chancellor's new house [1] that is building, and went with trouble up to the top of it, and there is there the noblest prospect that ever I saw in my life, Greenwich being nothing to it; and in every thing is a beautiful house, and most strongly built in every respect; and as if, as it hath, it had the Chancellor for its master. [2] Thence with him to his paynter, Mr. Hales, who is drawing his picture, which will be mighty like him, and pleased me so, that I am resolved presently to have my wife and mine done by him, he having a very masterly hand. So with mighty satisfaction to the 'Change and thence home, and after dinner abroad, taking Mrs. Mary Batelier with us, and they set me down at my Lord Treasurer's, and themselves went with the coach into the fields to take the ayre. I

---

[1] See 18th Feb. 1665, and 9th May, 1667.

[2] Two years after, he was in exile.

staid a meeting of the Duke of York's, and the officers of the Navy and Ordnance. My Lord Treasurer
lying in bed of the gowte. Our business was discourse
of the straits of the Navy for want of money, but after
long discourse as much out of order as ordinary
people's, we came to no issue, nor any money promised, or like to be had, and yet the worke must be
done. Here I perceive Sir G. Carteret had prepared
himself to answer a choque of Sir W. Coventry, by
offering of himself to shew all he had paid, and what
is unpaid, and what money and assignments he has in
his hands, which, if he makes good, was the best thing
he ever did say in his life, and the best timed, for else
it must have fallen very foule on him. The meeting
done I away, my wife and they being come back and
staying for me at the gate. But, Lord! to see how
afeard I was that Sir W. Coventry should have spyed
me once whispering with Sir G. Carteret, though not
intended by me, but only Sir G. Carteret came to me
and I could not avoyde it. So home, they set me
down at the 'Change, and I to the Crowne, where
my Lord Brouncker was come and several of the
Virtuosi, and after a small supper and but little good
discourse I home, where I find my wife gone to Mrs.
Mercer's to be merry, but presently came in with
Mrs. Knipp, who, it seems, is in towne, and was
gone thither to danse, and after eating a little supper
went thither again. I to bed.

15th. At noon to Starky's, a great cooke in Austin
Friars, invited by Collonell Atkins, and a good dinner,

among others Sir Edward Spragg, but ill attendance. Before dined, called on by my wife in a coach, and so I took leave, and then with her and Knipp and Mercer to Mr. Hales, the paynter's.[1] Here Mr. Hales begun my wife's portrait in the posture we saw one of my Lady Peters, like a St. Katharine.[2] While he painted, Knipp, and Mercer, and I, sang; and by and by comes Mrs. Pierce, with my name in her bosom for her Valentine, which will cost me money. But strange how like his very first dead colouring is, that it did me good to see it, and pleases me mightily, and I believe it will be a noble picture. Thence with them all as far as Fleete Streete, and there set Mercer and Knipp down, and we home. We hear this night of Sir Jeremy Smith, that he and his fleete have been seen at Malaga; which is good newes.

16th. Up betimes, and by appointment to the Exchange, where I met Messrs. Houblons, and took them up in my coach and carried them to Charing Crosse, where they to Collonell Norwood to see how they can settle matters with him, I having informed them by the way with advice to be easy with him, for he may hereafter do us service, and they and I are like to understand one another to very good purpose. I to my Lord Sandwich, and there alone with him to talke

---

[1] John Hayls, or Hales, a portrait-painter remarkable for copying Vandyke well, and being a rival of Lely.

[2] It was at this time the fashion to be painted as St. Catherine, in compliment to the Queen. The so-called Lady Bellasys, among the beauties of Charles II., now at Hampton Court, is thus represented.

of his affairs, and particularly of his prize goods, wherein I find he is wearied with being troubled, and gives over the care of it to let it come to what it will, having the King's release for the dividend made, and for the rest he thinks himself safe from being proved to have anything more. Thence to the Exchequer, and so by coach to the 'Change, Mr. Moore with me, who tells me very odde passages of the indiscretion of my Lord in the management of his family, of his carelessnesse, &c., which troubles me, but makes me rejoice with all my heart of my being rid of the bond of 1,000*l.*, for that would have been a cruel blow to me. With Moore to the Coffee-House, the first time I have been there, where very full, and company it seems hath been there all the plague time. So to the 'Change, and then home to dinner. Then to the office, and out by coach to White Hall, thinking to have spoke with Sir W. Coventry, but did not, and to see the Queene, but she comes but to Hampton Court to-night. I walked a good while to-night with Mr. Hater in the garden, talking about a husband for my sister, and reckoning up all our clerks about us, none of which he thinks fit for her and her portion. At last I thought of young Gauden, and will thinke of it again.

17th. Up, and to the office, where busy all the morning. Late to dinner, and then to the office again, and there busy till past twelve at night, and so home to supper and to bed. We have newes of Sir Jeremy Smith's being very well with his fleete at Cales.

18th (Lord's day). Lay long in bed discoursing with pleasure with my wife, among other things about Pall's coming up, for she must be here a little to be fashioned, and my wife has a mind to go down for her, which I am not much against, and so I rose and to my chamber to settle several things. At noon comes my uncle Wight to dinner, and brings with him Mrs. Wight, sad company to me, nor was I much pleased with it, only I must shew respect to my uncle. After dinner they gone, and it being a brave day, I walked to White Hall, where the Queene and ladies are all come: I saw some few of them, but not the Queene, nor any of the great beauties. Met with Creed and walked with him a turne or two in the Parke, but without much content, having now designs of getting money in my head, which allow me not the leisure I used to have with him. Thence took coach, and calling by the way at my bookseller's for a booke writ about twenty years ago in prophecy of this year coming on, 1666, explaining it to be the marke of the beast,[1] I home, and there fell to reading, and then to supper, and to bed.

19th. To White Hall with some of the rest of our brethren, and thence to my Lord's, to see my Lord

---

[1] The book purchased by Pepys is entitled: "An Interpretation of the Number 666, wherein not only the manner how this Number ought to be interpreted is clearly proved and demonstrated; but it is also shewed that this number is an exquisite and perfect character, truly, exactly, and essentially describing that state of Government to which all other notes of Antichrist doe agree. With all knowne objections solidly and fully answered, that can be materially made against it." By Francis Potter, B.D., Oxford, 1642, 4to. A

Hinchingbroke, which I did, and I am mightily out of countenance in my great expectation of him by others' report, though he is indeed a pretty gentleman, yet nothing what I took him for, methinks, either as to person or discourse discovered to me, but I must try him more before I go too far in censuring. Hence to the Exchequer from office to office, to set my business of my tallys in doing, and there all the morning. So at noon by coach to St. Paul's Church-yarde to my Bookseller's, and there bespoke a few more books to bring all I have lately bought to 10*l.* Here I am told for certain, what I have heard once or twice already, of a Jew in town, that in the name of the rest do offer to give any man 10*l.* to be paid 100*l.*, if a certain person now at Smyrna be within these two years owned by all the Princes of the East, and particularly the grand Signor as the King of the world, in the same manner we do the King of England here, and that this man is the true Messiah. One named a friend of his that had received ten pieces in gold upon this score, and says that the Jew hath disposed of 1,100*l.* in this manner, which is very strange ; and certainly this year of 1666 will be a year of great action ; but what the consequences of it will be, God knows ! Thence to the 'Change, and from my stationer's thereabouts carried home by coach two books of Ogilby's, his Æsop and Coronation, which fell to my lot at his

copy of this work in the British Museum contains the book-plate of " William Hewer, of Clapham, in the county of Surrey, Esq., 1699." See 4th and 10th Nov., 1666, *post*.

lottery.[1] Cost me 4*l*. besides the binding. So home.
I find my wife gone out to Hales, her paynter, and I
after a little dinner do follow her, and there do find
him at worke, and with great content I do see it will
be a very brave picture. Left her there, and I to my
Lord Treasurer's, where the state of our Navy debts
was laid open, there being but 1,500,000*l*. to answer
a certaine expense and debt of 2,300,000*l*. Thence
to White Hall, and there saw the Queene at cards with
many ladies, but none of our beauties were there. But
glad I was to see the Queene so well, who looks
prettily; and methinks hath more life than before,
since it is confessed of all that she miscarried lately;
Dr. Clerke telling me yesterday of it at White Hall.[2]

20th. Up, and to the office; where, among other
businesses, Mr. Evelyn's proposition about publique
Infirmarys was read and agreed on, he being there:
and at noon I took him home to dinner, being desirous of keeping my acquaintance with him; and a
most excellent humoured man I still find him, and
mighty knowing. After dinner I took him by coach
to White Hall, and there he and I parted, and I to
my Lord Sandwich's, where coming and bolting into
the dining-room, I there found Captain Ferrers going
to christen a child of his born yesterday, and I came
just pat to be a godfather, along with my Lord Hinch-

---

[1] At the old theatre, between Lincoln's Inn Fields and Vere Street.

[2] The details in the original leave no doubt of the fact, and exculpate the
Chancellor from the charge of having selected the Queen as incapable of bearing children.

ingbroke, and Madam Pierce, my Valentine, which for that reason I was well contented with, though a little vexed to see myself so beset with people to spend me money, as she of a Valentine and little Miss Tooker, who is come to my house this day from Greenwich, and will cost me 20s., my wife going out with her this afternoon, and now this christening. Well! by and by the child is brought and christened Katharine, and I this day on this occasion drank a glasse of wine, which I have not professedly done these two years, I think, but a little in the time of the sicknesse. After that done, and gone and kissed the mother in bed, I away to Westminster Hall, and thence home, where little Miss Tooker staid all night with us, and a pretty child she is, and happens to be niece to my beauty that is dead, that lived at the Jackanapes, in Cheapside.

21st. Up, and with Sir J. Minnes to White Hall by his coach, by the way talking of my brother John to get a spiritual promotion for him, which I am now to looke after, for as much as he is shortly to be Master in Arts, and writes me this weeke a Latin letter that he is to go into orders this Lent. There to the Duke's chamber, and find our fellows discoursing there on our business, so I was sorry to come late, but no hurte was done thereby. Here the Duke, among other things, did bring out a book of great antiquity of some of the customs of the Navy, about 100 years since, which he did lend us to read and deliver him back again. Thence to Trinity-house, being invited to an Elder Brother's feast; and there met and sat by Mr. Prin, and had good discourse about the privileges of Parliament, which, he says, are few to the Commons' House, and those not examinable by them, but only by the House of Lords. Thence with my Lord Brouncker to Gresham College, the first time after the sicknesse that I was there, and the second time any met. And here a good lecture of Mr. Hooke's about the trade of felt-making, very pretty. And anon alone with me about the art of drawing pictures by Prince Rupert's rule and machine, and another of Dr. Wren's;[1] but he says nothing do like squares, or, which is the best in the world, like a darke roome,[2] which pleased me mightily.

22nd. Up, and to the office, where sat all the morning. At noon home to dinner and thence by coach with my wife for ayre principally for her. I alone stopped at Hales's and there mightily am pleased with my wife's picture and with Mr. Hill's, though I must owne I am not more pleased with it now the face is finished than I was when I saw it the second time of sitting. My wife to Mrs. Hunt's, who is lately come to towne and grown mighty fat. We are much troubled that the sicknesse in general (the town being so full of people) should be but three, and yet of the particular disease of the plague there should be ten encrease.

23rd. To my Lord Sandwich's, who did lie the last

---

[1] Sir Christopher Wren.   [2] The camera obscura.

night at his house in Lincoln's Inne Fields. It being fine walking in the morning, and the streets full of people again. There I staid, and the house full of people come to take leave of my Lord, who this day goes out of towne upon his embassy towards Spayne. And I was glad to find Sir W. Coventry to come, though I know it is only a piece of courtshipp. I had much discourse with my Lord, he telling me how fully he leaves the King his friend and the large discourse he had with him the other day, and how he desired to have the business of the prizes examined before he went, and that he yielded to it and it is done as far as it concerns himself to the full and the Lords Commissioners for prizes did reprehend all the informers in what related to his Lordship, which I am glad of in many respects. But we could not make an end of discourse, so I promised to waite upon him on Sunday at Cranborne and took leave and away hence to Mr. Hales's with Mr. Hill and two of the Houblons and saw my wife's picture which pleases me well, but Mr. Hill's picture never a whit so well as it did before it was finished, which troubled me and I begin to doubt the picture of my Lady Peters my wife takes her posture from, and which is an excellent picture, is not of his making, it is so master-like. I set them down at the 'Change and I home to the office and at noon dined at home and to the office again. Anon comes Mrs. Knipp to see my wife, and I spent all the night talking with this baggage, and teaching her my song of " Beauty retire," which she

sings and makes go most rarely, and a very fine song
it seems to be.   She also entertained me with repeating many of her own and others' parts of the play-
house, which she do most excellently; and tells me
the whole practices of the play-house and players,
and is in every respect most excellent company.   So
I supped, and was merry at home all the evening, and
the rather it being my birthday, 33 years, for which
God be praised that I am in so good a condition
of healthe and estate, and every thing else as I am,
beyond expectation, in all.   So she to Mrs. Turner's
to lie and we to bed.   Mightily pleased to find myself in condition to have these people come about me
and to be able to entertain them, and have the pleasure of their qualities, than which no man can have
more in this world.

24th.   All the morning at the office till past three
o'clock.   At that houre home and eat a bit alone, my
wife being gone out.   So abroad by coach with Mr.
Hill, who staid for me to speake about business and
he and I to Hales's, where I find my wife and her
woman, and Pierce and Knipp and there sung and
was mighty merry, and I joyed myself in it; but vexed
at first to find my wife's picture not so like as I
expected; but it was only his having finished one
part, and not another, of the face; but, before I went,
I was satisfied it will be an excellent picture.   Here
we had ale and cakes and mighty merry, and sung my
song, which she [Knipp] now sings bravely, and
makes me proud of myself.   Thence left my wife to

go home with Mrs. Pierce, while I home to the office, and there pretty late, and to bed, after fitting myself for to-morrow's journey.

25th (Lord's day). My wife up between three and four of the clock in the morning to dress herself, and I about five, and were all ready to take coach, she and I and Mercer, a little past five, but, to our trouble, the coach did not come till six. Then with our coach of four horses I hire on purpose, and Lechmere to ride by, we through the City to Branford and so to Windsor, Captain Ferrers overtaking us at Kensington, being to go with us, and here drank, and so through, making no stay, to Cranborne,[1] about eleven o'clock, and found my Lord[2] and the ladies at a sermon in the house; which being ended we to them, and all the company glad to see us, and mighty merry to dinner. Here was my Lord, and Lord Hinchingbroke, and Mr. Sidney,[3] Sir Charles Herbert,[4] and Mr. Carteret, my Lady Carteret, my Lady

---

[1] Cranbourne Lodge. Sir G. Carteret's official residence, as Vice-Chamberlain. See 20th July, 1665.

[2] Sandwich.

[3] Sidney Montagu, Lord Sandwich's second son.

[4] This person, erroneously called by Pepys Sir C. Herbert, will be best defined by subjoining the inscription on his monument in Westminster Abbey: — "Sir Charles Harbord, Knight, third son of Sir Charles Harbord, Knight, Surveyor-General, and First Lieutenant of the Royall James, under the most noble and illustrious Captaine, Edward, Earle of Sandwich, Vice-Admirall of England, which, after a terrible fight, maintained to admiration against a squadron of the Holland fleet, above six hours, neere the Suffolk coast, having put off two fire-ships; at last, being utterly disabled, and few of her men remaining unhurt, was, by a third, unfortunately set on fire. But he (though he swome well) neglected to save himselfe, as some did, and out of perfect

Jemimah, and Lady Slaning.[1]   After dinner to talk to and again and then to walk in the Parke, my Lord and I alone, talking upon these heads; first, he has left his business of the prizes as well as is possible for him, having cleared himself before the Commissioners by the King's commands, so that nothing or little is to be feared from that point, he goes fully assured, he tells me, of the King's favour.   That upon occasion I may know, I desired to know, his friends I may trust to, he tells me, but that he is not yet in England, but continues this summer in Ireland, my Lord Orrery is his father almost in affection.   He tells me my Lord of Suffolk, Lord Arlington, Archbishop of Canterbury, Lord Treasurer, Mr. Atturny Montagu, Sir Thomas Clifford in the House of Commons, Sir G. Carteret, and some others I cannot presently remember, are friends that I may rely on for him.   He tells me my Lord Chancellor seems his very good friend, but doubts that he may not think him so much a servant of the Duke of York's as he would have him, and indeed my Lord tells me he has lately made it his business to be seen studious of the King's favour, and not of the Duke's, and by the King will stand or fall, for factions there are, as he tells me, and God knows how high they may come.   The Duke of Albemarle's

love to that worthy Lord, whom, for many yeares, he had constantly accompanyed, in all his honourable employments, and in all the engagements of the former warre, dyed with him, at the age of xxxii., much bewailed by his father, whom he never offended; and much beloved by all for his knowne piety, vertue, loyalty, fortitude, and fidelity."

[1] Sir G. Carteret's daughter Caroline.

post is so great, having had the name of bringing in the King, that he is like to stand, or, if it were not for him, God knows into what troubles we might be from some private faction, if an army could be got into another hand, which God forbid! It is believed that though Mr. Coventry be in appearance so great against the Chancellor, yet that there is a good understanding between the Duke and him. He dreads the issue of this year, and fears there will be some very great revolutions before his coming back again. He doubts it is needful for him to have a pardon for his last year's actions, all which he did without commission, and at most but the King's private single word for that of Bergen; but he dares not ask it at this time, lest it should make them think that there is something more' in it than yet they know; and if it should be denied, it would be of very ill consequence. He says also, if it should in Parliament be enquired into the selling of Dunkirke (though the Chancellor was the man that would have it sold to France, saying the King of Spayne had no money to give for it) ; yet he will be found to have been the greatest adviser of it; which he is a little apprehensive may be called upon by this Parliament. He told me it would not be necessary for him to tell me his debts, because he thinks I know them so well. He tells me, that for the match propounded of Mrs. Mallett for my Lord Hinchingbroke, it hath been lately off, and now her friends bring it on again, and an overture hath been made to him by a servant of her's, to compass the thing without consent of friends, she herself having a respect to my Lord's family, but my Lord will not listen to it but in a way of honour.[1] The Duke has for this weeke or two been very kind to him, more than lately, and so others, which he thinks is a good sign of faire weather again. He says the Archbishopp of Canterbury has been very kind to him, and has plainly said to him that he and all the world knows the difference between his judgment and brains and the Duke of Albemarle's, and then calls my Lady Duchesse the veryest slut and drudge and the foulest worde that can be spoke of a woman almost. My Lord having walked an houre with me talking thus and going in, and my Lady Carteret not suffering me to go back again to-night, my Lord to walke again with me about some of this and other discourse, and then in a-doors and to talke with all and with my Lady Carteret, and I with the young ladies and gentlemen, who played on the guittar, and mighty merry, and anon to supper, and then my Lord going away to write, the young gentlemen to flinging of cushions, and other mad sports; at this late till towards twelve at night, and then being sleepy, I and my wife in a passage-room to bed, and slept not very well because of noise.

26th. Called up about five in the morning, and my Lord up, and took leave, a little after six, very kindly of me and the whole company. Then I in, and my wife up and to visit my Lady Slaning in her bed, and

---

[1] She afterwards married Lord Rochester.

there sat three hours, with Lady Jemimah with us, talking and laughing, and by and by my Lady Carteret comes, and she and I to talke, I glad to please in discourse of Sir G. Carteret, that all will do well with him, and she is much pleased, he having had great annoyance and fears about his well doing, and I fear has doubted that I have not been a friend to him, but cries out against my Lady Castlemaine, that makes the King neglect his business and seems much to fear that all will go to wracke, and I fear with great reason; exclaims against the Duke of Albemarle, and more the Duchesse for a filthy woman, as indeed she is. Here staid till 9 o'clock almost, and then took coach with so much love and kindnesse from my Lady Carteret, Lady Jemimah, and Lady Slaning, that it joys my heart, and when I consider the manner of my going hither, with a coach and four horses and servants and a woman with us, and coming hither being so much made of, and used with that state, and then going to Windsor and being shown all that we were there, and had wherewith to give every body something for their pains, and then going home, and all in fine weather and no fears nor cares upon me, I do thinke myself obliged to thinke myself happy, and do look upon myself at this time in the happiest occasion a man can be, and whereas we take pains in expectation of future comfort and ease, I have taught myself to reflect upon myself at present as happy, and enjoy myself in that consideration, and not only please myself with thoughts of future wealth and forget the pleasure we at present enjoy. So took coach and to Windsor, to the Garter, and thither sent for Dr. Childe;[1] who came to us, and carried us to St. George's Chappell; and there placed us among the Knights' stalls (and pretty the observation, that no man, but a woman may sit in a Knight's place, where any brass-plates are set) ; and hither come cushions to us, and a young singing-boy to bring us a copy of the anthem to be sung. And here, for our sakes, had this anthem and the great service sung extraordinary, only to entertain us. It is a noble place indeed, and a good Quire of voices. Great bowing by all the people, the poor Knights in particularly, to the Alter. After prayers, we to see the plate of the chappell, and the robes of Knights, and a man to show us the banners of the several Knights in being, which hang up over the stalls. And so to other discourse very pretty, about the Order. Was shown where the late King is buried, and King Henry the Eighth, and my Lady Seymour.[2] This being done, to the King's house, and to observe the neatness and contrivance of the house and gates : it is the most romantique castle that is in the world. But, Lord ! the prospect that is in the balcone in the Queene's lodgings, and the terrace and walk, are strange things to consider, being the best in the world, sure. Infinitely satisfied I and my wife with all this, she being in all points mightily pleased

---

[1] William Child, Doctor of Music, Organist of St. George's Chapel, at Windsor. Ob. 1696, aged 91.

[2] Henry VIII.'s wife, Jane Seymour. (M. B.)

too, which added to my pleasure; and so giving a great deal of money to this and that man and woman, we to our taverne, and there dined, the Doctor with us; and so took coach and away to Eton, the Doctor with me. Before we went to Chappell this morning, Kate Joyce, in a stage-coach going towards London, called to me. I went to her and saluted her, but could not get her to stay with us, having company. At Eton I left my wife in the coach, and he and I to the College, and there find all mighty fine. The school good, and the custom pretty of boys cutting their names in the shuts of the window when they go to Cambridge, by which many a one hath lived to see himself a Provost and Fellow, that had his name in the window standing. To the Hall, and there find the boys' verses, "De Peste;" it being their custom to make verses at Shrove-tide. I read several, and very good ones they were, and better, I think, than ever I made when I was a boy, and in rolls as long and longer than the whole Hall, by much. Here is a picture of Venice hung up, and a monument made of Sir H. Wotton's giving it to the College. Thence to the porter's, in the absence of the butler, and did drink of the College beer, which is very good; and went into the back fields to see the scholars play. And so to the chappell, and there saw, among other things, Sir H. Wotton's stone with this Epitaph:

> Hic jacet primus hujus sententiæ Author: —
> Disputandi pruritus fit ecclesiæ scabies.

But unfortunately the word "Author" was wrong writ,

and now so basely altered that it disgraces the stone. Thence took leave of the Doctor, and so took coach, and finely, but sleepy, away home, and got thither about eight at night, and after a little at my office, I to bed; and an houre after, was waked with my wife's quarrelling with Mercer, at which I was angry, and my wife and I fell out. But with much ado to sleep again, I beginning to practise more temper, and to give her her way.

27th. Up, and after a harsh word or two my wife and I good friends, and so up and to the office, where all the morning. At noon late to dinner, my wife gone out to Hales's about her picture, and, after dinner, I after her, and do mightily like her picture, and think it will be as good as my Lady Peters's. So home mightily pleased, and there late at business and set down my three last days' journalls, and so to bed, overjoyed to thinke of the pleasure of the last Sunday and yesterday, and my ability to bear the charge of these pleasures, and with profit too, by obliging my Lord, and reconciling Sir George Carteret's family.

28th (Ash Wednesday). Up, and after doing a little business at my office I walked, it being a most curious dry and cold morning, to White Hall, and there I went into the Parke, and meeting Sir Ph. Warwick took a turne with him in the Pall Mall, talking of the melancholy posture of affairs, where every body is snarling one at another, and all things put together looke ominously. This new Act too putting us out of a power of raising money. So that he fears as

I do, but is fearfull of enlarging in the discourse of an ill condition in every thing, and the State and all. We appointed another time to meet to talke of the business of the Navy alone seriously, and so parted, and I to White Hall, and there we did our business with the Duke of York, and so parted, and walked to Westminster Hall, where I staid talking with Mrs. Michell and Howlett long and her daughter, which is become a mighty pretty woman, and thence going out of the Hall was called to by Mrs. Martin, so I went to her and bought two bands, and so away home and there find Mrs. Knipp, and we dined together, she the pleasantest company in the world. After dinner I did give my wife money to lay out on Knipp, 20s., and I abroad to White Hall to visit Collonell Norwood, and then Sir G. Carteret, with whom I have brought myself right again, and he very open to me ; is very melancholy, and matters, I fear, go down with him, but he seems most afeard of a general catastrophe to the whole kingdom, and thinks, as I fear, that all things will come to nothing. Thence by coach home and to the office, where a while, and then betimes to bed by ten o'clock, sooner than I have done many a day. And thus ends this month, with my mind full of resolution to apply myself better from this time forward to my business than I have done these six or eight days, visibly to my prejudice both in quiett of mind and setting backward of my business, that I cannot give a good account of it as I ought to do.

March 1st. Up, and to the office and there all the

morning sitting and at noon to dinner with my Lord Brouncker, Sir W. Batten and Sir W. Pen at the White Horse in Lumbard Streete, where, God forgive us! good sport with Captain Cocke's having his mayde sicke of the plague a day or two ago and sent to the pest house, where she now is, but he will not say anything but that she is well. But blessed be God! a good Bill this week we have; being but 237 in all, and 42 of the plague, and of them but six in the City: though my Lord Brouncker says, that these six are most of them in new parishes where they were not the last week. Here was with us also Mr. Williamson, who the more I know, the more I honour. Hence I slipt after dinner without notice home and there close to my business at my office till twelve at night, having with great comfort returned to my business by some fresh vowes in addition to my former, and more severe, and a great joy it is to me to see myself in a good disposition to business. So home to supper and to my Journall and to bed.

2nd. Up, as I have of late resolved before 7 in the morning and to the office where all the morning, among other things setting my wife and Mercer with much pleasure to worke upon the ruling of some paper for the making of books for pursers, which will require a great deale of worke and they will enter a good deale of money by it, the hopes of which makes them worke mighty hard. At noon dined and to the office again, and about 4 o'clock took coach and to my Lord Treasurer's and thence to Sir Philip Warwick's new house by appointment, there to spend an houre in talking and very good discourse about the state of the King as to money, and particularly in the point of the Navy. He endeavours hard to come to a good understanding of Sir G. Carteret's accounts, and by his discourse I find Sir G. Carteret must be brought to it, and what a madman he is that he do not do it of himself, for the King expects the Parliament will call upon him for his promise of giving an account of the money, and he will be ready for it, which cannot be, I am sure, without Sir G. Carteret's accounts be better understood than they are. He seems to have a great esteem of me and my opinion and thoughts of things. After we had spent an houre thus discoursing and vexing that we do but grope so in the darke as we do, because the people, that should enlighten us, do not helpe us, we resolved for fitting some things for another meeting, and so broke up. He shewed me his house, which is yet all unhung, but will be a very noble house indeed. Thence by coach calling at my bookseller's and carried home 10*l.* worth of books, all, I hope, I shall buy a great while. There by appointment find Mr. Hill come to supper and take his last leave of me, and by and by in comes Mr. James Houblon to bear us company, a man I love mightily, and will not lose his acquaintance. He told me in my eare this night what he and his brothers have resolved to give me, which is 200*l.*, for helping them out with two or three ships. A good sum and that which I did believe they would give me, and I did expect little less. Here we talked and very good company till late and then took leave of one another, and indeed I am heartily sorry for Mr. Hill's leaving us, for he is a very worthy gentleman, as most I know. God give him a good voyage and successe in his business. Thus we parted and my wife and I to bed, heavy for the losse of our friend.

3rd. All the morning at the office, at noon to the Old James, being sent for, and there dined with Sir W. Rider, Cutler, and others, to make an end with two Scots Maisters about the freight of two ships of my Lord Rutherford's. After a small dinner and a little discourse I away to the Crowne behind the Exchange to Sir W. Pen, Captain Cocke and Fen, about getting a bill of Cocke's paid to Pen, in part for the East India goods he sold us. Here Sir W. Pen did give me the reason in my eare of his importunity for money, for that he is now to marry his daughter. God send her better fortune than her father deserves I should wish him for a false rogue. Thence by coach to Hales's, and there saw my wife sit ; and I do like her picture mightily, and very like it will be, and a brave piece of work. But he do complain that her nose hath cost him as much work as another's face, and he hath done it finely indeed.

4th (Lord's day). All day at my Tangier and private accounts, having neglected them since Christmas, which I hope I shall never do again ; for I find the inconvenience of it, it being ten times the labour to remember and settle things. But I thank God I did it at last, and brought them all fine and right; and I am, I thinke, by all appears to me, and I am sure I cannot be 10*l.* wrong, worth above 4,600*l.*, for which the Lord be praised! being the biggest sum I ever was worth yet.

5th. I was at it till past two o'clock on Monday morning, and then read my vowes, and to bed with great joy and content that I have brought my things to so good a settlement, and now having my mind fixed to follow my business again and sensible of Sir W. Coventry's jealousy, I doubt, concerning me, partly my siding with Sir G. Carteret, and partly that indeed I have been silent in my business of the office a great while, and given but little account of myself and least of all to him, having not made him one visitt since he came to towne from Oxford, I am resolved to fall hard to it again, and fetch up the time and interest I have lost or am in a fair way of doing it. Up about eight o'clock, being called up by several people, among others Mr. Moone with whom I went to Lumbard Streete to Colvill, and so back again and in my chamber he and I did end all our businesses together of accounts for money upon bills of Exchange, and am pleased to find myself reputed a man of business and method, as he do give me out to be. To the 'Change at noon and so home to dinner. Newes for certain of the King of Denmark's declaring for the Dutch, and resolution to assist them.

6th. Up betimes and did much business. Then to

the office and there till noon and so home to dinner and to the office till night. In the evening being at Sir W. Batten's, stepped in for I have not used to go thither a good while, I find my Lord Brouncker and Mrs. Williams, and they would of their own accord, though I had never obliged them (nor my wife neither) with one visit for many of theirs, go see my house and my wife; which I showed them, and made them welcome with wine and China oranges, (now a great rarity since the war, none to be had.) My house happened to be mighty clean, and did me great honour, and they mightily pleased with it. They gone I to the office and did some business, and then home to supper and to bed. My mind troubled through a doubtfulness of my having incurred Sir W. Coventry's displeasure by not having waited on him since his coming to towne, which is a mighty faulte that I can bear the fear of the bad effects of till I have been with him, which shall be to-morrow, God willing. So to bed.

7th. Up betimes, and to St. James's, thinking Mr. Coventry had lain there; but he do not, but at White Hall; so thither I went and had as good a time as heart could wish, and after an houre in his chamber about publique business he and I walked up, and the Duke being gone abroad we walked an hour in the Matted Gallery: he of himself begun to discourse of the unhappy differences between him and my Lord of Sandwich, and from the beginning to the end did run through all passages wherein my Lord hath, at any time, gathered any dissatisfaction, and cleared himself to me most honourably; and in truth, I do believe he do as he says. I did afterwards purge myself of all partiality in the business of Sir G. Carteret, (whose story Sir W. Coventry did also run over,) that I do mind the King's interest, notwithstanding my relation to him; all which he declares he firmly believes, and assures me he hath the same kindnesse and opinion of me as ever. And when I said I was jealous of myself, that having now come to such an income as I am, by his favour, I should not be found to do as much service as might deserve it; he did assure me, he thinks it not too much for me, but thinks I deserve it as much as any man in England. All this discourse did cheer my heart, and sets me right again, after a good deal of melancholy, out of fears of his disinclination to me, upon the differences with my Lord Sandwich and Sir G. Carteret; but I am satisfied thoroughly, and so went away quite another man, and by the grace of God will never lose it again by my folly in not visiting and writing to him, as I used heretofore to do. It being a holyday, a fast-day, I to Greenwich, to Captain Cocke's, where dined, he and Lord Brouncker, and Matt. Wren,[1] Boltele, and Major Cooper, who is also a very pretty

---

[1] Mathew Wren, eldest son of the Bishop of Ely, of both his names, M. P. for St. Michael's, 1661, and made Secretary to Lord Clarendon, after whose fall he filled a similar office under the Duke of York, till his death in 1672. According to Pepys's " Signs Manual," Wren was mortally wounded in the battle of Solebay. He was one of the earliest members of the Royal Society, and published two tracts in answer to Harrington's " Oceana."

companion ; but they all drink hard, and, after dinner, to gaming at cards. So I provoked my Lord to be gone and he and I to Mr. Cottle's and met Mrs. Williams (without whom he cannot stir out of doors) and there took coach and away home. They carry me to London and set me down at the Temple, where my mind changed and I home, and to writing and heare my boy play on the lute and a turne with my wife pleasantly in the garden by moonshine, my heart being in great peace and so home to supper and to bed. The King and Duke are to go to-morrow to Audly End, in order to the seeing and buying of it of my Lord Suffolke.[1]

8th. Up betimes and to the office, where all the morning sitting and did discover three or four fresh instances of Sir W. Pen's old cheating dissembling tricks, he being as false a fellow as ever was born. Thence with Sir W. Batten and Lord Brouncker to the White Horse in Lumbard Streete to dine with Captain Cocke, upon particular business of canvas to buy for the King, and here by chance I saw the mistresse of the house I have heard much of, and a very pretty woman she is indeed and her husband the simplest looked fellow and old that ever I saw. After

---

[1] The King took possession of Audley End the following autumn, but the conveyance of the estate was not executed till May 8th, 1669; of the purchase money, which was 50,000*l.*, 20,000*l.* remained on mortgage of the Hearth Tax in Ireland; and in 1701, Henry Howard, fifth Earl of Suffolk, was allowed by the Crown, upon the debt being cancelled, to re-establish himself in the seat of his ancestors. It seems very doubtful whether the interest of the mortgage was ever received by the Suffolk family.

dinner I took coach and away to Hales's, where my wife is sitting; and, indeed, her face and necke, which are now finished, do so please me that I am not myself almost, nor was not all the night after in writing of my letters, in consideration of the fine picture that I shall be master of. Thence home and to the office, where very late and so home to supper and to bed.

9th. Up, and being ready to the Cockpitt to make a visit to the Duke of Albemarle, and to my great joy find him the same man to me that [he has been] heretofore, which I was in great doubt of, through my negligence in not visiting of him a great while; and having now set all to rights there, I am in mighty ease in my mind and I think I shall never suffer matters to run so far backwards again as I have done of late, with reference to my neglecting him and Sir W. Coventry. Thence by water down to Deptford, where I met my Lord Brouncker and Sir W. Batten by agreement, and to measuring Mr. Castle's new third-rate ship, which is to be called the Defyance. And here I had my end in saving the King some money and getting myself some experience in knowing how they do measure ships. Thence I left them and walked to Redriffe, and there taking water was overtaken by them in their boat and so they would have me in with them to Castle's house, where my Lady Batten and Madam Williams were and there dined and a deale of doings. I had a good dinner and counterfeit mirthe and pleasure with them, but had but little, thinking how I neglected my business.   Anon, all home to Sir W. Batten's and there Mrs. Knipp coming we did spend the noon together very merry.   She and I singing, and, God forgive me ! I do still see that my nature is not to be quite conquered, but will esteem pleasure above all things, though yet in the middle of it, it has reluctances after my business which is neglected by my following my pleasure.   However musique and women I cannot but give way to, whatever my business is.   They being gone I to the office awhile and so home to supper and to bed.

10th.   Up, and to the office and there busy sitting till noon.   I find at home Mrs. Pierce and Knipp come to dine with me.   We were mighty merry ; and, after dinner, I carried them and my wife out by coach to the New Exchange, and there I did give my Valentine, Mrs. Pierce, a dozen payre of gloves, and a payre of silke stockings, and Knipp for company's sake, though my wife had, by my consent, laid out 20*s*. upon her the other day, six payre of gloves. Thence to the Cakehouse hard by, and there sat in the coach with great pleasure, and eat some fine cakes and so carried them to Pierce's and away home. It is a mighty fine witty boy, Mrs. Pierce's little boy. Thence home and to the office, where late writing letters and leaving a great deale to do on Monday, I home to supper and to bed.   The truth is, I do indulge myself a little the more in pleasure, knowing that this is the proper age of my life to do it ; and out of my observation that most men that do thrive in the world, do forget to take pleasure during the time that they are getting their estate, but reserve that till they have got one, and then it is too late for them to enjoy it with any pleasure.

11th (Lord's day). Up, and by water to White Hall, there met Mr. Coventry coming out, going along with the Commissioners of the Ordnance to the water side to take barge, they being to go down to the Hope. I returned with them as far as the Tower in their barge speaking with Sir W. Coventry and so home and to church, and at noon dined and then to my chamber, where with great pleasure about one business or other till late, and so to supper and to bed.

12th. Up betimes, and called on by abundance of people about business, and then away by water to Westminster, and there to the Exchequer about some business, and so homeward and bought a silver salt for my ordinary table to use, and so home to dinner, and after dinner comes my uncle and aunt Wight, the latter I have not seen since the plague; a silly, froward, ugly woman she is. We made mighty much of them, and she talks mightily of her fear of the sicknesse, and so a deale of tittle tattle and I left them and to my office where late. This day I hear my Uncle Talbot Pepys died the last week. All the news now is, that Sir Jeremy Smith is at Cales [1] with his fleete, and Mings in the Elve. [2] The King is come this noon to towne from Audly End, with the Duke of York and a fine train of gentlemen.

---

[1] Cadiz.   [2] Elbe.

13th. Up betimes, and to the office, where busy sitting all the morning, and I begin to find a little convenience by holding up my head to Sir W. Pen, for he is come to be more supple. At noon to dinner, and then to the office again where mighty business, doing a great deale till midnight and then home to supper and to bed. The plague encreased this week 29 from 28, though the total fallen from 238 to 207, which do never a whit please me.

14th. Mr. Povy carried me in his chariot to White Hall, where we had a meeting before the Duke. Thence with my Lord Brouncker towards London, and in our way called in Covent Garden, and took in Sir John (formerly Dr.) Baber; who hath this humour that he will not enter into discourse while any stranger is in company, till he be told who he is that seems a stranger to him. This he did declare openly to me, and asked my Lord who I was, giving this reason, that he has been inconvenienced by being too free in discourse till he knew who all the company were. Thence to Guildhall (in our way taking in Dr. Wilkins), and there my Lord and I had full and large discourse with Sir Thomas Player,[1] the Chamberlain of the City (a man I have much heard of for his credit and punctuality in the City, and on that score I had a desire to be made known to him) about the credit of our tallys, which are lodged there for security to such

---

[1] One of the City Members in the Oxford and Westminster Parliaments. See more of him in the Notes, by Scott, to "Absalom and Achitophel;" in which poem he is introduced under the designation of "railing Rabsheka."

as should lend money thereon to the use of the Navy.
I had great satisfaction therein : and the truth is, I
find all our matters of credit to be in an ill condition.
Thence, I being in a little haste walked before and
to the 'Change a little and then to Trinity house to
dinner, where Captain Cox made his Elder Brother's
dinner. But it seemed to me a very poor sorry dinner.
I having many things in my head rose, when my belly
was full, though the dinner not half done and home
and there to do some business, and by and by out of
doors and met Mr. Povy coming to me by appointment, but it being a little too late, I took a little pride
in the streete not to go back with him, but prayed
him to come another time, and I away to Kate Joyce's,
thinking to have spoke to her husband about Pall's
business, but a stranger, the Welsh Dr. Powell, being
there I forebore and went away and so to Hales's, and
there had the pleasure to see how suddenly he draws
the Heavens, laying a darke ground and then lighten-
ing it when and where he will. Thence to walk all
alone in the fields behind Grayes Inne, making an
end of reading over my dear " Faber fortunæ," of my
Lord Bacon's. And so anon by invitation to Mrs.
Pierce's, where I find much good company, that is to
say, Mrs. Pierce, my wife, Mrs. Worshipp and her daughter, and Harris the player, and Knipp, and Mercer,
and Mrs. Barbary Sheldon, who is come this day to
spend a weeke with my wife ; and there with musique
we danced, and sung and supped, and then to sing
and dance till past one in the morning ; and much

mirthe with Sir Anthony Apsley and one Collonell Sidney, who lodge in the house; and above all, they are mightily taken with Mrs. Knipp.

15th. Lay till it was full time to rise, it being eight o'clock, and so to the office and there sat till almost three o'clock and then to dinner, I and my cozen Anthony Joyce, and he and I to discourse of our proposition of marriage between Pall and Harman and upon discourse he and I to Harman's house and took him to a taverne hard by and we to discourse of our business and I offered 500*l.* and he declares most ingenuously that his trade is not to be trusted on, that he however needs no money, but would have her money bestowed on her, which I like well, he saying that he would adventure 2 or 300*l.* with her. I like him as a most good-natured, and discreet and, I believe, very cunning. We came to this conclusion for us to meete one another the next weeke, and then we hope to come to some end, for I did declare myself well satisfied with the match. Thence to Hales's, where I met my wife and people; and do find the picture, above all things, a most pretty picture, and mighty like my wife; and I asked him his price: he says 14*l.* and the truth is, I think he do deserve it.

16th. At noon to the 'Change, and did several businesses, and thence to the Crowne behind the 'Change and dined with my Lord Brouncker and Captain Cocke and Fenn, and Madam Williams, who without question must be my Lord's wife, and else she could not follow him wherever he goes and kisse

and use him publiquely as she do. In the evening
called on by Povy, and he and I staid together in my
chamber till 12 at night ending our reckonings and
giving him tallys for all I was to pay him and so
parted, and I to make good my Journall for two or
three days and begun it till I come to the other side,
where I have scratched so much, for, for want of
sleep, I begun to write idle and from the purpose. So
forced to breake off, and to bed.

17th. Up, and to finish my Journall, which I had
not sense enough the last night to make an end of,
and thence to the office, where very busy all the morning. At noon home to dinner and presently with my
wife out to Hales's, where I am still infinitely pleased
with my wife's picture. I paid him 14*l.* for the picture, and 1*l.* 5*s.* for the frame, and I think it not a
whit too deare for so good a picture. It is not yet
quite finished and dry, so as to be fit to bring home
yet. This day I began to sit, and he will make me, I
think, a very fine picture. He promises it shall be as
good as my wife's, and I sit to have it full of shadows,
and do almost break my neck looking over my shoulder to make the posture for him to work by. Home,
having a great cold; so to bed, drinking butter-ale.
This day W. Hewer comes from Portsmouth and gives
me an instance of another piece of knavery of Sir
W. Pen, who wrote to Commissioner Middleton, that
it was my negligence the other day he was not acquainted, as the board directed, with our clerks coming down to the pay. But I need no long argument

to teach me that he is a false rogue to me and all the world besides.

18th (Lord's day). To church, and then home to dinner, and so walked out to St. James's Church, thinking to have seen faire Mrs. Butler, but could not, she not being there, nor, I believe, lives thereabouts now. So walked to Westminster to Mrs. Martin's. She tells me as a secret that Betty Howlet of the Hall, my little sweetheart, that I used to call my second wife, is married to a younger son of Mr. Michell's (his elder brother, who should have had her, being dead this plague), at which I am glad, and that they are to live nearer me in Thames Streete, by the Old Swan. Thence by coach home and to my chamber about some accounts, and so to bed. Sir Christopher Mings is come home from Hambro' without anything done, saving bringing home some pipestanes for us.

19th. Upon a meeting extraordinary at the office most of the morning upon the business of the accounts. Where now we have got almost as much as we would have we begin to lay all on the Controller, and I fear he will be run down with it, for he is every day less and less capable of doing business. Thence with my Lord Brouncker and Sir W. Coventry to the ticket office, to see in what little order things are there, and there it is a shame to see how the King is served. Thence to the Chamberlain of London, and satisfy ourselves more particularly how much credit we have there, which proves very little. Thence to Sir Robert Long's, about much the same business, but have not the satisfactlon we would have there neither. So Sir W. Coventry parted, and my Lord and I to Mrs. Williams, and there I saw her closett, where indeed a great many fine things there are, but the woman I hate. Here we dined, and Sir J. Minnes came to us, and after dinner we walked to the King's play-house,[1] all in dirt, they being altering of the stage to make it wider. But God knows when they will begin to act again; but my business here was to see the inside of the stage and all the tiring-rooms and machines; and, indeed, it was a sight worthy seeing. But to see their clothes, and the various sorts, and what a mixture of things there was;[2] here a wooden-leg, there a ruff, here a hobby-horse, there a crown, would make a man split himself to see with laughing; and particularly Lacy's[3] wardrobe, and Shotrell's.[4] But then again, to think

---

[1] " Soon after Charles II.'s entry into London, two theatrical companies are known to have been acting in the capital. One of these had been formed by a bookseller of the name of Rhodes (said to have been formerly Wardrobe Keeper in the Blackfriars' company), who had obtained a licence from the authorities already, at the time when General Monk was advancing upon London. For this company a patent was granted to Sir William D'Avenant in August, 1660, under the name of ' The Duke [of York]'s servants,' while for the other, known as ' The Old Actors,' another patent was, under the name of ' The King's Servants,' granted to one of the Killigrews, either Thomas, or his less-known younger brother, Dr. Henry Killigrew. Of the companies, the former from 1662 acted at Lincoln's Inn Fields, then at Dorset Garden in Salisbury Court; the latter from 1663 at the ' Theatre Royal,' near Drury Lane, though the house was not yet called by that famous local name." — *English Dramatic Literature to the death of Queen Anne*, by A. W. WARD, M.A., vol. ii. pp. 447, 448. (M. B.)

[2] Compare 5th October, 1667.

[3] John Lacy, the celebrated comedian, author of four plays. Ob. 1681.

[4] Robert and William Shotterel both belonged to the King's Company at the opening of their new Theatre in 1663. One of them had been Quarter-

how fine they show on the stage by candle-light, and how poor things they are to look now too near hand, is not pleasant at all. The machines are fine, and the paintings very pretty. Thence mightily satisfied in my curiosity I away with my Lord to see him at her house again, and so take leave and by coach home and to the office, and thence sent for to Sir G. Cartaret by and by to the Broad Streete, where he and I walked two or three hours till it was quite darke in his gallery talking of his affairs, wherein I assure him all will do well, and did give him (with great liberty, which he accepted kindly) my advice to deny the board nothing they would aske about his accounts, but rather call upon them to know whether there was anything more they desired, or was wanting. But our great discourse and serious reflections was upon the bad state of the kingdom in general, through want of money and good conduct, which we fear will undo all. Thence mightily satisfied with this good fortune of this discourse with him I home, and there walked in the darke till 10 o'clock at night in the garden with Sir W. Warren, talking of many things belonging to us particularly, and I hope to get something considerably by him before the year be over. He gives me good advice of circumspection in my place, which I am now in great mind to improve; for I think our office stands on very ticklish terms, the Parliament likely to

---

master to the troop of horse in which Hart was serving as Lieutenant under Charles I.'s standard. He is called by Downs a good actor, but nothing further is recorded of his merits or career. — *Note to Cibber's Apology.*

sit shortly and likely to be asked more money, and we able to give a very bad account of the expence of what we have done with what they did give before. Besides, the turning out the prize officers may be an example for the King giving us up to the Parliament's pleasure as easily, for we deserve it as much. Besides, Sir G. Carteret did tell me to-night how my Lord Brouncker himself, whose good-will I could have depended as much on as any, did himself to him take notice of the many places I have; and though I was a painful man, yet the Navy was enough for any man to go through with in his owne single place there, which much troubles me, and shall yet provoke me to more and more care and diligence than ever. This day by letter from my father he propounds a match in the country for Pall, which pleased me well, of one that hath seven score and odd pounds land per annum in possession, and expects 1,000*l.* in money by the death of an old aunt. He hath neither father, mother, sister, nor brother, but demands 600*l.* down, and 100*l.* on the birth of first child, which I had some inclination to stretch to. He is kinsman to, and lives with, Mr. Phillips, but my wife tells me he is a drunken, ill-favoured, ill-bred country fellow, which sets me off of it again, and I will go on with Harman. So after supper to bed.

20th. Busy all the morning. At noon dined in haste, and so my wife, Mrs. Barbary, Mercer, and I by coach to Hales's, where I find my wife's picture now perfectly finished in all respects, and a beautiful picture it is, as almost I ever saw. I sat again, and had a great deale done, but, whatever the matter is, I do not fancy that it has the ayre of my face, though it will be a very fine picture. Thence home and to my business, being post night, and so home to supper and to bed.

21st. First by coach to my Lord General to visitt him, and then to the Duke of York, where we all met and did our usual business with him; but, Lord! how everything is yielded to presently, even by Sir W. Coventry, that is propounded by the Duke, as now to have Troutbecke,[1] his old surgeon, and intended to go Surgeon-General of the fleete, to go Physician-General of the fleete, of which there never was any precedent in the world, and he for that to have 20*l.* per month. Thence with Lord Brouncker to Sir Robert Long,[2] whom we found in his closett, and after some discourse of business he fell to discourse at large and pleasant, and among other things told us of the plenty of partridges in France, where he says the King of France and his company killed with their guns, in the plain de Versailles, 300 and odd partridges at one bout. Thence I to the Excise Office behind the 'Change, and there find our business of the tallys in great disorder as to payment, and thereupon do take a resolu-

---

[1] John Troutbecke, in 1661, was surgeon to the Life-Guards, commanded by the Duke of Albemarle.

[2] Sir Robert Long, Secretary to Charles II. during his exile, and subsequently made Auditor of the Exchequer, and a Privy Counsellor, and created a Baronet, 1662. Ob. unmarried, 1673.

tion of thinking how to remedy it, as soon as I can. So to Gresham College, where I staid half an houre, and so away home to my office, and there walking late alone in the darke in the garden with Sir W. Warren, who tells me that at the Committee of the Lords for the prizes to-day, there passed very high words between my Lord Ashly and Sir W. Coventry, about our business of the prize ships. And that my Lord Ashly did snuff and talk as high to him, as he used to do to any ordinary seaman. And that Sir W. Coventry did take it very quietly, but yet for all did speak his mind soberly and with reason, and went away, saying, he had done his duty therein, and so left it to them, whether they would let so many ships go for masts or not. Here he and I talked of 1,000 businesses, all profitable discourse, and late parted, and I home to supper and to bed, troubled a little at a letter from my father, telling me how he is like to be sued for a debt of Tom's, by Smith, the mercer.

23rd. Up, and going out of my dressing-room, when ready to go down stairs, I spied little Miss Tooker, my pretty little girle, which, it seems, did come yesterday to our house, but I did not know of it till now. I was glad of her coming, she being a very pretty child, and now grown almost a woman. I out by six o'clock to Hales's. Anon comes my wife and Mercer and little Tooker, and having done with me we all to a picture drawer's hard by, Hales carrying me to see some landskipps of a man's doing. Thence by coach to Anthony Joyce to receive Harman's answer, which did for me to receive, for he now demands 800*l.*, whereas he never made exception at the portion, but accepted of 500*l.* This I do not like; but, however, I cannot much blame the man, if he thinks he can get more of another than of me.

24th. To the office, where all the morning. After dinner I to White Hall to a Committee for Tangier, where the Duke of York was, and I acquitted myself well in what I had to do. After the Committee up, I had occasion to follow the Duke into his lodgings, into a chamber where the Duchesse was sitting to have her picture drawn by Lilly, who was there at work. But I was well pleased to see that there was nothing near so much resemblance of her face in his work, which is now the second, if not the third time, as there was of my wife's at the very first time. Nor do I think at last it can be like, the lines not being in proportion to those of her face.

25th (Lady day and Sunday). Up, and to my chamber in my gowne all the morning about settling my papers there. At noon to dinner, where my wife's brother, whom I sent for to offer making him a Muster-Master and send to sea, which the poore man likes well of and will go, and it will be a good preferment to him, only hazardous. I hope he will prove a good discreet man. After dinner to my papers and Tangier accounts again till supper, and after supper again to them, but by my mixing them, I know not how, my private and publique accounts, it makes me mad to see how hard it is to bring them to be understood, and my head is confounded, that though I did sweare to sit up till one o'clock upon them, yet, I fear, it will be to no purpose, for I cannot understand what I do or have been doing of them to-day.

26th. Up, and a meeting extraordinary there was of Sir W. Coventry, Lord Brouncker, and myself, about the business of settling the ticket office, where infinite room is left for abusing the King in the wages of seamen. Our meeting being done, my Lord Brouncker and I to the Tower, to see the famous engraver,[1] to get him to grave a seale for the office. And did see some of the finest pieces of work in embossed work, that ever I did see in my life, for fineness and smallness of the images thereon, and I will carry my wife thither to shew them her. Here I also did see bars of gold melting, which was a fine sight. So with my Lord to the Pope's Head Taverne in Lumbard Streete to dine by appointment with Captain Taylor, whither Sir W. Coventry came to us, and were mighty merry, and I find reason to honour him every day more and more. Thence alone to Broade Street to Sir G. Carteret by his desire to confer with him, who is I find in great pain about the business of the office, and not a little, I believe, in fear of falling there, Sir W. Coventry having so great a pique against him, and herein I first learn an eminent instance how great a man this day, that nobody would think could be shaken, is the next overthrown, dashed

---

[1] Rotier, a German. See 9th March, 1662-63. (M. B.)

out of countenance, and every small thing of irregularity in his business taken notice of, where nobody the other day durst cast an eye upon them, and next I see that he that the other day nobody durst come near is now as supple as a spaniel, and sends and speaks to me with great submission, and readily hears to advice. Thence home to the office, where busy late, and so home a little to my accounts publique and private, but could not get myself rightly to know how to dispose of them in order to passing.

27th. All the morning at the office busy. At noon dined at home, Mr. Cooke, our old acquaintance at my Lord Sandwich's, came to see and dine with me, but I quite out of humour, having many other and better things to thinke of. Thence to the office to settle my people's worke and then home to my publique accounts of Tangier, which it is strange by meddling with evening reckonings with Mr. Povy lately how I myself am become entangled therein, so that after all I could do, ready to breake my head and brains. I thought of another way, though not so perfect, yet the only one which this account is capable of. Upon this latter I sat up till past two in the morning and then to bed.

28th. Up, and with Creed, who came hither betimes to speake with me about his accounts, to White Hall by water, mighty merry in discourse, though I had been very little troubled with him, or did countenance it, having now, blessed be God! a great deale of good business to mind to better purpose than chatting with him. Waited on the Duke, after that walked with Sir W. Clerke into St. James's Parke, and met with Mr. Hayes, Prince Rupert's Secretary, who are mighty, both, briske blades, but I fear they promise themselves more than they expect. Thence to the Cockpitt, and dined with a great deal of company at the Duke of Albemarle's, and a bad and dirty, nasty dinner. So by coach to Hales's. Hither came my wife and Mercer and Knipp, we were mighty merry and the picture goes on the better for it. This night, I am told, the Queene of Portugall, the mother to our Queene, is lately dead, and newes brought of it hither this day.

29th. All the morning hard at the office. At noon dined and then out to Lumbard Streete, to look after the getting of some money that is lodged there of mine in Viner's hands, I having no mind to have it lie there longer. This day, poor Jane, my old, little Jane, came to us again, to my wife's and my great content, and we hope to take mighty pleasure in her, she having all the marks and qualities of a good and loving and honest servant, she coming by force away from the other place, where she hath lived ever since she went from us, and at our desire, her late mistresse having used all the stratagems she could to keepe her.

30th. Up, and away goes Alce, our cooke-mayde, a good servant, whom we loved and did well by her, and she an excellent servant, but would not bear being told of any faulte in the fewest and kindest words and would go away of her owne accord, after having given her mistresse warning fickly for a quarter of a yeare together. I out to Lumbard-streete, and there received 2,200*l.* and brought it home ; and, contrary to expectation, received 35*l.* for the use of 2,000*l.* of it for a quarter of a year, where it hath produced me this profit, and hath been a convenience to me as to care and security of my house, and demandable at two days' warning, as this hath been. To Hales's, and there sat till almost quite darke upon working my gowne, which I hired to be drawn in ; an Indian gowne.

31st. All the morning at the office busy. At noon to dinner, and thence to the office and did my business there as soon as I could, and then home and to my accounts, where very late at them, but, Lord ! what a deale of do I have to understand any part of them, and in short do what I could, I could not come to any understanding of them, but after I had thoroughly wearied myself, I was forced to go to bed and leave them much against my will and vowe too, but I hope God will forgive me, for I have sat up these four nights till past twelve at night to master them, but cannot. Thus ends this month, with my head and mind mighty full and disquiett because of my accounts ; however, I do see that I must be grown richer than I was by a good deale last month. Busy also I am in thoughts for a husband for my sister, and to that end my wife and I have determined that she shall presently go into the country to my father and mother, and consider of a proffer made them for her in the country, which, if she likes, shall go forward.

April 1st (Lord's day). To Charing Cross, to wait on Sir Philip Howard; whom I found in bed: and he do receive me very civilly. My request was about suffering my wife's brother to go to sea, and to save his pay in the Duke's guards; which after a little difficulty he did with great respect agree to. I find him a very fine-spoken gentleman, and one of great parts, and very courteous. Much pleased with this visit I to White Hall, where I met Sir G. Downing, and to discourse with him an houre about the Exchequer payments upon the late Act, and informed myself of him thoroughly in my safety in lending 2,000*l.* to Sir W. Warren, upon an order of his upon the Exchequer for 2,602*l.* and I do purpose to do it. Thence meeting Dr. Allen,[1] the physician, he and I and another walked in the Parke, a most pleasant warm day, and to the Queene's chappell; where I do not so dislike the musique. Here I saw on a post an invitation to all good Catholiques to pray for the soul of such a one departed this life. The Queene, I hear, do not yet hear of the death of her mother,[2] she being in a course of physique, that they dare not tell it her. At noon my uncle and Aunt Wight dined with me and very merry. After dinner my uncle and I abroad by

---

[1] Probably Thomas Allen, M.D., of Caius College, Cambridge, and member of the College of Physicians. Ob. 1685.

[2] Donna Luiza, the Queen Regent of Portugal. The Court wore the deepest mourning on this occasion. The ladies were directed to wear their hair plain, and to appear without spots on their faces, the disfiguring fashion of patching having just been introduced. — STRICKLAND'S *Queens of England,* vol. viii. p. 362. (M. B.)

coach to White Hall and I did some business and thence with him and a gentleman he met with to my Lord Chancellor's new house, and there viewed it again and again and up to the top and I like it as well as ever and think it a most noble house. So all up and down my Lord St. Albans his new building and market-house,[1] and the taverne under the market-house, looking to and again into every place of building. I this afternoon made a visit to my Lady Carteret, whom I understood newly come to towne; and she took it mighty kindly, but I see her face and heart are dejected from the condition her husband's matters stand in. But I hope they will do all well enough. And I do comfort her as much as I can, for she is a noble lady.

2nd. Up, and to the office and thence with Mr. Gauden to Guildhall to see the bills and tallys there in the chamber (and by the way in the streete his new coach broke and we fain to take an old hackney). Thence walking with Mr. Gauden in Westminster Hall to talke of his son Benjamin; and I propounded a match for him, and at last named my sister, which he embraces heartily, and speaking of the lowness of her portion, that it would be less than 1,000*l.*, he tells me

---

[1] Jermyn Street and St. Alban's Market, which was afterwards called St. James's Market. "A large place with a commodious Market House in the midst, filled with Butchers' shambles, besides the Stalls in the Market-Place for country Butchers, Higglers, and the like; being a market now (1720) grown to great account, and much resorted unto, as being well served with good provisions."—STRYPE, b. vi. p. 83. CUNNINGHAM'S *Handbook of London*. (M. B.)

if everything else agrees, he will out of what he means to give me yearly, make a portion for her shall cost me nothing more than I intend freely. This did mightily rejoice me and full of it did go with him to London to the 'Change; and there did much business and at the Coffee-house with Sir W. Warren, who very wisely did shew me that my matching my sister with Mr. Gauden would undo me in all my places, everybody suspecting me in all I do; and I shall neither be able to serve him, nor free myself from imputation of being of his faction, while I am placed for his severest check. I was convinced that it would be for neither of our interests to make this alliance, and so am quite off of it again, but with great satisfaction in the motion. So to Westminster Hall, where I purposely tooke my wife well dressed into the Hall to see and be seen; and, among others, met Howlet's daughter, who is newly married, and is she I call wife, and one I love mightily. So to Broad Streete and there met my Lady and Sir G. Carteret, and sat and talked with them a good while and so home.

3rd. Up, and Sir W. Warren with me betimes and signed a bond, and assigned his order on the Exchequer to a blank for me to fill and I did deliver him 1,900*l.* The truth is, it is a great venture to venture so much on the Act, but thereby I hedge in 300*l.* gift for my service about some ships that he has bought, prizes, and good interest besides, and his bond to repay me the money at six weeks' warning. So to the office, where busy all the morning. At noon home to dinner, and there my brother Balty dined with me and my wife, who is become a good serious man, and I hope to do him good being sending him a Muster-Master on one of the squadrons of the fleete. After dinner and he gone I to my accounts hard all the afternoon till it was quite darke and I thank God I do come to bring them very fairly to make me worth 5,000*l.* stocke in the world, which is a great mercy to me. At night a while to the office and then home and supped and to my accounts again till I was ready to sleepe, there being no pleasure to publish them, if they are not kept in good order. So to bed.

4th. Up, and with Sir W. Pen in his coach to White Hall, in his way talking simply and fondly as he used to do, but I find myself to slight him and his simple talke, I thank God, and that my condition will enable me to do it. Thence, after doing our business with the Duke of Yorke, with Captain Cocke home to the 'Change in his coach. He promises me presently a dozen of silver salts, and proposes a business for which he has promised Mrs. Williams for my Lord Brouncker a set of plate shall cost him 500*l.* and me the like, which will be a good business indeed. After done several businesses at the 'Change I home and being washing day, dined upon cold meate, and so abroad by coach to Hales's, and there sat till night, mightily pleased with my picture, which is now almost finished. So by coach home, it being the fast day and to my chamber and so after supper to bed, consulting how to send my wife into the country to advise about Pall's marriage, which I much desire and two or three offers are now in hand.

5th. Up, and before office time to Lumbard Streete, and there at Viner's was shewn the silver plates, made for Captain Cocke to present my Lord Brouncker; and I chose a dozen of the same weight to be bespoke for myself, which he told me yesterday he would give me on the same occasion. To the office where the falsenesse and impertinencies of Sir W. Pen would make a man mad to think of. At noon would have avoided, but could not, dining with my Lord Brouncker and his mistresse with Captain Cocke at the Sun Taverne in Fish Streete, where a good dinner, but the woman do tire me, and indeed how simply my Lord Brouncker, who is otherwise a wise man, do proceed at the table in serving of Cocke, without any means of understanding in his proposal, or defence when proposed would make a man think him a foole. After dinner home, where I find my wife has on a sudden, upon notice of a coach going away to-morrow, taken a resolution of going in it to Brampton. So she to fit herself for her journey and I to the office all the afternoon till late and so home and late putting notes to " It is decreed, nor shall thy fate &c." and then to bed. The plague is, to our great grief, increased nine this week, though decreased a few in the total. And this encrease runs through many parishes, which makes us much fear the next year.

6th. Up mighty betimes upon my wife's going this day towards Brampton. I could not go to the coach with her, but W. Hewer did and hath leave from me to go the whole day's journey with her. To White Hall and there met by agreement with Sir Stephen Fox and Mr. Ashburnham, and discoursed the business of our Excise tallys; the former being Treasurer of the guards, and the other Cofferer of the King's household. I benefitted much by their discourse. Home, where all things, methinks, melancholy in the absence of my wife. This day great newes of the Swedes declaring for us against the Dutch, and, so far as that, I believe it.

7th. To the office and there till noon. Thence with my Lord Brouncker home by coach to Mrs. Williams's, where Bab. Allen and Dr. Charleton dined. Bab and I sang and were mighty merry as we could be there, where the rest of the company did not over-please. Thence took her by coach to Hales's, and there find Mrs. Pierce and her boy and Mary. She had done sitting the first time, and indeed her face is mighty like at first dash. Thence took them to the cakehouse, and there called in the coach for cakes and drank, and thence I carried them to my Lord Chancellor's new house to shew them that, and all mightily pleased, thence set each down at home, and so I home to the office, where about ten of the clock W. Hewer comes to me to tell me that he has left my wife well this morning at Bugden, which was great riding, and brings me a letter from her. She is very well got thither of which I am heartily glad. After writing several letters, I home to supper and to bed.

The Bishop of Munster, every body says, is coming to peace with the Dutch, we having not supplied him with the money promised him.

8th (Lord's day). To the Duke of York, where we all met to hear the debate between Sir Thomas Allen and Mr. Wayth; the former complaining of the latter's ill usage of him at the late pay of his ship. But a very sorry poor occasion he had for it. The Duke did determine it with great judgement, chiding both, but encouraging Wayth to continue to be a check to all captains in any thing to the King's right. And, indeed, I never did see the Duke do any thing more in order, nor with more judgement than he did pass the verdict in this business. The Court full this morning of the newes of Tom Cheffins's [1] death, the King's closett-keeper. He was well last night as ever, playing at tables in the house, and not very ill this morning at six o'clock, yet dead before seven : they think, of an imposthume in his breast. But it looks fearfully among people now-a-days, the plague, as we hear, encreasing every where again. To the Chappell, but could not get in to hear well. But I had the pleasure once in my life to see an Archbishop [2] (this

---

[1] Sir E. Walker, Garter King at Arms, in 1644 gave a grant of arms *gratis*, to Thomas Chiffinch, Esq., one of the Pages of His Majesty's Bed-chamber, Keeper of his private Closet, and Comptroller of the Excise. His brother William appears to have succeeded to the two first-named appointments, and became a great favourite with the King, whom he survived. There is a portrait of William Chiffinch at Gorhambury.

[2] Richard Sterne, Bishop of Carlisle, elected Archbishop of York, 1664. Ob. 1683.

was of York) in a pulpit. Then at a loss how to get home to dinner, having promised to carry Mrs. Hunt thither. At last got my Lord Hinchingbroke's coach, he staying at Court; and so took her up in Axe-yard, and home and dined. And good discourse of the old matters of the Protector and his family, she having a relation to them. The Protector [1] lives in France: spends about 500*l.* per annum. Thence carried her home again and then to Court and walked over to St. James's Chappell, thinking to have heard a Jesuite preach, but came too late. So got a hackney and home and there to business. At night had Mercer comb my head and so to supper, sing a psalm, and to bed.

---

[1] Richard Cromwell. (M. B.)

PEDIGREE OF THE EARL OF SANDWICH.
[See footnote, p. 151.]

EDWARD MOUNTAGU,
Lord Chief Justice, temp. Henry VIII., died 1557.

EDWARD MOUNTAGU, Knt.,
"A worthy patriot in the reign of Queen Elizabeth," died 1602.

EDWD. MOUN-TAGU, Knt., First Lord Mountagu of Boughton.	WALTER, Knt.	HENRY, Lord Mountagu, First Earl of Manchester.	CHARLES, Knt.	JAMES, Bishop of Bath 1605, and Winchester 1616.	SIDNEY, Knt. M.P. for Huntingdon in the Long Parliament, whence he was expelled. Mar. PAULINA, daughter of John Pepys, of Cottenham, Camb., died 1644.

HENRY, drowned at sea.	EDWARD, a distinguished Parliamentary Captain. M.P. for Huntingdon, Admiral, *First Earl of Sandwich*, died 1672.	ELIZABETH, mar. Sir Gilbert Pyckering, of Titchmarsh.

(M. B.)

VOL. V.   LIST OF PRINCIPAL MISTAKES IN THE FOURTH EDITION, 1854.

PAGE		LINE						
24	..	16	For flatly	.	.	read	*desolately.*
29	..	6	" 18th	. . .		"	*28th.*
29	..	9	" 13th	. .		"	*23rd.*
29	..	9	" 14th	. . .		"	*24th.*
38	..	17	" at one	. .		"	*I alone.*
40	..	13	" matter	. .		"	*letter.*
40	..	15	" possible	.		"	*pardonable.*
45	..	2	" good	. . .		"	*gold.*
45	..	3	" bands	. .		"	*hands.*
53	..	28	" writ	. . .		"	*right.*

PAGE		LINE				
54	..	25	For respect . .	read	*aspect.*
60	..	15	" Burying Hall .	"	*Bazing Hall.*
79	..	19	" nearly . .	"	*newly.*
87	..	13	" 100 . . .	"	*1,000.*
90	..	22	" thing . .	"	*wedding.*
92	..	18	" slight . . .	"	*sleight.*
95	..	11	" knowing .	"	*liking.*
97	..	5	" silk . . .	"	*sick.*
105	..	17	" mean to .	"	*must.*
121	..	18	" greetings . .	"	*gettings.*
131	..	19	" family . .	"	*fellow.*
142	..	28	" they would not .	"	*or fit to.*
157	..	22	" drunkard .	"	*drinker.*
173	..	19	" dinner . .	"	*linen.*
219	..	15	" brought . .	"	*bought.*
241	..	29	" about . . .	"	*above.*
254	..	27	" less . .	"	*else.*
257	..	10	" first . . .	"	*finest.*
258	..	26	" £800 . .	"	*£8,000.*
261	..	16	" musique . .	"	*mimique.*
266	..	23	" not fear . .	"	*fear.*
271	..	7	" make leagues .	"	*make legs.*